With a degree in English and American Literature, Julie Haworth worked as an English teacher for a number of years, specializing in working with learners with literacy difficulties, before launching her own freelance copywriting business. She is a member of the Romantic Novelists' Association.

Also by Julie Haworth

Always By Your Side

New Beginnings at the Cosy Cat Cafe

JULIE HAWORTH

**SIMON &
SCHUSTER**

London · New York · Sydney · Toronto · New Delhi

First published in Great Britain by Simon & Schuster UK Ltd, 2024

1 3 5 7 9 10 8 6 4 2

Simon & Schuster UK Ltd
1st Floor
222 Gray's Inn Road
London WC1X 8HB

Simon & Schuster: Celebrating 100 Years of Publishing in 2024

Simon & Schuster Australia, Sydney
Simon & Schuster India, New Delhi

www.simonandschuster.co.uk
www.simonandschuster.com.au
www.simonandschuster.co.in

A CIP catalogue record for this book
is available from the British Library

Paperback ISBN: 978-1-3985-2748-5
eBook ISBN: 978-1-3985-2746-1
Audio ISBN: 978-1-3985-2747-8

Typeset in Bembo by M Rules
Printed and Bound in the UK using 100% Renewable
Electricity at CPI Group (UK) Ltd

MIX
Paper | Supporting
responsible forestry
FSC® C171272
FSC
www.fsc.org

To Chris (and the cats)
I'm hoping you might get as
far as reading this page!
Love you lots xx

Chapter 1

Tori stared at the luggage carousel as the bags from Flight 231 were carried around the conveyor belt with a hypnotizing quality. She squeezed between two men who were at least twice her size and pretending not to see her to avoid losing their spot at the front of the crowd. They were clearly poised and ready to pounce on their luggage as soon as it appeared.

'Excuse me,' she said loudly, making her presence known.

'Oh, sorry, love,' the larger of the two men replied, as he moved sideways to let Tori through. 'Didn't see you there.'

'No worries,' Tori replied with a half-smile, thinking that the man most definitely *had* seen her there but had simply chosen not to move. She could hear the ear-crunching thud of bags hitting the conveyor belt as the baggage handlers sorted through the luggage behind the flimsy plastic curtain that was shielding them from view.

'Honestly, can't they be more careful? Some of us have got breakables in there, you know,' she muttered, running her hands through her long brown hair and scooping it back into a ponytail with the hairband she had around her wrist.

'Oh, you'd think they were throwing around bags full of rocks, the way they carry on.' A woman's voice came from behind her. Tori turned her head to see who had spoken. It was a woman in her late fifties, with jet-black hair and the brightest red lipstick Tori had ever seen. 'When we came back from Marbs, my miniature sherries were smashed to pieces by the time that lot were through with them,' the woman continued, folding her arms. 'I was livid, wasn't I, Gary?' A short, balding man, standing next to her, nodded silently.

'Nightmare,' replied Tori, giving the woman a vague nod of agreement.

'Well, I hope you don't have anything breakable in there? I've learnt my lesson, haven't I, Gary?' Gary nodded again. Tori got the sense that he knew there was no point in arguing. 'All my breakables are right here, safely tucked away,' she said, tapping her pink shoulder bag proudly.

Tori smiled weakly; she didn't feel like getting involved in a conversation with anyone right now, not in the mood she was in. This had been one of the worst weeks of her life. She couldn't believe things with Ryan were *really* over. When they'd set off together on the adventure of a lifetime just over a year ago, things between them couldn't have been better. She'd thought their future together was mapped out. She'd been so excited to see the world with Ryan, before they returned home to start their life together in Blossom Heath, the East Sussex village in which Tori had grown up.

She'd had it all planned out. They'd come home, save for the deposit on a house, move in together and get engaged. It was the perfect life plan. She even knew exactly the type of wedding she wanted; she'd been planning it since she was a little girl. She'd done everything she was supposed to do, she'd done everything *right*.

When Ryan had broken the news to her a week ago that he wasn't going to return to England, she had been shocked, but it wasn't the end of the world if he wanted to stay in Thailand a bit longer. When he'd told her that he didn't plan on coming back *at all*, that he wanted to end things between them because he wasn't a 'relationship guy', the bottom had fallen out of her world. *Not a relationship guy?* What did that even mean? They'd already been together for just over four years, after meeting on a night out in London; if that wasn't a relationship, she didn't know what was.

Tori turned her head back towards the luggage. Still no sign of her bag. She let out a long, deep breath. Where was her rucksack? There were less people clambering for a spot at the side of the carousel now the number of bags had reduced. Eventually there was just a single bag left, a bright pink wheely suitcase covered in gold flamingos, circling around unclaimed. Tori looked around her and realized that she was the only passenger from Flight 231 left in the baggage reclaim hall. She pressed her fingers into her temples; she could feel the beginnings of a headache forming at the base of her skull. Her bag wasn't coming, was it? She sighed. Why did this kind of stuff always happen to her? If she'd known a bag was going to go missing, she would have placed a bet on it being hers. As if she wasn't already exhausted from the flight home and the emotional turmoil of being dumped, now she was going to have to deal with a visit to the lost luggage desk. Great. Just great.

Tori fired off a quick text to her mum, Joyce, who she knew would be waiting for her in the Arrivals terminal. *I'm back safe and sound! Can't wait to see you!!! Got to detour to lost luggage first, I'll be as quick as I can xx* Tori felt slightly queasy when she thought about the prospect of breaking the news about Ryan to her mum. She hadn't told anyone about the break-up yet, not even her friends from her business degree course at university. With the split coming out of nowhere, she hoped there was still a chance that Ryan would come to his senses, change his mind and follow her home, telling her he'd made a terrible mistake. That was still possible, right? What was the point of upsetting everyone when there could still be a chance of things working out? She didn't want her mum's opinion of Ryan to be clouded in the future, and she knew if she told her about the way he'd behaved this week, it would be. She loved her mum dearly, but she wasn't one to forgive and forget, particularly when it came to men. When Joyce had asked her why Ryan wasn't flying home, she'd invented an excuse about him having found some temporary work and said that he'd be joining her in Blossom Heath in a few weeks. She felt dreadful lying to her mum; it wasn't something she'd usually do, but surely these were exceptional circumstances? If she didn't say the words out loud, she could still pretend that it hadn't really happened, that she wasn't single. That just felt easier somehow.

Tori had hopped straight on a plane the day after Ryan had broken the news that their relationship was over. There was no way she was hanging around to see him embark on his newly single life. *No way in hell.* Even though she hoped their split was just a blip and Ryan would feel differently once he'd got whatever this was out of his system, she couldn't wait to get back home. Tori knew her mum would worry when she discovered that things hadn't worked out as planned for her and Ryan. They were supposed to be arriving home *together*, ready to get started on the next chapter in their lives. Finding work … moving in together … perhaps even a wedding. She shook her head. There was no point in going over what might have been, she needed to stay positive; she was sure if she let things settle, she could speak to Ryan … convince him to change his mind. And if not, well, she'd have to choose her moment wisely and tell her mum when the time was right. She couldn't cope with seeing the disappointment on her face when she found out.

Tori followed the signs from the baggage hall leading her to the lost luggage desk and she knew she was in the right place as soon as she spotted a queue of people who looked irate and exhausted simultaneously. Oh well, at least she wasn't the only unlucky passenger in baggage reclaim today. She could hear the man at the front of the queue shouting at the attendant behind the desk.

'What's the point of paying for first class if you can't even be trusted to get my bags here? Do you know how much this flight cost me?' the man shouted, turning redder and redder in the face.

Tori bristled slightly and found her grip on her handbag tightening. Whatever had happened to this man's luggage, she was pretty sure that screaming at the woman behind the desk wasn't going to make it appear any faster. Honestly, why are some people so rude? No one *wants* to lose their luggage but it's not the poor girl behind the desk's fault. Tori decided to make sure she was as nice as possible to the desk clerk when it was her turn; it was the least she could do to make up for her having to deal with that dreadful man. As she stepped forward to speak to the luggage clerk, she made a mental note to never apply for a job on a lost luggage desk. Think of all those angry people you'd have to deal with every day. She shuddered.

As Tori made her way out of the Arrivals gate, she spotted her mum instantly.

'Mum!' she shouted, as she ran towards her with her arms outstretched.

'There's my girl,' said Joyce, engulfing her daughter in a hug. 'Oh, I've missed you. Come on, let me have a look at you,' she said, taking a step back to examine Tori full in the face. 'You look gorgeous as always, a bit too skinny and your hair has got so light,' she said, ruffling her daughter's long brown hair.

'Ah, that'll be all the sunshine in Thailand,' Tori replied, smiling.

'Well, it suits you, love, it's a very . . . sun-kissed look.'

'Thanks, Mum.'

'What a shame about your bag, though. What did the lost luggage people say?'

'Oh, I've filled out a form and they've given me a reference number. Fingers crossed they'll be able to track it down. They'll send it on to the house if they find it, so I won't need to come back.'

'That's something at least,' Joyce replied. 'It's such a shame that Ryan couldn't fly back with you, love. I bet you're going to miss him.'

'Oh, yeah,' she said, not quite meeting her mum's eye. 'I miss him already.'

'What is it you said that's keeping him out there?'

'Just some bar work, but it's really good money,' she added quickly, 'and what with us saving up for a place of our own, he couldn't really turn it down,' she lied.

'Of course not, love. It's good that he's thinking about your future – you've found yourself a good one there.'

'Yeah, I have,' Tori said, trying hard to blink away the tears that she could feel pooling at the backs of her eyes.

'What's wrong, love?'

'Oh, just my allergies,' said Tori, wiping her eyes with the back of her hands. 'I think the air conditioning on the plane has flared them up.'

'Here, use this,' said Joyce, passing Tori a pack of tissues from her handbag.

'Thanks, Mum,' said Tori with a sniff.

'Now, would you like to grab a coffee here or head home and I'll make you one of my hot chocolates?' Joyce was the owner of Blossom Heath's only tearoom, the Cosy Cup, and her calorific cakes and treats were legendary.

'With all the trimmings?'

'Obviously. Cream, marshmallows *and* chocolate sprinkles.'

'Like it's even a choice, Mum,' said Tori, taking her mum's arm.

'Home it is, then,' Joyce laughed. 'I can't tell you how good it is to have you back for good, love. It's such a relief to know that you're safe and sound, and you and Ryan are here to stay.'

'Hmm, yep . . . me and Ryan,' Tori said, nodding in agreement. Her hands felt shaky as they walked back towards the car. She really hoped she wasn't going to have to break it to her mum just yet that things between her and Ryan were over. She knew how much her mum loved Ryan and how upset she'd be that things hadn't worked out for the pair of them. She wanted to wait a while in case there was a chance of her and Ryan getting back together. Why worry her mum if it wasn't really necessary? As she put her bags into the car, she realized that her return home was going to be harder than she thought. Much harder.

Chapter 2

The drive from the airport whizzed by. Tori had so much to tell her mum about; she hadn't seen her for just over a year and the pair of them had always been close. Tori's dad had left when she was fifteen and he hadn't kept in touch much since. She got the obligatory Christmas and birthday cards and the odd phone call, but they hadn't seen much of each other over the past few years. Tori had found it hard to forgive him after he left Joyce for another woman and her dad had made little effort to stay in contact with her. The way she saw it, if he couldn't be bothered to make the effort then neither could she. Perhaps he was embarrassed about the way he'd treated her mum and was too ashamed to show his face? Either way, they were better off without him; things were easier, just the two of them against the world.

As they pulled up outside the Cosy Cup, Tori smiled. It felt good to be back with her mum again, to be back in Blossom Heath, even if it wasn't in the circumstances she'd hoped for.

'It's so good to be back, everything looks exactly the same,' said Tori as she walked into the tearoom and eyed the cakes behind the counter. 'How come you're closed this afternoon? I thought Cathy would be holding the fort?'

'Oh, I thought I'd told you, love – it must have slipped my mind. Cathy left a couple of weeks ago – she met a new man and moved to Northampton. I've been on my own since. As it's Sunday, I thought I'd close early.'

'On your own? But Mum, that's way too much for one person – you can't possibly manage to bake, serve and keep up with all the orders at the same time,' said Tori, her brow furrowed.

'I manage. I've reduced the opening hours and I've scaled the menu back a bit. Anyway, I only needed to get through a couple of weeks until you were home and I'd have reinforcements.'

'Oh, I see,' said Tori, exhaling. She wasn't sure that working at the Cosy Cup was exactly what she had planned for her future now she wasn't with Ryan. *What exactly was her plan?* She felt her heart beat slightly faster when she realized that she didn't know. She hadn't thought that far ahead.

'Now you're back for good, there's no need to worry about hiring someone new. It's all worked out perfectly,' Joyce said with a smile.

'Perfectly, yes.' Tori nodded, feeling a queasy sensation in her stomach, she really didn't know how long she'd be staying in Blossom Heath. 'Ooh, you've got coffee and walnut cake,' she said, keen to change the subject.

'You could give me a chance to get my coat off,' Joyce laughed. 'You know where everything is – grab yourself a slice and I'll get to work on the hot chocolates.'

Tori threw her handbag down on her favourite chair by the window, picked up a plate and cut a huge slice of cake. She was ravenous. The meal she'd had on the flight had been awful, congealed pasta with a sauce that had some kind of meat in it, although she couldn't tell what. She picked up a fork and sat down at the window table. It had always been her favourite spot as she could see all the comings and goings on the village green and over the years, she'd spent countless hours watching the world go by. She was just getting comfy when she saw a large ginger cat, around the size of a small dog, appear at the café door, meowing frantically, hoping to be let in.

'Ernie!' cried Tori, jumping up from her seat.

'You know the rules – he's not allowed in here,' Joyce called out. Tori and Joyce lived in the house next to the Cosy Cup and one of the rules was that Ernie was never allowed in the tearoom.

'Oh, come on, Mum, it won't hurt just once. He hasn't seen me for a year!'

'Go on, then,' Joyce said, relenting. 'As long as it's just this once.'

Tori opened the front door and scooped Ernie up in her arms, which was no mean feat considering he was a Maine Coon who weighed in at just over eight kilograms. Tori rubbed him gently under the chin and the cat immediately began purring contentedly.

'Oh, I missed you, Ernie, I'd forgotten just how adorable you are,' she said as she popped him down on the floor so he could begin exploring. Tori looked around the little tearoom fondly; she loved how warm and inviting the place had always been. Although, she had to admit, it was starting to look a little dated. The pretty gingham tablecloths, intricate handmade doilies and mismatched boho furniture were all looking tired and in need of replacement. Tori took a huge bite of her cake. 'Mmm, I can't tell you how much I've missed your baking, Mum,' she said, closing her eyes as she savoured the rich frosting.

Joyce laughed. 'Well, now you're back home you can eat all the cake you want, love. You can stand to gain a few pounds, you know.'

'Honestly, Mum, my jeans are finally feeling roomy and I'm planning on keeping it that way. Turns out after all those fad diets I've tried, all I needed was to live off rice and beans for six months.'

'Well, no fear of that here,' Joyce said with a smile as she placed two mugfuls of hot chocolate and whipped cream on the table and pulled up a chair opposite Tori. 'I've made your favourite for tea later – lasagne.'

'Aw, thanks, Mum.'

'So, tell me. Now you've explored Asia, what was the highlight, the number one thing that you loved more than anything else?'

'That's tough, I mean the whole thing was just, well . . . amazing. It really opens your eyes, seeing other cultures, seeing what else is out there. I loved Tokyo, it's so bright and vibrant, all the neon lights and pop culture, it's such a special place – it has a real buzz about it.'

'A bit like London?'

'That's the thing, though, it really isn't like London at all. It's hard to explain but it's a city of contrasts, I suppose,' said Tori, stirring her hot chocolate. 'You've got gorgeous temples with so much history right next door to skyscrapers and markets that are twenty-four hours next to the most beautiful, tranquil gardens. Everything there just feels so ... cutting edge and the shopping is, well, it's out of this world. You'd love it, Mum, honestly you would.'

'I'm sure I would, love. It might be tricky getting holiday cover for this place, though.'

'You'd be in your element. There are quirky coffee shops everywhere, and they sell these delicious, sweet buns filled with red-bean paste called anpans,' she said, smiling at the memory. 'Oh Mum, you'd love them!'

'Anpans, eh? Sounds interesting. I'll look up a recipe.'

'You should! I'm happy to give them a taste test.'

'No surprises there,' Joyce chuckled.

'Hang on, let me grab my phone and I'll show you some pictures.' Tori reached for her bag, dug out her iPhone and flicked through her photo gallery of Tokyo to show her mum some of her favourite images.

'It certainly sounds as though it was a wonderful experience,' said Joyce.

'You know what you'd *really* love about the café culture in

Tokyo, though, Mum?' Tori said, leaning in towards Joyce. 'The cat cafés!'

'The what?'

'Cat cafés. They have loads of them in Tokyo; lots of people can't have their own pets, they all live in small apartments you see, so it's a way for them to spend time with cats if they can't have one of their own. It's a genius idea.'

'And the cats just wander around while people are drinking their coffee?'

'Exactly. There are rules and stuff, though, you can't stroke the cats unless they come up to you and there are lots of welfare regulations to make sure that they're well looked after. I couldn't get enough of visiting while I was out there, I missed Ernie so much,' she said, bending down to scoop up the ginger cat and place him on her lap.

'Doesn't sound very practical to me. Cats are into everything; they'd cause chaos. Climbing curtains, knocking over cups ... the mind boggles.'

'Well, somehow they make it work and the customers absolutely love it.'

'Each to their own, I suppose.'

'I'll take you there one day and you can see for yourself.'

'I'd love that,' said Joyce, she reached across the table and gave Tori's hand a squeeze. 'If we can get someone to look after this place,' she quickly added.

'Deal! So what's been going on in Blossom Heath since I've been away, then? There must be tons of gossip?' Tori asked, popping the last pink marshmallow into her mouth.

'Oh, I don't know about that – not much changes around here.'

'Come on ... spill,' Tori giggled.

'Actually, there is something that'll interest you.'

'What?'

'Well, Rose Hargreaves has moved back to the village! Permanently!'

'What? Jean's niece, from Jasmine Cottage? Wow! I thought she was engaged and living in London ...'

'She was, but she came back last spring to help out when Jean had her fall—'

'Jean had a fall? Is she okay?'

'She's fine now; she fractured a hip but she's fully recovered. Anyway, Rose came down to help out and ended up falling for a local lad and breaking up with her fiancé.'

'Seriously? Who?'

'Jake Harper!'

'Jake! No way!'

'They fell head over heels for each other by all accounts. Rose's living with Jean at Jasmine Cottage but I don't think it'll be too long before she's moved in at Harper Farm with Jake.'

'Wow! That's amazing, I can't believe Rose is back for good. I've not spoken to her properly since I went to Japan; being on the move all the time makes it harder to stay in touch.'

'She's got a job locally too, teaching up at the school. I told her you're back this weekend and she's dying to see you.'

'I can't wait to catch up with her. I'll drop her a message – it's been too long.'

'Just you wait until Ryan flies back and then the four of you can go out on double dates!'

Tori felt her mouth go unbearably dry at the mention of Ryan's name.

'Oh, yeah, maybe.'

'He's a lovely lad is Ryan – I'm sure he'll get on well with Rose.'

'Uh-huh,' Tori agreed, nodding. This was ridiculous. She needed to tell her mum the truth; she'd never lied to her mother before and it wasn't a habit she wanted to get into. It was one thing not wanting to tell her over the phone but another to keep it from her now she was home. She needed to be brave, she took a deep breath and—

'You know, I was thinking. I know it's early days as you've only just got back and Ryan's not even here yet but, well, I've got a bit of cash put by and I'd like to help you out with the deposit on a house.'

'Mum, no, we couldn't accept anything like that,' Tori said quickly, her voice catching.

'Now, let me stop you there, love. I know how hard it is for young couples nowadays getting their foot on the property ladder. I *want* to do this for the pair of you, so just let me, will you? No arguments?' Joyce took Tori's hand again and locked eyes with her. 'Please, love? Let me help?'

Tori felt physically sick. What could she say? *Sorry Mum, but the man you think is the perfect boyfriend dumped me a week ago and isn't flying back to England at all. In fact, I've pretty much wasted the last four years of my life with him.* No. It would break her mum's heart. She'd have to bide her time before she broke the news. If there was any chance of a reconciliation, any chance at all, she needed to keep her lips sealed.

'Sure, Mum, that would be great,' she said, blinking back tears.

'Oh, come here, love,' said Joyce, standing and flinging her arms around her. 'You know we could even go and have a look at a few places before Ryan gets back? Just see what's available? They're building some lovely starter homes up on that estate past the school. Jake's sister Kate bought one recently and it's lovely apparently.'

'Why not?' Tori agreed. What was wrong with her? Why was she saying yes? She was just digging herself a deeper and deeper hole that she'd have to find her way out of eventually. She couldn't keep lying forever.

Chapter 3

Tori woke up the next morning feeling refreshed yet sad, after one of the best night's sleep she'd had in over a year. There really was nothing like your own bed after months spent sleeping in youth hostels and budget hotels.

'Morning, Ernie,' she said, reaching down to scratch the cat on the top of the head. There was something comforting about Ernie's presence at the foot of her bed; she hadn't got used to sleeping alone again – her break-up with Ryan was so recent. *Ryan.* She sat up and placed her head in her hands. Why hadn't she told her mum the truth about him when she'd first stepped off the plane? Putting off breaking the news to her mum had seemed easier when she was still in Thailand, but now all she'd done was create even more problems for herself. She knew deep down that clinging to hopes of a reconciliation was, at best, a long shot. Now her mum was offering the pair of them cash for a deposit on a house and they weren't even together anymore. *Oh God!* She slumped back onto the bed and covered her head with the pillow. Her mum even wanted to go to look at houses with her this week. What a mess.

Tempting as it might be, staying in bed all day wasn't going to fix anything, she told herself. No, she needed to face things head-on. Tori could hear her mum moving around in the kitchen below. She decided to take action. She took a deep breath, threw back the duvet and pulled on her dressing gown. She'd go downstairs right now and tell her mum the truth. Honesty really was the best policy. As she descended the stairs, she could hear her mum in the kitchen singing along to the radio.

'Since when did you become a Ronan Keating fan?' Tori giggled, pulling up a chair at the kitchen table.

'It's a catchy tune and, anyway, I've got a good singing voice.'

'I know, I'm only messing,' said Tori, smiling. 'What's all this anyway? Looks like you're cooking up a feast.'

'Pancakes with fresh blueberries and maple syrup, love.'

'You're going to have to stop spoiling me like this. I've been back less than twenty-four hours and I've already eaten more than a week's worth of calories. You know I'd be happy with a slice of toast in the café, like we usually have.'

'If I can't make a fuss of my only daughter on her first morning back, who can?' said Joyce, placing a stack of pancakes on the table in front of Tori.

'I guess, but I'm making *you* dinner tonight, okay?' said Tori, picking up the bottle of maple syrup and pouring a generous amount over her stack. Joyce smiled. 'Listen, Mum, can I talk to you about something?' Tori asked. She wanted to seize the moment to break the news about Ryan while she was still feeling brave.

'Sorry, what, love? Look, I wanted to show you this – I grabbed a brochure for that new development I was telling you about when I was passing last week,' said Joyce, pulling a glossy brochure out of one of the kitchen drawers.

Tori looked at it; it was emerald green and shiny with the words MEADOWGATE MEAD emblazoned across the front in gold lettering. She swallowed hard. 'But, Mum—'

'Oh, just have a look – don't spoil my fun, love. It looks stunning, doesn't it? I think it would be the perfect place for you and Ryan to start out.'

Tori smiled weakly and stuffed a huge forkful of pancakes into her mouth. She couldn't say anything to her mum now, could she? God, her timing was awful. 'Yeah, I mean it looks . . . nice.'

'Nice? Oh, it's more than nice. Look at this,' she said, 'on page eighteen it shows you all the facilities they've got on site – see? There're tennis courts, even an on-site gym.'

'Wow, yep, I can see that,' said Tori, taking the brochure to flick through. All she could see were pictures of good-looking couples smiling and walking together arm in arm around a man-made lake or laughing on a bike ride together. They looked so . . . happy . . . so . . . perfect. Suddenly Tori wasn't feeling hungry anymore. She pushed her plate away.

'I'm going to grab a shower,' she said, standing up abruptly.

'But you've not finished your breakfast,' said Joyce.

'I think I'm still full after that lasagne last night,' she lied.

'Okay, well, just let me know what you fancy doing today. I wasn't planning on opening until later, what with it being your first day home. We could always take a drive over to Meadowgate Mead if you like? The opening times are on the back of the brochure there, see?'

'Oh,' Tori replied, her brain frantically trying to come up with something, anything, that would mean she didn't have to go and view a new house that she'd never move into. 'Actually, I was planning to . . . go and visit Rose. Yes, I thought the two of us could have a catch-up.'

'Rose? But won't she be teaching? It's Monday morning.'

'Oh.' Damn, her mum was right – Rose *would* be teaching today. A sudden thought struck her. 'But isn't it the Easter holidays? It's Good Friday this week, isn't it?'

'Of course! You're right, love, I'm sure Rose would love to see you.'

'I'll just go and give her a quick ring.' As Tori climbed the stairs back to her bedroom to find her phone, she prayed with every inch of her being that Rose was going to be at home this morning.

Tori knocked hard on the front door of Jasmine Cottage and was greeted by the sound of a dog barking. A dog? Had Rose got a dog since she'd moved back to Blossom Heath? The door opened and a smile broke across Tori's face as soon as she saw her childhood friend.

'Tori!' cried Rose, pulling her into a hug. 'It's been way too long!'

'It really has,' Tori agreed as she became aware of a wet nose pressed up against her knees. 'And who do we have here?' she asked, bending down to stroke the black and white Border Collie that was jumping up excitedly around her.

'This is Scout. She's gorgeous, isn't she?'

'Well, hello, Scout,' said Tori, 'aren't you a cutie?' As if on command, Scout rolled onto her back in the hope of a belly rub.

'That's her favourite trick,' said Rose, laughing. 'I'm afraid it's mandatory for all visitors to give Scout a tummy tickle before they're allowed in.'

Tori laughed. 'Well, I'm more than happy to oblige,' she said, giving Scout the fuss she was after before standing up again. 'She's a sweetheart. I can't believe you've already got a dog – you've only been back five minutes.'

'A lot's happened since we last saw each other,' said Rose. 'Why don't I stick the kettle on and we'll catch up?'

'Sounds perfect,' said Tori, as she stepped over the threshold of Jasmine Cottage.

After Rose had made a pot of tea, the pair of friends sat down at the kitchen table and began chatting animatedly about everything that had been happening since they'd last met.

'I was trying to remember the last time we saw each other,' said Tori, cupping the mug in both hands before drinking her tea.

'I reckon it's been nearly five years. You've been off travelling when I've been back the last few summers.'

'That long? Wow. It feels like so much has happened since then. You first. How have you gone from being engaged to a City banker and teaching in London, to being back in Blossom Heath and dating Jake Harper?'

Rose laughed. She explained that she'd returned to Blossom Heath in spring last year to care for her aunt and, after losing her teaching job in London, she'd ended up taking a temporary job at Blossom Heath Primary School.

'I found Scout when I first got back; she was a stray and I ended up adopting her. Let's just say that Blossom Heath won my heart and I couldn't go back to London.'

'Sounds like it wasn't just Blossom Heath that won your heart,' said Tori, with a sly smile.

'Well, no, Jake had a lot to do with it. I don't think I'd realized how badly things were going with my ex until I met Jake. Being back here made me see what I really wanted out of life, I guess. Then, when Mrs Connolly, the headteacher at the village school, offered me a permanent job, I knew that I just couldn't leave.'

'Wow. That must have been tough, though, breaking off your engagement, I mean?'

'It was, and I did question whether I was doing the right thing, but I knew deep down that Jake was the one I wanted to be with. I know it sounds corny, but maybe you just *know* somehow, when you meet *the one*.'

'Oh, so Jake's "the one" now, is he?' Tori teased; she noticed Rose's cheeks turning redder.

'Well, yeah, I think he actually is.'

'That's amazing, Rose. I'm really happy for you both and I'm so pleased you're back. I can certainly do with all the friends I can get right now . . .'

'Why, what's up?' Rose replied quickly, her eyes narrowing.

Tori hung her head; she wasn't sure where to start. She'd made such a mess of things.

'It's not you and Ryan, is it?'

Tori could feel the tears about to flow. This time she didn't hold back, she let them fall freely. Rose pulled her chair closer and placed an arm around Tori's shoulders.

'Tori, what is it? What's wrong?'

'Oh God, Rose, I'm such an idiot,' Tori whispered in between sobs. 'Things with Ryan are . . . well, they're over.'

'Oh no, I'm so sorry. What happened?' Rose asked, pulling a tissue out from the pocket of her jeans and passing it to her friend.

'That's the thing – nothing. I don't even know what I did wrong. Everything was fine and then he just turned around and said he didn't want to be in a relationship anymore. No reason, no explanation . . . nothing. He just said, "I'm not a relationship guy." But what does that even mean, Rose?'

'And he didn't say anything else? Just that he wanted to end things?'

'No, nothing. I've literally got no clue what went wrong. He just seemed to change his mind about everything overnight. I mean, we had plans. We were coming back home to start looking for our own place together; I was going to move out of Mum's and he was going to leave his houseshare in London to move here. I thought we'd end up getting engaged before Christmas and then ... this happens.'

'It just doesn't make any sense,' said Rose. 'I'm not surprised you're feeling confused. I would be too.'

'We were talking about all the plans we had for when we got back from travelling and then ... he just ends it. I thought we were happy, at least *I* was.'

'God, Tori, I'm so sorry. You don't deserve to be treated like that. He owes you a reason at least; you can't just end things out of the blue after four years together without some sort of explanation.'

'I just don't understand,' said Tori, balling up the tissue she had in her left hand and clasping it hard. 'But it's even more complicated.'

'How?'

'I couldn't face telling Mum the news over the phone ... I still haven't explained things to her. If there's a chance that Ryan and I could make things up, I don't want Mum to have a bad opinion of him. Especially after how Dad let her down; I'm not sure she'd ever forgive Ryan if she knew ... I've said he got offered some work in Thailand and is staying on a bit longer.'

'Oh Tori,' said Rose, rubbing her friend's arm.

'I know. At first, I thought I'd break the news once I got home but I couldn't bear to do it. She was so excited about us being back in Blossom Heath for good and looking for a house together ...' Tori paused. 'Last night she even offered to pay the deposit for us. Oh, Rose, she had a brochure and everything and she wants to take me to Meadowgate Mead today to look around the show home. What am I going to do?' She looked up at Rose, her eyes wide and her face streaked with tears. 'I know I shouldn't have lied – I've just made it all a thousand times worse.'

'Don't be daft,' said Rose, handing her friend another tissue. 'Your mum will understand. All she wants is for you to be happy and you know she'll support you whatever. This whole thing is Ryan's fault, none of the blame lies with you. You do know that, Tori, don't you?'

Tori sat quietly for a moment.

'But Mum *loves* Ryan. She'll be heartbroken,' Tori replied.

'I think her opinion of him will change pretty quickly when she hears how he's treated you. I know mine has,' Rose said firmly.

'I guess,' said Tori, shrugging.

'I know,' replied Rose, taking Tori's hand. 'You just have to bite the bullet and tell her the truth. She'll be on your side.'

'But what if this whole thing is just a silly wobble and I work things out with him?'

'And you think it could be?'

'Oh, I don't know,' said Tori, dropping her head. 'It all happened so suddenly; I don't feel like I've really processed it. I keep checking my phone and he's not been in touch. No phone calls, messages . . . nothing. I'm determined not to be the first one to make contact.'

'Even so, Tori, I don't think you can keep something like this from your mum. She knows you too well – she'll figure it out. She'll understand.'

'You're right,' Tori agreed, relaxing slightly as she sat back in her chair. She blew her nose hard. 'Thanks, Rose, I can't tell you how much better I feel for sharing all this with you.'

'Glad I could help,' said Rose. 'Now get these Bourbons down you, you look like you could do with a sugar fix.' She smiled, offering the plate of biscuits to Tori. 'You know, just because Ryan wasn't the one, doesn't mean your perfect man isn't just around the corner—'

'No way!' Tori replied sharply. 'I'm done with men ...'

'Ah, you say that now but when your perfect guy—'

'I'm serious, Rose, I'm not looking to date *anyone* right now. Mr Darcy could literally walk through that door', she said, gesturing towards the kitchen door, 'and I'd tell him to get lost.' Rose rolled her eyes towards the ceiling. 'I mean it, Rose, Ernie's pretty much the only guy I want around, and he has fur and a tail.' And, as she said those words out loud, Tori realized that she had never been more serious about anything in her life.

Chapter 4

When Tori returned to the Cosy Cup, her mum had already opened up and was busy dealing with the mid-morning rush.

'Oh, Tori, thank goodness. Can you make a start clearing tables four and eight for me?' Joyce called from behind the counter where she was busy making lattes at the coffee machine. Every table in the tearoom was occupied and Joyce looked rushed off her feet. She had a pencil tucked behind her left ear, a notepad wedged into the waistband of her apron and her face was red with exertion.

Tori made quick work of clearing the tables that had empty cups and plates on them, piling everything up onto one tray and taking it through to the kitchen.

'Mum, why's it so busy? It's only Monday morning.' she said as she returned to the counter.

'The WI have just turned out from the village hall; they always pile in here for a cuppa and catch-up after their meetings.'

'Just tell me where you want me and I'll pitch in,' said

Tori, grabbing herself an apron from the hook next to the cash register and tying it around her waist.

'I was hoping you'd say that, love. Can you get these coffees over to table seven? And then take the orders from tables one and six – they've been waiting ages.'

'I'm on it.' As Tori took a tray of lattes over to table seven, she was greeted by three familiar faces beaming up at her.

'Tori dear, it's lovely to see you home again,' said Jean Hargreaves. Although in her early eighties, you'd never have guessed it. Her grey hair was stylishly cut into a mid-length bob and she was wearing an emerald green chiffon top with a necklace in the exact same shade.

'Hi, Jean. I've just been catching up with Rose at the cottage – I can't believe she's back!' said Tori, placing the coffees down on the table.

'Oh, I'm over the moon to have her here, dear. I can't tell you how much her being around has lifted my spirits. Jasmine Cottage feels like a different place with her and Scout there and it's not just me rattling around,' Jean said, her eyes glowing. 'But how are you? How were your travels, dear? We've all missed you.'

'Oh, good. Really good. I'll come over and tell you about it properly when things aren't so hectic here,' said Tori.

'Oh, to be young and off having adventures,' said Jean, with a wistful look in her eye.

'And you're feeling better, are you? After your fall?' Tori asked.

'Oh, that,' Jean said, waving her hand dismissively. 'I'm right as rain, dear. Don't you worry about me.'

'It'll take more than a fractured hip to keep Jean Hargreaves out of mischief,' laughed Beth, the landlady of the Apple Tree. 'It's good to have you back, Tori, sweetheart.'

'Never mind how *she* is,' said Maggie, the owner of Harrison's general store, 'I want to know when that boyfriend of yours is getting here – Ryan, isn't it? Joyce said he's been delayed and we're all dying to see him again.' Jean, Beth and Maggie all looked up at her expectantly.

'And to hear more about your travels, of course,' Beth added quickly.

Tori felt her mouth go dry and her shoulders tense. She'd not even been back in the village ten minutes and already people were quizzing her over Ryan. She couldn't tell them the truth; well, not yet anyway. She needed to explain things to her mum first.

'Oh, in a couple of weeks hopefully,' she said, twisting the strings of her apron tightly around her fingers. 'I'd best get on, we're really busy this morning,' she added quickly, picking up her tray.

'Well, make sure you bring him along to the pub when he arrives – your first drink's on the house,' said Beth.

Tori nodded, gave Beth a weak smile and walked away silently.

The rest of the morning passed quickly, and before Tori knew it, the lunchtime rush was over and she was ready to collapse in a heap.

'Please tell me it's not this busy every day?' Tori asked her mum, untying her apron strings and throwing herself into the nearest chair. 'I don't know how you've been managing on your own since Cathy left . . . I've only worked one shift and I'm done in.'

'Well, it's a good thing I'm made of stronger stuff,' Joyce laughed, putting a steaming hot mug of tea and a cheese and sundried tomato toastie down in front of Tori. 'Now the new housing estate is up, we're busier than ever. Plus, it's practically holiday season and you know we always get tourists popping in on their way over to Rye.'

'It's good that new estate is bringing in business,' Tori said, taking a large bite of her toastie. 'Ow, that cheese is like molten lava,' she said, pursing her lips and blowing hard.

Joyce laughed. 'It has just come off the grill, what do you expect?' said Joyce, taking a seat opposite her daughter and tucking into a ham sandwich.

'What's the plan for the rest of the day?' Tori asked.

'I'll close up here at three and then I thought we could take a drive up to that new retail park if you fancy it? They've got a Dunelm, so you could get some ideas for your new place . . .'

Tori decided to be brave and take Rose's advice. She was going to tell her mum the truth about Ryan. Even if they did get back together, she wanted her mum to know the full story. She hated not being straight with her; it wasn't how their relationship worked.

'Mum, listen, I've got something I need to talk to you about actually . . .'

'Oh, hang on, love, I've forgotten the sugar.' As Joyce stood up and walked over to the counter, she staggered and grabbed hold of the corner of the nearest table to steady herself.

'Mum!' cried Tori, leaping up and grabbing Joyce around the waist. 'What's wrong? Come back and sit down,' she said, helping Joyce to her seat.

'I stood up too quickly, that's all,' said Joyce, fanning herself with the menu that was on the table. 'I just got a bit dizzy, nothing to worry about.'

'Are you sure?'

'Don't make a fuss, love, I'm fine. Like I said, I just stood up a bit too fast. It's nothing a bit of a sit-down and some food won't sort out.'

'Well, if it happens again, you're getting checked out by the doctor. Deal?'

'Oh, you're making something out of nothing, love.'

'I'm serious, Mum. Deal?'

'Oh, okay. Deal,' Joyce said, nodding her head reluctantly.

Tori banished all thoughts of breaking the news about Ryan from her mind. The last thing she wanted to do was to add to her mum's stress. It looked like she'd be going to the retail park to do some shopping for her imaginary new house after all . . .

The shopping trip didn't turn out as badly as Tori had feared. She'd managed to steer Joyce away from the idea of shopping for items for a new house by focusing on buying accessories to spruce up the tearoom. The Cosy Cup was decorated in a pastel colour palette of pale pink and mint green and Tori had spotted the cutest little pink and green bud vases which would be perfect for fresh flowers. She persuaded her mum to invest in one for every table in the café under the proviso that *she* would be the one responsible for keeping the floral arrangements fresh each day.

Tori could feel herself drifting off in the passenger seat of her mum's Toyota Yaris on the journey back to Blossom Heath. She was still feeling jet-lagged from the flight home and the busy shift in the tearoom had helped to edge her into a state of slumber. As she felt the car pull to a stop, she opened her eyes to see that they weren't back home at all. They were parked outside the sales office of the Meadowgate Mead housing development. Tori rubbed her eyes.

'Mum? What are we doing here?' she asked, panic flicking across her face. 'I thought we were going straight home?'

'Ah, I spotted the signs for Meadowgate and I just couldn't resist, love. I wanted to see what all the fuss is about. We might as well have a look around the show home while we're here.'

'But I'm shattered, Mum,' said Tori. She really didn't want to get in any deeper with her lies and dragging herself around the show home would only make things worse. She'd still heard nothing from Ryan; she needed to face facts and drop the idea that he'd come after her, realizing he'd made a dreadful mistake. It was time to be straight with her mother, to tell her the truth. 'Mum, listen—' But before she could begin to explain, Joyce was already walking briskly towards the sales office. 'Oh God,' Tori groaned, doing her best to unfasten her seat belt and catch up with her. But it was too late – Joyce had already opened the door and was shaking the hand of the suited man behind the desk. She'd have to keep up the charade a little longer. She took a deep breath, plastered on her best smile and followed Joyce into the office.

'Ah, you must be Tori,' the man said, holding out his left hand for Tori to shake. 'I'm Dan, Dan Carver. It's a starter home you're interested in, is it? For you and your partner?'

Tori opened her mouth but no words came out. She closed it again.

'Yes, that's right,' Joyce answered, giving Tori a shove with her left elbow. 'It's a two bed we'll need to look at . . .'

'Perfect, that will be the Bedford then. The show home is stunning, they've really thought of everything when it comes to space,' said Dan, handing Tori a glossy brochure. 'If you buy off-plan you'll be able to choose your own kitchen and bathroom design too, which is a huge bonus.'

'Ooh, wouldn't that be lovely, Tori? You could have your pick of any colour scheme you like.'

'Great,' Tori agreed, nodding.

'We've got four plots left for the Bedford, so that would be numbers 84, 88, 90 and 96, and you'd have the option of being mid or end terrace,' Dan explained eagerly, pointing at the site map with his pencil. 'Of course, the show home itself will be available in a few months' time, so that could be an option too.'

'Uh-huh,' Tori nodded.

'Let me just grab the keys and we'll get started with the tour,' said Dan, reaching over to the cabinet behind his desk. 'This way, ladies,' he continued, opening the office door and leading the way along the path.

'Isn't this exciting?' said Joyce, linking her arm through Tori's. 'Just think, this could be your first proper home.'

As they walked into the house, Joyce oohed with delight. The front door opened straight into a spacious living and kitchen area, which was decorated in shades of cream and grey, with a large plush corner sofa occupying one side of the room and fluffy rugs covering the dark wooden flooring. The dining table had been set up with plates and glasses as though it was ready and waiting for guests to arrive. It looked like something out of a magazine. It was stunning. It was everything Tori had imagined her first home with Ryan would be. A home that she knew she would never share with him.

Tori couldn't hold it in any longer. She felt the pressure building in her chest, her breathing became faster and shallow, and she was aware of a wet track of tears running down her face. Her sobs gathered force, becoming more audible, until both Joyce and Dan turned around.

'Tori, love, what on earth's wrong?' Joyce said, putting her arm around her daughter's shoulders. 'What's happened?'

'I can't do this, Mum. It's all … lies,' Tori mumbled in between sobs.

'What's lies? What are you talking about, love?'

'Er, I think I'll give you two a minute, shall I?' said Dan, backing away quickly. 'I'll be in the office if you want to talk figures,' he continued, exiting hastily through the front door.

'Everything is, Mum. Nothing I've said since I got home is true.'

'But I don't understand,' said Joyce. 'Let's sit down, shall we?' She guided Tori towards the sofa and passed her a pack of tissues she'd dug from her handbag. 'Just take a minute and calm down. Whatever's wrong, we can fix it.'

'That's what Rose said you'd say,' Tori said, sniffing. 'She said I just needed to be honest with you and you'd understand.'

'I'll always understand, love. But first, don't you think you'd better explain what all this is about?'

Tori hesitated.

'It's me and Ryan, Mum. We're ... over. He dumped me, last week. I just couldn't bear to tell you.' Tori dissolved into sobs.

'Oh, love, come here,' said Joyce, pulling Tori in towards her for a hug.

'I'm so sorry, Mum. I didn't want to tell you over the phone and then I just couldn't face telling you in person either. You were so ... *happy* and I just ... well, I guess I didn't want to ruin it. I thought he'd realize he'd made a mistake and we'd work things out. I didn't want you to think badly of him, I guess. Then you offered to pay the deposit on a house, and I just got in deeper—'

'Oh, forget all that,' said Joyce, waving her hands in the air.

'What happened exactly though, love? Why on earth would he end things? I thought things were going so well between the two of you?'

'I don't even know myself, not really. It was totally out of the blue – I can't explain it. I don't know what I did wrong . . .'

'Hey!' said Joyce, her tone suddenly stern. 'I'll not have you talking like that – I'm sure it's nothing *you've* done. Don't start second-guessing yourself, okay? All that matters to me is that you're happy.'

'Thanks, Mum,' Tori sniffed.

'And as for a house, the offer stands. If you still want a place of your own, I'll help you with the deposit when the time comes.'

'But . . .'

'It doesn't have to be now,' Joyce added quickly. 'Whenever you're ready, the offer's there.'

'Thanks, Mum,' said Tori, blowing her nose hard. She paused and looked up. 'Listen, after everything with Ryan, I'm just not sure what my plans are now I'm back. I don't know what I'll do . . .'

'It's fine, love,' said Joyce, taking Tori's hand in hers. 'You don't need to start mapping out your entire future today now, do you?'

'I guess not.'

'Exactly. There's no rush for you to decide what's next, is there? Blossom Heath isn't going anywhere and neither am I.'

'Thanks, Mum,' said Tori, her shoulders relaxing.

Joyce looked around the living room of the show home, her eyes narrowed. 'You know, after all the hype over this new development, I can't see what all the fuss is about personally. This house is bland, if you ask me. You may as well just move into Ikea.'

'Do you know what? I completely agree,' Tori replied, patting her mum's hand and wiping away the remainder of her tears. 'When I'm ready to live on my own, I want something with a bit more character.'

'Maybe something with an inglenook fireplace and a few oak beams?'

'And stairs that creak when you walk up them.'

'Sounds perfect,' Joyce agreed. 'Come on, let's get out of here, shall we?'

'Let's,' said Tori, standing up and pulling Joyce off the sofa with a heave.

'I can tell you one thing, though,' said Joyce as they walked out of the front door, 'I don't think Dan's going to be best pleased about losing out on his commission. Do you?'

Tori laughed.

'No, well, we'd better break it to him gently on the way out,' Tori replied.

'Or we could just make a run for it?' said Joyce with a conspiratorial wink.

'Mum!' said Tori, putting her hands on her hips. 'I'm *shocked* that you would even suggest such a thing ...' She paused. 'Let's do it!'

Giggling, Tori and Joyce clasped hands and made a run

for the car, ducking beneath the window of the sales office to escape unseen. As Joyce started the Toyota's ignition to make their getaway, Tori saw Dan look up from his desk. What would he think of them now they'd done a runner? She smiled and realized that she didn't really care.

Chapter 5

As Tori lay in bed the next morning, she felt as though a huge weight had been lifted. *She'd done it.* She'd told her mum about Ryan and, just as Rose had known she would, her mum had been there to support her. Tori sat up in bed and reached across the bedside table to find her phone. She typed out a message to Rose. *I've told Mum about Ryan. Thanks for your advice and being there when I needed to talk. If you're around today, there's a mocha with your name on it at the Cosy Cup xx*

Tori looked down at the foot of her bed. Where was Ernie? She could always rely on him being curled up there every morning, even after she'd been away travelling. How odd. Tori pulled on her jeans and a T-shirt and headed downstairs.

'Morning, Mum. Have you seen Ernie?' she asked.

'Now you mention it, no. I don't think he's been in yet.'

'Weird. He doesn't usually stay out all night these days, does he?' said Tori.

'Not usually. He's probably just out getting up to mischief somewhere. He'll turn up,' Joyce replied.

'I hope so.'

'I'm heading next door to open up,' said Joyce, grabbing the keys to the café.

'I'm going to have some cereal first; I don't fancy toast this morning,' said Tori, filling a bowl with cornflakes. Before she poured in the milk, Tori stopped and picked up the box of dried cat food next to the bread bin and opened the back door. 'Ernie! Ernie!' she called, shaking the box of food. 'Ernie, breakfast!' She stood at the door for a few minutes shaking the box and calling Ernie's name. 'Where are you, little man?' she wondered, closing the door. As she poured milk over her cereal, she hoped that, whatever Ernie was up to, he hadn't got himself into any trouble.

Tuesday morning at the Cosy Cup flew by, and before Tori knew it, it was already twelve thirty. She was just catching her breath, when a petite brunette woman, dressed in designer clothes, approached the counter.

'Any chance I could grab a quick baguette to go? I've got to be back at the salon in five, but I'm starving,' said the woman.

'Yeah, of course. I think Mum's got some made up,' said Tori, looking in the glass display cabinet. 'Any preference?'

'If you've got tuna, that would be great.'

'Tuna and cucumber?'

'Perfect,' the woman said, beaming at her. 'I don't

think we've met before, I'm Claire. I run the salon over the road,' she explained, pointing across the village green towards her shop.

'Lovely to meet you. I'm Tori, Joyce's daughter.'

'Ah! Of course. I've heard all about you, you're just back from travelling aren't you?' Claire asked, tapping her card to pay.

'That's right.'

'Sorry, I've got to dash,' she said, glancing at her watch, 'but you should pop by the salon some time, say hello.'

'I'll do that. I could do with a bit of a trim,' said Tori, fanning out her hair.

'Perfect, I'll see you soon then,' said Claire, waving goodbye.

'Was that Claire?' asked Joyce, appearing from the kitchen with a tray of freshly cooked biscuits.

'Ooooh, they smell good,' said Tori, attempting to steal one. Joyce batted her hand away.

'These are for the customers,' said Joyce. 'So, was that Claire?'

'Oh, yes, sorry,' said Tori distractedly.

'She's a lovely girl, I've been meaning to introduce the pair of you.'

'She seemed friendly. I said I'll pop over to the salon for a trim at some point.'

'Good idea. I'm sure the two of you will hit it off. It'll be good for you to get out and about more, you don't want to be stuck at home with me every night.'

'I don't mind, Mum. Honest.'

'You're a good girl, Tori,' said Joyce, squeezing her hand.

Tori looked away when she heard a familiar voice call her name.

'Tori,' said Rose, waving from across the counter.

'You made it,' said Tori, leaning over to give her friend a hug.

'Well, you did say that there's a mocha with my name on it,' Rose laughed.

'I did! Grab a table and I'll see if I can join you.'

'Of course you can,' said Joyce, rolling her eyes. 'Great to see you, Rose, love.'

Tori busied herself at the barista machine, before heading to the window table to join Rose.

'I'm so glad you came clean with your mum. Didn't I tell you everything would be okay?' said Rose.

'I know. I should have done it as soon as I got off the plane, but I guess we're always wiser after the event.'

'Have you heard from Ryan?' asked Rose.

'Nope, nothing. I'm not expecting to. He was pretty clear things are over; I just didn't want to accept it. I can't think what else there is to say,' replied Tori, shrugging.

'Perhaps it's better that way? At least it'll be a clean break and you can get on with your life?'

'Maybe. Oh, I don't know. To be honest, I've not really thought much about the future. Staying here without Ryan just feels so strange. I don't know what I'm going to do work-wise. Ryan was going back to his old job, so I thought I'd have time to look around properly, find something that really appealed. I was so caught up in the idea of our shiny new future together, I didn't look beyond that.'

'You've got options. I know Blossom Heath isn't exactly London, but you've got your business degree, so it shouldn't be too hard to find something that suits,' said Rose.

'You think?' asked Tori, smiling widely.

'I do. What about that place you were working before you went away?'

'Andersen's?' Rose nodded. 'The marketing department of a discount furniture warehouse wasn't exactly the dream.'

'No, I get that. There's a couple of new tech start-ups in Ashford. Jake mentioned something about one of his football mates getting a job there. I can ask if you'd like?' Rose reached across the table and took Tori's hand.

'Oh, I don't know,' Tori said quickly. 'I don't want to make any decisions right now; everything just feels so up in the air.'

'I get it, no pressure. But if you want me to ask, just let me know.'

The door of the tearoom banged open, and Tori looked up to see who had made such a dramatic entrance. It was Maggie Harrison. She looked red in the face and was clearly out of breath. Her eyes scanned the room and stopped when they spotted Tori.

'Tori, it's Ernie . . .'

'Ernie? What's happened, Mags?'

'He's at the top of that huge sycamore tree on the green; you know, the one next to the duck pond? Ted and I have tried to coax him down but he's not having it. I think he's stuck.'

Tori and Rose stood up and made towards the door.

'Oh, Ernie! Come on, Rose, we'd best go rescue him.'

Tori could hear Ernie yowling before she could see him.

'See, there he is,' said Maggie, pointing at the sycamore's uppermost branches.

'Oh Ernie! How did you manage to get all the way up there?' said Tori.

'Those branches look too thin to support him. He's huge,' said Rose, concern etched on her face.

'I know, right?' said Tori.

'How are we going to get him down?' asked Rose.

'Ted's gone back to the shop for a ladder. Hopefully we can reach him that way,' said Maggie.

'Great. Look, here's Ted now,' said Rose, pointing towards a tall man with salt and pepper hair making his way across the green towards them with a ladder tucked awkwardly under his arm. She turned towards Tori. 'He'll be fine – we'll get him down.'

Ted huffed and puffed as he extended the ladder as far as it would go. He tried to secure it against the tree with a length of rope, but he was all fingers and thumbs.

'Honestly, give it here, would you?' said Maggie, rolling her eyes. She tied the rope quickly and with minimal fuss. 'There, that should hold firm,' she said, patting the ladder.

'It's not as long as I would have liked,' said Ted. 'He's still way too high for us to reach.'

'I'll go,' said Tori quickly. 'He's my cat and if he hears my voice, hopefully he'll come down.'

'I'm happy to give it a go, Tori. Mags has always got me up and down that ladder doing some repair or other,' said Ted.

'Don't be daft. He's my cat – I'll go,' Tori replied.

'I'll hold it steady,' said Ted, 'just take it slow and try not to spook him.'

Tori nodded and took a deep breath. She'd been rock climbing on her travelling adventures so a medium-sized tree should be easy enough.

'Piece of cake,' she said under her breath. As she climbed the ladder, she whispered to Ernie encouragingly, 'Come on, little man, just a bit closer.' She stretched out an arm. Ernie yowled and shifted his weight awkwardly. 'That's it, this way . . .' But Ernie turned his back and, much to Tori's frustration, climbed even higher up the tree. 'Seriously, Ern? You do get I'm trying to rescue you, right? I'm not climbing this tree for fun,' she muttered. Finally admitting defeat, she made her way back down. 'We'll have to think of something else. Whether he's scared or just being bloody-minded, there's no way he's coming down.'

'That's cats for you,' laughed Rose. 'Fickle.'

'I think we're going to have to call the fire brigade out on this one,' said Maggie.

'You're not serious?' said Tori, half laughing.

'I think Mags is right,' agreed Ted.

'But surely they've got actual emergencies to be dealing with. Won't they think this is a waste of time?' said Tori.

'I bet you'd be surprised how often they deal with things like this,' Ted explained. 'Honestly, Tori, they've got the right equipment to get high enough and they'll have Ernie down in a flash. The last thing you want him to do is panic and injure himself.'

'Well, I guess so,' said Tori.

'Grace!' shouted Rose, in the direction of a woman in her late twenties, wearing skinny jeans and a T-shirt, striding across the green towards them. Her hair was pulled back into a messy bun and she was waving as she approached.

'Grace?' asked Tori.

'She's the local vet. She helped me when I found Scout last year,' said Rose.

'Hi, all,' said Grace, smiling, 'I was just popping out for a coffee – what's going on?'

'It's Tori's cat, Ernie. He seems to have got himself well and truly stuck,' explained Rose, pointing up to the branches of the tree.

'Should I call the fire brigade?' asked Ted.

'I'm guessing that ladder won't reach him?' Grace asked, craning her neck to look up.

'Afraid not,' said Tori.

'Officially speaking, the fire service will only come out if the RSPCA call, but they owe me a favour so I'll see what I can do,' said Grace, pulling her phone out of her pocket.

'Brilliant, thanks, I'd appreciate that,' replied Tori.

'Who would have thought a cat could cause this much trouble?' said Ted.

'You should introduce Ernie to Scout,' said Rose, smiling. 'Honestly, if I had a pound for every time she managed to get herself in trouble . . .'

'All part of owning a pet,' replied Mags. 'You should hear some of the near misses Grace has to deal with. Ernie will be fine,' she said, giving Tori's arm a squeeze.

'They're on their way,' said Grace, putting her phone away. 'I'll hang on if you like, give him a once-over when they've got him down to put your mind at rest, Tori.'

It wasn't long before Tori heard sirens approaching and she spotted a fire engine closing in on the green.

'Did they really need to switch the sirens on?' said Tori; she could feel her face burning hot. 'It's not exactly a life-or-death situation, is it?'

'Maybe it's a quiet day,' replied Grace with a shrug. 'Come on, I'll introduce you.' She grabbed Tori by the arm and walked with her towards the fire engine. 'Hi, Leo,' she said, waving at one of the firefighters.

'Hi, Grace,' replied one of the most attractive men Tori had ever seen. Leo was at least six foot four with broad shoulders, piercing blue eyes and a mop of curly brown hair peeking out beneath his firefighter's helmet. 'Let me guess? You've got a cat stuck in a tree for us?'

'You've got it in one,' laughed Grace. 'This is Tori, Ernie's owner. Tori, this is Leo Walker.'

'Thanks for coming out so quickly,' Tori stammered, her face burning hot. 'I know it's not exactly a real emergency, well, compared to what you usually deal with, I mean . . .'

'Oh, you'd be surprised, we get called out to all sorts,' Leo replied, smiling warmly at her. 'Cats have a knack of getting themselves into scrapes. My own two are a right pair of troublemakers.'

'He's not wrong,' said Grace. 'He's always at the surgery with Tallulah and Tinkerbell.'

'Tallulah and Tinkerbell?' said Tori, struggling to stifle a laugh.

'My cats,' said Leo. 'And I didn't come up with those names,' he added quickly. 'They were rescues and Grace is right, they've cost me a fortune in vet's bills already this year.'

'And I welcome the business,' Grace teased.

'Right then, Tori. Shall we get Ernie's paws firmly back on the ground?' Leo asked.

'Please,' Tori replied as she walked back towards the tree.

Leo and the rest of the fire crew worked quickly to set up the tallest ladder Tori had ever seen. Leo climbed it in no time at all and he soon reached the tree's uppermost branches, where Ernie was camped out. Tori could hear Leo talking quietly and softly; he was trying hard to coax the cat into the carrier without frightening him. His gentleness took her by surprise; he seemed such an imposing figure that his tone almost seemed at odds with his physical appearance. As Ernie leapt for the higher branches, Leo was ready. He caught the cat in mid-air, in one swift and fluid movement, and was soon on his way back down.

Grace, Rose, Ted and Mags began cheering and clapping,

and before Tori knew it, Leo was handing her one very indignant feline. Tori couldn't account for what happened next – perhaps it was relief or gratitude, she flung her arms around Leo and hugged him tightly.

'Oh, thank you, thank you,' she found herself saying breathlessly. 'I can't believe you managed to catch him. When he leapt into the air, I thought . . .'

'Hey,' said Leo, fixing his eyes directly on her, 'he's okay. Cats are pretty hardy things despite what they'd have you believe.'

'Oh God, sorry, I don't know why I'm so upset,' said Tori, wiping her eyes. 'What must you think?'

'I think that you clearly love your cat, and that's a pretty good character trait if you ask me,' said Leo, holding her gaze again. Tori looked back at him. *Why couldn't she look away?*

'Ahem,' said Rose, clearing her throat.

'Why don't I take Ernie back to the clinic now and give him a proper once-over? I can pop him back to the tearoom in a little while,' said Grace.

'I honestly can't thank you enough, Grace. You've been such a help,' replied Tori, finally breaking eye contact with Leo.

'We'd best be getting off too,' said Leo, nodding towards the fire engine.

'Oh yeah, of course. Well, thanks again for everything you've done,' said Tori.

'Ah, it's all part of the job. I hope Ernie's okay,' said Leo. As he turned to walk away, Leo paused. He stopped and looked back at her. 'I hope I see you again, Tori.'

'You'll find her at the Cosy Cup tearoom,' shouted Rose. 'Your next coffee is on the house,' she added. Leo gave her a thumbs-up.

Tori felt her pulse begin to quicken and something told her that it wasn't entirely down to the chaos that Ernie had caused today.

'What was that?' Rose asked, as she walked with Tori back to the tearoom.

'What was what?' replied Tori, shaking her head.

'Don't give me that,' said Rose. 'You and Leo?'

'What about Leo?' said Tori blankly.

'Uh, what about those sparks flying between the two of you?'

'Sparks?'

'Oh, come on, you're not completely blind. Talk about chemistry,' said Rose, 'I've never seen anything so obvious.'

'Obvious?'

'The obvious attraction between the pair of you. Oh, come on, Tori, you two were totally vibing!'

'You're imagining things.'

'I am not,' said Rose, coming to a standstill and putting her hands on her hips. 'Don't tell me you genuinely didn't feel it?' Tori shifted awkwardly on the spot. 'I knew it!' said Rose, jumping up and down. 'You like him, don't you?'

'Look, I'm not saying I felt nothing . . . I mean, obviously he's gorgeous, I'm not blind. But I meant what I said the yesterday. I'm *over* men. And anyway, I'm sure he's got a whole line of women queuing up for him. He's not going to be interested in me.'

'Oh, stop it! He was definitely checking you out . . .'

'Rose! I said I'm not interested, okay?'

'You know, he plays football with Jake,' Rose continued. 'I'll get him to put some feelers out, make sure he's single—'

'No! I mean it, Rose. Don't meddle, okay?'

'But—'

'Rose!' said Tori, glaring at her friend.

'Okay, okay. I promise I won't meddle,' said Rose, kicking at the ground with her foot.

'Thanks.'

'But you're an idiot if you ask me, Tori Baxter, you just don't ignore chemistry like that.'

'Well, I can certainly try to,' Tori said determinedly, and, as she strode back towards the tearoom, her thoughts were firmly fixed on Ryan. Whatever kind of spark she had felt just now with Leo, it wasn't something she was ready to think about just yet.

Chapter 6

The next few days whizzed past and Tori soon found that she'd been back in Blossom Heath for over a fortnight. She had slipped back into the routine of helping her mum out at the tearoom each day as though she'd never been away, which helped keep her mind occupied and she realized that she'd hardly thought about Ryan at all in the last twenty-four hours. That was definitely progress. She couldn't believe how much her feet throbbed and her lower back ached after a shift waiting tables and serving coffees. She honestly didn't know how her mum had been managing to run things on her own since Cathy had left. She paused. What would her mum do when she got another job? She really didn't want to leave Joyce in the lurch but the thought of working there indefinitely didn't leave her feeling inspired. Now her plans for the future had been thrown into chaos, she wasn't sure how she felt about being in the village long term. If she was going to get over Ryan, she knew she needed something new, an adventure or distraction that was just for her, a chance to feel like herself again, and that wasn't going to happen if she stayed stuck working at the tearoom.

After another long day on her feet, Tori sat curled up on the sofa at home, her legs tucked underneath her, as she scrolled through Instagram on her phone. She had insisted on cooking for her mum tonight; Joyce had looked exhausted when they had finally left the Cosy Cup and Tori noticed the dark shadows under her eyes with concern. Joyce was watching her favourite soap on TV and Ernie was purring contentedly on her lap. After being away for so long, the soap's storyline was completely lost on Tori and she had focused all her attention on her phone. So far she'd avoided checking social media since she'd been home; she didn't want to stumble across a post from Ryan, showing off how fabulous his newly single life was in Thailand. *A life that no longer included her.* Ryan Wicks. She hovered her index finger over his name as it appeared in her friends list. Should she unfollow him? Or would that look weird? She really didn't want him to think that she cared enough to go to the trouble of unfollowing him. She stared at the screen intently. What to do . . .

'Earth to Tori?' said Joyce.

Tori looked up abruptly, her concentration broken.

'Sorry, what?'

'I said, do you want a cuppa?'

'Oh, yeah, sorry,' Tori replied.

'Honestly, you young ones with your phones. You're

practically glued to them,' said Joyce, as she walked out of the living room.

'It's nothing important,' Tori shouted through to the kitchen, 'just Instagram.'

Bang!

Tori heard a loud crash from the kitchen.

'Mum?' she called, leaping up from the sofa. 'Mum?' When she reached the kitchen doorway, Tori saw Joyce lying on the floor, a ceramic mug smashed into pieces around her. Ernie was next to her meowing loudly. She was out cold. 'Mum!' yelled Tori, dropping to her knees and taking Joyce's hand. 'Mum, what's wrong?' She squeezed her mum's fingers and gently tucked her hair back behind her ear.

Joyce began to stir, she murmured and her eyes slowly opened. She looked confused. 'Tori, love? What?' asked Joyce quietly, trying to sit herself up.

'Mum, thank God!' replied Tori, exhaling. 'Don't try and move, just take a minute. I think you fainted.'

'Fainted?'

'I think so. Shall I call Dr Marshall?' said Tori.

'Just wait will you, love,' said Joyce breathlessly, grabbing Tori's arm. 'Let me just get my bearings. I'll be fine in a minute.'

'But, Mum, I really think that—'

'I'm fine, honestly,' said Joyce, pulling herself up into a sitting position with Tori's help. Ernie was quick to nuzzle into her. 'Oh, Ernie, are you checking up on me?'

'He knows something's wrong too. You were out cold, Mum!'

'And now I'm fine. This just happens from time to time and I'm always fine after a few minutes.'

'This has happened before?'

'A couple of times,' replied Joyce, not quite meeting Tori's eye.

'If this has happened before, that's even worse!'

'Help me up, will you?' said Joyce, her left arm outstretched. Tori took it gently, helped her mum to her feet and sat her down in one of the dark oak kitchen chairs. 'These things just happen when you get to my age. It's nothing to worry about, love. I've just been overdoing things.'

'That's not true, Mum, and you know it. You need to see the doctor. What if it's something serious?' Joyce was silent. 'What would you do if it was me? You'd march me up to Dr Marshall's in the blink of an eye and I'd have no say in the matter, would I, Ernie?'

'Well . . .'

'You know you would, Mum.'

'Fine,' said Joyce, her shoulders slumping. 'I guess it can't hurt to get checked, if it puts your mind at rest.'

'It will,' said Tori firmly.

'I'll give the surgery a call in the morning.'

'It's only just gone six – the surgery's still open. Why don't I give Dr Marshall a call now and see what he says?'

'You know, you remind me of someone,' said Joyce, smiling weakly.

'Yeah? Who?'

'Me,' Joyce laughed. 'I don't give up easily either.'

*

Tori put in a call to the surgery and Sheila, the receptionist, was as helpful as ever. She rang Tori back within five minutes and said that, given the special circumstances, the doctor, who lived in the village himself, would make an exception to the home visits rule and pop in to see Joyce on his way home after surgery. Joyce, who thought a home visit was completely over the top given that she'd only had a 'dizzy turn', was wrapped up in a blanket on the sofa, at Tori's insistence, with her feet up on a footstool and a cup of sugary tea at her side. By seven thirty, there was a knock at the door, and Tori sprang up from the sofa to answer it.

'Tori,' said Dr Marshall with a smile, as he stepped over the threshold. He was a tall man, with jet-black hair, which was greying around his temples, despite the fact that he was only in his late thirties.

'Thanks for coming out, Doctor, I can't tell you how much we appreciate it,' said Tori. 'I know you don't generally do home visits as a rule.'

'It's no bother, you're on my way home. Now, where's the patient?' he asked, and Tori led him through to the living room. 'Good evening, Joyce,' he said as he sat down next to her on the sofa and opened his medical bag. 'Why don't you tell me what's been going on?'

'I'm sure it's nothing. Tori shouldn't have bothered you,' said Joyce, waving her hands dismissively. 'I just had a bit of a funny turn, that's all.'

'Why don't you let me be the judge of that?' he replied with a smile.

Joyce went on to explain everything that had been happening with her health in recent months and Tori was shocked to learn about the tiredness, weight gain, sensitivity to the cold, as well as muscle aches and pains.

'Honestly, sometimes I feel as though I just can't keep my eyes open,' Joyce explained, 'but surely, it's just part of getting older?'

'She was running the Cosy Cup on her own before I got back,' Tori explained. 'I know she's been under a lot of pressure and working too hard.'

'I'd like to run some tests,' replied Dr Marshall. 'Come into the surgery tomorrow and we'll get some blood work done – that will give us a clearer picture of what's going on.'

'Thanks, Doctor,' said Tori.

'Give Sheila a call in the morning and she'll get you booked in. Once I've got the results, I'll give you a call. In the meantime, make sure that you're taking things easy. I'm sure Tori can look after the Cosy Cup for a few days?' he said, turning to face Tori directly.

'Of course ...'

'But—' Joyce interjected.

'No arguments I'm afraid, Joyce. Doctor's orders, okay?'

Joyce nodded silently.

'I'm perfectly capable of running things for a few days, Mum. Trust me.'

'There we are, then,' said Dr Marshall, closing his bag and standing up. 'I'll see you in the morning, Joyce.'

'Thanks again, Doctor,' said Tori as she led him out, closing the front door behind him. She walked back into the lounge and slumped down on the sofa next to her mother.

'Are you sure you're going to be okay running things tomorrow, love?' Joyce asked. 'It's been a while since you've opened up on your own.'

'I'll be fine – I don't want you worrying about me, okay? I've been helping out every weekend and summer holiday since I was at secondary school. Let's just focus on getting you right. Everything else will sort itself out.'

'I'll only be next door if you need me, I can—'

'Mum! You're to rest and that's doctor's orders. I might not have your baking skills, but I can make sandwiches, rustle up some scones and a Victoria sponge or something.'

'Tori?' Joyce paused. 'What if the test shows something serious?'

Tori took both of her mum's hands and looked her in the eyes. She could see her mum was anxious. She wasn't used to that. Her mum was always *her* tower of strength; no problem was ever too great for her to solve.

'Then we'll deal with it together. Let's not get ahead of ourselves, though,' she added quickly. 'Like you say, it's probably nothing.'

'I hope so, love.'

Tori nodded. She looked away and bit her lower lip hard. *But what if it wasn't?* The thought of her mum facing a health problem was more than she could bear to contemplate. She was sure of one thing, though: she was going to be running the Cosy Cup single-handedly for the next few days and she was determined to do her mum proud.

Chapter 7

Tori's first morning running the Cosy Cup solo had been eventful to say the least. Before she'd even begun to think about surviving the lunchtime rush, she'd already burnt her hand getting a batch of cheese scones out of the oven, spilt coffee over Maggie Harrison, given three tables the wrong orders and messed up the change for Mrs Connolly. No matter how busy the tearoom was, though, Tori just couldn't stop thinking about her mum and what her test results might show. Fear gripped her whenever she thought about it. She looked at the polka dot clock on the wall. It was 11.30am. Her mum should be done by now. All she could do was keep busy and hope they didn't have to wait too long for the results.

'Rose!' she said in surprise as she saw her friend standing at the counter in front of her. 'What can I get you?'

'Absolutely nothing. I'm not here for coffee – I'm here to help,' Rose said with a smile, stepping behind the counter and grabbing an order pad.

'Help? I don't understand . . .'

'I've just seen Maggie. She told me about your mum and said you were struggling.'

'I'm managing just fine,' said Tori, stiffening slightly.

'Well, the coffee stain on Mags's T-shirt tells a different story,' said Rose, raising her eyebrows. Tori's cheeks burned hot. 'Hey, I'm not judging, lovely. I just thought you could do with a hand, that's all. I may as well make myself useful seeing as I'm working part time.'

Tori pulled her friend into a firm hug.

'Thanks, Rose,' she said. 'Mags is right, though. I'm in well over my head here.'

'You've had a lot to process in the last twenty-four hours. It's natural to feel a bit flustered. Just let me know where you want me and let's turn this day around, okay?'

'Okay, thank you,' said Tori, taking a deep breath. 'If you can take orders, I'll focus on barista and food duties – that should make things easier. I've put together a smaller menu, which is up on the specials board, so if you could just direct everyone to that ... It's not perfect, but it's the best I can do right now.'

'Got it,' said Rose, looking up at the board. 'This looks great! Ooh, smashed avocado and eggs on sourdough – that's new!'

'I thought I'd mix things up a bit, and it's one of the few things I know I can make. Do you think people will go for it?'

'Definitely! In fact, I'm putting my lunch order in now, so you better save me some,' Rose laughed.

'Consider it done.'

'Wow, that Vicky sponge looks impressive – I wouldn't have spotted Joyce hadn't made it.'

'Really?' said Tori. 'I'll take that.'

'Right, let's do this,' said Rose, taking a deep breath and stepping out from behind the counter to take her first order.

Rose and Tori worked non-stop through the lunchtime rush and their system worked perfectly. Rose took and delivered orders, cleared tables and kept the customers smiling, while Tori focused on making coffees and getting orders out of the kitchen. Just as Rose had predicted, the smashed avocados on sourdough had been a huge hit. Before they knew it, the pair of them were working together seamlessly and they'd almost made it through the busiest part of the day. *Almost.*

'Hey, Tori. Could you speak to that woman over in the window seat for me?' said Rose.

'Oh God,' said Tori, looking over.

'What?'

'That's Violet Davenport,' Tori groaned.

'And that's bad because?'

'Because she's Vicious Violet, literally the fussiest woman in the world. Even Mum can never get anything right for her.'

'Do you want me to speak to her? She did ask for you by name, though.'

'No, it's fine, I'll go,' said Tori, walking over to Violet's table. Tori forced her face into a smile. 'Mrs Davenport, hello. What can I help you with?'

'It's this cheese scone. It's *dry*,' Violet said, picking the scone up and then dropping it back onto her plate. 'Are you sure it's freshly baked?'

'Quite sure, yes. I baked it myself this morning,' said Tori, doing her best to keep her smile in place.

'*You* baked it?' replied Violet, screwing her face up to inspect the scone more closely. 'Well, that explains it. You clearly don't know what you're doing.'

'I'm sorry, Mum's out of action today, so it's just me running things, I'm afraid,' said Tori, trying her best to be pleasant. 'Can I get you something else instead?'

'No, thank you,' said Violet, pushing the plate away from her. 'I'd like a full refund. I can't imagine anything else you've baked is edible either.'

'Oh, erm, right, sorry,' said Tori, feeling flustered. She noticed a few of the other customers had turned to look. 'I'll just get that for you, Mrs Davenport.' Tori walked towards the cash register. It was taking every ounce of self-control she had not to lose her rag and remain professional. She collected the money and returned it to Violet. 'I'm sorry you didn't enjoy your scone. Mum will be back soon and I'm sure you'll find everything will have returned to normal.'

'I certainly hope so,' said Violet, scooping the change into her purse and standing up abruptly to leave.

'See you next week, then,' said Tori, doing her best to muster a cheery wave as Violet departed. 'It's no wonder everyone calls you Vicious Violet behind your back,' she muttered under her breath as soon as Violet was out of earshot.

She turned as she heard a voice whisper, '*Vicious* is a bit harsh. She seems more of an old prune to me.'

Tori spun around to find herself face to face with Leo. 'Make a habit of eavesdropping on other people?' she said, her suppressed annoyance towards Violet suddenly spilling over.

'God, no, sorry, that's not what I was doing,' said Leo, holding his hands up and taking a step backwards. 'I just thought I'd lighten the mood a bit, that's all.'

'Oh, I'm sorry. I'm just angry with Violet – I didn't mean to take it out on you, Leo,' she said, her tone quickly softening.

'Forget it,' said Leo, his face reddening. 'I thought I'd pop in after we met, I thought we . . .' His voice trailed off and he looked away.

'Ah, okay,' said Tori awkwardly.

'I thought we got on, that's all, and, after you invited me here . . .'

'I think technically it was Rose who invited you,' she smiled, gesturing towards Rose, who was looking at Tori with interest from behind the counter. 'But we're always happy to see new customers at the Cosy Cup,' she said, picking up the remains of Violet's discarded scone and clearing the table. 'Have a seat and I'll send Rose over to take your order.'

'Tori? What was that about?' said Rose as she banged through the door to the kitchen.

'What do you mean?' said Tori, throwing the tea towel she was holding down on the worktop.

'With Leo, what were you chatting about?' she asked, eyebrows raised.

'Oh, nothing. He just caught me bad-mouthing Violet, that's all.'

'That's all?'

'Of course,' said Tori, rubbing her temples. 'We'd best get back out there,' she continued, nodding towards the door.

'What's the deal with "Vicious Violet" anyway?'

'The nickname?'

Rose nodded.

'Oh, it's just something we used to call her when we were kids. She's always just so ... well, so *rude*. She can't seem to stand anyone having fun. When we were younger, she'd moan about ball games on the green or the noise we were making playing outside. I can't think of a single time she's spoken to me kindly.'

'Hence the name?'

'Exactly,' said Tori. 'I wasn't too hideous to Leo when he came in, was I? I almost bit his head off after my run-in with Violet,' she said nervously.

'I'm sure he'll forgive you.'

'Oh God, I'm such an idiot.'

'Well ...' Rose said, laughing. 'Look, why don't you just take him some cheese scones and you can smooth things over.'

'Do I have to?'

'Yep.'

'Let's hope they're not as bad as Violet says, then.' Tori

poked her tongue out at Rose, laughed and picked up a plate of scones in one hand and a cappuccino in the other. 'Here goes nothing.' She took a deep breath and walked out of the kitchen towards Leo's table.

'Here you go,' she said, placing the scones and coffee down in front of him.

'But I didn't order this . . .'

'I know, but you look like a cheese scone and cappuccino kind of guy. Think of it as a peace offering.'

'A peace offering?'

'For me biting your head off when you came in.'

'Don't worry about it,' he said, smiling at her. 'I don't suppose I could persuade you to take a break for five minutes and join me?'

'Er, no, sorry, I really can't, we're busy with—'

'Of course she can,' said Rose, coming round from behind the counter. She ushered Tori towards the empty seat at Leo's table and put a herbal tea down in front of her. 'It's quieter now. I can manage, just take a break.'

Tori threw a steely stare in Rose's direction.

'Erm . . . okay, sure, why not? I guess I can spare a few minutes,' said Tori, pulling off her apron and sitting down.

'Great!' Leo smiled broadly. The pair of them sat staring at each other awkwardly for a few moments. Leo broke the silence first. 'So, how's Ernie doing?'

'Oh, he's good, thanks. Totally forgotten about his run-in with the fire brigade,' she said, smiling.

'That's cats for you, isn't it? Nine lives and all that? They certainly don't dwell on things, do they? Just off on their next adventure. We could learn a lot from them, I reckon.'

'I know what you mean. Life's all about chasing mice and persuading us that it's dinner time again,' Tori laughed.

'That's a good look on you,' said Leo, his gaze lingering.

'What is?'

'A smile. The first time I met you, you were panic-stricken over Ernie.' He added quickly, 'Understandably, of course. And, today, well, today you were ...'

'Biting your head off?'

'Hey, you said it,' said Leo, holding his hands up and laughing.

Tori felt butterflies surge in her stomach despite herself. There was something about the way Leo's whole face lit up when he smiled, it was so natural, so ... perfect. It made her feel ... well, something, despite the fact that she was absolutely certain that she wasn't ready to feel something for anyone just yet, even if it was for someone like Leo.

Chapter 8

The next few days passed in a blur as Tori and Rose managed the running of the Cosy Cup between them while Joyce was out of action. Tori was exhausted by the time she got home each evening, but was determined not to show it; the last thing she wanted was for her mum to worry. Before she knew it, Thursday morning had come around and she was sitting in the waiting room at Blossom Heath Medical Centre with her mum, waiting for her results. The door to Dr Marshall's consulting room swung open.

'Joyce Baxter?' he called, in a deep, low voice. Joyce and Tori entered the consulting room. 'Have a seat, please, Joyce,' he said, pointing at a chair. 'How are you feeling? Any more fainting episodes?'

'None and I've been doing exactly as you said, Doctor. I've kept away from work and have been taking it easy. Tori's been doing a great job of looking after me,' Joyce said, beaming at her daughter. 'I can't say it's been easy, though,' she added quickly, 'I've watched enough daytime TV to last a lifetime.'

'Well, I've got your results here.' Tori took her mum's hand. 'Your thyroid levels are lower than they should be – it seems you have an underactive thyroid.'

'What does that mean?' Tori asked quickly, her heart beating faster.

'It's nothing to worry about – it's quite common as you get older. Your thyroid gland doesn't make enough thyroid hormone anymore. We can prescribe you tablets to bring your thyroid levels back to where they should be.'

'And then I'll start to feel better?' asked Joyce.

'It'll take a few weeks to kick in, but then you'll start to feel an improvement,' he said.

'At least it's treatable, that's the main thing,' Joyce replied.

'Your vitamin D and B12 levels are also low. I'll write you a prescription for the vitamin D and the B12 is given as an injection. You'll need one every other day for the first two weeks and then one every three months going forward.'

'Every other day?' said Joyce, her face falling. Tori felt her mum's grip on her hand tighten. 'But I don't really like needles, Doctor . . . Isn't there another option? Tablets?'

'Afraid not,' he said, shaking his head. 'We need to give the dose intramuscularly when the levels are this low. It's by far the most effective method.'

'You'll be fine, Mum. You're the bravest person I know. What chance has a little needle got against you?'

Joyce smiled weakly and nodded.

'I can give you the first dose now,' he said.

'Now?' said Joyce, her eyes widening.

'There's no time like the present, Mum – you may as well get it over with.'

Joyce nodded and began rolling up her sleeve.

'Excellent. I'll write the prescription for your vitamin D and thyroxine and, Tori, if you could take a seat in the waiting room? We'll have this jab done in no time, Joyce.'

Tori took a seat in the waiting room, pulling her phone out of her pocket and typing *underactive thyroid*. Scrolling down the page, she clicked on the NHS website and read: *thyroid gland not producing enough hormone ... treated by daily hormone tablets ... symptoms include tiredness, dizziness, muscle aches ...* That certainly sounded like everything her mum had been experiencing. An underactive thyroid and vitamin deficiencies. This she could deal with. It could have been worse. So much worse. It was going to take her mum time to get back on her feet, but she should make a full recovery. Tori looked up as the consulting room door opened.

'Hey, how was it?' she asked.

'Not as bad as I thought,' said Joyce, rolling her sleeve down. 'I've just got to book in for another blood test in two weeks' time and then we can go and get my prescription.'

'Why don't we pop in at the Cosy Cup first? I think you deserve a sugar fix after your jab.'

Joyce laughed. 'Sounds like a plan. I've missed the place. Plus, I want to say thank you to Rose for holding the fort. I hope she's been okay.'

'Rose is used to wrangling a class of thirty kids; I reckon running the tearoom for an hour is a breeze compared to that!'

When Tori and Joyce arrived at the Cosy Cup, Rose had two large slices of chocolate fudge cake and a couple of lattes waiting to greet them.

'Rose, love, were you expecting us?' asked Joyce, taking a seat at the table nearest to her.

'Oh, you know me, I've got an incredible sense of intuition,' said Rose, tapping her nose.

'Or you're just really good at reading your WhatsApp messages,' laughed Tori, waving her phone in the air.

'Busted!' giggled Rose, holding her hands up. 'The cake is from Jean, in case we needed extra supplies, but Tori's got it covered – she's doing a great job with the baking.'

'I can see that,' said Joyce, smiling as she looked around the packed tearoom. 'So, what's on this new menu of yours, then, love?' she asked, looking up at the specials board. 'Green tea, smashed avocado and eggs, cheese and Marmite toasties, strawberry and banana smoothies ...'

'Those have been going down a storm, haven't they, Tori?' said Rose encouragingly.

'And the green tea has been really popular with the yoga club, when they come in early morning after class. I was thinking ... we could add a few more smoothies and even some shots like ginger or spinach,' added Tori.

'Spinach! Blimey. Well, it may not be my cup of tea, but

they certainly sound interesting,' said Joyce, taking a sip of her latte.

'I hope you don't mind me making a few changes, but I thought if—'

'You go for it. I'm excited to try some new flavours and see what you discovered on your travels,' said Joyce, with an encouraging smile.

'How did everything go with Dr Marshall?' asked Rose.

'Good, thank you, love. I've got an underactive thyroid apparently, but I've got some meds and I'm having vitamin injections. I'll be back on my feet in no time, don't you worry.'

'Well, that *is* a relief,' said Rose. 'I'll leave you both to it. I've managed not to burn the place down, so I'm taking that as a win.'

'As if I'd let you near the kitchen,' said Tori, laughing. 'You're a disaster zone when it comes to actual cooking.'

'Hey!' cried Rose, 'I'll have you know that Jake is a big fan of my Eton mess and I make it from scratch!'

'Let me guess – your idea of "from scratch" means meringues out of a packet, double cream, some strawberries and . . . voila,' said Tori.

'Exactly – from scratch!'

Rose and Tori paused for a moment, looked at each other and burst out laughing. 'Hey, life's too short for cooking, okay?' said Rose.

'Oh, Rose, love, you do know how to put a smile on my face. I needed that today,' said Joyce. 'I hope you realize how much I appreciate you standing in for me this week; I don't think Tori could have coped without you.'

'Of course I do,' replied Rose. 'Honestly, Joyce, it's been an absolute pleasure. Tori and I have had a real blast together this week, haven't we?'

'We really have, Mum. It's been like old times.'

'You pitched in when Aunt Jean was poorly and when Scout went missing,' said Rose. 'You were there for me, Joyce, and the least I can do is repay the favour.'

'Well, that's just what we do in Blossom Heath, isn't it? We look out for each other,' said Joyce.

'We certainly do,' Rose agreed.

As Rose rushed off to serve Simon and Anya, the couple from the gift shop, the Pink Ribbon, Tori spotted a familiar face walk through the door.

'Look who it is!' cried Kate, Jake's younger sister.

'Kate!' said Tori, jumping up to give her friend a hug.

'It's so good to see you! I meant to pop in sooner but mum life kinda got in the way,' said Kate, shaking her head.

'Ah, you're here now. How are you? And Ben and the girls?'

'I'm good. Life is crazy as always! Ben's working all hours, so I feel like I hardly see him, Lily wants to be a mermaid and Hannah is pony crazy, she's almost as bad as us when we were her age,' said Kate.

'I hope your bank balance is up to the challenge, Kate. Those riding lessons nearly bankrupted me,' laughed Joyce.

'Tell me about it,' replied Kate. 'I'm going to need to take out a second mortgage at the rate she's going through jodhpurs!'

'Kate, hi!' cried Rose, from behind the counter.

'Hiya! Jake told me you were here,' said Kate, with a wave.

'If Kate and Rose are free later, why don't you all go to the pub for a drink?' said Joyce. Tori opened her mouth to object. 'Listen,' insisted Joyce, holding up a hand. 'You've been working too hard recently, you deserve a night out.'

'I'm free,' said Kate.

'What if you have another funny turn, Mum?' said Tori.

'Rose? Have you got plans later?' Joyce shouted across the room.

'You mean other than spending the night glued to my phone while Jake watches Spurs lose?' said Rose.

'Fancy the pub?' asked Joyce.

Rose beamed. 'Definitely! I'll see if Grace is free too. We can make a night of it,' said Rose.

'Perfect,' said Joyce, smiling. 'There you are then. All sorted.'

'Mum, you really don't take no for an answer, do you?' Tori laughed.

As Kate headed to the counter to place her order, Tori pulled up a chair opposite her mum and took a large swig of her coffee.

'So how *are* you feeling, Mum? About the test results I mean.'

'Relieved, to tell you the truth. I know I put on a brave face, but ... well, I guess part of me was worried sick that there was something really wrong. Something that couldn't be fixed with a few pills and some vitamin injections.' Joyce sniffed and rubbed her eyes.

'Oh, Mum! Why didn't you say anything? We could have talked about it.'

'Oh, you know me, I like to hope for the best and, anyway, I didn't want to burden you with my worries.'

'Why not? That's exactly what I'm here for!'

'You've got enough on your plate. What with everything that's happened recently with Ryan and . . .'

'And what?'

'And . . . I didn't want you to feel as though you *had* to look after me.'

'But Mum—'

'No, Tori. I didn't . . . I don't want you to feel as though I'm a burden. I'm not sure what you've got planned now that you're home, but I don't want to be the one holding you back, if you've got other things you want to do.' Joyce hung her head.

'Oh, Mum. I'd never feel like that. I love being back here. You're stuck with me for a good while yet, okay?'

'Well, I appreciate you looking after this place while I get back on an even keel,' said Joyce.

'It's the least I can do. You're always there when I need you and I'm glad I can be the one to look after you for a change.'

'I'll put an ad in the local paper to hire a replacement for Cathy. It's just not practical to think that I can run this place on my own.'

'There's no rush – I can pitch in for now. Running this place is definitely a two-person job.'

'I know we've never really talked about it properly, but I'd always hoped you'd want this place permanently one day,' said Joyce, looking around the Cosy Cup fondly.

'I've never really given it much thought. It's one thing to help out now and again but if it's what I'll be doing *forever . . .*'

'Well, don't dismiss the idea. If you want to be involved properly, the Cosy Cup has your name written all over it.'

'Thanks, Mum, I don't know why we've never really talked about it before. I assumed I'd end up living in London or somewhere, but I'll definitely give it some proper thought,' said Tori, taking a huge bite of the chocolate fudge cake sitting on her plate.

Chapter 9

Tori and Rose walked to the Apple Tree together that evening. Their route from Jasmine Cottage was filled with the scent of fragrant blossom trees, the early evening sunshine glinting through in pretty patterns. Tori could almost feel the long, lazy days of summer within reach.

'So, how are things with you and Jake?' Tori asked, as she looped her arm through Rose's.

'Really good, thanks. I can't believe how lucky I am really. When I think how things were with Ollie, how wrong we were for each other . . . I don't think I realized how unhappy I was until I met Jake. And now? Things couldn't be more perfect. Oh God, sorry, that's so tactless of me, what with you and Ryan . . .'

'Don't be daft, I'm happy for you, Rose. It sounds like you went through a lot with Ollie, but you've come out the other side. I can't imagine dating again – the thought fills me with horror.'

'Don't say that, I'm starting to get seriously concerned

you're off men for life. Your perfect someone is out there somewhere ...'

'Well, maybe I'll find them one day ... in the *very* distant future.'

'That's more like it.'

'Don't get your hopes up – I'm thinking a few decades ahead. Maybe when I hit seventy? Then I might *think* about dating again.'

'God, if we're still dating at that age, you can count me out!'

'You'll be married to Jake with about ten grandkids by then,' Tori laughed. 'I can see you both now, sitting on the porch up at Harper Farm ...'

'Oh, stop! Even *I'm* not thinking that far ahead,' Rose said. 'You need to take the pressure off, stop thinking about dating and just enjoy the moment. Who knows how many gorgeous men we'll spot in the pub?'

'Hey! You're spoken for!'

'I know! But if I spot any hotties, I'll send them your way.'

'Listen, I've got something for you,' said Tori, pulling a package wrapped in shiny gold paper out of her bag.

'What's this?'

'Open it and you'll see,' laughed Tori.

Rose pulled at the wrapping paper to reveal a stack of pretty notebooks and pens wrapped with a silver bow.

'Oh, Tori, they're gorgeous.'

'I know how much you love your stationery, and I thought they'd be perfect for journalling.'

'You know me too well,' Rose said with a smile.

'You're still journalling, right?'

'Of course, I never miss a day.'

'The pink one's a proper gratitude journal, it's got inspirational quotes and space to write down your thoughts ...'

'I love it!' said Rose, taking a deep breath. 'Ah! That new notebook smell!'

'I just wanted to let you know how much I've appreciated your help in the café; I don't think I could have got through this week without you, Rose.'

'Oh, it's no bother, honestly. You didn't have to get me anything, but I love them. Ooh, new pens too,' said Rose, opening a pack of pastel ballpoints.

'I'm grateful, and I wanted you to know.'

'Hey, maybe you should start a gratitude journal too?' laughed Rose.

'Well, you'd definitely be in it,' replied Tori, linking her arm back through Rose's.

The Golden Pippin trees in the front of the pub were already starting to show their pink and white flowers, and Tori smiled as she walked through the main entrance. Just how many evenings had she spent in this place as a teenager? Too many to count. Nightlife in Blossom Heath was limited to say the least, so the pub had been the focus of her social life in her younger years. She'd had her first pint of beer here on her eighteenth birthday and shared her first kiss with Tom Pollard under one of the huge apple trees in the pub garden. God, she'd had such a crush on him. Her face burned hot at the memory. What was Tom Pollard up to now? He'd probably left the village and was making a life for himself somewhere like London or Manchester. Hardly any of Tori's school friends still lived in Blossom Heath; it was one of the hazards of growing up in such a rural location.

'Rose! Tori!' called Grace from the other end of the bar. 'What are you having?'

'I'll get them,' said Tori, pushing her way through the crowd.

'Thanks,' said Grace, 'mine's a pint of Sussex Best.'

'I'll join Kate,' said Rose, gesturing towards the booth in the corner of the pub where Kate was sitting.

'G and T?' asked Tori, nodding in Rose's direction. Rose gave her a thumbs-up.

'What can I get you, Tori, sweetheart?' asked Beth. Tori placed her drinks order. 'How's Ernie after his adventure the other day?'

'I was going to ask exactly the same thing,' said Grace.

'Oh, he's good, thanks. Completely oblivious to the chaos he caused,' said Tori, taking a sip of her Sauvignon Blanc.

'That's cats for you,' said Grace.

'Isn't it just,' agreed Beth. 'That Leo's a bit of a dish, isn't he?'

Tori blushed; she hoped no one had noticed.

'Is he? I can't say I really took much notice ...' said Tori, fishing around in her handbag for her debit card.

'Not really my type,' said Grace, 'but I can see the attraction. He's very handsome, isn't he?'

'Er,' said Tori, struggling to respond. 'I guess so. Like I said, I wasn't really taking much notice.' She found she couldn't quite look Grace in the eye.

'Well, you had bigger fish to fry, I expect,' said Beth, passing Grace her drink. 'Ernie was stuck up a tree at the time.'

'Exactly,' agreed Tori, almost too quickly. She stuffed her purse back into her bag. 'Thanks for these, Beth, lovely to see you,' she said, nodding as she made her way over to Rose.

'How are you all?' said Grace, shuffling along the bench to get comfy in the corner.

'I've been helping out at the café this week, actually, just while Joyce is resting up,' replied Rose.

'She's okay, though?' asked Grace, concerned.

'Hopefully. She's having some thyroid issues,' Tori explained, 'so she's taking it easy until her pills kick in.'

'Sounds sensible. Are you back for good, then, Tori?' asked Grace.

'Maybe. I'm just settling back into village life; it's a bit of a culture shock after Thailand,' said Tori.

'I bet!' said Kate.

'I haven't really decided what to do now I'm back on my own.' Tori shrugged.

'Ah, Rose told me about your ex. Ryan, is it?' said Grace.

'I hope you don't mind?' said Rose quickly.

'Course not,' said Tori.

'Is he completely out of the picture?' asked Kate, picking up her pint.

'Completely. I've not heard a word from him since I got home. I did think about messaging him, but I don't want to be *that* girl,' said Tori.

'Meaning?' asked Grace, raising her eyebrows.

'You know, the one pining after her ex, looking for answers. He wanted to end things and now he has. What more is there to know?' said Tori.

'It might help you move on, though,' Grace suggested.

'I have moved on. I'm off men,' said Tori, taking a large swig of wine. 'Life's a whole lot simpler without them.'

'Simpler, maybe, but definitely less fun,' Kate laughed.

'Well, here's to simplicity then,' said Tori, raising her drink. They all clinked their glasses in agreement. 'Cheers,' they chorused.

The four friends spent the next few hours drinking and laughing together. Tori found she had a lot in common with Grace; they both loved travelling and Tori liked her carefree attitude and the way she listened without feeling the need to judge or advise. She was happy to see how well Rose and Kate got along too. Perhaps they'd even be sisters-in-law one day? As she made her way through the packed pub on her way back from the ladies, she saw a familiar face at the jukebox and beamed, despite herself.

'Kings of Leon or Lewis Capaldi?' asked Leo, when he saw her. He beckoned her over.

'Huh?' said Tori.

'Kings of Leon or Lewis Capaldi?' repeated Leo, inclining his head towards her.

'Oh, always Kings of Leon.'

'Right answer!' He punched his selection into the juke-box, and 'Use Somebody' began blaring out through the speakers. He smiled at her, and Tori's stomach did a little flip. 'I don't know about you, but I could use a drink. What can I get you?' he said, nodding towards the bar.

'Oh no, you don't have to, I'm—'

'I *want* to,' he said, holding her gaze.

'Sauvignon Blanc, please.' She followed Leo towards the bar and perched herself on the nearest stool. Why hadn't she reapplied her lip gloss when she was in the ladies? More to the point, why did she care? She wasn't interested in Leo, was she? He sat down next to her and smiled. She felt butterflies surge in her belly. Honestly, she had to stop this; she wasn't interested in dating again.

'To Ernie,' he said, raising his pint glass. 'May he long continue causing chaos.' He smiled at her. He really did have the perfect smile. Tori raised her glass and laughed.

'Listen, I'm sorry about the way I spoke to you the other day. I was so rude to you ...'

'Forget it,' he said, waving his hand. 'You've already apolo-gized. I'm a big boy, I can take it. Plus, there was free food involved. I'm happy for you to insult me daily if you always say sorry with a cheese scone.'

'That's good to know,' said Tori, laughing. *Damn!* He was sweet too. Sweet *and* sexy.

'So, how long are you back for? Jake mentioned you'd been off travelling.'

Tori stiffened. What else had Jake been telling him? 'Oh, did he?'

'He just mentioned it in passing,' Leo added quickly.

'Er, I'm not really sure yet, it depends on a few things . . .'

'Like . . .'

'Oh, there you are!' said Rose, on her way to the bar. 'Grace and I wondered where you'd got to.'

'Sorry, I can go . . .' said Leo, making to stand up. Rose held a hand up to stop him.

'You're fine where you are. Tori looks much happier talking to you anyway . . .'

'I came here with you and the girls, I'd better—' said Tori.

'We'll come and find you before we leave,' Rose cut in, mouthing the word 'hottie' and gesturing wildly at Leo behind his back. Tori rolled her eyes and ushered Rose away.

'Sorry about that,' she said, feeling her insides fizz.

'No worries,' laughed Leo. 'Have you and Rose been friends long?'

'Since we were kids. She used to come and stay here every summer with her Aunt Jean; we got on instantly, like kids do. What about you? You're not from around here, are you? I mean . . . I think I'd have remembered if I'd seen you before . . .' *God, why did she say that?* She sounded like a stalker. She took a big glug of wine.

'I'm from Ashford, so fairly local. When the job came up in Rye I applied straight away and . . . here I am.'

'And do you like it? Being a firefighter, I mean.'

'Oh, yeah, I love it. It's really interesting work—'

'Although less interesting when you're called out to rescue a cat from a tree . . .'

'Well, I met you, didn't I?' He reached to pick up his pint glass. There was a pause. He cleared his throat. 'Listen, Tori. I was wondering—'

'Sorry, I think Rose wants me,' she lied, jumping up from the bar stool as if it was red hot. 'It was lovely to see you, Leo – thanks again for the drink.' She grabbed her glass of wine and dashed across the packed pub as quickly as she could.

Had Leo been about to ask her on a date? She hoped not. It was too soon. Besides, Leo couldn't be interested in *her*. She shook her head. She'd run off like a petrified rabbit in the headlights and now he probably thought she was a total idiot. She exhaled slowly. Well, whatever he'd planned to ask, she was glad she hadn't hung around to find out. Single life was most definitely the way forward and she didn't plan on changing her mind about that anytime soon.

Chapter 10

Sleep evaded Tori that night. Not only did she keep coming back to what Leo might have been about to ask her in the pub, she also couldn't stop thinking about what her mum had said. Could she really consider taking the Cosy Cup on permanently? Did she even want to? She looked at the clock. It was 3am and she hadn't slept a wink. She sat up, threw back the duvet, flicked on the bedside lamp and reached for her phone. Ernie looked up at her from the foot of the bed, bleary-eyed.

'Sorry Ern, I can't sleep.'

The huge ginger cat made his feelings known by slowly turning his head away and curling up into an even tighter ball. His message was clear: just because Tori was up at an ungodly hour, it didn't mean he had to join her.

Tori opened the photo app on her phone and began scrolling through her most recent set of pictures. They were all of Tokyo, her favourite place from her travels with Ryan. She smiled as she flicked through image after image of historic temples and picturesque gardens. When she came across a photo of Ryan, a wave of sadness swept over her. The photo was taken in front of the Sensō-ji Temple, and Ryan was smiling broadly with his arms spread skyward. She exhaled deeply, her grip constricting around the phone. Had it really been just a few weeks since they'd been in Tokyo, looking forward to their future together? It felt like a lifetime ago. She almost didn't recognize the man in the picture. Had she ever *really* known him? She had trusted him, and he had let her down . . . why? She didn't know. The feeling of nausea in her stomach turned to a red-hot fury. She jabbed her finger on the delete button and pressed down hard. The picture of Ryan vanished. If only it was that easy to delete Ryan from her mind too.

She knew trying to sleep now would be pointless; she may as well get up and make some hot milk. The sight awaiting her when she got to the kitchen surprised her. Joyce was sat at the kitchen table, laptop open, surrounded by Post-it notes.

'Mum? What are you doing up?' Tori asked, rubbing her eyes. 'What's all this?' She pointed to the mess of notes strewn across the table. 'You look exhausted. Have you been here all night?'

'Pretty much. Listen, Tori, I've got something really important to talk to you about, I've had this idea—'

'Slow down, Mum. I was going to make some hot milk. Fancy some?'

'No, look, just sit down for a second, will you?'

'What *is* all this?' repeated Tori, pulling up a seat. 'Looks like you've been busy—'

'I have, I've come up with a genius idea. I've been up all night thinking about it—'

'Thinking about what?'

'Well, it's about that money I'd set aside for the deposit for you ... Why don't we do something else with it instead? Something exciting?'

'Okay ...' said Tori hesitantly. 'What have you got in mind?'

'Well, I'm not getting any younger—'

'You're hardly—'

'Just let me finish, would you?' Tori nodded silently. 'I'm not going to be running the Cosy Cup forever. It's been playing on my mind a bit recently, what's going to happen when it's time for me to take a backseat—'

'But, Mum—'

'So,' continued Joyce, holding a palm up to silence her, 'if you're not going to be looking for a house right now, why don't we turn the Cosy Cup into one of those cat cafés, like the ones you went to in Tokyo?'

'A cat café? In Blossom Heath?' said Tori, stunned.

'Exactly,' replied Joyce, smiling broadly.

'You're serious?'

'Deadly.'

'But, Mum, it would take so much work.'

'I know, but I'm pretty sure we're both up to the challenge. The Cosy Cup is crying out for a revamp.'

'It's lovely as it is . . .'

'That's kind of you, but we both know that's not strictly true. It's looking more than a little tired around the edges and I think you're exactly the person to give it a facelift.'

'Me?'

'Yes, you.'

'I'm no Mary Berry, though, Mum. My cakes aren't exactly up to your standards.'

'There's more to running the Cup than baking, Tori. Much more. It's a business and needs someone with a business brain to run it.'

'And you think that's me?'

'I *know* it is. That business degree of yours has given you all the skills you need. And I'll still be next door to bake cakes and help serve. You can manage the business and sort out the cats! We'll keep the character of the Cosy Cup, but with a new twist.'

Tori's brain was whirring. *Could she?* Would it even work? It was a mad idea but . . . They would have to get planning approval, of course, she had no idea what welfare measures would need to be put in place for the cats; she'd have to look into health and safety too, and then there was the financial side of things – how much would a project like this even cost? But, well, she had been looking for a project, a new adventure to take her mind off things. What if? What if Joyce's idea could work? A cat café was unique, she was sure people would travel to visit; there was certainly nothing else like it anywhere locally, was there? A sudden thought struck her. *What if there already was?*

'But, Mum, what if there's already a cat café?'

'In Sussex?' Tori nodded. 'What do you think I've being doing all night?' said Joyce, pointing at the laptop screen and angling it towards Tori. The words *cat café, Sussex* were visible in the search bar. Tori's heartbeat quickened as she scrolled through the results page . . . *London, Yorkshire, Essex, the Lake District, Devon* . . . nope, she couldn't see any results in Sussex, that had to be a good thing, right? But could they really do this? Was it even an option? They'd need to do more research, come up with a proper business plan. But she could do that. She'd spent three years at university studying business, if not for this project, then for what? A job back at the furniture warehouse?

'And you think it could work? Here? What would the regulars make of a load of cats in the Cosy Cup?'

'It would certainly make us unique, and I can't see why our regulars would mind; we'd still be the same Cosy Cup they know and love, just with cats. We'd attract new customers too, people who would travel here specifically for the cats.'

'I guess there'd be nowhere quite like us nearby.'

'There only seems to be a handful of cat cafés in the whole of the UK and none of them are in Sussex . . .'

'There's still an awful lot to think about – logistics, planning permission, welfare regulations, my head's swimming with it all – but, you know what, I think we could make this work, Mum, I really do,' said Tori, reaching for Joyce's hand.

'You like the idea, then?' said Joyce.

'Yes! I think it's the best idea ever!' Tori's voice cracked with excitement. 'And you really think this is something you want to do? It's a big step and—'

'Absolutely,' said Joyce. 'We'll need to do our research, though, but we can worry about that tomorrow.'

'But what about Ernie? Do you think he'll get jealous with a load of new cats next door? I wouldn't want to put his nose out of joint . . .'

'Oh, he'll be fine, love. He likes other cats, doesn't he?'

'Well, yes, he plays with that little tortoiseshell cat from a few doors down – they're always in the garden together.'

'Mags said he's snuck into their place a few times and cuddled up with Troilus, their Siamese, she's found them asleep together on the bed.'

'Really? The cheek of him!' Tori laughed. 'But that's why we love him.'

'Don't worry about Ernie, he'll be fine, and he won't be mixing with the café cats anyway, he'll only get a glimpse of them through the window.'

'True,' Tori agreed.

'Now how about you put that milk on and then maybe we can both try and get some sleep?'

'Is it too late for champagne?' asked Tori, as she opened the fridge.

'Champagne?' said Joyce, smiling up at her. 'I thought you wanted something to help you sleep?'

'I did, but now we've got a reason to celebrate, sleeping seems less important.'

'You're on! I'll get the glasses, love,' said Joyce.

When Tori finally made it back to bed, she was giddy with champagne and excitement at her mum's plans for the tearoom. She scrolled through her pictures of Tokyo on her phone and her face broke into a smile when she found a whole album devoted to the cat cafés she had visited during her time in the city. There were cats of all shapes and sizes: thin ones, fat ones, super-fluffy ones and hairless ones, pedigrees and moggies alike. Tori stopped scrolling when she reached a small, grey cat with a streak of white fur across his chest.

'Kenzo! Oh, I'd forgotten just how cute you are!' She reached across the bed and held her phone out towards Ernie, who still hadn't moved from his spot at the end of the bed. 'Hey, Ern, look! This is Kenzo. He kept me company in Tokyo when I was missing you.' Ernie opened his eyes and pawed at the screen. 'You two would get on great, you know. Kenzo reminds me a lot of you.'

A cat café in Blossom Heath. She couldn't believe it. She had been looking for a project, a new adventure to take her mind off things but she'd never expected ... *This*.

'Come on, Ernie, we need to get some sleep, tomorrow we've got work to do.'

*

By eight o'clock the next morning, Tori was back in the kitchen surrounded by a mountain of notes. She rubbed her eyes and looked down at her empty coffee cup. She needed more coffee, much more. Tori flicked through her notebook and looked at everything she had researched since she'd been up. The more she had read online, the more certain she had become that she *could* do this. That it would work. She'd even come up with a new name, if her mum was happy with the tearoom being rebranded . . . The Cosy Cat Café. It was the perfect blend of old and new. She heard footsteps padding down the stairs towards the kitchen.

'Morning, love. You're up bright and early,' said Joyce, stifling a yawn.

'Well, there's lots to do today,' said Tori brightly, 'plus I needed to check.'

'Check what?'

'That you really did suggest we open a cat café in the middle of the night – that I didn't dream the whole thing.'

'You didn't dream it. I'm just pleased you're as excited about it as I am.'

'Oh, I am. Honestly, it was something I'd never even thought about before, but I think it sounds brilliant!'

'And you're up for putting the hard work in?' said Joyce, reaching for the orange juice.

'Absolutely! I can't wait to get started actually,' said Tori, nodding.

'We'll need a back-up plan – what happens to the cats if things don't work out?'

'I've been thinking about that. One of the cat cafés I was reading about teamed up with a local rescue, and all the cats in their café are looking for forever homes. Customers register their interest in adopting them with the rescue centre, so the time they spend in the café is like a halfway house.'

'What a lovely idea,' said Joyce, reaching down to stroke Ernie, who was wrapping himself around the table legs and mewing for his breakfast.

'I know! It's so clever. If we operated in the same way then, worst-case scenario, if things don't work out, we'd just need to get all the cats we were looking after adopted before we switched back to being a regular tearoom again. What do you think?'

'I love it!'

'Seriously? Oh, Mum, that's great news!' Tori leapt up and threw her arms around her mother.

'There's still a lot to think about and we need to investigate the idea properly, but we'll do some more planning, get some expert advice and then we can make a decision . . . together.'

'I've already got some contact details for people who might be able to help,' said Tori, displaying a wide grin, 'and I thought I could talk to Grace and see if she can advise us on the animal welfare side of things?'

'That sounds like a great starting point.'

'I'm going to put together a full business plan to show you, but I just need to get all the ideas worked out in my head first.'

'Perfect. Now, how would you feel about officially becoming manager of the cat café?'

'Manager? Seriously?'

'If you're going to take ownership of this, then I think it's only fair. You're going to be the driving force behind the project, and I want to recognize that.'

'Oh, thanks, Mum,' said Tori. 'I won't let you down. I know the cat café is a new idea, but I want you to know how important it is to me that we keep the essence of the Cosy Cup alive. People love it and it's important we don't lose that with the revamp.'

'Of course, love. I've got every faith in you. Now, can we get some breakfast sorted? I'm starving.'

'I'm just heading next door to open up. I'll get some eggs on the go.'

'Great.'

'Jump in the shower and I'll have breakfast ready by the time you arrive.'

'Thanks, love.'

When Tori arrived at the Cosy Cup to make a start on breakfast, she felt her face break into a grin. Was she really about to embark on a new adventure, right here in Blossom Heath?

Chapter 11

After surviving the lunchtime rush, Tori headed straight over to Brook House to see Grace. She'd managed to consume enough coffee to just about stave off last night's lack of sleep, and she wanted to seize the moment while the idea was still fresh. Now that the plan was to turn the Cosy Cup into a cat café, she was keen to talk the idea over with an expert.

'Hi there,' she said to Tara, the receptionist behind the desk. 'I don't suppose Grace is about?'

'You're in luck – she's just finishing her lunch. Let me see if she's free,' replied Tara, disappearing through the door that led to the consulting rooms. She reappeared with a beaming Grace at her side.

'Tori! It's not Ernie again, is it?'

'No, Ernie's fine but I've got an idea that I wanted to run past you, if you've got five minutes?'

'Sure, afternoon surgery doesn't start for a bit. Come through and I'll make you a cuppa?'

'Perfect. If you've got coffee, the stronger the better,' said

Tori, following Grace through the door leading to the clinic's staffroom.

'Everything okay?'

'Actually, everything's great – Mum's had this great idea for the Cosy Cup, and I wanted to pick your brains before we start making plans.'

'Pick *my* brains? Are you sure you're asking the right person? I don't know much about—'

'You're the *perfect* person, Grace, trust me. What do you know about cat cafés?' Grace stopped adding milk to her coffee.

'Cat cafés? You mean like the ones in Asia?'

'Yes! Exactly that. There are a few in the UK now too.'

'Well, I've never actually been to one, but I think they're a great idea in theory … Wait, you're not thinking about turning the Cosy Cup into a cat café?' She turned to face Tori. Tori held her breath. Oh no. Was Grace about to tell her this was a terrible idea?

'Maybe? Mum suggested it last night.' She added quickly, 'But it's really early days.' She shifted her weight forwards to perch on the very edge of her chair. 'I've done a bit of research and I think it could work …'

'I think it's a brilliant idea, Tori,' said Grace.

'Seriously?' replied Tori.

'Seriously. They're a great way for people to spend time around cats when they can't commit to keeping a pet themselves. They help kids learn how to interact with animals and I've even heard of some that work alongside rescues and have cats that are adoptable—'

'That's *exactly* what we were thinking!' Tori clapped her hands together, almost sending her coffee flying.

'Which part?'

'Well, all of it, but I'd really like to find a rescue to work alongside so that we could offer a temporary home to cats that need adopting.'

'Really? That's great. I know the perfect organization to put you in touch with – New Beginnings Animal Rescue. It's run by a lady called Izzy and she does amazing work. She usually has around thirty cats looking for homes; I'm sure there might be one or two who would be happy living a café life.' Grace passed Tori a pale blue business card. 'All her contact details are on there.'

'Hang on a minute. Izzy Sullivan?'

'That's right.'

'I think I know her. If it's the same Izzy I'm thinking of, we went to school together!'

'I can't imagine there's more than one Izzy Sullivan in Blossom Heath.'

'She moved to Hastings a few years ago and we never really kept in touch, but it must be her.'

'Maybe it's a sign?' suggested Grace. 'The stars are trying to tell you something?'

'Maybe they are,' laughed Tori.

'Café life won't be suitable for all of the cats at the centre, I suspect, not if they're nervous or not happy living with other cats or shy with people, say.'

'I get that. I guess it's a case of trying to find the right match, isn't it? Making sure that any of the cats that do stay with us are happy to be petted, and comfortable in a busy environment, would be my main priorities, I think.'

'Exactly, but Izzy and I can help you get that right.'

'Thanks, Grace. I can't tell you how much I appreciate this.'

'There'll be a lot of hoops to jump through with the council, though,' said Grace, her tone serious. 'You'll have to adhere to Animal Welfare Regulations *and* have a visit from an inspector. I'll help you as much as I can, Tori, but don't underestimate the work involved.'

'I get it. I'm totally up for the challenge, though – I really want to get it right.'

'Some of the older cats can be at the rescue for months, if not years. Black cats find it harder to get adopted too, as everyone wants the more unusual colourings like ginger and tortoiseshell.'

'Really? That's so sad. I love black cats – they look like mini panthers.'

'Have a chat with Izzy and see what she thinks. If she's on board, let me know and maybe we can go and meet some of the cats together.'

'That sounds amazing, thanks so much, Grace. I'll call Izzy as soon as I get home.'

'Perfect. I take it this plan means you're staying in Blossom Heath permanently?'

'Definitely! If I can get this to work, I'll be staying for good.'

'I can't see why it wouldn't, as long as you follow all the advice and rules around cat welfare. You can certainly count on me as a regular customer.'

'Aren't you already?' Tori laughed.

'Well, yes, but if hanging out with cats is part of the package, I might be having fewer takeaways!'

'I'll save you a seat.'

'Is that the time?' said Grace, glancing at her watch. 'I'm going to be late for afternoon surgery! Sorry to rush you out, but if there's anything you need help with, you know where I am.'

'Thanks, I'll take you up on that. Swing by the café when you're free – we've got some new tea blends on the menu.'

'You realize you'll never get rid of me in that case.'

'Well, if all goes to plan, we're going to need a resident vet,' laughed Tori. 'See you soon, and thanks again, Grace, I really appreciate this.'

As Tori walked across the village green back to the café, she felt her phone buzz in her pocket. It was a text from Rose. *Dinner at Harper Farm tonight?* Tori typed out her reply: *Count me in xx* Before she'd had time to put it back in her bag, her phone buzzed with Rose's reply. *Perfect! 8pm, bring a bottle xx* Tori's face broke into a smile. She hadn't seen Jake since she'd been back in the village, and she couldn't wait to share her travelling adventures with one of her oldest friends. It would also be the first time she'd seen Rose and Jake together as a couple. Two of her closest friends in a relationship – who would have thought? She couldn't wait to tell Rose about the plans for the cat café and share the news that she might be staying in Blossom Heath after all.

Tori arrived at Harper Farm just before eight. She couldn't wait to spill the beans about the plans for the tearoom; she just *knew* that Rose was going to be as excited as she was.

'Tori!' said Jake, opening the front door and pulling her into a bear hug. 'It's been ages!' Jake's two Border Collies, Tagg and Finn, were jumping up around Tori's knees, eager to greet her.

'Jake! It's been so long! How are you?' said Tori, standing on tiptoes to give him a kiss on the cheek.

'I'm good, it's great to have you back – Friday nights in the Apple Tree haven't been the same without you.'

'I've missed you too – it's good to be home,' she said, bending down to fuss the two dogs. The front door to Harper Farm opened straight into the large kitchen and Tori spotted Rose, oven gloves on, pulling a huge casserole pot out of the Aga. Scout was sitting at her feet, clearly hoping there were titbits in the offing. 'Please tell me *you* haven't cooked dinner?' said Tori.

'Now, there's gratitude for you,' said Rose, pulling off the oven gloves.

'Don't worry,' said Jake, 'I'm the resident chef tonight.'

'Thank God for that,' said Tori, laughing. 'The last time Rose cooked for me I nearly ended up at the doctor's.'

'Hey! It wasn't my fault the fish was out of date,' said Rose, taking the bottle of red wine out of Tori's outstretched hand and kissing her friend on the cheek.

'And that's not something she should have noticed?' Tori asked Jake. He laughed.

'I couldn't possibly say,' he replied, putting his arms around Rose's waist and kissing her gently on the neck. 'Although food does tend to come in two distinct varieties when Rose is cooking. Burnt or frozen.'

'Hey!' said Rose, flicking Jake across the back of his legs with a tea towel.

'Ow!' said Jake in mock outrage.

'Don't be such a meanie, then,' Rose chuckled as she opened the wine. 'Large or small?'

'Large, obviously,' replied Tori. 'So how are Blossom Heath's hottest couple? I'm so excited for the pair of you! I can't believe you're official! Kate clearly approves too.'

'Happy,' said Jake, raising a glass, 'very happy. In fact, I propose a toast. To Rose! The best girlfriend a bloke could wish for.'

'To Rose!' agreed Tori, clinking her glass against Jake's. 'Honestly, Rose, you've been a lifesaver in the café while Mum's been poorly. Have I told you how much I appreciate you?'

'Once or twice,' replied Rose, taking a glug of wine, 'but I'm always happy to hear it. I still can't believe I made it through the week without breaking anything; I'm definitely not a natural waitress.'

'Well, there was that near miss with Ted's full English almost ending up in his lap,' laughed Tori. 'Seriously though, Rose, I don't know what I would have done without you.'

'Thankfully you don't have to worry about that,' replied Rose, raising her glass.

'Actually, I've got some news I want to share— Oh, there's four places set – is someone joining us?'

Rose and Jake exchanged an awkward glance.

'You'll see,' said Rose, tapping her nose. 'Here you go,' she said, passing Tori the largest glass of wine she had ever seen.

'So, Mum's had this great idea for the Cosy Cup—' There was a knock at the door and all three dogs leapt up barking. 'Shall I get it? I'm closest,' said Tori, getting up from her seat.

'Thanks,' said Jake. 'If this goes pear-shaped, it's on you,' he whispered to Rose.

'If what goes pear-shaped?' Tori asked. She opened the front door and found herself face to face with Leo. He was grinning, holding a bottle of wine in one hand and a cheese-cake in the other. She stood completely still, in stunned silence. *Leo?* What was he doing here? Surely, *he* wasn't the mystery dinner guest?

'Tori, hi!' he said, leaning forward and kissing her on the cheek as he stepped over the threshold. 'Sorry I'm a bit late guys, I got halfway here and remembered Rose had asked me to bring dessert.'

Leo was the fourth dinner guest! Tori threw Rose a confused look. Rose shrugged and mouthed a half-hearted 'sorry' in her direction.

'Brilliant, thanks, Leo,' said Jake, stepping forward to break the silence. 'Cheesecake, my absolute favourite.'

'It's only shop-bought, but I didn't want to turn up empty-handed. Rose was pretty specific,' said Leo.

Why had Rose invited Leo? She thought tonight was just about catching up with old friends. What were they up to? After everything she'd said about not being ready to date again, was Rose trying to throw her and Leo together?

'Sorry,' she said quickly, 'I need to use the loo.' She wanted a moment to gather her thoughts. She headed for the bathroom and splashed her face with cold water. Within seconds, Rose appeared in the doorway.

'Please tell me this isn't a set-up. I thought I explained I wasn't ready to date,' groaned Tori.

'I'm sorry, I know it looks bad . . .'

'You're right – it does!'

'Listen, this is absolutely *not* a set-up.'

'It's not?'

'No, I promise. I just thought the two of you would get along. You've been away for a while and Leo's pretty new to the village too. I just thought it couldn't do any harm for you to get to know each other better, that's all.'

'As friends?'

'Just friends. Seriously, I never meant to upset you. I guess it does kinda look like a set-up but that wasn't the plan.'

Tori perched on the edge of the bath and took a deep breath.

'Okay,' she sniffed. 'Sorry, I've not had much sleep, I was up most of last night thinking about—'

'Ryan?'

'Actually, no. Mum's had this idea for the tearoom . . .'

'What idea?' asked Rose, perching precariously alongside Tori on the edge of the bath.

'Well, you have to promise not to think we're crazy.'

'As if!' said Rose. Tori's eyes narrowed. 'I promise.'

Tori took a deep breath. 'Well, Mum's suggested turning the Cosy Cup into a cat café, like the ones I saw in Japan.'

'Ooh, I've heard about them,' said Rose, her eyes widening.

'And?'

'I think it's a great idea.'

'Honestly?'

'Honestly. Especially if it means you'll be staying in Blossom Heath.'

'It does.'

'Well, I'm all in then. Why don't we go back to the kitchen, and you can tell us all about it. It's exciting news.'

'As long as you promise not to play matchmaker.'

'Pinky swear,' said Rose, her little finger outstretched.

'Deal,' said Tori, hooking her own finger around Rose's and shaking.

'Tonight's just four friends having dinner. No pressure.'

'No pressure sounds good,' agreed Tori, standing up.

'Now, let's get some food dished up, shall we? I'm starving!'

'When aren't you?' said Tori, laughing, as she followed Rose out of the bathroom.

After her initial surprise at Leo's arrival, Tori had an enjoyable evening catching up with her friends. She chuckled hearing Jake talk about Rose's disastrous attempts at cooking, which led to Rose suggesting he take full responsibility for all the meals they ate in the future. Tori talked about the plans for the cat café and her friends shared in her excitement and made offers of help. Tori found that she enjoyed Leo's company, he was witty and good-humoured, and she was surprised at how much they had in common. He'd travelled a lot and they'd visited many of the same far-flung locations; he was an animal lover too and they had the same taste in music, with his album collection ranging from the Spice Girls to AC/DC. She liked how genuinely kind he was; he'd even offered to drop by the Cosy Cup and help her with fire regulations. Rose had been right: it couldn't hurt to be friends with Leo, could it?

As Leo drove home from Harper Farm, he found himself smiling. When Rose had called him that afternoon to ask him to join them for dinner, he wasn't sure how Tori would react. He had thought they were getting on well when he'd seen her last night in the pub, but she couldn't get away from him fast enough when he'd fudged an attempt to ask her out. He really couldn't read her.

When he'd arrived at Jake's farm, he could tell that Tori

hadn't expected him to be there. Jake had said as much when she fled to the bathroom. He didn't know much about Tori's past, he didn't want to pry, but Jake had told him that she'd just got out of a long-term relationship with the boyfriend she'd been travelling with. It seemed as though things were still pretty raw, and he wanted to make sure he didn't come on too strong.

Tonight was different, though. He sensed that Tori felt more at ease in his company. The conversation between them had flowed naturally and, if he hadn't had an early shift the next day, he'd still be at the farmhouse listening to stories of her adventures. He loved how passionate she was when she told him about the plans for the Cosy Cup too; her face had been so animated when she'd talked about it and her enthusiasm was infectious. A cat café in Blossom Heath! What an idea! He really hoped that Tori could make it work. And he was happy to do whatever he could to help her. As he pulled his BMW onto the driveway of his terraced house on the outskirts of the village, he spotted his cats sitting on the doorstep waiting for him, their green eyes shining brightly in the reflection of the car's headlights.

'Hey, you two,' he said, as he got out of the car. 'Waiting for dinner?' Tinkerbell ran over to him meowing. 'I know, I know, don't worry, food's on its way.' He opened the front door and the cats darted across the threshold. 'Okay, okay, at least give me a chance to take my shoes off,' Leo laughed as they yowled at full volume. 'Honestly, anyone would think I never feed you,' he said, picking their empty food bowls up from the kitchen floor. Each pink bowl had the word 'Princess' and a tiny golden crown embossed on the side of it. They had been chosen by Leo's eight-year-old niece, Lara, as a Christmas present for his feline duo. Lara loved the cats just as much as he did and was always begging her mum for a cat of her own, without success. Leo grabbed some cat food and Tinkerbell's patience ran out when she spotted the sachets being opened and she jumped onto the kitchen worktop. 'Honestly, Tinks, patience young lady,' said Leo, placing her back on the kitchen floor. 'There you go, girls,' he said, putting the bowls down as the cats dived in eagerly. Tallulah was purring while she ate. 'Tally, I swear you have the loudest purr ever,' he said, reaching down to stroke her on the back.

Leo, loosening the belt on his jeans, grabbed a beer from the fridge and settled himself on the sofa. He fired off a text to Jake. *Thanks for tonight, mate. Great to see you both.* Jake had been a good friend to Leo since he'd arrived in the village almost a year ago. They'd met when Leo had signed up for the local Sunday league football team, Rye Rangers, and they discovered they were both Spurs fans. Jake had been quick to include Leo in his circle of friends and they'd often go to the Apple Tree together or hang out and watch the footie. As he reached down to finish his beer, his phone buzzed. *Our pleasure. See you at football next weekend.* Next weekend? Leo had almost forgotten. Their upcoming match was the biggest of the season, against Ashford Albion. The two teams were fierce rivals and Rye hadn't beaten them in the last couple of matches. Leo hoped that the next match would put an end to their losing streak. He typed out a reply: *Deffo. We're due a win!!!* Perhaps Rose would come and bring Tori too. Since Rose and Jake had been together, Rose would usually come to matches and cheer Jake on from the sidelines. Leo had often wished he could find his 'Rose', someone he could talk to, maybe even settle down with? Although he'd never been short of dates, finding his 'person' was something that had eluded him so far. There had been girlfriends, but no one that he'd ever felt he wanted to commit to, build a life with. Maybe he just wasn't ready to settle down yet? He took another sip of beer. Tallulah hopped up onto the sofa and quickly made herself comfortable in his lap, purring away contentedly.

Tori seemed different to most of the women he had dated. He couldn't quite put his finger on it, but there was something about her that intrigued him. She was obviously gorgeous with her green eyes and beautiful smile, but it was more than just that though ... She had a certain spark about her that he couldn't quite quantify, but it drew him to her. Maybe he should ask Jake for her number? Was that too much? He didn't want to come across as pushy ... To hell with it, he fired off a text: *No worries if not mate, but do you think I could have Tori's number?*

As Tori was about to turn off her bedroom light, she heard her phone vibrate on the bedside table next to her. She had a message from a number she didn't recognize. *Hi Tori, it was great to see you this evening, I can't wait for the cat café to open! Leo xx* Surprising herself, Tori found that she was pleased to hear from him. It was pointless denying it, there *was* something there between her and Leo and she'd be a fool if she didn't explore it. She replied: *Lovely to see you too, next time you're passing the Cosy Cup, pop in and say hi, the coffee is on me xx* Before she'd even managed to put it back down, her phone buzzed again. *I'll hold you to that xx* She smiled, flicked off the bedside lamp and fell into the most contented sleep she'd experienced since she'd been back in Blossom Heath.

Chapter 12

The following week passed in a blur. Tori was busy running the café single-handedly as Rose had been kept busy at school, and she collapsed into her bed after every shift, exhausted. She didn't know how her mum had managed to run the place alone since Cathy had left. It all meant that she hadn't made as much progress with her plans for the cat café as she would have liked, but she'd get there. She had a long to-do list and she was determined to spend Sunday night at home, working through it. Her mum wasn't due back at the café until the following Monday as Tori was adamant that she wasn't to return until her medication had properly kicked in and she was feeling better. Despite this, Joyce made an appearance on Saturday morning.

'Mum! What are you doing here?' Tori asked, as she spotted Joyce walking through the door. 'You're not supposed to be back until next week?'

'Oh, I'm feeling so much better now, love. There's no

sense in me sitting at home twiddling my thumbs while you're rushed off your feet, is there?'

Joyce did look so much better than she had a couple of weeks ago. The medication was clearly kicking in as her energy levels were virtually back to normal.

'Well, only if you're *sure* you're feeling up to it?' Tori stared at her mum, eyes narrowed.

'I am,' replied Joyce, 'I promise.'

Tori got the sense that, whatever her objections might be, her mum was going nowhere. She sighed. 'Okay then, but I'll be keeping my beady eye on you and any signs that it's getting too much too soon and I'm sending you home. Deal?'

'Have you forgotten that *I'm* the parent?'

'Deal?'

'Okay, fine. Now where do you want me?'

'Taking orders would be great,' said Tori, passing Joyce a notepad and pencil. 'And Mum?'

'Yes?'

'It's great to have you back, you know,' said Tori, hugging her tightly.

'It's good to be back,' replied Joyce. 'Now, let's get to work, shall we?'

Tori nodded.

Joyce was in her element back at the tearoom. The regulars were happy to see her, and she chatted away to them, taking and delivering orders and catching up on all the gossip she'd been missing out on. Tori stood and watched her for a while.

She looked so happy and full of life. Her eyes were brighter, her energy levels restored, and Tori felt truly grateful that she was on the mend.

'Tori! I didn't know you were back,' cried a familiar voice from the other side of the counter.

'Melissa! Hi!' said Tori, looking up to see another of her oldest childhood friends standing in front of her with a pram. 'How are you? And how's the new arrival?' she asked, stepping out from behind the counter and peering inside at the sleeping baby.

'Oh, she's good. I, on the other hand, am feeling a little ragged around the edges.'

'A girl? How lovely. What's her name?'

'Annabel.'

'That's such a pretty name! I'm sorry I've not been in touch, I've only been home a few weeks and life has been . . . well, let's just say, a little crazy.'

'Oh, don't worry, I know what it's like. I'm totally out of the loop, what with this one keeping me up half the night,' replied Melissa, rubbing her eyes.

'Caffeine?'

'I wish, I'm still breastfeeding. Can I grab a fruit tea? Berry if you've got it?' said Melissa, pulling out her purse.

'Sure, grab a table and I'll bring it over. If I get five minutes, I'll join you,' said Tori, handing over the card machine.

As soon as the tearoom was quieter, Tori made her way over to Melissa's table and pulled up a chair.

'She's still asleep,' said Melissa in a hushed voice, rocking the pram gently back and forth.

'How are things? You must be exhausted.'

'Oh, I am, but she's totally worth it,' replied Melissa, her face lighting up. 'I'm completely in love with her, so's Harry.'

'I bet! She's absolutely gorgeous, Mel, congratulations. I'm so happy for you both.'

'Thanks, lovely. But how are you? How was travelling? And Ryan? Is he back too?'

'Ah well, travelling was amazing, thanks. But Ryan ... well, we're not actually together anymore,' said Tori, dropping her gaze.

'Oh, Tori, I'm so sorry! Are you okay?'

'I'm getting there ... It's good to be home and with friends again. It's helping.'

'Break-ups suck. If you need to talk, I'm usually up doing feeds most of the night, so ring any time, day or night.'

'Thanks, Mel.'

'Who would have thought it, eh? When we started in reception class together, that we'd be still be friends all this time later?' said Melissa.

'It's crazy to think how long we've known each other. All those ups and downs ...'

'Like when we both had a crush on Paul Jones; I seriously thought our friendship was doomed.'

'Well, we were all of eight years old so obviously we both thought he was husband material,' said Tori, snorting with laughter.

'You know, I still see a lot of Harriet too.'

'I thought she'd moved away?'

'She did, but she's back again. Her little lad, Henry, is eighteen months now; we go to the same mother and baby group at the village hall. Although the drinks there suck, not a patch on this strawberry and vanilla tea!'

'Hey, why don't you hold it here?' said Tori, her eyes widening.

'The mother and baby group?'

'Why not?'

'The little ones can get quite noisy; I think we might drive away your other customers . . .'

'We could have a child-friendly morning, once a week, and then no one needs to worry about how loud they are or how much mess they make?'

'Seriously, Tori? That sounds wonderful.'

'Really?'

'Yes! I always feel so self-conscious when I'm out, like what if Annabel starts screaming the place down or has a nappy explosion? It's not just me; I know a lot of the other mums feel the same.'

'I'll pitch it to Mum, but I'm sure she'll be on board. I could do babyccinos for the older kids, and child-friendly snacks, hummus and carrot sticks, that kind of thing?'

'You know you'll *have* to do it now you've told me about it; I'll be on your case otherwise! I'll be telling the other mums too,' said Melissa.

'Do! I'm so glad you popped in and I got the chance to meet the gorgeous Annabel. If you need a night off, you know where I am. I'm happy to babysit anytime.'

'You might regret that – I'll definitely hold you to it.'

'You must, and say hello to Harriet for me, would you?'

'Of course,' said Melissa, draining the last of her tea.

When Melissa and Annabel left, Joyce pulled Tori to one side.

'Listen, love. There's something I wanted to give you,' she said, passing Tori a pink pastel envelope.

'What's this?'

'Just open it, will you?'

Tori opened the envelope and inside was a gift voucher for a hair appointment at Claire's salon, Snippers.

'You're all booked in for four o'clock,' said Joyce, smiling.

'But, Mum, you didn't need to …'

'You've been working far too hard these past couple of weeks and I wanted to treat you. It's my way of saying thank you for everything you've done since you've been home.'

'It wasn't any trouble, I wanted to help.'

'I know, but I wanted to treat you so do me a favour, will you? Let me.'

'Thanks, Mum. These split ends could do with a refresh,' Tori said, pulling a few strands of hair out to the side and examining them.

'There you are, it's perfect timing then.'

Tori walked through the shiny silver doors of Snippers at exactly four o'clock. Located almost opposite the Cosy Cup on the other side of the village green, the salon was sand-wiched between the Pink Ribbon and Harrison's. It had changed hands just before Tori had set off on her travels and was now under Claire's ownership. As she looked around the slick black and silver interior, she guessed that no expense had been spared on the refurbishment. The reception desk was decorated with sparkling diamanté tiles and a gorgeous crystal chandelier was hanging from the ceiling. Tori was excited at the prospect of undergoing a makeover. She couldn't remember the last time she'd had a proper haircut; spending money on luxuries like that hadn't been something she'd been able to afford while she was travelling.

'Hi, Tori,' said Claire from behind the counter.

'Mum's booked me in for a bit of a refresh,' said Tori, waving her voucher.

'That's right,' said Claire, flashing a brilliant white smile in her direction. Tori nodded. 'She said she wanted to treat you. Come and take a seat.'

Tori followed Claire across to one of the black leather stylists' chairs and sat down in front of the mirror. She couldn't help noticing how chic Claire was. She was dressed in tight leather trousers with an animal print blouse, her make-up was flawless, and her eyes sparkled from under her glossy brown fringe. She really was stunning. Tori could never pull off a look like that. She'd look ridiculous.

'Now what are we doing today?' Claire asked.

'I'm not too sure ... I was thinking just a trim but now I'm wondering if I should do something a bit more daring?'

Claire's eyes twinkled and she gave a little clap of delight.

'Do it! You've got great bone structure, so your face can handle most styles.'

'Oh, I don't know,' said Tori, 'maybe I should just go for the usual . . .'

'How about we take a couple of inches off the length at the back?' said Claire, fanning Tori's hair out across her back. 'And I can take the front a little shorter and feather it, like this' – she lifted some shorter strands level with Tori's chin – 'and let's add some colour. You've got beautiful highlights.'

'That's from travelling; my hair always goes lighter when I'm in the sun.'

'Well, it looks fabulous, so let's add a few more strands to really bring that out. What do you say?'

Tori paused for a moment. 'Go for it – you only live once.'

'It'll look gorgeous – just leave it to me,' said Claire, tilting her head to one side. Claire bustled away at the trolley beside her, mixing up a paste and she painted strands of Tori's hair with a small brush, before carefully wrapping them in foil. She left Tori to sit for a while with a magazine to allow the colour to take, before calling 'Alice?' to a girl in her late teens who was sweeping up the floor. 'Can you give Tori here a wash and condition and pop her back in my chair when you're done?'

'Sure,' said Alice, putting her broom away and walking towards the row of basins on the back wall of the salon.

'Alice will take great care of you and I'll see you in ten,' said Claire, flashing her bright white smile again.

Claire wasn't wrong; Alice's hair-washing skills were sublime. The products she used smelt heavenly, a combination of lavender and patchouli, and Alice finished the treatment off with a head massage. Tori could feel all the stress and tension from the last couple of weeks floating away. Her mum was right: this really was just what she had needed. Alice led Tori back towards Claire who was ready and waiting, comb and scissors in hand. She began snipping away at Tori's wet hair with expert precision.

'So how are you settling back into village life?'

'Good, thanks. It's taken a while to readjust but travelling feels like a lifetime ago now.'

'Who did you go with? Your boyfriend?' Claire asked, almost too quickly.

Tori hesitated. Did she really want to share her dating history with someone she didn't really know? She closed her eyes and decided, why not? Wasn't that what people did? Tell their deep, dark secrets to their hairdresser? Claire probably knew more about what was going on in the village than Maggie Harrison did, although Tori hoped she was more discreet.

'Ex-boyfriend. We broke up just before I got back.'

'Oh, I'm sorry. Men, eh? More trouble than they're worth half the time.'

'I guess . . . I'm trying not to think about it. Anyway, I've got a lot to keep me busy right now; I've got big plans for the tearoom.'

'Really? What?'

'Well, I've only told a couple of people but I'm hoping to turn it into a cat café!'

'Wow! Seriously? That sounds exciting!' said Claire, pausing her scissors mid snip to stop and look at Tori in the mirror.

'It is. I mean, I've still got a lot of research to do first but I'm hoping I'll get the go-ahead from the council.'

'Well, if you need any help, just let me know. Us local businesses have to stick together, right?'

'Thanks, Claire, I appreciate that.'

'So, this ex of yours, were you together long?'

'Just over four years.'

'Do you think you'll get back together? I mean, maybe this is just a bump in the road?'

'I doubt it; I've not even heard from him since I've been back.' Was Tori imagining it, or did Claire's face fall a little at this news? She shook her head; don't be silly, she doesn't even know Ryan.

'Well, never say never.' Claire began running her fingers through Tori's wet hair, checking the cut was even and snipping away any stray hairs that were out of place. 'That's looking great.' While Claire was working, Tori chatted away happily to her, talking more about her plans for the café, and Claire filled her in on all the improvements she'd made to the salon since she took over.

After Claire had worked her magic with the blow-dry, Tori looked at her reflection in the mirror.

'Wow, Claire, this looks amazing, you've done a great job. Honestly, this is just what I needed.'

'It's my absolute pleasure – I'm so glad you love it!'

'I do!'

'Joyce paid in advance so you're all set, but pop on over to the counter and I'll give you one of our loyalty cards.' Claire's patent heels click-clacked on the smooth black and white tiled floor as she walked towards the reception desk and Tori couldn't help but wonder how she managed to stay upright in those shoes, let alone stand in them all day; the heels must be at least five inches.

'Your shoes are gorgeous,' said Tori, 'but how on earth do you manage to stay on your feet all day?'

'Oh, these?' she said, standing on one foot and pointing the other out towards Tori. 'They're Christian Louboutins. Cost me an absolute fortune but totally worth the sore feet. Do you like them?'

'They're stunning but I'm more of a Converse kind of girl,' said Tori, flashing her blue and white Converse trainers in Claire's direction.

'Right, I've stamped your loyalty card for you. If you get six stamps you get twenty per cent off your next cut and blow-dry.'

'Thanks.'

Just as Tori was about to turn and leave, Claire added, 'Oh, I meant to ask. Did I spot you having coffee with that new fireman? Oh, what's his name? Lee? Lance?'

'Do you mean Leo?'

'Oh yes, I think that's the one. Know him well?'

'No, not really. He rescued my cat, Ernie, when he got stuck up that tree,' said Tori, pointing at the offending syca-more through the window.

'Oh, I see,' said Claire. Was it Tori's imagination or did her shoulders seem to relax a little? 'Listen, Tori, why don't we grab lunch soon? You can tell me more about your plan for the cat café.'

'Sure, that would be great.'

'How about the twenty-eighth at the Apple Tree? One o'clock? It's on me.'

'I'm pretty sure that should work but I'll just need to check that Mum's okay to manage on her own.'

'Of course, well, my number's on the card. Great to meet you properly.'

'You too,' said Tori.

As she walked away from the salon, Tori stopped to admire her shiny new haircut in the window. Claire really had done a great job; she barely recognized herself and she couldn't remember the last time she'd felt so buoyed when she'd looked at her reflection. Things really did feel like they were starting to turn around. Her mum was on the mend, she had big plans for the Cosy Cup, a glossy new haircut, and she was finally starting to feel happy to be back in Blossom Heath. Ryan or no Ryan.

Chapter 13

Tori spent most of Sunday afternoon sitting in the Cosy Cup glued to her laptop, making plans for the cat café in her notebook. She'd already submitted the relevant paperwork to the council, and she didn't want to lose momentum while she was waiting for permission to be granted. Grace had messaged her earlier in the week with links to websites that would help her understand all the animal welfare regulations. Tori had listed all the things she'd need to think about and what adjustments would need to be made to the Cosy Cup to make it cat-friendly. She had everything on a spreadsheet and her business plan was well under way. By the time she got home that evening, her mind was swimming with ideas and she was feeling more than a little overwhelmed with the enormity of the task she was undertaking.

'Earth to Tori?' said Joyce, clicking her fingers from across the dinner table.

'Sorry?'

'I said, what's on your mind? I can tell you're miles away – you've barely touched your dinner.'

'Sorry, Mum. I'm thinking about the business plan. It's so much more involved than I thought. There's a lot of work to do to make sure we've got everything covered. I don't want to get too far ahead of myself, though, while we're still waiting for the go-ahead from the council.'

'Why don't you talk me through things? That might help make it all a little clearer?'

'Hang on, let me grab my notebook,' said Tori, pushing her plate of spaghetti aside. She leafed through a few pages until she came to the checklist she'd made that afternoon. 'We need to make sure the café is escape-proof. I was thinking an additional set of doors, almost like a kind of lobby area.'

'Okay, that sounds doable. What else?'

'We need to create quiet spaces for the cats away from customers. Other cat cafés have shelves and hidey-holes high on the walls so they can sleep undisturbed.'

'That seems easy enough.'

'We should put some walkways up too, like rope bridges suspended from the ceiling. Something like this maybe?' Tori reached for her phone and pulled up some pictures she'd spotted online.

'How clever!'

'We've got to make things as cat-friendly as possible.'

'Agreed. Why don't you let me have a chat with Greg Ellis? I've always used him when I've needed work doing on the tearoom and his prices are fair. Let's get him out to have a look and once we have his quote, we'll know what we're dealing with.'

'If you're sure? I can show him some of the designs I've seen online and see if we can have something similar.'

'I'll call him this evening.'

'I've not had a chance to speak to Izzy at New Beginnings yet, so I'll try her mobile tonight. She might be able to advise us on the welfare side of things too?'

'Let's finish dinner, we've got calls to make!'

After their meal, Tori sat at the dining-room table with her notebook at hand and dialled Izzy's number. She picked up on the first ring.

'Hello?'

'Hi. Is that Izzy?' Tori asked.

'Speaking.'

'I'm Tori Baxter, from the Cosy Cup. If you're the same Izzy Sullivan I'm thinking of, then you might remember me from school?'

'Hi, Tori! Yes, of course I remember you! It's been ages!'

'How are you? I don't think we've seen each other since the school-leaving ball!' said Tori.

'It's been forever, hasn't it? I never thought I'd end up back in Blossom Heath running a rescue, but here I am!'

'Well, you always loved animals; I remember those kittens you helped your mum to hand-rear when we were kids. She brought them into school once, remember?'

'Oh, yes! I'd forgotten about that,' said Izzy.

'I hope you don't mind but Grace suggested I give you a call.'

'Grace was here yesterday; she mentioned your plans for the tearoom. It certainly sounds like an interesting project.'

'Thanks. I've been doing my research and I'd love for the café's residents to be rescues looking for homes. I wonder if you might consider teaming up with us?'

'Can I be totally honest with you, Tori?'

'Please.'

'I do have some reservations. The welfare of the cats in my care comes first. I'm not interested in them being used as a gimmick. I'd want to make sure they get more enrichment than they'd get here at the centre before finding them forever homes.'

'I totally get that. Of course, for us, ultimately, it's about adding something different and unique to the Cosy Cup, but I want to be able to help the cats in the process too.' There was silence at the other end of the phone. Tori's grip on it tensed. Had she said too much? Could Izzy be convinced her motives were genuine?

After what seemed like an eternity, Izzy finally spoke. 'Well, Grace seems to believe in you, so that definitely goes in your favour. How about the pair of you come and visit this week, meet some of the cats and then we can take it from there.'

'Perfect. Thank you, Izzy.' Tori punched the air as relief flooded through her. 'I'll bring some plans along with me, so you can have a look at the designs and see if there's anything you think we should add or change. I really want to work with you on this, Izzy, you're the expert and I promise I'll take your advice on board. If you're not happy with what we've got planned, I totally respect that too.'

'That sounds like a good starting point. I'll check with Grace, and we'll fix a time. It'll be good to see you again.'

'Thanks, Izzy. I can't wait.' As Tori hung up the phone, she couldn't remember the last time she'd felt so excited.

Things tended to happen quickly once Joyce was involved in something, and, true to form, by four o'clock Monday afternoon, Greg Ellis was knocking on the door of the Cosy Cup just as they were getting ready to close for the day.

'Greg!' said Joyce, shaking his hand firmly. 'Thanks for coming out so quickly, I really appreciate it.'

Greg was a tall, stocky man in his early sixties with a full head of bright white hair. He was dressed as you'd expect a builder to be, in scruffy jeans streaked with paint, with a red plaid shirt. He carried an A4 notebook, a tape measure and a calculator.

'Happy to help, especially if there's a cuppa in the offing,' he said.

'Of course; let me throw in a sandwich too. I'm guessing you've not had lunch?' asked Joyce.

'I have, but there's always room for one of your special ham and pickle sarnies,' Greg replied.

'Oh, stop!' replied Joyce, blushing. *Was Tori imagining things or was Joyce flirting?* 'I'll make you up a plate and I'll let Tori talk to you about her plans.'

'Good to see you again, Tori,' said Greg, shaking her hand.

'I'm guessing Mum's told you a bit about our plans?'

'A cat café,' he said, whistling. 'Can't say I've ever heard of anything like it before.'

'We'll be the first in Sussex, but there are a few dotted around the UK. Let me show you what we're thinking.'

Tori sat down with Greg and took him through some of the designs she'd found for the café. He listened patiently and added some thoughts of his own.

'Well, I certainly think it's doable. It's just a case of getting the design right and looking at materials and pricing. Have you got a budget in mind?' He directed his question at Joyce.

'I was thinking along the lines of five thousand; I really don't want to go much over that,' said Joyce, taking a sip of her milky tea.

'I think we should be able to come in under that,' replied Greg. 'Let me get some measurements and that will give me a clearer idea.' He stood up and walked towards the front door with his tape measure. Tori followed. 'We'll need to put up a stud wall next to the entrance here, to create that lobby area that you wanted. There'll be a second door here,' he said, stepping back and outlining the shape in the air with his arms, 'and that will lead through to the main café. That's going to be the biggest expense. I've been doing some research into cat cafés online since Joyce told me about your plans and we could put a cat flap in this wall and create an area for litter trays so they're concealed from the public, but the cats can access them whenever they need to. Is that what you were thinking, Tori?'

'That's exactly it.'

'Adding the shelves and walkways higher up shouldn't be too difficult. I've got a fantastic carpenter working for me and he'll be able to build anything you'd like.'

'And what about timescales?' asked Joyce.

'You're in luck there,' said Greg. 'We've just had a big job cancel on us that was booked in for a few weeks' time, so we can pencil you in while you're waiting to get the go-ahead from the council.'

'Wow! Really? I didn't expect it could all happen so quickly,' said Tori, her heart rate quickening. 'We're still waiting to hear from the council; they've said they'll aim to respond within four weeks, but I'll ring them to see if we can get an answer any sooner.'

'Might as well strike while the iron's hot,' said Joyce. 'How long do you think we'll have to close, Greg?'

'Around a fortnight, could be quicker, but it's hard to say for certain until we get started.'

'What do you think, Mum?' Tori swallowed hard.

'When are you off to see Izzy?'

'Tomorrow afternoon,' said Tori.

'Why don't we see how that goes and then we can let Greg know one way or the other tomorrow evening. If that's okay with you, Greg?'

'Tomorrow evening's fine. I'll hold the spot in my diary until then and just let me know if you want to go ahead. You don't need to pay a deposit until the council gives you approval, if that helps.'

'It does. We'll make a final decision tomorrow night then,' said Joyce.

'You're sure about the money side of things, though, Mum. It's a big expense ...'

'You let me worry about that, love. You just focus on getting us the green light,' said Joyce.

As Tori let Greg out of the café, she locked the door behind him. She swept a hand across her forehead. She was one step closer to making the cat café a reality. One very big step. A wave of self-doubt swept over her. A cat café in Blossom Heath. Could she really do this? Was she up to the challenge? She wasn't sure. One thing she was sure of, though: she was going to give it her best shot.

Chapter 14

As Tori drove along the lane on the outskirts of Blossom Heath that led up to New Beginnings Animal Rescue Centre, the road gradually became narrower until it was just a single track. She navigated the potholes carefully, not wanting to knock out her suspension, and followed the signs marked 'Reception'.

'Hello?' she said, knocking as she entered the small, timber-framed building. She could hear voices but couldn't see anyone behind the reception desk.

'Hi, can I help you?' A woman dressed in faded blue jeans, a bright orange gilet and dark green wellies, sporting a smile that lit up her whole face, emerged from a side door. 'Tori!' said Izzy, holding out her hand. 'Great to see you, you haven't changed at all! Come through, Grace and I are having coffee before we get started. Can I get you something?'

'Coffee would be lovely. It's got to have been twelve years seen we last saw each other?' replied Tori.

'At least! We've got some serious catching up to do!' said Izzy.

'So much has happened, school feels like a lifetime ago.'

'Doesn't it just.'

'I still can't believe you run this place,' said Tori. 'I knew you'd end up working with animals – it makes total sense.'

'I can't imagine doing anything else, to be honest,' Izzy agreed. 'I love it too much. I'm excited to hear about your plans for the cat café, though!'

'Thanks. I can't really take the credit, it was Mum's idea.'

'But it was inspired by your travels, right?'

'Definitely. I loved the cat cafés in Japan, so I guess the whole trip was inspiration for the idea.'

Izzy took Tori through to a small staffroom, with two worn-out brown leather sofas, one of which was occupied by a large black greyhound, who lifted his head and wagged his tail when he spotted Tori.

'Tori, hi!' said Grace, patting the empty space beside her on the sofa.

'There you go,' said Izzy, passing Tori a mug of coffee. 'If I can move this lump out the way,' she said, wiggling into the tiny space left on the sofa next to the greyhound, 'I might actually be able to sit down too.'

'The *lump* is called Duke,' said Grace, laughing, 'and as you can tell, he likes his home comforts.'

'Doesn't he just,' agreed Izzy. 'He came in a couple of years ago as an ex-racer and managed to worm his way into my heart, so he's never left.' She stroked Duke gently under the chin and the greyhound nestled his head into her hand appreciatively.

'He's gorgeous,' agreed Tori, 'I'm not surprised you couldn't let him go. I don't know how you do it – I'd want to keep all of them.'

'It's tough but you get used to it. You have to think of it as helping them on their way to their forever homes – we're just a stopgap,' explained Izzy.

'How many animals do you have here?' asked Tori.

'It's mainly cats. We have around forty at any one time but that can go up in the summer months when we're coming into kitten season. We do take dogs, but we only have eight kennels, so we're limited on how many. And then there's the rabbits and guinea pigs, hamsters and mice, and we even get reptiles sometimes too.'

'Wow! That's a lot to manage,' said Tori.

'I'm lucky – I have a great team of volunteers who help out with daily cleaning and dog walking, and they spend a lot of time with the cats, playing with them, grooming them, that kind of thing.'

'Izzy does a great job,' said Grace. 'I can't tell you how many times she's helped out when we've had a stray that needs somewhere to go.'

'You more than make up for it by the discount you give us,' replied Izzy. 'Vet bills are our biggest expense. We fund-raise as much as we can to try and keep things going, but all it takes is one seriously ill animal and that can drain all our savings overnight.'

'If there's anything I can help with on the fundraising side of things, I'd be happy to. Maybe a coffee morning? We could have a collection tin on the counter too,' said Tori.

'That would be great – I'll hold you to that, you know!' said Izzy, laughing. 'Right, shall we kick off this tour then? We can meet some of the cats that I think could be suitable for café life and take things from there.'

'Sounds like a plan,' agreed Grace, heaving herself up off the sofa.

As soon as Izzy opened the door to the cattery, the visitors were greeted with a chorus of meows. Tori stopped at the first pen and read the card pinned to the door telling her about a cat called Magic, who had arrived at the centre when her owner had become ill. Tori peered into the pen, but she couldn't spot Magic anywhere.

'There she is,' said Izzy, from behind her.

'Where?'

'If you look closely at the pyramid bed, you'll see a pair of green eyes shining,' said Izzy, pointing towards the domed cat bed.

'Oh yeah!' said Tori, spotting a pair of bright eyes peering out at her. 'I see her.'

'Magic is super-nervous; she'll always hide away when we have visitors. She's the type of cat that would find café life too stressful. She's been used to living with the same owner her whole life and she's finding all the changes unsettling.'

'I can imagine, poor little mite,' replied Tori.

'Don't worry, Izzy will find her the perfect home,' said Grace.

'I've already got one in mind. Do you know Bill Grayson?' Grace and Tori nodded. 'His wife died recently, and he's been looking for a cat for company. Magic here will be perfect for him. He's coming in to meet her this afternoon.'

'See! I told you! Izzy is a feline matchmaker extraordinaire. She always manages to match the right cat to the right human. I don't know how she does it,' said Grace.

'It's so important to get it right, Tori.'

'Izzy's got a great success rate. Hardly any of her adoptions fall through,' added Grace.

'We're always here if things don't work out, though. Any animal that's adopted has full rescue back-up for life,' said Izzy.

'Wow, Izzy, that's great,' Tori agreed.

'Now, let me introduce you to this gentleman,' said Izzy, striding ahead down the corridor. 'Tori, I'd like you to meet Mr Wiggles. I think he'd absolutely love café life.'

As Tori stopped in front of the pen that Izzy had pointed out, she was met by the largest and most handsome black cat she had ever seen. He was purring loudly and rubbing his fur up and down the bars of his enclosure.

'He's adorable,' said Tori, bending down and pushing her fingers through the pen's bars to tickle Mr Wiggles under the chin. 'Why's he called Mr Wiggles? It's such a strange name.'

'Can't you tell?' said Izzy. 'Just look at him, his whole body is wiggling to get your attention.'

'Oh yeah, I see what you mean!' Tori laughed.

'Why don't you go in and get to know him?' said Izzy, opening the pen door to let Tori inside.

'Well, hello there, little man,' said Tori, scooping Mr Wiggles up in her arms. 'Aren't you just adorable.'

'You'd think so,' said Izzy, 'but he's been with us for nearly a year now with zero interest.'

'Really? Why?' said Tori.

'He's a black cat for starters, they always tend to stay with us for a bit longer, plus he's an older chap and needs daily thyroid meds, which puts a lot of people off,' explained Izzy.

'He sounds just like my mum! She's just started on thyroid meds too,' said Tori.

'I won't tell Joyce you just compared her to a stray cat,' laughed Grace.

'You'd better not,' said Tori, in a hushed voice.

'He was a stray so we've got no background on him but, as you can see, he loves people, he's confident and cuddly, and I think he'll lap up all the attention your customers can throw at him. He's a really chilled-out boy,' said Izzy.

'Does that mean you're happy to work with us?' asked Tori, holding her breath. Izzy paused for a second.

'It does. I know I said I had some reservations but now we've discussed things in person, I couldn't be any happier. I think working with the Cosy Cup would be perfect for us.'

'That's fantastic news! Oh, we're going for a name change too – what do you think of the Cosy Cat Café?' said Tori.

'I like it!' said Izzy, smiling.

'It certainly does what it says on the tin,' said Grace.

'Did you hear that, Mr Wiggles?' whispered Tori. 'It looks like you're going to be moving to the Cosy Cat Café very soon. What do you think?' Mr Wiggles stared at Tori and meowed. It looked like the Cosy Cat had found its first official resident.

Chapter 15

Since her visit to New Beginnings, Tori had been working hard to finish her business plan ready to show Joyce. Between that and working flat out at the tearoom every day, she'd had little time for much else. It had been a quiet afternoon at the Cosy Cup and Joyce had left early to get her regular B12 injection. Tori was working at her laptop and the last few customers of the day were chatting away happily and enjoying their tea and cake. Tori looked up as the bell on the door chimed. It was Leo. Her eyes were drawn to his smile.

'Slacking off?' he asked, grinning broadly.

'As if! This is the first time I've had a minute to myself all day.' Tori hadn't seen Leo since they'd had dinner with Rose and Jake, and she was surprised by how happy she was to see him.

'Sorry it's taken me so long to drop by, but I remember you saying that the coffee was on you?'

'Someone has a good memory,' she laughed.

'I do whenever there's a freebie involved.'

'What can I get you?' she asked, standing up.

'A flat white would be great.'

'Grab a seat,' she said, indicating the chair opposite her. 'I'll be back in a sec.'

Tori soon arrived back at the table with a tray of coffee and scones.

'Wow, these look impressive,' said Leo, taking the largest scone on the plate and biting into it, 'and they taste even better!' he continued, sighing with pleasure.

'I can't take the credit. Mum does most of the baking, but you're right, her scones are the best.'

'You'll never get rid of me with food this good.'

'Well, we'd love to see you.'

'It's not *just* the scones that are good here,' said Leo as their eyes met, something flickering between them.

'Well, no, we do have great coffee too,' she said quietly.

A tension hung in the air around them and neither of them spoke.

Leo finally cleared his throat. 'How's it all going with the plans for the cats?' he asked, pointing at Tori's laptop.

'Good, thank you. I've submitted all the paperwork to the council, and Greg's starting on the building work once we get approval.'

'Wow! You *are* a fast worker.'

'There's no point hanging around. Once we've got the green light, I'm going up to New Beginnings with Grace to choose five cats for the café. We've already got one in mind called Mr Wiggles—'

'Mr Wiggles?' Leo spluttered his coffee and began coughing.

'Because he's just sooo wiggly!' Tori laughed.

'Now I've heard everything . . .'

The door to the café banged opened and Violet Davenport stood framed in the doorway.

'Oh God. Not Vicious Violet again,' groaned Tori.

'What's all this I hear about you turning this place into a *cat* café?' Violet demanded.

'Sorry?' said Tori, baffled. How did Violet even know about the plans for the café? Only a handful of people knew so far. The Cosy Cup's other customers stopped what they were doing and turned to stare.

'A cat café? Here in Blossom Heath? I've never heard anything like it,' said Violet.

Tori stood up and took a deep breath. She wanted to explain things calmly and answer any questions Violet might have about her plans for the tearoom.

'Well, we *are* planning to turn the Cosy Cup into a cat café, but can I ask how you found out?' Tori asked, trying her best to keep her tone polite.

'I will not divulge my source,' said Violet, tapping her nose. 'Let's just say it's someone who has the village's best interests at heart.'

'We've submitted our application to the council so—'

'If you think your plans are going to sail through without a fight, you've got another thing coming, Missy. It's not hygienic having cats and food together, and imagine the sort of people who'll turn up – tourists and day-trippers, clogging up the roads and filling up the parking spaces. I won't be the only one who's against this, you know!'

Tori closed her eyes and exhaled slowly. *Just breathe.* You can handle Violet Davenport. She's just looking to stir up trouble, that's all. The next thing she heard was Leo's voice next to her.

'I think you've made your views quite clear, Mrs Davenport. Perhaps it's time you leave and let Tori see to her *paying* customers.'

Violet took a deep breath, stood up straight, turned and left the tearoom, slamming the door behind her. Tori slumped down in her chair.

'Why is it whenever you visit, Violet is in here shouting about something?' she said.

'I've just got impeccable timing,' laughed Leo.

'Thanks for stepping in, I was about to lose my rag with her.'

'All part of the service,' said Leo, taking another sip of his coffee. 'I'm used to staring danger in the face.'

'I think I'd rather face a fire than Violet Davenport any day of the week,' said Tori, wrinkling her nose. As she took a bite of her scone, a sinking feeling hit the pit of her stomach. Would the rest of the village feel the same way as Violet about the cat café? Was she going to have a fight on her hands?

*

Tori woke the next morning to a message from Rose. *Sorry to be the bearer of bad news, hun, but have you seen these? They're plastered all over the village xx* Rose had sent an image of a flyer that read *Stop the cat café! Meeting tonight, 8pm Village Hall, All Welcome.* Tori stared at the phone, her brain whirring. *What? Who?* She felt sick. Violet Davenport must be behind this! Was she set on turning the whole village against her? Tori threw back the duvet, got showered, dressed and headed next door.

'Morning, love,' said Joyce, as a batch of toast popped up from the toaster. 'What's wrong? You look fit to burst!'

'Look!' said Tori, passing her phone across. 'Just look!'

Joyce made a face as she read the message. 'Oh dear.'

'It *must* be Violet Davenport, don't you think?' said Tori quickly.

'Hold your horses, love. Let's not go jumping to conclusions.'

'It has to be Violet. She came in yesterday and said I was going to have a fight on my hands. Just because she doesn't like the idea of a cat café, she's going to try and turn the rest of the village against the idea as well!' Tori felt the urge to cry and bit her lower lip hard in an attempt to stop herself. She couldn't, she wouldn't let Vicious Violet ruin things for her before she'd even got started.

'Just because there's a meeting doesn't mean everyone's going to be against you. I'm sure there's plenty of people in the village who will love the idea.'

'I hope so, Mum. I really hope so. I couldn't bear it if—'

'That's enough with the what-ifs,' said Joyce, gripping Tori's hand firmly. 'I'm sure if you explain things, everyone will see how great it's going to be. We'll both go along tonight and show everyone the plans. I've lived here a long time and this is just what village life is like. People care when they think things might change.'

'Do you think people will listen, though, Mum? What if we can't convince them?'

'I'm sure we can, love. It'll take more than Violet to stop us.'

'You're right,' said Tori, standing up quickly and grabbing her phone. 'I'll get in touch with Grace and Izzy and see if they can come along. We've already got their support and if anyone has any concerns about the welfare of the cats, it would be great to have their expert opinions in the room. We can cover all the new additions to the menu we're planning but reassure everyone that the essence of the Cosy Cup isn't going to be lost just because we're having cats there.'

'Great idea, love. I'm sure having Grace and Izzy there and on board will hold a lot of sway in the village. People trust their judgement and know they'll have the cats' best interest at heart.'

'I wonder if we should have a chat with the other business owners? It would be great if they could come along tonight and show their support. I'm hoping most of them will be in favour of our plans.'

'That's the spirit, love. Let's get started – we've got work to do.'

As Tori searched for Grace's number in the Contacts list on her phone, she was certain of one thing. She wasn't going to give up on her plans that easily.

Chapter 16

As Tori walked with Joyce into the packed village hall just before eight o'clock, she tried to quash the nerves that were building inside her. What if the rest of the village took Violet's side? Would the cat café be doomed before they'd even been given permission to open its doors? As they walked towards the row of chairs at the front of the hall, a hush descended around the room.

'Don't worry, love. Just be calm, share the plans as thoroughly as you can, and I'm sure it won't be as bad as you think,' Joyce whispered.

'I really hope so,' said Tori. She spotted Grace and Izzy waving at her from their chairs, and she hurried towards them, eager to escape the limelight.

'We thought we'd get here early, see what we're dealing with,' said Izzy.

'I didn't think there'd be so many people here,' replied Tori, her eyes darting around the room. 'I don't even recognize half of them.'

'It's the new-build estate; we've got so many more people in the village now than we did when you left. It might not necessarily be a bad thing, though,' said Joyce.

'Don't worry,' said Izzy, 'you know what this place is like – it doesn't mean people are against you.'

'What else is there to do in Blossom Heath on a Tuesday night?' Tori looked up to see Rose, followed by Jake, Kate and Leo, taking their seats in the row directly behind her. Rose leant forward and gave her an encouraging smile. 'It's going to be fine.'

'Exactly,' said Joyce. 'It's either this or watching a repeat of *Midsomer Murders*.' Tori let out a weak laugh.

Violet Davenport stood up in her front-row seat and turned to face the assembled crowd. She coughed and the audience looked up at her expectantly.

'Good evening, everyone. I'm sure many of you are aware of the shocking news for the plan to open a cat café here in our village. No doubt most of you were as horrified as I was to hear about it. A cat café will likely bring even more tourists to the village and create utter chaos on our roads.'

Tori heard a few shouts of 'Hear, hear!' from the crowd. She threw Grace a panicked look. Violet beamed and nodded approvingly.

'A cat café in Blossom Heath will attract all sorts of strange people to the village. The place will be full of millennials wanting to take *selfies*.' She put great emphasis on the word and shook her head. 'Our roads will be clogged up with traffic. Just think how parking around the village green will be affected. It's bad enough, without hordes of tourists cluttering up the place.' A murmur of agreement reverberated through the audience.

'This is bad,' Tori whispered to Grace through gritted teeth. 'Look! Everyone agrees with her.' She cast her eyes around the room, pointing out all the heads that were nodding thoughtfully at Violet's words.

'They've not heard your side yet,' said Kate. 'Don't panic.'

'I don't know if I can get up there in front of everyone,' Tori said quietly, sliding further down into her seat. 'Maybe this really *is* a crazy idea . . .'

Izzy had clearly heard enough and jumped up from her chair.

'Seeing as we've listened to Mrs Davenport's concerns, how about we hear Tori and Joyce's point of view?'

'And what's it got to do with you, Izzy Sullivan?' Violet snapped. 'Tori should be able to speak for herself, seeing she's the one behind all this,' she said, waggling an accusatory finger in Tori's direction. Tori's face turned scarlet.

'It has quite a lot to do with me, actually,' Izzy replied, straightening up to her full height, 'seeing as New Beginnings is going to be working with the Cosy Cup and all of the cats in the café will be available to adopt through us.'

Tori heard words of encouragement from the crowd. 'Aw.' 'How lovely.' 'Great idea.' Violet seemed to notice too and quickly changed tack.

'I can't see how that's relevant, Izzy,' she said, waving a hand dismissively.

'I'd say it's very relevant,' said Grace, rising to stand alongside Izzy. 'Hello, everyone, I'm Grace Ashworth, owner of Brook House Vets and I've been advising Tori on the necessary welfare issues with regards to the cats that are going to be living at the café. It's wonderful that some of the long-term residents at New Beginnings are going to be given the chance to live there while they're searching for a new home.'

Grace and Izzy went on to explain that the opportunity for some of the cats to get their chance in the spotlight and find a new home might save them from being stuck at the rescue centre for even longer.

'That's all well and good, Grace, but none of that addresses the issues around increased traffic and parking. Everyone here knows how busy it is on market day – it's hard enough trying to park as it is. Do we really want to make it worse?' said Violet, who was not easily discouraged.

Tori shifted in her seat; she gripped the sides of her chair until her knuckles turned white. Joyce whispered in her ear.

'Tori, I think it's time you got up there. You can't leave all of this to Grace and Izzy.'

'I don't think I can. My legs feel like jelly . . .'

'I believe in you,' said a soft voice in Tori's ear. She turned around to see Leo looking right at her. 'You've gone through all of this in the plans you submitted to the council, you know this stuff inside out.'

'I can't—'

'I promise you can. You've got this, Tori,' said Leo, smiling.

Tori looked back at him and nodded. She took a deep breath and got to her feet. Fear gripped her as she turned to face the crowded room.

'I understand why you might have concerns, Violet,' she said, her voice brittle with nerves. 'Having a cat café in the village *is* something different. But I think the cats will help to make the café even more fun for everyone. The fundamentals of the Cosy Cup won't change. We'll still have Mum's amazing bakes and the best cream tea in Sussex! And who knows? Maybe bringing new customers to the café will have a positive knock-on effect for other businesses in the village?'

'We could always do with more passing trade,' said Simon, from the Pink Ribbon.

'We'd certainly welcome some extra business too,' agreed Ted from Harrison's.

'Exactly!' said Tori, emboldened by the responses. 'The cat café might attract more customers for *all* of us, not just the Cosy Cup. And maybe some visitors will want to stop in at the Apple Tree for a drink or pop into the Pink Ribbon for a souvenir.'

'Well, they'll certainly find a warm welcome with us,' shouted Pete, the pub's landlord.

Violet Davenport looked fit to burst. Leo gave Tori an encouraging thumbs-up.

'I'm sure the kids at school will be queuing up to visit.

Those that don't have pets themselves can learn about them with you,' said Eileen Connolly.

'Definitely,' said Tori, bouncing on her toes. 'We'll be educating people about responsible pet ownership too.'

'In that case, maybe you could come into school and do a talk for us, Tori? Izzy? It's National Pet Day soon and I'm sure the children would love to hear about what you're trying to do to find the cats from the rescue centre new homes,' suggested Mrs Connolly.

'I'd love to,' replied Tori, nodding thoughtfully.

'Great idea,' shouted Izzy.

'I'm not saying we don't have things to work out. We're planning on operating a booking system, but we'll still be open to walk-in customers, so all our regulars can drop in as usual. I know more visitors who arrive by car will have a knock-on effect to parking in general around the village, but we're looking at solutions.'

'That's right,' said Joyce, standing up. 'There are already some parking spots next to the shop and the village council have said that customers can use the village car park. We're going to encourage customers to travel by bike too. Jake's putting up some bike racks in front of the café. That should give us more than enough parking for all the café's visitors.'

'We'll make sure there are clear instructions on our booking page too, that way everyone will know exactly where to park to minimize disruption,' said Tori.

'We'd be happy for your customers to use the pub car park

too,' said Ted helpfully. 'We've usually got room, and who knows, they might stay for a pint?'

'Thanks, Ted,' said Tori. 'We'll take you up on that. And if anyone has any concerns, please just come and speak to me. The door to the Cosy Cup is always open. I want this to be a positive thing and I hope you'll believe me when I say that I would never do anything to harm Blossom Heath. I love this place – it's my home.'

'Well, I hardly think—' said Violet.

'We *all* know that, dear,' said Jean Hargreaves, her steely tone silencing Violet. 'I think Tori should be applauded for her tenacity. We need more of our youngsters to stay in the village, instead of having to move away to find work. I say the more diverse businesses we have in Blossom Heath, the better!'

'Well said!' shouted Beth, applauding.

'Hear, hear!' agreed Maggie, joining in.

Before Tori knew it, the entire hall was nodding in approval and clapping. She couldn't quite believe it – had she really won the village over? The expression of shock on Violet's face was priceless, she was almost the shade of purple her name suggested.

'Sorry to throw you under the bus there, Jake, love,' whispered Joyce. 'I promise I was going to ask you about installing the bike racks, but I got a bit caught up in the heat of the moment.'

'It's no problem, Joyce. I'll be over first thing in the morning to take a look.'

'I don't think it's a big job,' said Joyce.

'I'm on it,' said Jake, grinning back at her.

Tori turned to see Leo, a smile plastered across his face.

'Well, I'd say that went pretty well, wouldn't you?' he said.

Tori had to admit it – he was right.

Chapter 17

Tori was still waiting for a response to her plans from the council, and running to check the post when she heard the daily thud of letters hitting the doormat had become somewhat of a ritual.

'Morning, Mum,' said Tori, rushing into the kitchen to grab a glass of juice.

'Before you ask, no, there hasn't been any post yet,' replied Joyce.

'Am I that predictable?'

'Afraid so, love. Just be patient, I'm sure it won't be too much longer.'

'I just don't know why it has to take so long,' she said, pulling her hair back into a ponytail.

'It's just how it is and worrying isn't going to make it turn up any faster.'

'I know. It's hard not to think about it, though. What if our application gets turned down? What are we going to do then, after all the work we've done?'

'Like I said, worrying isn't going to make a blind bit of difference – you just have to be more patient. I'm sure everything will be fine. You know what these council offices can be like.'

'I'll try.'

'Well, you're having lunch with Claire today, aren't you?' Tori nodded, gulping her juice. 'That'll keep you occupied. It'll be nice for you to make some more friends now you're home.'

'Yeah, I know. She seems nice. I probably won't get to see much of Melissa and Harriet now they've got kids.'

'Oh, Claire's lovely. I've been going to her since she took over the salon last year. Always got a smile on her face. She's not a gossip either. She must hear half the village's secrets but she's not one to repeat things.'

'Ooh, you're right – they say people tell their hairdresser secrets they don't tell anyone else. Just *think* of what she must know . . . I wonder if she's got any dirt on Violet?'

'Don't go asking!'

'Why not?'

'You don't want to put her in an awkward position.'

'But she might know something that could be useful in case Violet kicks off again—'

'Tori!'

'Honestly, Mum. She's a hairdresser, not a priest.'

'Tori!'

'Fine, I won't ask her,' said Tori, offering a bowl of kibble to Ernie, who sniffed it suspiciously and sauntered away. 'Oh,

Ern, stop being such a fussy pants, will you?' laughed Tori, shoving her used glass into the dishwasher.

When Tori arrived at the Apple Tree at one o'clock, Claire was already at the bar.

'Tori! What can I get you?' asked Claire, pointing at her wine.

'We're going straight for the wine, are we?'

'Why not? It's not often I get away from the salon for a proper lunch break – may as well make the most of it.'

'Sensible girl,' said Pete from behind the bar. 'What'll it be, Tori?'

'Oh, go on then. I'll have whatever she's having,' said Tori, reaching for her purse.

'Today is on *me*,' said Claire, placing a hand over Tori's to stop her opening her bag.

'At least let me get the drinks?'

'Absolutely not. I said lunch was on me and I meant it. It's my treat.'

'Thanks, Claire, that's really lovely of you.'

'There you go, Tori,' said Pete, placing a large glass of white wine in front of her. 'Beth has got table six ready for you – make yourselves comfortable and someone will be over to take your order.'

'Thanks, Pete,' replied Claire.

As Tori followed Claire towards the table, she noticed again just how flawless she looked in another pair of gravity-defying heels and a tailored green jumpsuit. Tori looked down at her own clothes: a pale blue ditsy floral dress with her favourite, and rather battered, stonewash denim jacket and her navy Converse trainers, which had undoubtedly seen better days. She pulled her jacket around her more tightly. She suddenly felt self-conscious. It wasn't just her outfit, though. Claire was successfully running her own business, striking out on her own and turning her dream into reality. Tori wondered if she'd ever be able to do the same. Did she really have what it took to succeed in business and make the cat café a success? Would people take her seriously? Somehow, she didn't think Claire was ever not taken seriously.

'So, how's it all going with the plans for the café?' asked Claire, the chunky gold bracelets rattling on her wrist as she swept a lock of immaculately highlighted hair behind one ear.

'Good . . . I think. I'm still waiting for the final go-ahead from the council, but hopefully I should hear any day now.'

'That's par for the course, I'm afraid. Nothing happens quickly when it comes to the council.' Claire paused and tapped a red manicured nail against the side of her glass. 'You know, I do have a contact there . . . I'd be happy to give them a ring, see if they could chase things for you?'

'Wow, Claire, that would be amazing,' said Tori, leaning forwards. 'Are you sure you don't mind, though – I don't want to put you out?'

'It's no bother.'

'Thanks, I really appreciate it. By the way, did you hear about the meeting Violet called at the village hall about the café? I still can't fathom out how she knew anything about it, to be honest. It just doesn't make sense.'

'Oh, what does it matter now? Anyway, what's good here?' said Claire, changing the subject and turning her attention to the menu on the table in front of her.

'Pretty much everything,' replied Tori, laughing, 'but the hunter's chicken has to be one of my favourites.'

'Oh no, far too many calories for me, all that cheese and bacon. Let's see . . . what about . . .' Claire ran her finger down the menu and stopped when she landed on the *salade niçoise*. 'Ah, there we are, *salade niçoise*. Don't you find that's the problem with pub food? Hardly any healthy options on the menu. Everything's smothered in cheese or served with chips . . .'

'I guess,' replied Tori, although she didn't have a problem with smothering everything in cheese and serving it with chips. Wasn't that half the fun of eating out? Although you probably didn't get a figure like Claire's by eating anything that wasn't salad.

Beth was quick to come and take their orders and the food arrived swiftly. Tori and Claire chatted about Tori's plans for the café and the story behind Claire's arrival in Blossom Heath. It turned out that she was from London and had worked her way up the ladder at a rather famous chain of salons. An affair with her married boss had gone badly wrong, so when the chance came up to strike out on her own, she'd taken it.

'He always promised he'd leave her, of course, but then I found out his wife was pregnant again. I knew I had to get out. He was never going to leave – it just took me a while to realize that.'

'God, Claire, that must have been awful. I'm so sorry.'

'You don't think I'm ... a terrible person? For having an affair with a married man? It's not something I'm proud of, but I'd fallen in love with him before I even knew he had a wife.'

'We all make mistakes. And anyway, he's the one who was married, not you,' said Tori.

Claire nodded. 'The thing is, I want to settle down, have a family and that was never going to happen if I stuck with Damian. I'm thirty next birthday – I can't afford to be wasting time.'

'Sounds like you did the right thing. How are you finding Blossom Heath, though? It must seem a bit dull after living in London?'

'I love it here,' said Claire, her face breaking into a smile. 'I'd had enough of London to be honest. Like I said, I'm ready to settle down and I don't want to raise my kids in the city.'

'And what about the Blossom Heath dating scene? If you're looking to settle down, there aren't many options—'

'Oh, I don't know about that. I might have already found someone,' she said, not quite meeting Tori's eye.

'Really? Who? Do I know him?'

'Let's just say I'm playing my cards close to my chest for now. We had a couple of dates a while back, but things didn't quite work out as I'd hoped.'

'I'm sorry to hear that.'

'Ah, it's just a matter of time before he realizes what he's missing,' said Claire, running a hand through her hair. 'What about you, though? Have you heard from that ex of yours?'

'Ryan? No, nothing.' Tori put her knife and fork down.

'Is that a good or bad thing?'

'Oh, I don't know. To be honest, I've been so busy with all the plans for the café, I haven't had too much time to think about him, which is probably a good thing . . .'

'And have you got your eye on anyone else?' Claire asked casually. Tori looked away.

'Uh . . .'

'Sorry, I don't mean to pry, only I've noticed you chatting to that fireman guy, a few times, he's hot, I wouldn't blame you if you . . .'

'Oh, Leo?' Tori's face flushed red.

'That's the one. Nothing going on there, then?' asked Claire, leaning forwards, her fork paused halfway to her mouth.

'Nope, absolutely nothing.' Why was she suddenly feeling so warm? 'We're just friends,' she said in a high-pitched voice that sounded unfamiliar to her.

'Oh well, that's probably for the best. I've heard he's a bit of a player.'

'Really? Leo?' said Tori, stiffening.

'Yep, definitely not boyfriend material. I don't know the guy personally,' said Claire, holding up her hands, 'it's just what I've heard. I'd hate for you to get involved with some-one else who might break your heart.'

Was Tori imagining it, or did it sound like Claire was warning her off?

'Well, like I said, we're just friends, so it's not an issue.'

'That's good to hear; I wouldn't want you getting hurt after what you've just been through with your ex.'

'No danger of that – I'm one hundred per cent single.'

'Cheers to that,' said Claire, raising her glass, 'and cheers to friendship.'

'To friendship,' said Tori, clinking her glass against Claire's.

When Tori arrived back home, she spotted a letter on the kitchen table with a pink Post-it note stuck to the top: *I think this is what you've been waiting for.* Was this it? Had the letter from the council finally arrived? Tori's hands turned clammy. What if it was bad news?

'God, this is worse than getting my exam results,' she said to Ernie, who had just jumped up on the kitchen table to greet her. Tori tickled him under the chin, and he began purring instantly. 'I know the café might be full of cats soon, but you'll always be my number one, you do know that don't you, Ern?' Ernie continued purring contentedly. 'Good, just checking.' She nodded. 'Well, here goes nothing,' she said, picking up the letter and tearing it open. She took a deep breath before unfolding the sheet of paper in front of her. *Dear Ms Baxter, Thank you for your planning application in relation to the Cosy Cup tearoom, Blossom Heath. We are pleased to inform you that your licence to turn the premises into a cat café has been granted.* Tori stared at the letter. She scanned it again to ensure there was no mistake ... *pleased to inform you ... licence ... granted* ... there could be no doubt. The Cosy Cat Café had officially been given the green light. She ran next door to the café, the letter firmly clutched in her hands.

'Mum! Mum!' she cried, as she entered the kitchen. 'It's a yes from the council!'

'Oh, love, that's brilliant news, come here,' said Joyce, throwing her arms around her daughter.

'So, this is really happening, then?' said Tori, taking a step back.

'It really is, my darling, it really is.'

Tori pulled her phone out of her jacket pocket and fired off a text to Leo. *The cats are officially a go! Fancy coming along to the rescue to help me choose some kitties?*

Chapter 18

Tori sat across from her mum at the kitchen table that evening with bated breath.

'What do you think?'

'Hang on, love. I'm on the last page, let me finish,' said Joyce, as she leafed through Tori's business plan.

Tori had worked so hard putting the business plan together. She wanted to make sure that she'd thought of everything, covered all the bases. She wanted to impress her mother, to let her know she'd be right to trust her with the tearoom's future. Tori knew the key to success was in seamlessly merging old with new; the last thing she wanted to do was erase all trace of the Cosy Cup's roots. It was important that the new café offered all the old favourites, as well as her new additions to the menu, and that customers could still expect the same friendly atmosphere and warm welcome. She ran through the plan again in her mind; she'd included cash-flow forecasts, a marketing plan, expenditure, strategies to diversify and grow the business. Was there anything she'd forgotten?

'I can certainly see the work you've put into this,' said Joyce, closing the spiral-bound presentation book. 'I'm impressed,' she continued, taking off her reading glasses.

'You are? Seriously?' said Tori, who was perched on the edge of her seat.

'I am. You've got some great suggestions here; I love all the ideas for expanding the menu, and bringing in some healthier options . . .'

'You do?'

'Absolutely. And the idea of a child-friendly morning and reaching out to clubs and groups in the village is great. I don't know why I've never thought of it before, to be honest – the WI are always moaning about how bad the coffee is at the village hall. Having gifts too – I'm sure that would go down well; mugs and bags people can buy.'

'Exactly, and I was thinking we could always give a percentage of the profit from the merchandise to New Beginnings, so people wouldn't just be buying stuff, they'd be helping the rescue at the same time.'

'I like it,' said Joyce, nodding. 'The idea of having bakes inspired by your travels is brilliant . . . I'll research Japanese recipes. I'll really enjoy that too.'

'I'd love that, Mum! I've been looking at ways we could support local makers. I'm going to speak to Jake and see if any of his farm contacts could supply us with their cheese, milk, yoghurt and bacon, for example, and we could do a "local" ploughman's, with everything coming from local farms, or a Blossom Heath Apple Pie, from the crop of Pippins at the

Apple Tree,' said Tori, almost in one breath. 'Really make the café part of the village. What?' she asked, aware that Joyce was staring at her.

'I was just wondering, that's all.'

'What?'

'When exactly did you grow up and become so smart?'

'So, does that mean you're okay with the plan?' asked Tori, holding her breath.

'One hundred per cent, love. Now we've got the go-ahead from the council, I'm going to call Greg and sort out the deposit to get the work started.'

'And you like the new name too?'

'The Cosy Cat Café? I do. You've kept the "cosy" but given it a new twist – it's very clever, love.'

'I wanted to give a little nod to the café's history and everything you've done here. It has a certain ring to it, don't you think?'

'The Cosy Cat Café,' Joyce repeated. 'You'll get no arguments from me. The Cosy Cat Café it is.'

A few days later, Tori was driving back up the bumpy road to New Beginnings Rescue Centre. When she pulled into the car park, she saw that Leo was already there. He was with a young girl of around seven or eight years of age. Her hair was styled in a long plait, and she was jumping up and down excitedly, clapping her hands together. Tori pulled into the parking bay alongside his car and the girl ran over and tapped on her window.

'Are you Tori?' the girl asked.

'Lara, come here. Give Tori a chance to get out the car first,' said Leo, taking the girl by the hand.

'I am indeed,' said Tori, smiling. 'And I'm guessing you're Lara?'

'Yes, and this is my Uncle Leo,' replied Lara, tugging at the sleeve of Leo's T-shirt. 'But I think you already know him,' she said, giggling.

'I hope you don't mind; Lara was desperate to come along. Her mum's finally said she can have a kitten and Izzy's got a litter we can take a look at apparently,' he said, taking Lara, who looked fit to burst, by the hand.

'Wow, a kitten! How exciting!' said Tori. 'Of course I don't mind.' She bent down to speak to Lara directly. 'I need some help choosing cats to come and live at my café. Do you think you could help me?' Lara nodded enthusiastically.

'Can we go and see the kittens first, though?' she asked.

'We need to help Tori first, *then* we can go and see the kittens,' said Leo.

'Pleeeeease Uncle Leo,' said Lara, 'pleeeeease can we see the kittens first?' She looked up at him with a pleading expression.

'We talked about this, Lara. I said if you came along, we'd see the kittens after we'd helped Tori,' said Leo.

'I bet Tori doesn't mind, do you?' asked Lara, looking up at Tori and flashing her best smile. 'Pleeeeeease can we see the kittens first?'

'Don't look into her eyes,' said Leo, scooping Lara up in his arms and swinging her around as she squealed with delight. 'She'll get you to agree to anything that way. How do you think I ended up with cats named Tallulah and Tinkerbell?' Leo put Lara back down and she turned to engulf him in the biggest of hugs.

'Let's go and see the kittens first,' Tori agreed, nodding her head.

'Yes!' screamed Lara, punching the air. She ran over and hugged Tori firmly. 'Tori, you're the best!'

'That must be some kind of record,' said Leo, shaking his head.

'What is?' asked Tori.

'How quickly she managed to twist you round her little finger,' he chuckled. 'She's pretty hard to say no to.'

'Seeing a bunch of adorable kittens is no hardship. I'd say it's a win-win,' Tori laughed.

'What's this I hear about kittens?' said Izzy, opening the door to reception.

'Izzy!' cried Lara, 'Tori said we can go and see the kittens first.'

'Oh, did she?' said Izzy, raising her left eyebrow. Tori held her hands up and laughed. 'Well, I guess we'd better go and find them, then. Do you know how to handle kittens, Lara?'

'Yes,' said Lara, nodding her head eagerly. 'Uncle Leo told me. Because they're so little, I need to be gentle with them. And I mustn't be too noisy, even though I'm excited, because that might scare them, and I need to wait and let them come to me.' Lara looked up at Leo expectantly, he gave her an approving smile and mouthed *well done*.

'That's right, Lara. Do you think you can remember to do all of that?' asked Izzy.

'Yes. I don't want to frighten them, I'll be really gentle,' replied Lara seriously.

'Let's head to the nursery, then,' said Izzy, leading the way into the rescue centre. As she opened one of the side gates and led them along a narrow path, Tori felt a tiny warm hand slide into hers and grip it tightly. She looked down to see that Lara was holding her hand. Leo noticed too and gave a wink of approval.

'We keep the kittens and their mums in this separate nursery block to lower the infection risk. They're too young to be vaccinated, so we keep them away from the rest of the adult cats,' explained Izzy, stopping in front of the door of a large, timber-framed cabin.

'Makes sense,' replied Leo.

'The kittens you're going to meet are eleven weeks old. There's six of them: four girls and two boys. They'll be ready to go to their forever homes in around a week, so that gives us plenty of time to organize your home check.'

'What colour are they?' asked Lara quickly, hopping up and down.

'They're all tabbies and a few of them have white patches too,' said Izzy.

'Oh, tabbies are my favourites,' said Lara, gripping Tori's hand and looking up at her.

'*All* cats are your favourites, Lara. Izzy could show us a bald, three-legged one with bad breath and that would be your favourite too,' Leo said. Lara giggled, shaking her head.

'When we go inside, you need to dip your shoes in the tray of disinfectant by the door. That's to keep the kittens safe.' Lara nodded eagerly, clearly determined to show Izzy that this was her number one priority. 'Here we go,' said Izzy, opening the cabin door.

Lara spotted the kittens immediately and squealed in delight, before remembering her promise to be quiet and clasping a hand over her mouth in excitement.

'Uncle Leo, Tori, look!' said Lara, pointing towards the pen. Inside were six gorgeous tabby kittens, with blue eyes, all wide awake and mewing. A couple were play-fighting and rolling around, two were frantically chasing a toy ball and the final two kittens were sat calmly next to their mum, who looked up towards the pen door at the sight of Izzy.

'This is their mum, Angel. She came in as a stray, heavily pregnant. She's a really friendly girl, loves human attention, as you can see.' Angel rubbed her cheek against the pen's mesh, purring loudly. 'As the babies were born in our care, they're all well socialized and used to being handled, so they'll be ideal for Lara.'

'They're beautiful,' said Tori, her eyes widening.

'Can we go in with them?' asked Lara.

'Of course. I'll leave you guys alone and let Lara make her choice. You can have the pick of the litter.'

'Perfect. Thanks, Izzy,' said Leo.

'Oh Lara, how are you ever going to choose?' laughed Tori as Lara plonked herself down in the middle of the pen, all six kittens making an instant beeline for her.

'I don't know!' said Lara, picking up a fishing rod toy and waving it around. All six kittens sprung into action, eagerly chasing the toy and attempting to pounce on it. 'I love them all.'

'You're a natural kitten wrangler, Lara,' said Leo. 'You've got the whole bunch of them entertained.'

'And what about you, Angel?' Tori said to the small tabby cat, who was weaving around her ankles, purring happily. 'What do you make of us?' Angel stood up on her back legs and placed her front paws gently on Tori's shins, letting out a tiny mew. 'Do you want me to pick you up?' Tori bent down and scooped Angel up in her arms. The cat's purr intensified. 'Isn't she gorgeous?'

'Uh-oh,' said Leo, scratching his head.

'What?' asked Tori, cradling Angel in her arms like a baby.

'I know we're meant to be looking at the kittens, but I'd say you might have found a resident for the café right there.' He nodded at Angel.

'Angel?'

'Angel,' said Leo, nodding his head. 'I'd say you're smitten.'

'She is lovely, isn't she? Do you think Izzy would agree?'

'You can only ask,' said Leo, stroking Angel under the chin.

'What do you think, Angel? Would you like to live at the café until you find your forever home?' Tori asked.

'How's it going, Lara?' said Leo, sitting on the floor next

to his niece. He was instantly set upon by two kittens, who climbed up his shirt and started squeaking at him. 'Ouch, their little claws are so sharp!' He pulled the kittens' claws gently away from his shirt and threw a ball for them; they raced off in hot pursuit.

'Don't be such a baby, Uncle Leo,' said Lara. Tori tried hard not to laugh. 'I can't decide between these two.' She pointed at the two kittens who had fallen asleep in her lap. One was fluffy, the biggest of the bunch, and the other was much smaller, with four white socks and a flash of white across its chest.

'You've got to narrow it down to one, I'm afraid,' said Leo, his brow furrowed. 'Your mum won't be impressed if I tell her you're getting *a pair* of kittens.'

'But look, they love each other,' said Lara, her eyes wide. 'We *can't* split them up, Uncle Leo, we just can't.'

'If you're going to get one kitten, why not two? You never know, they might keep each other out of mischief?' said Tori, casting a conspiratorial wink in Lara's direction. The little girl beamed at her.

'Or they could be double trouble?' said Leo, laughing. 'Aren't you supposed to back me up, not side with Lara?'

'Tori's right, Uncle Leo. *You've* got two cats. Two is the perfect number of cats to have.'

'I get the sense that I'm outnumbered here,' said Leo, scooping up both kittens in his arms. 'And what do you think, sleepy kittens? Do you want to live with Lara? She's very messy and never does as she's told. Do you think you can handle that?' He held the kittens up to his ears, as though they were talking to him. 'Well, it's a yes from them.' Lara leapt up and threw her arms around Leo's neck. 'So long as it's okay with your mum, then two kittens it is!'

'Thanks, Uncle Leo. I know Mum won't mind.'

The door to the cabin swung open and Izzy reappeared. 'How are we getting on?' she asked.

'Well, it looks as though we came in for one kitten and, somehow, we're now looking to adopt two,' said Leo, nodding towards the pair of sleeping kittens nestled in his arms.

'Ah, amazing!' replied Izzy. 'That often happens and if you're planning on having more than one cat, adopting a sibling pair is the best option. They'll grow up together and keep each other entertained.'

'See, Tori was right,' replied Lara, pointing over at Tori, who was still cradling Angel in her arms.

'Now, let's see who you've chosen,' said Izzy, stepping into the pen, with her handheld microchip scanner at the ready. 'Yep, thought so. This little guy is Dexter, he's the biggest and fluffiest of the bunch, but the gentlest too. I reckon that means ... yep, thought as much,' said Izzy, scanning the microchip of the second kitten in Leo's arms. 'This is his little sister, Domino.'

'Dexter and Domino,' repeated Lara.

'These two are always together, they're such a funny pair ... they adore each other,' Izzy explained.

'Aw, I'm so pleased they're getting to stay together,' said Tori.

'And I see you've made a friend too,' Izzy said to Tori, who was still cuddling Angel.

'Erm ... well, yes, I wanted to talk to you about that. I don't suppose there's any chance that—'

'Angel would be suitable for the café? Izzy finished.

'Well, yes,' said Tori. 'I know you said not all of the cats would be suited to café life,' she added quickly, 'but I was wondering, well, hoping ...'

'Definitely!' said Izzy. 'Angel was top of my list of suggestions for you.'

'Really?' said Tori, her shoulders relaxing.

'I thought if you spent some time with her ...'

'Izzy! Was this a set-up?' asked Leo, raising his eyebrows.

Izzy shrugged. 'I knew once you met Angel, you'd fall in love with her.'

'Well, I did. You were right, Izzy.'

'She loves other cats too, so she'll be happy in a group environment. I'm sure she won't be with you for long before someone snaps her up,' said Izzy, stroking Angel on the top of her head. 'If only all my adoption visits were this easy,' she laughed. 'Five minutes in and we've already got three cats sorted.'

'Lara, now we've found Dexter and Domino, can we go and look at some of the other cats for Tori?' asked Leo, putting the kittens back down in her lap.

'Oh, but I want to stay with my kittens,' said Lara, hanging her head.

'It's their dinner time now, anyway,' said Izzy, taking

Angel from Tori's arms and putting her back with her babies. The kittens headed straight for their mum and began feeding. 'And then they'll need another nap soon. It's best if we leave them alone for a while.'

'Oh, okay,' said Lara. 'Bye Dexter, bye Domino. I can't wait for you to come live with me.'

'Aw, she's so sweet,' Tori whispered to Leo as they left the nursery.

'You wouldn't say that if you saw her kicking off at bed-time,' he replied.

Izzy began running Tori through the list of cats she thought would be suited to life at the café, most of whom were long-stayers and unlikely to be rehomed before the cat café opened its doors. As well as Mr Wiggles, there was Daisy, a petite tortoiseshell who was around a year old; Norris, a middle-aged ginger who had a chunk missing from his left ear; and Valentine, a young grey male of around eight months who was playful, energetic and into everything, despite having a metal plate in his leg after a road accident. As soon as Tori met the cats individually, she just knew that Izzy had got it right. Although they were all very different, they all seemed to be relaxed, friendly and gentle.

'You know, I was thinking about what you said the last time I was here, Izzy, about needing to raise funds for the centre,' said Tori.

'If you've got any ideas, that would be great. Our vet bills have been crazy this month,' said Izzy.

'A coffee morning at the Cosy Cat is one idea and we can have a collection tin on the counter, but I'm sure there's more we can do. Maybe a few of us can put our heads together? See what we can come up with?' said Tori.

'I'd be up for that,' said Leo, 'to say thanks to Izzy for making Lara so happy. Why don't we rope Rose and Jake in too, have a brainstorm at the pub?'

'Excellent idea,' said Izzy. 'Seriously, anything you could do would be a great help.'

'I'll spread the word,' said Tori, 'and I'll keep you posted.'

'Perfect,' said Izzy.

Lara, who had been struggling to contain her excitement all morning, pleaded with Tori to let her work at the café.

'Erm, I think you might be a bit young for that, Lara,' Tori said. 'How old are you? Eight?'

'Yes, but I'm nearly nine,' Lara added quickly, standing up tall.

'Wow, nearly nine. I'm sorry, Lara, but you aren't allowed to have a job for a few years yet, I'm afraid,' Tori explained.

'How about I take you to visit the cat café once it's open?' said Leo, fishing his car keys out of his pocket.

'Really?' said Lara.

'Really,' replied Leo.

'And I'd get to see Angel and all the other cats?'

'Oh, absolutely,' said Tori. 'You never know, your uncle might even treat you to a hot chocolate with cream and marshmallows.'

Lara's eyes widened. 'Deal,' she said, holding out her hand for Tori to shake.

'Deal.'

'And we can talk about getting a job when I'm a bit older?' said Lara.

'Oh, definitely. As soon as you're old enough,' Tori replied.

Lara took a few moments to consider this. 'Okay, then. That sounds fair. Uncle Leo?'

'Yes, Lara.'

'Can we stop off at the pet shop on the way home to get stuff for Dexter and Domino?'

'Sure. I take it I'm paying?'

'I'm too young to have a credit card, silly,' Lara laughed.

'She's got you there,' said Tori, chuckling.

'Seeing as I've got to break the news to your mum that we're bringing two kittens home next week instead of one, I think arriving with a car full of pet supplies might help soften the blow.'

'Good thinking,' Tori agreed.

As Lara and Leo climbed into their car and Tori waved them off, she realized just how much she'd enjoyed spending time with Leo again today. Lara clearly doted on him, and he seemed to be absolutely devoted to her too, acting like the perfect uncle – patient, funny, kind. The perfect family man. Underneath all that, could he really be the cold-hearted player that Claire had suggested he was?

Chapter 19

Building work at the Cosy Cup started the following week and Greg was doing a fantastic job bringing Tori's vision for the cat café to life. His team had worked tirelessly to get the job completed in time for the reopening and Tori and Joyce were delighted with the results. The café now had its new entrance lobby, the walls had been painted in muted lemon and turquoise shades, and walkways, ledges and hidey-holes were almost finished. Jake had installed bike racks out the front and Ted had added a sign to the pub car park, stating that café customers were welcome to park there. If that wasn't enough to silence Violence Davenport's concerns about parking once and for all, Tori wasn't sure what would. Although it had felt strange since the tearoom had closed its doors temporarily to customers, Joyce had quickly refocused her energies on supervising the renovation work and Tori had noticed that Greg and her mum were enjoying spending time in each other's company.

'Morning,' called Tori, as she entered the café. 'How's everything going?'

'Morning, boss,' replied Greg, with a mock salute. He was halfway up a ladder drilling holes in the wall. 'All good here.'

'Tori? I thought I heard your voice, love. Fancy a cuppa?' said Joyce, appearing from the kitchen with two mugs in hand.

'I should have known you'd already be here,' said Tori.

'Oh, you know me, I like to keep busy,' replied Joyce, her face reddening. *Was her mum blushing?*

'Cheers, Joyce,' said Greg, climbing down the ladder and taking one of the mugs on offer. 'Milk and two sugars, just how I like it,' he continued, slurping his tea. 'Your mum's been doing a grand job of keeping us all fed and watered.'

'It's her forte,' said Tori, raising an eyebrow.

'Well, me and the lads really appreciate it,' said Greg. 'Some of the jobs we're on, we don't see as much as a chocolate digestive.'

'Isn't that awful, Tori?' said Joyce, shaking her head.

'Shocking,' replied Tori distractedly. 'How's things going? Are we still on track to finish by the twenty-first?'

'Absolutely,' replied Greg, taking another swig of tea.

'Honestly, Greg, the place looks amazing. I can't tell you how pleased I am,' said Tori.

'He's a real craftsman, isn't he? It's hard to find workmanship like this nowadays,' said Joyce appreciatively.

'If you can't put some time and love into your work, you're in the wrong job,' said Greg, looking at Joyce fondly and smiling.

'I'm just glad you're happy.' Joyce returned his smile.

'Beyond happy,' said Tori. 'I'm just popping to Harrison's for some of Ernie's treats. I think he could do with some new toys to keep him entertained too. Either of you want anything?'

'No, we're good, love, but you do spoil that cat, you know,' said Joyce, not taking her eyes off Greg. 'Greg, why don't you sit down and enjoy that cuppa? I've got a Victoria sponge just out the oven if you're hungry?'

'When am I not?' Greg laughed.

'I'll grab you a slice and join you,' said Joyce, straightening her apron.

'Perfect,' said Greg, 'I look forward to our morning chats.'

'Me too,' said Joyce.

As Tori walked across the green towards Harrison's, she replayed the exchange between Greg and her mum in her head. Was she imagining it or was there something between the two of them? They seemed to enjoy each other's company, that much was obvious, but it was more than that, though. It was the way they looked at each other. There was something in her mum's expression that seemed, well ... different. Happier? Excited? Youthful? Was she interested in Greg? Tori had to admit, she'd never considered the possibility of Joyce dating again. The idea felt strange, but why shouldn't Joyce find someone new? She was barely sixty after all; lots of people found love later in life and Joyce certainly deserved to be happy after the way she'd been treated by Tori's father. Greg seemed like a good guy from what Tori had seen. She decided that if there *was* something between her mum and Greg, she'd do everything she could to encourage it.

As Tori walked through the door to Harrison's, the bell chimed to signal her entrance. She headed straight for the pet food aisle, grabbed a couple of packs of Ernie's favourite treats, a new fishing rod toy, a pack of toy mice and made for the till.

'Jess, hi! I wasn't expecting to see you here.'

'Hiya!' said the tall smiling girl behind the till. 'I've pretty much finished uni, so I'm back for the foreseeable. Mum being Mum, she put me straight back to work in the shop.'

'Really? Wow, that's gone quick! What was it you were studying again?'

'Art. I've just finished my MA at Cardiff.'

'Of course, I forgot you were an artist. I remember that mural you painted up at the school.'

'The one of the green man?'

'That's the one. I wish I was that talented. I wanted to try and do something arty for the café, but I really don't have the skills.'

'I heard about your plans for the Cosy Cup – it sounds exciting!'

'Can you tell that to Violet Davenport? She thinks re-opening as a cat café is the worst thing to ever happen in the village.'

'Ah, Vicious Violet. Mum told me she was trying to stir things up. Typical Violet. I wouldn't waste your time on her. She was in here the other day complaining that our multipacks of jammie dodgers were more expensive than the supermarket.'

'Sounds like Violet.'

'So, when are you reopening?'

'The cats arrive next week and we're opening the week after, so you'll have to come along.'

'You can count on it.' Jess paused for a second. 'You know . . .' she continued, slowly, 'I'm at a bit of a loose end these next few weeks, if you're looking for a bit of artwork at the café, how about I help you out?'

'Seriously? That would be amazing!'

'I don't need paying; I'm looking for projects to add to my portfolio and the café would be perfect.'

'I'm definitely paying you, Jess. Just let me know what the going rate is, send me an invoice and I'll sort it.'

'If you're sure?'

'I am.'

'I'll be grateful for an excuse to escape from the shop for a while, if I'm honest. Mum won't be able to say no if I tell her it's for my portfolio,' said Jess, tapping her nose.

'I like the way you think,' said Tori.

'How about a mural for the back wall?'

'Sounds great.'

'I can sketch out some designs this evening and head over tomorrow to show you first, before I make a start, if that works for you?' said Jess.

'That would be wonderful. Thank you!'

'Do you need any help with logos and stuff?'

'Definitely. It's on my to-do list but I've not made a start yet,' said Tori.

'What do you need? Web design, social accounts, that kind of thing?'

'All of the above!' laughed Tori.

'Not a problem – I can help with all that. Let's chat properly tomorrow – would eleven o'clock work?'

'That's fine. You're a star, thanks, Jess.'

'Happy to help. Like I said, if it gets me away from manning the till, I'm all in,' Jess laughed.

'Well, I owe you.'

'Listen, Mum told me about what happened with you and Ryan. How are you doing?'

'Oh, that,' said Tori, waving her hand dismissively. 'I guess it just wasn't meant to be.'

'No, but it still sucks, though.'

'True. I'll get over it, I guess. I've got the café to keep me busy at least.'

'Definitely. Throwing yourself into something new is great distraction therapy. Personally, I'd rather go for throwing myself at some*one* new, but whatever works for you.'

'You don't change, do you, Jess?' said Tori, laughing. 'I'm guessing you've still not found a man who can tempt you into a relationship?'

'No way! Being single is way too much fun.'

'If it's working for you, why change?' Tori agreed.

'My thoughts exactly.'

As Tori paid for her shopping and put her purse back

into her bag, she felt her phone vibrate with a message. She looked at the screen. It was from Leo. Her pulse raced. *Tori, I'm trying the direct approach. How about we go on a proper date? Dinner? Tomorrow night? 8pm? The Purple Prawn in Rye?* Tori felt all the blood drain from her face. Spending time with Leo recently had been, well, it had been amazing, but a date? No, that was something altogether different.

'Tori? I said, what's up?' Tori looked up from her phone, she could see Jess's face was full of concern.

'Oh, er ... sorry. I was just checking my messages,' Tori said distractedly.

'Something wrong?'

'No, I'm fine, honestly.'

'Well, you look pale as anything,' said Jess.

'Do I? Just tired, I guess. I'll see you tomorrow?'

'Looking forward to it,' said Jess.

As Tori walked back to the café, she fired off a reply to Leo. *Thanks for asking, sorry but I can't xx* As she put her phone back into her bag, Tori realized that she didn't feel the sense of relief that she'd expected to at having put Leo off. She felt as though she'd made a mistake. A huge one.

Chapter 20

Jess arrived at the Cosy Cat Cafe promptly at eleven the next morning, a large sketch pad under one arm and a laptop bag slung over her shoulder.

'Morning!' said Tori, leaping up from her seat in the window.

'Hiya!' replied Jess, grinning. 'Slacking off already, are you?' She nodded towards Tori's cup of coffee.

'You don't want to see me in the mornings if I've not had my caffeine fix.' Jess snorted with laughter. 'I'm not joking,' continued Tori, 'it's really not a pretty sight.'

'I'll take your word for it.'

'Grab a seat,' Tori said, indicating the chair opposite, 'get comfy and I'll get you a drink. What do you fancy?'

'Soy latte, thanks.' Tori nodded. 'Did Ernie like his new toys?'

'He did! I had to give up whisking the mouse on a string round the lounge, though, my arm nearly fell off.'

'Sounds like he's got you trained well,' laughed Jess.

'Doesn't he just, that's why they say dogs have owners, cats have staff.'

'You know,' said Jess, looking around the café, her eyes wide, 'this place looks amazing, Tori. You've done a brilliant job!'

'Really? Do you like it?' Tori asked, holding her breath, as she realized Jess was the first person to see the renovation works.

'I love it. The colour scheme is gorgeous, and all these walkways and dens are genius,' said Jess, walking around the room to take in the new look. 'This back wall here would be perfect for a mural, don't you think?'

'That's what I was thinking too.'

'Great minds, eh?'

'Exactly.'

'Let me show you what I came up with last night,' said Jess excitedly, reaching for her sketch pad and pulling up a chair.

'There you go,' said Tori, placing a mug on the table in front of Jess. Tori pulled her chair around to look over Jess's shoulder as she flicked through her sketch pad.

'Now, I've done a couple of different designs,' said Jess, thumbing through the pages, 'but this is the one I wanted to show you first,' she said, studying Tori's face as she scanned the page.

'Jess, it's, well, it's . . .' Tori stared at the design, taking in the artwork in front of her. It showed a sleeping cat, its tail curled up around a cup of coffee, steam rising from the top. Underneath the drawing were the words The Cosy Cat Café, in a fancy script.

'Yes . . . ?'

'It's . . . *perfect*, I love it.'

'Really?'

'Really!'

'I hoped you would,' replied Jess, exhaling. 'I've got a few other sketches to show you, but I thought this might be the one.'

'It is.'

'I was thinking it would work as a logo too. I'd obviously have to scale it down, but you could have it on all the menus and signage?'

'Definitely! That would look great, Jess.'

'And you could get it printed onto some branded merchandise too? Mugs, jute bags . . . that kind of thing?'

'Great idea! I was hoping to get some gift items to sell too,' said Tori.

'I'll finalize the design this afternoon and email it across, that way you can start using it straight away and I can come back tomorrow and get going on the mural if I'm not going to be in the way?'

'Greg will be here finishing up the last few bits, if you don't mind working around him?'

'Excellent – I can buy the paints this afternoon.'

'Honestly, Jess, I can't thank you enough. Don't forget to keep the receipts, so I can reimburse you. You're so talented, I can't see you helping out in the shop for long,' said Tori, stirring more sugar into her coffee.

'God, I hope you're right. It's doing my head in being back with Mum and Dad. It's not even like I'm going back to uni in September now my master's is done. It's time for the real world . . . unfortunately.'

'Don't feel too down about it. I know it's weird once you graduate – I was out of sorts for weeks. One minute you're surrounded by all your mates, having the time of your life and the next . . . well, you're back in Blossom Heath with no clue what you're going to do next.'

'It sucks,' said Jess, staring into her soy latte.

'It does, but it's exciting too. Who knows what's next for you? Have you thought about what you might want to do work-wise?'

Jess paused and drank her coffee. 'The dream would be to land a job at a London gallery, but the chances of that happening are . . . well, let's just say it's unlikely. The competition is ridiculous; I'm not sure it's even worth trying,' she said, her face falling a little.

'If it's what you really want, it's got to be worth a try? You'll only kick yourself in the future if you don't give it a shot now,' said Tori, reaching across the table to pat Jess on the arm.

'I know,' said Jess, sighing, 'but the rejection letters are pretty brutal.'

'I bet. Look, try not to worry about it too much, keep applying for all the jobs you fancy and, in the meantime, well, you've got the mural to focus on.'

'Thanks, Tori. A pep talk from you is a whole lot less judgemental than one from Mum.'

'I get that. My mum can be a bit pushy at times too, but it's only cos they want what's best for us, right?'

Jess smiled, tucking her hair behind her ear. 'Thanks, Tori, it's good to chat to someone who gets it.'

'Honestly, I'm around if you ever need to talk.'

'I'll hold you to that. Right, I'd best get off and get everything sorted for tomorrow,' said Jess, standing and picking up her sketch pad.

'It's going to look amazing. I'm so grateful – thanks, Jess.'

'Don't mention it.'

'See you tomorrow,' said Tori, locking the door behind Jess as she left.

Tori spent the rest of the day prepping the café for the cats' impending arrival. Greg was ticking things off the snagging list and making sure everything was ready for the reopening. Tori had the sneaking suspicion that Greg's work was more than done, but he seemed keen to hang around, and Tori wondered if this was so he could spend more time with Joyce. Tori noticed that her mum joined Greg on all his breaks, chatting happily and supplying him with endless cups of tea and cake. There was definitely something in the air between the pair of them.

Tori tried distracting herself by getting some admin done for the café. True to her word, Jess had emailed over the finished artwork for the new logo and Tori had been busy setting up social media accounts for the café ready to announce the grand opening. She uploaded pictures of the new interior to Instagram and Facebook. That done, she found her mind kept going over and over the reply she had sent to Leo yesterday. *Sorry but I can't.* The phrase kept bouncing around in her head. Leo hadn't replied. She wished she knew what he was thinking.

'Mum, I'm just popping out,' she said, grabbing her faded denim jacket from the coat rack.

'Okay, love,' replied Joyce, barely looking up from her conversation with Greg.

It was a warm June afternoon; school was already out for the day and the village green was packed with children playing football and enjoying the summer sunshine. Tori found herself squinting, so pulled her aviator sunglasses out of her pocket and put them on. Hang on ... if the kids were out of school, that must mean – yes! Hopefully Rose might be at Jasmine Cottage. Perhaps she would be able to give her some perspective over the situation with Leo.

As Tori knocked on the front door of the cottage for the third time, her heart sank. There was clearly no one in.

'Rose? Jean? Anyone home?' she called out, hoping for a response. Nope. Nothing. She couldn't even hear Scout barking. The cottage was deserted.

'Tori?' said a voice, making her jump.

'Rose! Oh, you're here,' she said, flinging her arms around her friend. 'And Scout too.' She bent down to fuss the Border Collie.

'What's up?' Rose asked quickly.

'Oh, it's nothing really, I'm just being silly,' said Tori, 'but I could do with a bit of advice, if you've got ten minutes?'

'I'll put the kettle on,' said Rose, pushing her key into the lock and opening the front door.

'I saw the kids were out of school and hoped you'd be home.'

'We had a staff meeting and I had to pick this little lady up from the dog-sitter. Teachers don't all run from the building when the bell goes at three, you know.'

Tori could tell from Rose's tone that she'd touched a nerve. 'Of course, sorry, I know you have loads still to do once the kids are gone,' she said quickly.

Rose's expression softened. 'Oh, don't worry, it's just a touchy subject. Ollie always used to try and tell me what an easy gig teaching was. How I had such a cushy number compared to all his City cronies.'

'He really was an idiot. Thank God you two split up.'

'It's crazy, isn't it? I look back now, and I don't know how we ever ended up engaged! Anyway, what's up?'

Tori went on to fill Rose in on what had happened with Leo. Their chats at the café, the trip to the rescue with Lara, how she found him so easy to talk to but how she'd been filled with panic when he'd asked her on a date.

'You really are stressing yourself out,' said Rose gently.

'I know, I just feel so confused. And Claire from the salon told me she'd heard he's a player—'

'Who? Leo?' said Rose, shaking her head.

'Yeah, she said he's a serial dater and pretty much warned me not to get involved.'

'Really?' said Rose, making a confused face. 'I mean, I

don't know Leo *that* well, but that doesn't seem like him at all from what Jake says and they're pretty tight.'

'That's what I thought too; he doesn't strike me as that type, but why would Claire say otherwise? She must know something we don't, and, let's be honest, after what happened with Ryan, I'm hardly the best judge of character, am I?'

'Is that what's putting you off? What Claire said?' Rose asked.

'No, yes . . . maybe, oh, I don't know,' said Tori, her head resting on her hands. Scout hopped up onto her back legs and placed her front paws in Tori's lap. 'Aw, don't worry, Scout, I'm okay.' She stroked the little dog gently on the head. 'She really is a sweetheart, isn't she?'

'She always knows when I'm upset,' said Rose fondly. 'Listen, you should take what Claire said with a pinch of salt. I don't even think she knows him very well, and you should only judge Leo by what *you've* seen of him.'

'That's the thing, though, I feel like I can't trust my gut after Ryan. I got him completely wrong. How can I trust my own judgement?' Tori took a deep breath in.

'Here,' said Rose, passing her a box of tissues. 'Don't beat yourself up – everyone feels like that after a break-up. It's only natural that you're wary about getting involved with someone again so soon.'

'I guess,' said Tori, blowing her nose hard.

'You know, it was a big risk for me to take a chance on Jake. I had my whole life mapped out in London. A job, a home, a fiancé. Moving here and dating Jake definitely wasn't the *safe* option . . .'

'But it was the right one.'

'Exactly. And look how everything's worked out – I've got a job I love, a wonderful home here with Aunt Jean and a future with the man I love.' Scout let out a short, sharp bark. 'Oh, and the best dog in the world,' she laughed.

'She really is the best, aren't you, girl?' said Tori, tickling Scout under the chin. She looked up at Rose. 'So, what do you think I should do?'

'It's got to be your decision, Tori, but I think you should give Leo a chance. Even if things don't work out, at least you can say you tried.'

Tori was immediately reminded of the advice she had given to Jess earlier: *You'll only kick yourself in the future if you don't give it a shot now.* Perhaps it was time she stopped overthinking things and started listening to her own advice?

Chapter 21

Tori decided to take a drive that evening to clear her head. She needed to pick up a few bits for the café that weren't stocked at Harrison's, so she headed for the retail park on the outskirts of the village to go shopping. As she locked the car, she scanned the shopping list: *litter trays, cat litter, dry kibble and wet food, scratching posts.* She'd put in a bulk order for supplies online, but who knew when that would arrive. Grabbing a trolley, she wandered the aisles, filling it as she went. As she rounded the corner, *bang* – she shuddered as she slammed into another trolley.

'Hey, careful,' said the man stood in front of her.

Tori looked up, straight into the eyes of Leo. 'Oh God, I'm so sorry. That was totally my fault.'

'Tori, don't worry about it, I wasn't looking—'

'No, it was me, honestly I—'

Leo started to laugh.

'How about we share the responsibility? I wasn't looking where I was going . . .' said Tori.

'And I wasn't paying attention?'

'Exactly.' Tori wasn't sure what to say next, but she was relieved to see that Leo was smiling. 'Listen, about that text I sent you yesterday . . .' she started.

'Forget it,' he said, waving a hand dismissively. 'I asked, you answered. There's no need to explain.'

'That's just it, though, I *want* to explain,' Tori continued. 'I panicked when I got your message, to be honest. It took me by surprise and I . . . kind of, well . . . reacted. It's not that I don't want to go on a date, it's just that I'm . . .'

'Not ready?' said Leo. Tori nodded. 'Don't worry, I understand,' he said. 'I guess my timing wasn't great?'

'I do like you, Leo, really, I do. That's not the problem,' she said, blushing. 'I'm just not sure I'm ready to date anyone yet.'

'That's fair enough, the last thing I want to do is pressure you,' he said, rubbing the stubble on his chin. 'How about this? Let's just hang out, see where things go? I promise not to ask you out again, and when you're feeling ready, you can ask me – if you want to, that is?'

'What? On a date?'

'Exactly. If you want to . . . in the future I mean,' he said quickly, 'you ask me.'

Tori thought about it for a moment. Her face broke into a smile. 'I like it,' she said, nodding in agreement. 'When I'm feeling ready to date again, you'll be the first to know.'

'Deal,' said Leo, holding his hand out for her to shake.

'Deal,' agreed Tori, taking his hand in hers.

'So, what are you shopping for?' asked Leo, surveying the contents of her trolley.

'Oh, you know, just the essentials to keep five cats in the lap of luxury, plus a few bits for Ernie – I don't want him feeling left out.'

'Anything I can help with?'

'Well, if you've got an opinion on whether to go for clumping or non-clumping cat litter, I'd love to hear it. Ernie's always changing his mind.'

'Oh, always clumping. Follow me, I'll show you which one Tinkerbell has given the seal of approval to.'

Leo wandered the aisles with Tori, giving his opinion on the must-have treats and the latest in interactive toys. Tori was impressed with the way he talked about his own two cats, and he'd even thrown a few presents into his shopper for Lara's new kittens, Dexter and Domino.

'Was your sister okay with Lara bringing home two kittens?' Tori asked.

'Not exactly, but we won her over pretty quickly.'

'I'm glad to hear it. Lara's adorable, by the way.'

'Isn't she? Her dad's not on the scene; actually that was one of the reasons I was so keen to take the job in Rye – I wanted to be around for her.'

Tori swallowed hard.

'Wow, Leo, that's lovely. I bet your sister's glad to have you around too.'

'Listen, seeing as I've bumped into you, I wanted to ask you something. Don't panic, I'm not going to ask you on another date,' Leo laughed. 'It's just I was wondering—'

'Uh-oh, that sounds ominous,' said Tori, pulling a face.

'Hey!'

'Sorry, I couldn't resist.'

'I was only wondering if you'd made any progress with hosting a coffee morning to raise funds for the rescue. I know we talked about getting together with Rose and Jake to think up some more ideas . . .'

'Oh, yes! I mentioned it to Beth yesterday. She's on board and I was going to suggest a few of us meet at the pub on Thursday to go through ideas.'

'Well, count me in. It would be good to help support Izzy; she does such a great job. Whenever we get an animal-related call-out, she's always ready to lend a hand.'

'I'm sure we can come up with some great ideas between us.'

'Definitely.'

'Well, we'd best get this lot through the checkout,' she said, noticing the sales assistant glaring at them both. 'Looks like we're the only customers left.'

As Tori began unloading her shopping onto the checkout, she was glad that she'd bumped into Leo again this evening and cleared the air. She didn't want there to be any awkwardness between them. If they were going to be friends, it was important they were both on the same page and getting involved again wasn't something she was ready to think about right now.

'Wow, Jess, this looks fantastic,' said Rose, as she studied the mural that was well under way on the back wall of the Cosy

Cat Café. 'In fact, the whole place is a triumph! Tori, you should be so proud of yourself.'

'It was a team effort,' replied Tori, as Joyce appeared with a tray of drinks and cakes.

'I don't know about that, love. Greg and the boys may have put in the labour, but all the design ideas were yours,' said Joyce.

'Your mum's right,' agreed Jess. 'The place looks stunning. Honestly, people are going to be lining up around the block to come here.'

'I hope you're right,' said Tori, biting her nails.

'It's only natural to feel a bit nervous about opening day, love, but you've done everything you can for now. Why don't you take a break and get these down you?' Joyce nodded towards the tray of treats.

'Ooh lovely, thanks, Joyce,' said Rose, pulling up a chair and grabbing a huge slice of carrot cake.

'I've got some bits to finish up in the kitchen, so I'll leave you girls to it,' said Joyce.

'Thanks, Joyce,' said Jess, throwing down her paintbrush and settling herself in the seat opposite Rose.

'How's things, Tori?' asked Rose. 'Have you spoken to Leo?'

'Leo? The hunky fireman?' said Jess quickly. 'Have you got your eye on him?' Tori looked away. 'You *have*, haven't you?' Jess thumped her hand on the table. 'Why am I always the last to hear the gossip?'

'Okay, fine,' replied Tori. 'There's nothing going on but—'

'But you're madly in love with him and want to have his babies?' said Jess quickly.

Rose laughed out loud. 'Sorry, Tori,' said Rose.

'Well, the thing is . . .' said Tori, taking a deep breath.

Before telling Jess about her encounters with Leo since she'd arrived back in Blossom Heath, Tori explained how she'd bumped into him at the pet superstore, which Rose was yet to hear about. Jess and Rose sat glued to the spot while Tori spilled the beans.

'So, that's it.' As she finished talking, Tori took a huge bite of the cake in front of her.

'I don't get it,' said Jess, looking confused. 'He's obviously into you, *you're* into him . . . so what's the problem?'

'Oh, to be twenty-two again,' said Rose, rolling her eyes.

'What?' said Jess.

'It's not quite as simple as that, Jess. I'm just not sure I want to date again right now. Let's just say I've got a few trust issues after what happened with Ryan . . .'

'Who said anything about dating? I'm talking about—'

'We *know* what you're talking about,' said Rose, 'but I don't think Tori's looking for that either – are you?'

'I mean, I've heard worse ideas,' said Tori, leaning back in her chair. Jess laughed. 'But Rose is right, I don't want to complicate things with a one-night stand.'

'Fair enough,' said Jess.

'I still think you should give Leo a chance,' said Rose. 'He clearly wants to get to know you and he's prepared to go slow. I know you've got a lot going on right now, what with the café opening and all, but don't dismiss the idea.'

'What's the worst that can happen?' asked Jess. 'Things

don't work out and you both move on. You're overthinking things, Tori.'

Tori pulled at a loose thread on one of the cushions.

'Maybe you're right . . . I'm just not in the right headspace for another knockback after Ryan.'

'Sod Ryan!' said Jess. 'He's not worth spending another minute thinking about. Seriously, Tori,' she said, her tone softening, 'don't let that idiot screw up your future. Just because he turned out to be a waste of space . . .'

'Doesn't mean that *all* men are. I know, I know . . . I've already heard that speech from Rose,' Tori said, jerking her thumb towards her friend.

'What can I say? Rose clearly knows what she's talking about,' said Jess, laughing.

'I'm with Jess. What's the worst that can happen?' agreed Rose.

'Let's just see how things go, shall we? I'm making no promises. I've got enough on my plate right now without worrying about men,' said Tori.

'When are the cats arriving?' asked Rose, taking pity on her friend and changing the subject.

'Funny you should ask . . .' said Tori.

'Uh-oh, this sounds like I'm about to be roped into something,' said Rose, screwing up her face.

'Fancy coming to New Beginnings with me on Saturday to collect them? Grace was going to but she's on call and I could do with an extra pair of hands,' said Tori.

'Name the time and I'll be there,' said Rose.

'Thanks, you're a star,' said Tori.

'We're going to give the cats a week to settle in and get their bearings, then do a little family and friends soft launch next Sunday before the grand reopening on Monday,' said Tori.

'Exciting!' said Jess.

'Terrifying!' said Tori.

'I take it we're on the soft launch guest list?' asked Jess.

'Obviously! I need all the moral support I can get,' said Tori.

'We'll be there to cheer you on,' said Rose.

'And I take it you'll be inviting a certain firefighter?' said Jess.

'Yes, I think so,' answered Tori, the warmth in her cheeks rising.

'I'm glad to hear it,' said Rose.

'I really hope he can make it,' replied Tori.

'Well, if he can't, he'll have me to answer to,' said Rose in her sternest teacher voice.

As she finished her hot chocolate, Tori realized that if Leo couldn't make the soft launch, the whole thing would seem a little bit less shiny.

When Tori arrived at the Apple Tree on Thursday evening, she was relieved to see that Rose, Jake, Jean and Leo had already grabbed a table and Grace, Maggie and Jess were at the bar. Even Pete and Beth had taken a break from bartending duties to join the group.

'Tori, Joyce! Over here!' called Rose, waving at them.

'I'll grab us a couple of Diet Cokes, love,' said Joyce, heading for the bar.

'Hi, everyone!' said Tori, automatically pulling up a chair next to Leo. 'Wow, what a great turnout.'

'Well, it's a great cause. Everyone knows what a brilliant job Izzy does,' said Leo.

'And how overworked she is too, poor dear,' added Jean.

'Thanks for coming, everyone. As you all know, we're going to team up with New Beginnings and we'd love to try and support Izzy and the rescue as much as possible, so we're going to start with a coffee morning once we reopen, but I'd love to do more if possible.'

'We're going to be selling branded merchandise at the café when we reopen – mugs, jute bags, that sort of thing, with a percentage of the profits going back to New Beginnings as well,' explained Joyce.

'Oh, I love that idea,' said Maggie. 'We'd be happy to stock them at the shop too.'

'That would be great, thanks, Mags,' said Tori, pulling out her notepad and scribbling away.

'Simon and Anya couldn't make it tonight, but I can ask them if they'd do the same in the Pink Ribbon,' said Jess.

'We've got a collection box at the café, but I wondered if some of the other shop owners might take one too?' said Tori.

'Definitely. I'll let Izzy know we can take a couple and put them on the bar,' said Beth.

'I've got another idea . . . I've been looking up recipes for dog and cat treats – I thought I'd do a few trial batches. I was thinking we could package them up and sell them on behalf of the rescue?' said Joyce.

'Brilliant!' said Rose. 'If you need any taste testers, I'm sure Scout, Tagg and Finn would be willing volunteers.'

'You're on,' replied Joyce. 'I'll pop over to the farm when I've got my first batch.'

'Don't forget Ernie. He'll have to give them the seal of approval first,' said Tori. 'If they pass his taste test, the cats at the café will love them.'

'If you're thinking of hosting a bigger event, Tori, we have lots of willing volunteers in the Blossom Heath Belles,' said Jean. 'Well, apart from Violet Davenport that is.'

'The Belles?' asked Tori.

'The WI ladies, dear,' Jean explained.

'Brilliant, thanks, that's good to know,' said Tori. 'I'm guessing Violet's still not on board with the cat café then?'

'Oh, you just leave Violet Davenport to me – she won't know what's hit her the next time I hear her bad-mouthing the café,' said Jean.

'Now that's a showdown you could sell tickets to, Auntie,' laughed Rose.

'My money's on Jean,' said Jake.

'Well, of course it is, Jake dear,' said Jean matter-of-factly. 'Now, Tori, Joyce mentioned that we might be able to hold our monthly WI meetings at the café once you reopen. The refreshments at the village hall are just dreadful,' said Jean.

'Of course! We'd love to have you,' said Tori, beaming.

'I'll talk to you afterwards and get your meeting dates in the café's diary.'

'Wonderful, thank you,' replied Jean.

'Actually, I've had a bit of an idea for an event . . .' said Leo tentatively. 'I might even be able to rope in some of the lads from the station to help.'

'Amazing!' said Tori. 'What did you have in mind?'

'Well, I've not run it past Jake yet,' said Leo quickly, glancing at his mate, 'but I was going to suggest holding a barn dance up at the farm? You've got a couple of barns up there that would be perfect.'

'I love it! That's such a fun idea. We could organize a band! Beth, Pete, maybe you could even run the bar?' said Tori.

'And we could sort out a hog roast or something?' suggested Jess.

'Ooh, I love a hog roast,' agreed Maggie.

'Like I said, it's just an idea. What do you reckon, Jake? Sorry to spring it on you, mate,' said Leo, clapping his friend on the back.

'Sounds like a plan to me. I'm more than happy for Izzy to use the barn,' said Jake. 'Actually, I think a farmer contact of mine is in a folk band; I'm sure if I twisted his arm, he'd probably play for mates' rates seeing it's for charity.'

'And the WI ladies could help with sorting out the food and decorating the barn,' added Jean.

'We could sell tickets at the café, couldn't we, Tori? I'm sure the other shops would do the same,' said Joyce.

'Count the surgery in too,' said Grace.

'I'm happy to design posters to put up; there's that community noticeboard in the village hall and I'm sure some of the locals would display them in their windows,' said Jess.

'Wow! This is all really exciting, but obviously I'll need to talk to Izzy about all this, before we get carried away,' said Tori, throwing her pen down.

'Is it just me or did that feel too easy?' laughed Rose.

'I'll call Izzy later and run it past her,' said Tori. 'She wanted to be here, but she's had an emergency rescue at the centre.'

'I propose a toast,' said Joyce, raising her glass, 'to Leo – he was the one who came up with the idea after all.'

'To Leo,' chorused the group, raising their glasses.

'And to our first New Beginnings Barn Dance!' added Tori. As she looked at the group of friends and family gathered around her, she felt truly happy to be back in Blossom Heath again. Ryan or no Ryan.

Chapter 22

When Saturday morning arrived, Tori drove up the now-familiar track to New Beginnings, with Rose beside her.

'Wow, these potholes need serious attention,' said Rose, grabbing the seat to steady herself. 'I'm glad we're risking your suspension, not mine.'

'Well, technically it's Mum's car,' Tori laughed. 'I just hope that those cupcakes she baked are still in one piece!'

'Have you spoken to Izzy about the barn dance idea yet?'

'No, I'll talk to her about it today.'

'It does sound like fun. What a great idea of Leo's!' Rose paused. 'Honestly, when are you going to agree to go on a date with him?'

'Not quite yet,' said Tori, shaking her head. She had to admit it, whatever her unresolved feelings towards Ryan, she did enjoy spending time with Leo.

Tori parked up next to a white New Beginnings van and spotted Izzy waving at them from behind the reception window.

'I can't believe the day's finally arrived,' Tori whispered to Rose, her voice catching a little. 'There's going to be actual cats living at the Cosy Cat Café today. Am I completely crazy?'

'Oh, definitely, but not about this, though,' said Rose. Tori threw her a confused look. 'This, Tori Baxter, is one of the best ideas you've ever had.'

Tori swallowed hard. 'Seriously?'

'Seriously. Look what you've done in just a few weeks! You've gone from arriving home without a plan, to completely refurbishing the Cosy Cup and relaunching with cats! I'm proud of you and you should be proud of yourself too.'

'Oh, stop it, anyone could have done it.'

'No. Anyone could *not* have done it. It takes a lot of resilience to pick yourself up when things have gone pear-shaped. And you, Tori Baxter, have done just that.'

'Don't go all mushy on me, Rose, you'll have me blubbing.'

'I'm just saying, look at everything you've managed to do in the last few weeks. It's not nothing, you know.'

'Point taken. I suppose it is pretty great, isn't it?'

'There's no suppose about it. Come on, let's get these cats home.'

They found Izzy waiting to greet them in the office.

'It's really happening! The cats are all ready to go!' said Izzy, pointing towards a row of cat baskets with five pairs of eyes peering out.

'Here, these are for you,' said Tori, putting a tray of cupcakes down on the counter. 'Mum insisted. I hope your volunteers are hungry.'

'These will go down a storm,' said Izzy, smiling. 'Thank Joyce for me, will you?' Tori nodded.

'Have you been to the Cosy Cat yet, Izzy? It looks amazing,' said Rose.

'I popped in yesterday to give everything a final once-over. It's fantastic – you've done a great job, Tori. I think the cats are going to love living with you.'

'Thanks, Izzy, and thank you for trusting me to look after them. I'll do my best to give them a great home until they're adopted.'

'Tori's got a suggestion for a fundraiser too, haven't you?' prompted Rose.

'Well, technically it was Leo's idea, but how do you feel about a gang of us putting on a barn dance to raise money for the centre up at Harper Farm?' said Tori.

'Wow! That sounds amazing – it'll be a lot of work to pull off, though; I'm always so busy, I'm not sure I'll be much—'

'Don't worry, we've got loads of volunteers already who really want to help with all the planning, so if you're happy with the idea in principle, we can get it going, and then I can just keep you in the loop before we firm up the details,' said Tori.

'Well, if you're sure, I don't see how I can say no,' laughed Izzy. 'Seriously, guys, I can't thank you enough. An event like this could really help to boost our funds.'

'Don't mention it,' said Tori. 'We all want to help.'

'Let's get this show on the road then, shall we?' said Izzy, reaching down to grab the basket containing Norris.

'Perfect,' said Tori, 'we'd love to see you.'

'I wonder what happened to his ear?' asked Rose, pointing to Norris. 'That's a huge chunk missing.'

'He was like that when he arrived. Unneutered males often fight over territory and, if he's lived most of his life on the streets, which I suspect he has, he'll have had to defend himself. He still loves other cats, though, despite everything he's been through,' explained Izzy.

'Well, he'll be spoilt rotten while he's with us,' said Tori, the thought of everything Norris might have been through tugging at her heart strings.

'Just give them time to explore and get used to their surroundings. Daisy and Norris have been sharing a pen the last couple of weeks and they get along great. Mr Wiggles and Angel love everyone and everything, and Valentine will definitely enjoy having a bit more space to burn off his excess energy,' said Izzy. 'Here are Mr Wiggles' thyroid meds – it's just one every morning before breakfast.'

'Brilliant, thanks,' said Tori, closing the boot of the car. 'Mum's going to give them to him as a reminder to take her own.'

'Good idea! And remember, any problems, I'm just a phone call away,' Izzy replied.

'It's going to be fine, isn't it, Tori?' said Rose.

'Uh-huh,' said Tori, nodding. As she pulled out of the car park, though, she hoped she hadn't bitten off more than she could chew.

*

Joyce was waiting to greet them when they arrived back at the Cosy Cat. She took Daisy's basket and peered through the bars.

'Oh, girls, isn't she a little love?' said Joyce, holding her index finger up against the mesh of the carrier for Daisy to sniff.

'That's Daisy,' said Tori, 'she's only a baby, just a year old. This is Norris and Valentine,' she added, holding up the two baskets she was carrying.

'And this is Angel and Mr Wiggles,' said Rose, nodding towards the baskets she had in her hands. 'I have got that right, haven't I?' Tori nodded.

'Ah, I've heard all about Mr Wiggles,' said Joyce, laughing. 'Come on, let's get them inside.'

Once the double doors were safely closed behind them, Tori suggested letting Daisy and Norris out first.

'Let's see how they get on, and then we can gradually introduce the others,' Tori suggested.

'I'll go first with Daisy then,' said Joyce. Daisy inched her head out of the basket gingerly, taking a tentative step forward. 'It's okay, Daisy, come out and explore,' she said, stretching her hand out towards the little tortoiseshell cat, who sniffed it gently.

'Wow, that didn't take long,' said Rose, opening the door to Norris's basket. Norris stepped right up to Rose, turned his head as Daisy meowed and ran towards her. The two cats began purring madly.

'Well, would you look at that,' said Tori. 'Izzy wasn't

wrong when she said those two were friends. Let's just give them a minute, see what they do.'

Norris started to explore the café, Daisy at his side. It didn't take him long to find the food bowls and tuck straight into the kibble that Joyce had put out. Daisy was eager to explore the toys on offer and was quick to pounce on a mouse and throw it up into the air.

'Shall we let you out next?' said Tori gently as she opened Angel's basket. The little tabby hopped straight into Tori's lap and settled herself there while Tori stroked her behind the ears. 'I appreciate the cuddles, but don't you want to explore? Do you think she's missing her kittens?' she asked.

'It must all seem a bit strange for her right now. I really hope she'll be happy here,' said Joyce.

'Valentine, are you ready to go exploring?' said Rose, opening the next basket. 'You've still got a metal plate in your leg remember, so be careful.' The grey boy was eager to start exploring. He seemed a little wary of approaching the other cats, but Daisy made the first move and gave him a gentle nudge, which seemed to help him relax. Although he did give Norris a wide berth when the ginger cat walked towards him, and scampered off in the other direction.

'I don't blame you, Valentine,' said Tori. 'If I were a cat and saw Norris for the first time, I'd run a mile too, he looks a right bruiser.'

'He does look like he's been around the block a few times, doesn't he?' Joyce agreed.

'Don't be fooled; Izzy says he's as soft as butter,' explained Tori.

'Last but not least, I guess it must be Mr Wiggles' turn,' said Joyce, opening his carrier. The large black cat was curled up, fast asleep inside.

'He looks pretty happy where he is,' laughed Tori. 'Leave him and I'm sure he'll make his own way out once he's ready.'

'Who fancies a cuppa?' said Joyce.

'Mine's a mocha if there's one going,' requested Rose.

'And if there's any cake . . .' said Tori.

'There's *always* cake,' laughed Joyce.

Tori and Rose settled themselves at one of the tables at the back of the café, watching the cats get used to their new surroundings. Valentine was into everything, sussing out all the hidey-holes and trying the scratching posts, with Daisy in hot pursuit. Angel had fallen asleep in the chair next to Tori and Norris was sunning himself on a shelf by the window and watching the world go by.

'They all seem to be making themselves at home, don't they?' said Joyce as she placed three large mugs and three enormous slices of ginger cake on the table.

'So far, so good,' agreed Rose.

'What about Mr Wiggles?' asked Tori, rubbing the back of her neck. 'He still hasn't made an appearance.'

'He seems fine, though,' said Joyce. 'Maybe he's just really relaxed?'

'Izzy did say that literally nothing phases him,' Rose reminded her.

'True. Let's give him a bit longer and see what he does,' agreed Tori, taking a mouthful of her drink.

'So, what's the plan now the cats have arrived?' Rose asked.

'Well, the soft launch is a week tomorrow. I figured that would give them enough time to settle in. I might invite a few people over for lunch first to see how the cats react – maybe Leo and Lara?' Tori avoided making eye contact.

'I think lunch would be the perfect first date, don't you agree, Joyce?' said Rose, nudging Joyce gently.

'Oh, I'm keeping well out of this,' said Joyce, holding up her hands. 'I've learnt not to offer Tori dating advice.'

'But anyway, this wouldn't be a date. If it was, I'd hardly be inviting his niece along, would I?' said Tori.

'Well, go on then,' said Rose, raising her eyebrows.

'What?' replied Tori.

'Message him. There's no time like the present,' said Rose, her eyes twinkling mischievously.

'You're not at school now, you know,' said Tori, laughing, 'I don't have to do everything you tell me.' Rose folded her arms and stared at Tori; her gaze was unwavering. 'Oh, fine,' said Tori, reaching for her phone and typing out a message. *Hi Leo, the cats are finally here! I don't suppose you and Lara fancy coming over for lunch tomorrow to meet them? Tori xx*
'Happy now?'

'Very,' Rose replied, popping the last pink marshmallow from her mocha into her mouth.

Tori's phone buzzed with a reply. *Love to. See you at 1ish? xx* Tori felt a wave of excitement course through her.

'Well,' said Rose, tapping her fingers on the table, 'what did he say?'

'He said yes,' said Tori.

'Oh, look who's made an appearance,' said Joyce.

'Mr Wiggles!' said Tori. 'He's finally woken up.' The huge black cat stretched out his front legs, yawned and sauntered around the café as though he had always lived there. He hopped straight up onto one of the viewing platforms and flopped down on the pink velvet throw that covered it. Within seconds he was snoring away again happily.

'Ooh, he's a character, isn't he?' said Rose, stifling a giggle.

'Isn't he just!' agreed Joyce. 'He's already found the best spot in the room.'

'You've got to admire him – he's got the measure of this place already,' said Tori. 'I hope he knows he's going to be well looked after here.'

'They all are,' confirmed Rose, looking around the room. 'They don't know it yet, but this place has put them one step closer to finding their forever homes.'

'Gosh, I really hope so,' said Tori, crossing her fingers.

'Hey, looks like we've got a visitor,' said Joyce, pointing to the window, where Ernie was sat looking in. He spotted Mr Wiggles immediately and pawed at the glass. Mr Wiggles wandered over and both cats sat looking at each other.

'Well, they're not hissing at each other, that's a good start,' said Rose.

Ernie pawed at the glass again and meowed.

'Sorry, little man, you know you're not allowed in the café and that goes double now it's full of cats,' said Tori.

'Aw, can't you let him in?' asked Rose.

'Afraid not – we can't risk him upsetting the rest of the group. Izzy's worked so hard to make sure they all get along, plus there's disease control measures we need to stick to,' explained Tori.

'Sorry, Ernie. Don't worry, Tori will spoil you at home later,' said Joyce, as Ernie eventually got bored and padded away towards the green.

'Ooh, I know! Let's get some pics of them settling in for your socials,' said Rose excitedly, grabbing Tori's phone. 'I bet they'll go down a storm.'

'Why didn't I think of that?' said Tori. 'I've set up the accounts, but I've only posted a few shots of the renovation so far and I can't wait to show these guys off.'

'If social media has taught us anything, it's that people can't get enough of a cute cat photo,' said Rose. 'Hold still and I'll take one of you and Angel while she's still snuggled in your lap.' Tori smiled for the camera. 'There! This one's perfect,' she said, holding the phone out for Tori to see.

'Aw, Angel looks adorable,' said Tori, tickling the sleeping cat underneath the chin.

'She's not the only one; that's a great pic of you. Here, get posting!' said Rose, passing the phone back to her.

Tori drafted out her Instagram post: *The cats have arrived at the Cosy Cat and we're getting ready for our grand opening on*

June 30th! *#sussexcatcafe* *#caturday* *#catsandcoffee* She hit the share button.

'There we go, Angel, you're live on Instagram!' said Tori.

'I don't think she's bothered, do you?' said Joyce.

'Nah, too busy sleeping,' agreed Tori. A ping alerted her to a notification on her phone: *The Cosy Cat Café has 1 new follower . . . Ryan Wicks* and Tori's stomach fell through the floor.

Chapter 23

Ryan? *Ryan?* What on earth was he doing? He hadn't made any contact since dropping her off at the airport in Thailand. How would he even know about the cat café? It didn't make any sense. Rose and Joyce had realized something was wrong when they saw the blood drain from Tori's face; they'd been as shocked as she was at seeing Ryan's name on her phone. Tori's head hadn't stopped pounding all afternoon and even though she'd gone to bed hours ago, it was no use, she just couldn't sleep. Her mind was whirring, trying to find an explanation, something, anything, which would explain why Ryan would make contact now. It just didn't add up. Should she message him? Follow him back? No, why should she? She shook her head. She'd forget it; if Ryan wanted to follow her on Insta, fine, that didn't mean she had to talk to him. She'd put him out of her mind and focus on the business.

When Tori's alarm went off the next morning, she woke with a dull headache. It felt as though she'd only just fallen asleep. Despite her resolution to put Ryan out of her head, he'd managed to remain very much lodged there when she'd eventually drifted off. She sat up, pulled back the duvet and gave Ernie, who was asleep in his usual spot at the end of her bed, a gentle scratch on the head.

'You don't have any trouble sleeping, do you, sweetheart?' she said. Ernie rolled on to his side, purring. 'You've been dreaming about chasing mice and eating tuna, right?'

Tori shuffled across the room and looked in the mirror. 'Eurrgh. Look at these bags, Ernie,' she said, pulling at the skin under her eyes. 'I look awful.' And then she remembered she had lunch plans with Leo today. She groaned. It was going to take a lot of make-up to make her feel presentable today. A whole lot.

She jumped in the shower, brushed her teeth and reached for her make-up bag. 'You don't know how lucky you are,' she said to Ernie, 'you just roll out of bed looking gorgeous.' Ernie hopped up onto her dressing table and began batting her mascara with his paws, almost knocking over the framed picture she had on display of him as a kitten. 'Hey, I need that,' she said, making a grab for the mascara. 'Gosh, were you ever this tiny?' she said, picking up the photo. 'You know, the Cosy Cup may be full of cats now, but you're still my number one boy,' she said, tickling him under the chin.

Make-up done, she pulled on her favourite pair of skinny jeans, one of the branded T-shirts with the café's logo on that had arrived yesterday, much to her delight, and grabbed her handbag. 'Come on, you, I need to go and see how our new kitties are getting on.' As she made her way down to the kitchen, she spotted a note on the table from her mum. *I couldn't wait to go next door and see how the cats are doing xx* Tori smiled. She knew Joyce was just as excited about their new residents as she was.

Tori spotted Joyce sitting at one of the window tables, coffee in one hand and Mr Wiggles fast asleep in her lap.

'How's it going?' she asked eagerly.

'Take a look around,' said Joyce. 'I'd say pretty well, so far.'

Tori scanned the room; all the cats seemed to be settling in fine. Valentine was flopped out on one of the tables, Angel was curled up asleep in the chair opposite Joyce and she could see two pairs of green eyes, presumably belonging to Norris and Daisy, peering out from one of the hidey-holes.

'Wow, everyone seems pretty relaxed!' said Tori.

'I know! They were quite lively when I arrived, but they've had breakfast and I've given Mr Wiggles his thyroid tablet.'

'Brilliant! I wasn't expecting them to be so chilled on their first day.'

'I've cleared out the litter trays, the water bowls have fresh water in them and it doesn't look like we've had any accidents overnight. I think Izzy's picked the perfect bunch for you!'

'I expected there might be teething problems, though.'

'There still might be; it's early days, so don't jinx it,' said Joyce, crossing her fingers. 'But I'd say, so far so good. What's your plan for today then?'

'Hang out with the cats till Leo and Lara get here for lunch.'

'I've got a few bits I need to get from the shops, so I'll leave you in peace when Leo arrives.'

'Oh no, Mum, you don't have to!' said Tori quickly. 'You're more than welcome to join—'

'No, love, I'd rather leave you to it. I need to catch up with Greg about something anyway.'

'Well, only if you're sure,' said Tori.

'I am.'

Tori and Joyce spent the rest of the morning in the café together, playing with the cats, putting the finishing touches to the tables and baking. Valentine was keen to investigate everything that was going on around him and no sooner had Tori put a bud vase on a table, he'd knocked it straight over.

'I can see you're going to be trouble, young man,' she said, picking Valentine up and popping him down on the floor. 'You're lucky these don't have water in them ... yet.' She riffled through one of the toy boxes and found a catnip banana that he could turn his attention to. She threw it up in the air and he chased it eagerly, pouncing on it and flipping it between his paws. 'That's more like it,' she said approvingly. Ernie appeared at the window a few times throughout the morning to check out the new arrivals and, much to Tori's relief, they all seemed happy enough to watch each other through the glass, without a hiss or a cross word between them.

Tori looked up as she heard a knock on the front door. She could see Lara peering through the glass and waving. Was it really one o'clock already? Where had the morning gone? As she unlocked the café door to let her visitors in, Lara looked fit to burst with excitement.

'Tori, are they here? Are they here?' she said, bouncing up and down on the spot.

'Who? The cats?' said Tori. Lara nodded. 'Erm, let me have a look . . .' she said, pretending to look around the room. 'Nope, no cats I'm afraid. I don't think they've arrived yet.'

'Don't be silly, Tori, I can see them!' Lara laughed.

'Can you, where?' said Tori, turning around.

'Right there,' squealed Lara, pointing at Norris, 'look, there's a ginger one.'

'Oh, you mean *this* cat?' said Tori, scooping Norris into her arms.

'Yes!' cried Lara.

'Sorry, Lara. I'm just messing. Come in and say hello,' said Tori.

'Sorry, she's been like this all morning,' said Leo, 'she's *so* excited. Anyone would think she'd not got two kittens of her own to play with.'

'Well, we're excited too,' said Tori.

As they entered the café, Lara spotted Valentine playing with his banana and she ran towards him.

'Careful, Lara, don't scare him,' Leo said.

'He's not scared, see?' said Lara, smiling as she threw the toy for him to chase. 'He wants to play.'

'Here, why don't you try using this,' said Tori, passing her a fishing rod toy with a shiny silver fish at the end of it. 'I bet he'll love that.'

'Yes! Domino and Dexter have one too, they love it,' replied Lara. She began waving the rod around animatedly and Valentine darted back and forth trying to catch his prey. It wasn't long before Daisy emerged from her hidey-hole and joined in with the game.

'She's doing a great job,' said Tori. 'That'll keep them occupied for hours. I wonder who'll get bored first, Lara or the cats?'

'Oh, definitely the cats,' laughed Leo. 'Lara's never given up on a game voluntarily.' He smiled and the lines around his mouth crinkled. She felt her insides do a little flip. Leo really did have a great smile . . . 'Earth to Tori?'

'Sorry, I was—'

'Miles away? I could tell. So, I was just wondering – what's for lunch?'

'Oh, right, yeah,' she said, snapping back to reality. Honestly, if she was that distracted by Leo's smile, there really was no hope for her. 'Mum was baking this morning, so I'll see what she's left for us. Make yourself at home,' she said, pointing to a corner table that she'd laid for three. 'Is there anything Lara doesn't like?'

'God no, she'll eat anything you put in front of her, especially if it has cheese or chocolate on it.'

'Well, that shouldn't be a problem – our entire menu comes covered in either cheese or chocolate,' she laughed.

As Tori made a couple of hot chocolates, she noticed that her hands were shaking. She took a deep breath. Why was she so nervous? It was only lunch. It wasn't like this was a proper date. Leo was only here so that Lara could meet the cats, right? It was no big deal. 'Get a grip, Tori,' she muttered under her breath. As she walked back to the table with the tray of drinks, she saw Lara's eyes widen.

'Wow, Tori, those look a-maz-ing!' said Lara, throwing the fishing rod toy to the ground and pulling up a chair.

'To be fair, they do look delicious,' agreed Leo with a nod of approval.

'They're a speciality of the house!' said Tori, returning to the kitchen to grab a plate of sandwiches. 'Wow, Lara, enjoying that, are you?'

'Oh yes,' replied Lara, wiping the cream from around her mouth with the back of her hand.

'I told you,' whispered Leo. 'Anything that contains cheese or chocolate and you're onto a winner.'

'Help yourself, guys,' said Tori, grabbing a tuna sandwich made with thick granary bread and plenty of butter for herself. 'How are your kittens getting on, Lara?'

'Oh, they're so naughty,' Lara said through a mouthful of cheese and pickle sandwich. 'Last night they climbed all the way up the curtains in the lounge and we couldn't get them down. Mum was soooo mad, but I thought it was funny.'

'Oh no!' said Tori, stifling a giggle. 'It sounds like they're getting into mischief already, then.'

'Too right!' said Leo. 'Their other favourite hobby is

climbing up my legs and their claws are insanely sharp. If I'm wearing shorts—'

'He screams like a girl,' said Lara, spluttering sandwich everywhere.

'Now that I would like to see,' said Tori, her hand brushing Leo's as they both reached for a napkin.

'You should, it's hilarious,' said Lara.

'I thought you put out fires for a living?' said Tori.

'He does, but that's not as scary as tiny kitten claws, is it, Uncle Leo?' Tori and Lara both burst out laughing. Lara jumped up from her seat and began hopping around the café impersonating Leo, squealing, 'Ouch! Ouch! Help! Save me from the tiny kittens! Their claws are sooooo sharp! Help!'

The more Tori laughed, the funnier Lara seemed to find it, and eventually, Tori was struggling for breath, especially when she saw Leo's face as he tried to look serious and disapproving as he watched Lara's impression of him.

'I'll have you know that tiny kitten claws are not to be messed with,' said Leo. 'Give me a fire to deal with any day of the week.'

'Well, perhaps you should make sure you're wearing jeans next time you visit? Even tiny kitten claws can't get through denim,' said Tori.

'Lesson learnt,' said Leo, nodding.

Lara was quick to polish off her lunch and pleaded to be excused from the table to play with the cats more.

'I think we all need a breather before I bring out the chocolate cake I spied in the kitchen,' said Tori.

'Chocolate cake!' said Lara, her eyes widening.

'But you've got plenty of time to play with the cats first. Why don't you see if Norris wants to make friends? Look, he's just woken up,' said Tori, pointing towards the large ginger cat who had just hopped down from the windowsill and was heading towards her. Lara got up from the table and began fussing Norris, who purred loudly.

'It looks like everything is going well then?' said Leo, as Valentine leapt onto the table and began investigating the remains of Tori's tuna sandwich.

'You were saying?' Tori laughed.

'Sorry, I think I might have jinxed it,' said Leo, giving a half-shrug.

'That's not for you, little man,' said Tori, placing Valentine gently back on the floor.

'I guess that must be one of the hazards of having them live in the café. There's lots of food up for grabs . . .'

'Well, yes, but I'm hoping people won't feed them. I've added a line on the new menus about how the cats have their own food and shouldn't be eating ours, which I hope will do the trick.'

'Best take tuna off the menu if you don't want them pestering people for scraps, though,' Leo laughed.

'Ah, good point,' agreed Tori.

As Tori got up to clear the plates, she glanced out of the window and saw Claire on the other side of the road, looking right at her. Tori smiled and waved, but Claire just kept staring, almost looking right through her. How rude!

'Someone you know?' said Leo, turning to see who Tori had been waving at, but Claire had already vanished.

'Yeah, my hairdresser, but I don't think she could have seen me. Weird.'

'Maybe the window was reflecting back at her or something?' Leo suggested, leaning back in his chair. 'Anyway, how are things going with the barn dance idea? I hear Izzy has given the go-ahead.'

'She did, yes, but there's going to be an awful lot to do, and I'm focused on the reopening plans at the moment. I think I might have taken on a bit too much by saying I can take charge of it.'

'If you need any help, I'd love to be involved,' Leo said enthusiastically.

'Thanks, Leo, I'd actually really appreciate your help.'

'How about you come over to mine one evening? We could get a pizza or something and talk through what needs to be done? It absolutely wouldn't be a date, though,' said Leo quickly, 'it would just be two friends hanging out and planning a barn dance,' he continued, reddening, 'for charity.'

'Oh, well, as it's for charity, how can I say no?' Tori laughed, taking a swig of her drink.

'Well, you can't really.'

'Exactly.'

'How about Wednesday night? Eight-ish?'

'And there's guaranteed pizza?'

'Absolutely.'

'Because that would be a dealbreaker you know,' she said, tilting her head to one side and smiling at him.

'As much pizza as you can eat.'

'Count me in then.'

'I'm messaging you my address now,' said Leo, pulling out his phone.

As Tori heard her phone beep with a message, she grinned. She knew she was already more excited for her 'non-date' with Leo than she should be for pizza with a 'friend'.

'I like Tori,' said Lara as she and Leo walked the short distance back home from the café. 'Do you like Tori, Uncle Leo?'

'Yeah, sure, she's nice,' answered Leo with a shrug.

'She's pretty, isn't she?' said Lara, her eyes shining.

'Erm ... I guess so, yeah,' replied Leo, scratching his head.

'You know,' said Lara tentatively, scuffing her trainers along the pavement, 'I think she likes you too, Uncle Leo. Why don't you ask her to be your girlfriend?'

'What?' said Leo, stopping in his tracks and letting go of Lara's hand. 'Why on earth would you say that?'

'Because you like her. And she likes you, I can tell,' replied Lara without blinking.

Leo's mind was whirring ... he knew Tori liked him but was it really so obvious that a eight-year-old child had noticed?

'If you ask her out, I bet she'd say yes,' said Lara, stopping to pick a daisy from the grass verge.

'She will?' Leo didn't tell her that he'd already tried that and she'd said no.

'Of course. You like her and she likes you. It's simple,' said Lara, looking up at him and sighing heavily.

'Lara, you're only eight, you're too young to understand this kind of stuff, it's complicated.'

'It isn't,' said Lara, laughing. 'Honestly, grown-ups can be so silly sometimes.'

'Who says I want a girlfriend anyway? I'm perfectly happy on my own.'

Lara stopped walking and took her uncle by the hand; she looked up at him, her face serious.

'But I want you to marry someone nice so I can be a princess fairy bridesmaid, and Tori's nice, isn't she?'

Leo knelt in front of his niece and hugged her close.

'How did you get to be so clever at eight years old?' Lara shrugged. 'You're right – Tori is nice, but there's a bit more to it than that. One day you'll understand . . .'

'Oh, grown-ups always say that,' said Lara, huffing. 'It's *so* annoying!'

'Okay, okay,' said Leo, standing up. 'How about we stop in at Harrison's on the way home. Get some treats for Domino and Dexter?'

'Oh, yes please!' replied Lara, pulling Leo towards the shop. 'And maybe some sweets for me too?'

'Sweets?' said Leo. 'You've just eaten a ton of cake!'

'Oh, pleeeease, Uncle Leo, pleeease!' she pleaded.

'We'll see,' said Leo, ruffling her hair. 'We'll see.'

As they walked through the door of Harrison's, Leo had a feeling that his niece's advice had been pretty accurate. He liked Tori and Tori liked him. Did it really need to be more complicated than that?

Chapter 24

On Wednesday night, on the dot of 8pm, Tori stood at the front door of Leo's mid-terrace house. She smoothed down her dress before knocking. Remember, this *isn't* a date . . .

'Hiya,' said Leo, swinging the door wide open. Two black and white cats darted between Tori's legs, making a break for freedom.

'Hello, sweetie,' she said, bending down to stroke the cat that was now weaving between her feet.

'Well, that's Tallulah – and Tinkerbell is the tail you saw scarpering down the road.'

'She's gorgeous, Leo,' said Tori, stepping over the cat and through the doorway. 'I brought wine,' she said, thrusting a bottle into his hand.

'Wine is good, thanks. Let's head to the kitchen and I'll grab some glasses.'

'Wow, this is nice,' she said, perching on one of the breakfast bar stools. 'Very modern.'

'I can't take the credit unfortunately,' said Leo, grabbing

two wine glasses from a cabinet and a corkscrew from the drawer. 'The previous owners had just had the whole place done up before they split and had to sell.'

'Ouch,' said Tori, screwing up her face.

'Definitely, but their loss is my gain,' he said, filling her glass. 'So, what do you fancy?' Tori spluttered her wine and coughed.

'Sorry ... pizza-wise?'

Leo pulled a pizza menu out of the letter rack on the worktop and waved it at her.

'Oh, yes ... of course,' she said, stumbling over her words. Obviously, he was talking about pizza. She pulled at the neck of her dress. 'Is it me, or is it hot in here?'

'It's you, I think. I can open the window, though, if you like,' said Leo, reaching for the handle.

'Thanks, some cool air would be good.'

'How do you feel about a meat feast?'

'Erm ...'

'Just tell me you're not one of those weirdos who likes pineapple on pizza,' he said seriously, pulling up a stool next to her at the breakfast bar.

'Oh God no! That's just wrong,' she laughed. 'I mean, fruit ... on a *pizza*.' She shuddered. 'A meat feast sounds perfect.'

'I knew you were my kind of girl,' he said, pulling out his phone to order. Tori raised her eyebrows. 'When it comes to pizza, I mean,' he added quickly. Tori laughed; perhaps she wasn't the only one who felt nervous tonight?

'Don't worry, I'm only messing,' she said. Leo's shoulders relaxed.

'I put my foot in it a lot – last week I asked a man if he wanted his mum to ride in the ambulance with him, only to find out it was his wife!' he said.

'Oh no, you didn't?' she asked, wincing.

'Oh, I absolutely did!'

Tori laughed, and Leo smiled broadly. 'Well, I'm glad my embarrassment amuses you.'

'Oh, it does,' said Tori. 'I'm sorry, I shouldn't laugh, but it *is* funny.'

'That's not what the six-foot-four, built-like-a-shed biker said. I honestly thought he was going to deck me.'

'I'm guessing his wife wasn't too pleased either!'

'Thankfully, she was pretty calm about it.'

'Well, at least the ambulance was already on the scene, just in case,' Tori teased, taking another sip of her wine.

'Just one of the hazards of the job.'

'But you love it, don't you?'

'My job?' asked Leo. Tori nodded. 'Oh yeah, it's what I've always wanted to do, ever since I can remember. Mum said one Christmas I wore the firefighter outfit she got me until New Year's Eve.'

'Aw, really? I bet you looked cute.'

'Yep, I went everywhere in that thing ... the supermarket, the dentist ... you name it. She did draw the line at me wearing it to my sister's christening, though.'

'So, you're the older brother then?'

'That's me. I'm four years older than Nina,' said Leo.

'Lara's mum?'

'That's right.'

'Do you get along?' Tori asked.

'We used to fight like cat and dog when we were kids. She was always getting me into trouble, but we've outgrown the bickering and have been a lot closer since Lara was born. Lara's dad didn't stick around once she arrived.' He pulled at the label on the wine bottle.

'That must be really tough on them both.'

'That's one of the reasons I wanted to take the job in Rye when it came up. So I could be around more for them both.'

'I remember you saying,' said Tori. 'Lara's an amazing kid – her dad's missing out, I'd say.'

'She really is. I can't even explain what she means . . . how much I . . . there aren't enough words . . .'

'To say how much you love her?'

Leo nodded.

'Don't worry, she knows,' whispered Tori.

'You think?'

'It's like me and Mum. She doesn't need to tell me every day for me to know that she'd jump in front of a bus for me. Dad left when I was fifteen; I was quite a bit older than Lara, but it still hurt. It took me ages to work out that I hadn't done anything wrong. Mum was the one who was there for me, even though she was dealing with him leaving her too.'

'Sorry, Tori, I didn't know.'

'Honestly, I'm fine with it now. A younger woman showed him a bit of attention and he ditched us without a second thought. That's on *him*, not me and Mum.'

'And you never hear from him?'

'We did at first, for a while, but he made less and less effort over the years until he finally stopped bothering at all.'

'Well, he sounds like an arse.'

'Cheers to that,' said Tori, raising a glass. Leo smiled, his eyes not leaving hers. Leo had shared some deeply personal stuff with her this evening, which made it even harder for her to believe that Claire was right when she had warned her he was a player. 'Seriously though, Lara is lucky to have you in her life, Leo; she clearly adores you and that kind of bond is something to treasure. Not everyone is that lucky.' She took a deep breath. 'Right, don't we have a barn dance to organize?' she said, just as the doorbell chimed to signal the arrival of their pizza.

'I don't think I've ever been so full in my whole life,' said Tori, pushing the empty pizza box away from her and grabbing one of the sofa cushions to put on her lap.

'You did put away an entire meat feast, plus chicken wings, garlic bread and I lost count of how many of those disgusting mozzarella sticks—'

'Hey! You ate just as much as me!' she said, batting him with the cushion.

'A fact I'm not denying, but *I've* still got room for the cheesecake in the fridge . . .'

'Cheesecake,' Tori groaned, 'you're not serious? You'll have to roll me out of here at this rate.'

'Or I could give you a fireman's lift?' said Leo, raising his eyebrows.

Tori reached for the bottle of wine on the coffee table at exactly the same moment as Leo, bumping hands with him. Her instinct was to pull her hand away, but she resisted. His skin felt, warm . . . soft. She realized that she didn't want this moment to end. Electricity pulsed through her and all she could think about was how much she wanted his lips to touch hers; nothing else seemed to matter. She slowly moved her head closer towards his and shivered as he ran a finger down the bare flesh on her arm. She closed her eyes, anticipating the moment their lips would finally touch—

'Eurgh!' she cried, jumping up from the sofa as something wet and slimy landed in her lap.

'Bloody hell, Tinks!' cried Leo. Sat in the middle of the sofa was a very proud-looking cat watching a small but very energetic frog.

'Shall I get Tinkerbell out the way?' asked a flustered Tori, scooping her up off the sofa.

'Can you shut her in the kitchen for now and grab me something to try and catch this thing?' replied Leo, making frantic and unsuccessful attempts to get hold of the frog.

Tori ran through to the kitchen, closing the door firmly behind her, putting a squirming Tinkerbell down on the floor. The cat yowled at her angrily. 'Don't give me that, young lady,' said Tori sternly. 'You have no idea what you've just interrupted.' Had she and Leo really been about to share their first kiss? And had they really just been interrupted by a *frog*? She'd heard of the frog prince, but this was ridiculous. Now what to use to pop the frog into ... Tori flung open Leo's kitchen cupboards, hoping to find something they could use. Settling on a salad spinner, she sprinted back to the lounge.

'Is this okay?' she asked, passing him the spinner.

'Let's hope so,' he replied. 'One, two, three ...' He pounced, placed the plastic tub over the frog and expertly slid the lid of the salad spinner underneath. 'Gotcha!'

'Let's see,' said Tori eagerly, peering over Leo's shoulder. He lifted the lid of the salad spinner, and she could see the tiny green frog inside. 'Aw, he's actually kind of cute—'

'Cute? If it wasn't for him, we would have—' He stopped himself and looked away. Tori cleared her throat.

'Well, at least it looks like he's not hurt, that's the main thing,' said Tori.

'True. I guess we should go and return him ...'

'You know where he's from?'

'Yep. Mrs Fisher down the road had a pond put in a few weeks ago and it's been raining frogs ever since,' explained Leo.

'That's hilarious! I can just imagine you coming home to a living room full of bouncing frogs after work,' said Tori, stifling a giggle.

'Tinkerbell seems to have a bit of a knack for catching them unfortunately ...'

'Well, I should be going anyway,' said Tori, reaching for her jacket.

'Really? But we've not even had the chance to talk about the barn dance ...'

'I've got to be up early tomorrow – I've got so much to do at the café before the soft launch,' she said, reluctantly putting her handbag over her shoulder. 'I guess we'll need to meet up again to talk about the dance ...'

'Great idea,' said Leo, smiling. 'How about I walk you home?'

'Don't be silly, it's only round the corner.'

'Honestly, it's no trouble,' said Leo. 'I've got to take this little fella home.' He tapped the lid of the salad spinner. 'I could do with stretching my legs.'

'In which case, that would be lovely, thank you,' she nodded. As they left the warmth of the house and stepped into the cool night air, they walked together in silence, their fingertips gently brushing. Tori waited for Leo under the streetlamp while he knocked on Mrs Fisher's front door.

'All good?' she asked, as he jogged back towards her.

'Yeah, I told Mrs Fisher she can keep the spinner – I never use it anyway.'

'Something tells me you're not much of a salad guy,' said Tori, tucking her hair behind her ears. She noticed that Leo's eyes were sparkling even more than usual in the moonlight. She looked away. They began walking slowly towards the Cosy Cat Café. 'He doesn't know how lucky he was.'

'Who?' said Leo, distractedly.

'The frog.'

'Ah.'

'Who knows what would have happened if you hadn't been home to save him. I'm guessing it would have been frogs' legs on the menu for Tinkerbell?'

'Oh, he'd have been fine. Tinks is all talk, no trousers.'

'She did a pretty good job of catching it.'

'Oh, yeah, she's great at catching them, but she hasn't got a clue what to do once she's brought them home,' he laughed.

'Ernie's exactly the same.'

'Last week she brought a snake home for me and I ended up having to chase it all over the house!'

'A snake?' said Tori, grabbing hold of his arm. 'You're joking?'

'I wish. It was only a grass snake thankfully, but I didn't know that when I was trying to get it into a pillowcase.' Tori threw her head back and laughed hard.

'Now, that is a sight, I'd pay to see,' she said, falling silent and fixing her gaze on his. For what felt like the longest time, neither of them spoke. Tori could sense the anticipation building as Leo took her by the hand and gently pulled her closer. He placed a hand on her cheek as she leaned in towards him and, this time, there were no interruptions and their lips met. As the kiss intensified, Tori threw her arms around Leo's neck, pulling him nearer. All she could think about now was how right it felt.

'Wow!' he said, when they finally broke apart. 'I wasn't expecting that.'

'Me neither!'

'I'm glad, though,' he said, gazing down at her.

'Me too,' said Tori. 'We couldn't let that frog spoil things for us,' she added breathlessly.

'No, I guess not,' he replied.

She stared at him.

'What?'

'Just checking,' she said, looking him up and down.

'For what?'

'Just making sure that you're not going to turn into a frog on me,' she laughed.

'Isn't it supposed to be the other way around? You kiss a frog, it turns into a prince?'

'Given my luck, I'd have the opposite effect.'

'I think we're good.'

'Now that *is* a relief.'

'You know,' he said, taking her hand in his, 'I'm pretty glad you ended up back in Blossom Heath.'

'Me too,' Tori agreed. 'Thanks for a lovely evening, the house is literally there; I'll be fine walking from here.'

'If you're sure?'

'I am,' she said, letting go of his hand.

'Tori?' he called as she got further away. 'Does this mean you're finally going to agree to that date?'

She turned and pulled her phone out of her bag, typing out a message. *Leo, would you like to have dinner with me next week?* Within seconds she had his reply: *Yes.*

Chapter 25

The next few days felt like the calm before the storm. Angel, Norris, Daisy, Valentine and Mr Wiggles continued to settle in well, and Izzy had been to visit and was satisfied that they seemed happy and well looked after. Sunday had come around far too quickly, and it was time for Tori to host the soft launch with family and friends before the Cosy Cat Café officially reopened on Monday morning. Tori hadn't had much chance to think about Leo in the last few days, although they'd been exchanging messages and she smiled when she thought about the kiss they had shared. She couldn't wait to see him again this afternoon, but she wasn't quite ready to share her news with anyone else just yet.

Joyce had been busy in the kitchen all morning, preparing platters of sandwiches, baking scones and tiny, delicate Japanese cakes, flavoured with matcha, sesame, cherry and red bean, which would make up the new special afternoon tea, blending the best of the Cosy Cup's traditional treats, with a few extras from the Cosy Cat's new menu.

'Wow, Mum, this looks amazing!' said Tori, as she walked into the kitchen. 'I feel like I'm back in Tokyo! These cakes look unreal!'

'Do you think so?' replied Joyce, wiping her hands on her apron. 'I want everything to be perfect today.'

'What is it you always say to me?' Joyce looked at her curiously. 'There's no such thing as perfect.'

'Ah I know, love, but it turns out I'm better at giving advice than taking it.'

'Everything looks fantastic – you've done a great job. Now will you come and sit down for five minutes before everyone arrives? You're still supposed to be taking it easy, you know.'

'Oh, I'm fine,' said Joyce. 'How do I look?' she asked, smoothing down her new Cosy Cat branded T-shirt.

'You look great, as always.'

'I nearly forgot,' said Joyce, reaching for her handbag, she pulled out a small, silver perfume bottle and sprayed scent onto her wrists.

'Since when do you put perfume on in the middle of the day?'

'Oh, it doesn't hurt to make a bit of an effort – it's a special occasion.'

'I've just opened some Prosecco – let's have a glass before anyone arrives.'

'Do you think there's enough?' Joyce asked, taking a large gulp from one of the crystal flutes, which were on loan from the Apple Tree.

'That depends. If you're planning to keep drinking at that speed then, no, definitely not,' Tori joked.

'It's just to settle the nerves, that's all.'

'You don't think Violet will make an appearance, do you? It would be just like her to turn up and try to ruin things.'

'I'm sure she wouldn't do that, love. She seems to have gone quiet since the meeting at the village hall. Hopefully that's the end of it.'

'Hmm ... I'm not so sure ...'

Tori spotted Rose, Jake and Grace through the window.

'They're here!' she squealed, grabbing her mum's arm.

'Well, don't just stand there, let them in!'

Tori, setting down her glass, dashed to unlock the front doors.

'Tori!' cried Rose, pulling her friend close. 'How's it all going? I'm so excited!'

'Me too!' said Tori, leaning back. 'Hi guys, thanks so much for coming.'

'Are you kidding? If there's free food, you can count me in,' said Jake, taking off his jacket.

'I remember,' said Tori, laughing.

'Oh, while I think of it, I mentioned to Nathan, my mate from the Young Farmers' Club, about you looking to stock some local cheeses, and he's up for it – I'll send you his number,' said Jake.

'Brilliant, thanks, Jake,' said Tori. 'I appreciate that.'

'How's everyone settling in?' asked Grace.

'Really well, I think, but come in and see for yourself,' said Tori warmly, leading the way through to the café.

'Oh, Tori! Everything looks fantastic, you've done an amazing job!' said Grace, taking everything in.

'Thanks, Grace, that means a lot coming from you,' said Tori.

'Has Violet been causing you any more problems?' asked Grace, eyebrows raised.

'Thankfully, no, so let's hope it stays that way,' replied Tori.

'I bumped into her in Harrison's the other day and she started moaning about the café as soon as she saw me. I couldn't get away fast enough,' said Grace.

'Oh no!' groaned Tori. 'Why can't she just let it go?'

'Well, forget about her for today – this is your moment, Tori, enjoy it,' said Grace.

Tori was busy handing everyone a glass of fizz, when she heard a knock on the door.

'Oops, hang on, let me get that,' said Tori.

The next twenty minutes passed by in a whirlwind of welcoming her closest friends and neighbours to the Cosy Cat Café. Finally, Leo was at the door, accompanied by Lara and a tall, slim woman with long, red, curly hair.

'Leo, Lara, hi! How are you?' said Tori. All she could think about was kissing Leo again, but now wasn't the time.

'Tori, this is my mummy,' said Lara excitedly. 'Mummy, this is Tori.'

'Hi, Tori, I'm Nina. Lara talks about you all the time – I feel like I know you already,' said Nina, with a smile that lit up her whole face. Wow, she really did look like her brother.

'Does she?' said Tori, trying to keep her eyes focused on Leo's sister.

'Oh yeah, but in a good way,' Nina explained.

'Well, she's adorable! Why don't you go through. I'm just going to grab a word with Leo if that's okay?' said Tori.

'Sure, come on Lara, you can show me the cats,' said Nina, taking Lara by the hand. As soon as they'd shut the door, Tori reached for Leo and pulled him close so they were out of sight.

'Hey, you,' he said, sliding an arm around her waist, 'I've missed you.'

The temptation to kiss him was overwhelming, but Tori knew she had to resist.

'Listen, I was thinking, let's not say anything to anyone about what happened the other night? It's still early days . . . I'd rather not deal with any questions yet, if you don't mind?'

'Sure, if that's what you want.'

'You know what people can be like. I just don't want to put any pressure on us – let's just see where things are going first.'

'I get it. We're taking this at your pace, Tori. Although the fact that I can't kiss you right now is killing me . . .'

'Me too.' She gripped his hand. 'Imagine their faces.' She nodded towards her friends through the window in the door.

'It would be priceless!'

'Almost worth it just to see the look on Maggie's face . . .'
Tori's breathing quickened, the urge to kiss Leo was intense.

The door to the lobby creaked open.

'Uncle Leo, Tori, come on! Everyone is waiting for you,' said Lara, oblivious to the conversation she had interrupted. Leo took a step away from Tori, letting go of her hand.

'Lead the way, Lara,' said Tori, snapping herself back to reality. Lara had done them both a favour. Imagine if they had given in to temptation and kissed in front of the whole village?

Tori picked up a glass of Prosecco and tapped the side gently with a knife to get everyone's attention.

'I just wanted to say thank you all for coming today. I know not everyone in the village was in support of turning Mum's tearoom into a cat café, so having you all here today means a lot. There are a few rules to follow, I'm afraid. Please don't feed the cats; they'll try and convince you they're starving – don't fall for it!' Laughter rang around the room. 'Let the cats come to you in their own time. If they're sleeping, please don't wake them up. There are toy boxes dotted around the café, so feel free to play as much as you like and when the cats are ready for cuddles, believe me, they'll let you know. You're all here as our guests today, so the food and drink from our new menu is on us, but if you did want to make a contribution to New Beginnings, the rescue centre we're working with, that would be fantastic. As you know, all the cats staying with us are available for adoption, and we're so grateful to Izzy and her team for not just letting us look after them, but for all their help in getting this venture off the ground. We couldn't have done it without you, Izzy, and I hope you'll all join me in raising a glass to the Cosy Cat Café.' Tori raised her glass and the room around her chorused, 'To the Cosy Cat Café.'

'Oh, well done, love. That was perfect, I couldn't have said it better myself,' said Joyce, wiping a tear from her eye. 'I'm so proud of what you've done here, I really am.'

'Oh, Mum,' replied Tori, 'don't, you'll set me off too!' She pulled a tissue from her pocket and blew her nose hard. 'Come here, will you,' she said, hugging her close. 'You know the only reason we've done this is because you suggested I go for it in the first place. Thank you for trusting me with the Cosy Cat. We're a team, I hope you know that.'

'Would you look at you two,' said Rose. 'You know you're both adorable, right?'

'Ha,' laughed Tori, wiping her eyes. 'You wouldn't say that if you saw us fighting over who gets the last custard cream in the pack.'

'The answer is me, of course,' said Joyce, winking. 'Right, I'm off to mingle.'

'See you in a bit, Joyce,' said Rose, turning to face Tori. 'So, what's going on with you and Leo?'

'What do you mean?'

'Don't give me that,' said Rose, rolling her eyes. 'I saw the two of you chatting in the lobby ... You looked pretty cosy if you ask me.'

'Don't be daft,' said Tori, looking over at Leo, who was now deep in conversation with Jake. 'We were just talking about fire safety.'

'Fire safety? Really? *That's* what you're going with?'

'It's true, he's been helping me out, making sure the café's up to standard, that's all.' Tori held her breath. It was a pretty weak lie, and she knew it. Rose was silent for a moment, weighing up the likelihood that Tori was telling the truth.

'Okay, fine,' she said exhaling, 'have it your way – you were talking about *fire safety*.' She drew speech marks in the air with her index fingers.

'What do you make of that?' said Tori, keen to change the subject.

'What?'

'Look at Mum talking to Greg. Is it just me or does it look like she's flirting with him?' said Tori.

Rose stared towards Joyce and Greg, who seemed to be absolutely smitten with one another. 'Do you know what, I think she is. She's touching his arm . . . laughing at whatever he's saying. See how he's looking at her?'

Tori looked more closely. Greg had eyes only for her mother, filling her glass, even though she didn't need a top-up and grinning at her. 'I think you're right,' Tori agreed, downing the last of her drink in one gulp.

'How do you feel about it?'

'It's weird processing the idea of Mum being interested in someone again, but she's been on her own for years now and

I want her to be happy. Greg seems like a decent bloke. I say good luck to them.'

'Cheers to that,' agreed Rose. 'Wouldn't it be lovely if they got together? Joyce deserves to be happy.'

'Well, don't jump the gun yet, we might have got it completely wrong.'

'Come on, there's definitely something there.'

'You say that about me and Leo too . . .'

'And I'm right!'

Tori's cheeks burned and she looked away.

'Well, if there is something between Mum and Greg, maybe I just need to give them a little push in the right direction?'

'What have you got in mind?'

'I'm not sure just yet, but leave it with me,' said Tori.

'If you need any help, you know where I am,' said Rose, tapping her nose. 'Listen, while I've got you, I wanted to ask how you'd feel about doing a talk at the school, with my class? You could tell them all about the cats, the partnership with the rescue, how you've transformed the tearoom. You could bring a couple of the cats along for the kids to meet, they'd love that.'

'A talk? In front of kids?' Tori felt the colour drain from her face. 'I'm not sure, Rose. I'm not good at that sort of stuff . . .'

'Oh, rubbish! You'll be great. You've made a speech in front of everyone today, haven't you?'

'But that's different, I didn't have to think about that.'

'And you won't have to think about this either. Just turn up and we'll figure it out on the day. You did say you wanted to make the café part of the community.'

'I did, didn't I?'

'You definitely did. I'll put something in the school diary and let you know when, okay?'

'I don't know how you've talked me into it but, okay, count me in!'

'Fabulous, you'll be great,' said Rose, taking a swig of Prosecco and heading off to find Jake.

'Tori!' said Melissa, beaming. 'Thanks so much for the invite. This place looks amazing!'

'Ah, thank you, it's been a lot of hard work, but totally worth it,' said Tori. 'Harriet, hi! It's lovely to see you again.'

'Oh, come here,' said Harriet, leaning in and kissing Tori on the cheek. 'It's been too long! Melissa's right, this place really does look fantastic. I love how you've kept the feel of the Cosy Cup but brought something fresh and new. It really is genius, Tori! I can't wait to bring the kids. They'll love it.'

'That reminds me, I spoke to Mum and we're going to be running a child-friendly slot just for parents and their kids every Wednesday between ten and twelve,' Tori explained.

'You are? Oh, I'm so pleased,' said Melissa.

'Kids are welcome all the time, of course, but Wednesday mornings will be specifically for them. There'll be colouring activities, babyccinos and supervised petting sessions with the cats,' said Tori.

'Brilliant!' said Harriet, smiling. 'Fancy making it a permanent day to meet up, Mel?'

'Try stopping me. We'll spread the word with the other mums too, Tori – you'll be packed out!' said Melissa.

'What's in these cakes, by the way?' asked Harriet. 'These green ones are phenomenal!'

'Ah, Mum made them specially. The green ones are matcha,' said Tori.

'Delicious!' said Harriet.

'Right, I'd better go but it was lovely to see you both – we must have a proper catch-up soon, though,' said Tori.

The soft launch was a triumph. Tori and Joyce served the perfect afternoon tea, and everyone was full of compliments on the new-look café and menu. The cats were adorable; there was a moment when Tori thought Valentine was about to pounce on an unsuspecting Jean's salmon sandwich, but Lara had averted the danger by the well-timed throw of a toy mouse. Norris had settled comfortably on Maggie's lap and refused to budge, while Jess kept Daisy and Angel amused all afternoon with a game of chase the string. Mr Wiggles had taken up residence on the chair next to Nina and was snoring loudly, which Lara found hilarious. '*I didn't know cats could snore, Mummy.*'

'How about we get some photos for social media?' said Jess, picking up Tori's phone. 'Show your followers how great the afternoon's been?'

'And I have to be in them, do I?' asked Tori, pulling a face. 'Can't it just be photos of the cats?'

'You're the face behind the business. People will want to get to know the woman at the heart of the café,' Jess insisted.

'Oh, go on then.'

'Here, take this,' said Jess, passing Tori another glass of Prosecco, 'and . . . *smile*.'

'To the Cosy Cat Café!' said Tori, flashing a cheesy grin for the camera.

'Perfect! Get these up on social media – you'll be fully booked in no time.'

'I really hope so,' replied Tori, crossing her fingers.

'Honestly, Tori, this place is going to be a great success, I just know it,' said Jess, encouragingly. 'You just need to believe in yourself.'

'Thanks, Jess, I appreciate your confidence in me,' said Tori, slipping her phone back into her pocket.

Tori tidied up the café alone that evening. Her mum had worked so hard, she'd wanted her to go home and put her feet up. Tori wanted to spend some time alone with the cats and make sure they were all relaxed after their first proper day with visitors. Luckily, they seemed to have taken it all in their stride, as if they'd always lived there. Tori finished the evening feeding routine and all five cats had found a cosy spot to settle down for the night; even Valentine had finally fallen asleep in Tori's lap.

She opened Instagram on her phone and started loading up the snaps Jess had taken. Posting: *Had our soft launch today and the cats loved every minute of it! Remember, they're all up for adoption, so if you'd like to meet them 'in the fur' why not come and pay us a visit! We open Monday!* Before she could even put her phone away, it started buzzing with notifications. Bryony249 had commented, *Aw they're so cute, can't wait to pop in for a cuppa.* Genie1989 wrote, *Wow, is this in Sussex? Can we book online?* Annie31 posted, *Let's check this place out @simone24, look at those cute cats!* Tori smiled, it looked like Jess was right, people really *were* keen to pay the café a visit. She typed out some replies. *Yes @Genie1989 we're in Sussex and you can book online, the link's in our bio. Thanks so much @ Annie31, we'd love to see you!*

This was better than she'd hoped for, she'd only put the pictures up ten minutes ago and she already had over thirty likes! Scrolling through the comments, her face turned ashen as she reached the latest one. Ryan Wicks. *Wow! Tori, you look amazing. I'm so proud of you xx* Before she had time to react, her DMs beeped with a new message. *I miss you xx*

Chapter 26

Tori's head was thumping when she awoke the next morning, and it wasn't just because of the Prosecco. She'd lain awake for hours thinking about Ryan's message. *I miss you.* How dare he! Just when she felt as though she was moving on with her life and getting to know Leo. She hadn't replied to his message, she didn't know how to respond ... Was he having regrets about ending things? *I miss you.* What did he expect her to do with that? If she was honest with herself, she knew that she still missed him too, but she was finally starting to accept things were over, finally starting to move on. She was moving forwards with her life, not backwards. She threw off the duvet, reaching for the glass of water at the side of her bed and looked at the clock – it was just gone seven. Today was the big reopening and one thing she did know was that she wasn't going to let thoughts about Ryan spoil things for her. *Today was her day.*

When Tori and Joyce arrived at the café, Tori dealt with getting the cats' breakfast ready and laying tables, while Joyce popped a few slices of bread into the toaster.

'Thanks, Mum!' said Tori, grabbing a piece of buttered toast from the pile, her hand trembling.

'I thought we should load up on toast, I imagine it's going to be non-stop today, who knows when we'll get another chance.'

'Good thinking. One thing I learnt travelling was, eat whenever you get the chance.'

'Always,' agreed Joyce. 'Don't be nervous about today, love, yesterday was a triumph and there's no reason to think today won't be the same.'

'I hope you're right,' said Tori, biting a nail. 'It's one thing having friends and family test us out, but I've no idea what paying customers are going to make of us.'

'They'll think it's the best café they've ever been to,' said Joyce, placing a hand over Tori's.

'Thanks, Mum. Speaking of yesterday ... I thought you and Greg looked like you were getting on well.'

'Jam?' Joyce asked, holding up a jar.

'No thanks – and don't change the subject! I'm not that easy to distract.'

'Worth a try,' said Joyce. 'Greg's lovely and we *do* get along; he asked me to go for dinner, but I'm not sure ...'

'Why not? You've got as much right to be happy as the rest of us. If you think there's something there, Mum, I think you should go for it.'

'Really? I wasn't sure you'd approve – I've not thought about dating since your father ...'

'For what it's worth, I think Greg seems like a lovely man.'

'Oh, I don't know . . .' said Joyce, pushing her toast aside. 'He might not even think of me in that way – why would he?'

'Because you're an attractive, intelligent, funny woman and he'd be mad not to fall for you.'

'I'm a firm believer that what's meant for you won't pass you by, so let's just see where things take us, eh? We've got enough on our minds today.'

'True, we'd better get a move on if we want to be ready for our first bookings at ten.'

Tori and Joyce spent the next couple of hours baking and adding finishing touches to the tables in preparation for the grand opening. Tori wanted everything to be perfect for opening day. The cats were relaxed, and Tori spent most of her time trying not to trip over Valentine, who wanted to be wherever she was. She scooped the little grey cat up in her arms.

'You really are into everything, aren't you, sweetheart?' she said as Valentine nestled into her arms purring loudly. 'Today's a big day, you know, your forever family might be about to walk right through those doors. Wouldn't that be something?' She buried her face into Valentine's soft fur and kissed him on the top of the head. 'Come on, I've got work to do, let's find you a playmate.' She put Valentine down in front of one of the puzzle toys and spun the balls inside around to entice him to play. Within seconds, he was happily batting the spheres around the track, and it wasn't long before Daisy and Angel joined in the game. 'That should keep you out of mischief for a while.'

By ten o'clock, a small queue had formed outside the café's doors.

'Looks like our first bookings are on time,' said Joyce, nodding in the direction of the window.

'I'd best let them in,' said Tori, taking a deep breath. 'Ready?'

'Ready!' said Joyce, nodding.

As Tori opened the doors and began welcoming the first few customers, she could see that most of the queue was made up of regulars, no doubt wanting to see what the fuss was about.

'Good morning, ladies,' said Tori, to a group of women she recognized from the local WI. 'If I can get you to have a quick read of the new rules before we sign you in?'

'Rules?' asked one of the women, bristling.

'They're just there to keep you and the cats safe and happy; nothing to worry about.'

'I can't say I've ever been to a café with rules before, Iris, have you?' the woman continued.

'Honestly, Elaine, stop making such a fuss,' said a tall, broad woman, pushing past her. 'Of course, we'll be happy to read the rules, dear. It's no big deal, is it, Iris?'

Iris shook her head silently and Tori took the group through to their seats.

The morning sitting was a sell-out. Not only had the online slots been fully booked in advance, they'd also had a few walk-ins that had filled the café to capacity, mainly tourists on their way to Rye, plus lots of regulars, intrigued to see what was happening at their beloved Cosy Cup. Tori hadn't had a chance to draw breath all morning, but from what she could see the customers had loved playing with the cats; there'd been lots of 'oohing' and 'aahhing' and everyone had stuck to the rules.

Valentine had made a beeline for a particular couple that Tori didn't recognize, who had spent their entire visit playing with him, and he'd fallen asleep in the woman's lap. Mr Wiggles had been strutting around like he owned the place, checking out each customer with a firm sniff and a nuzzle, much to everyone's amusement, and Daisy and Norris had provided the perfect Insta opportunity by curling up together in a heart-shaped pink basket. 'Don't forget to tag us in your posts,' called Tori to the customers who had leapt up to take a photo. As Tori was clearing tables and getting ready for lunchtime, the young couple Valentine had been sitting with approached her.

'Excuse me,' said the woman.

'Hi, how can I help? I hope you've enjoyed your visit?' asked Tori, praying she didn't have a customer complaint to deal with on day one.

'Is it true that all the cats are up for adoption?' the woman asked.

'Oh yes, absolutely. Has someone caught your eye? Let me guess, Valentine?'

'Is that the grey one?' asked the man.

'Yep, that's him,' replied Tori, pointing at Valentine, who

was curled up next to Angel on a shelf. 'I noticed he spent most of his time with you guys.'

'We'd love to adopt him,' said the woman. 'If we could?' she continued quickly.

'That's wonderful,' said Tori, grinning widely. 'If you give me your email address, I'll pass it on to Izzy, the manager of New Beginnings Rescue Centre, and she'll be in touch with the forms to start the adoption.'

'Awesome,' said the woman, clapping her hands together. 'I'm Simone and this is Tom,' she said, gesturing towards the man at her side. 'We saw your post on Instagram yesterday and I was desperate to come and meet Valentine before someone else snapped him up.'

'Are you local?' asked Tori. 'I don't think I've seen you here before.'

'Brighton; we thought it was worth the drive to visit,' said Tom.

'We've just bought our first house together and we've been desperate to get a cat for ages, but it was tricky when we were renting before,' explained Simone.

'I do have to tell you,' said Tori seriously, 'Valentine is recovering from a car accident, he's got a metal plate in his leg.'

'Oh, poor baby,' said Simone, a sad look passing across her face.

'Izzy can talk to you about what that means in the longer term, but I wanted to tell you in case that changes your minds at all,' said Tori.

'Not in the slightest,' said Tom, taking Simone's hand.

'It makes no difference to us. We'd love to give him a good home and if he needs a bit of extra help, we can certainly give it,' said Simone.

'Wonderful,' said Tori, passing a notepad across to her. 'Just pop your contact details on there for me and Izzy will be in touch.'

'I'm so glad we came in today,' said Simone. 'I've got everything crossed that Valentine can come and live with us; it will really make our new place feel like a proper home. I'm pleased we spotted your Instagram post.'

'Me too. It's good to know our social posts are working,' said Tori.

'Oh, they definitely are, and I'll make sure I tell all my friends about this place,' said Simone.

'I'd appreciate that,' said Tori, 'and I hope everything goes well with Izzy. Feel free to pop in anytime to see Valentine while you're waiting for the adoption to go through.'

'Great, we'll see you soon,' said Tom.

As soon as the couple left, Tori messaged Izzy. *We've got a potential home for Valentine already. Seem like a lovely couple, can you email an adoption form over to them?* If this morning was anything to go by, the Cosy Cat Café was well on its way to success.

Chapter 27

The week since the reopening had been so busy. There had been a steady flow of new customers and Tori was pleased to see that almost all their regulars had been coming in as usual. Apart from one. Violet Davenport hadn't shown her face once. What was her problem? For as long as Tori could remember, Violet had been the village loner and moaner. She didn't think she'd ever had a good word to say about anyone, and Tori was pretty sure she'd never married or had children. It must be a pretty lonely existence. Tori wondered if, now she was back permanently, it might be time to make peace with Vicious Violet, maybe take her some of the new Japanese-inspired cakes, show her some of the new logo merchandise, entice her into the Cosy Cat with the promise of a taste of their new smashed avocado on sourdough?

There was another regular Tori had been hoping to see, but so far Leo hadn't had time to pop in. They'd arranged to have dinner, on Thursday night at a new fish restaurant in Rye that Tori had been dying to try and she couldn't wait to see Leo again. Thankfully, she hadn't heard anything more from Ryan. She'd nearly replied to his message a couple of times, but something had stopped her. Things between them had ended so abruptly, they'd never talked things through. Was it possible he'd had a change of heart? Could being without her have made him realize that he'd made a mistake? Acted rashly? The not knowing was the hardest part. Every night this week she'd found herself staring at his message, *I miss you*, before she went to sleep, wondering if she felt the same. It was early days for her and Leo, but she'd been with Ryan for four years . . . If there was a chance for them, shouldn't she at least explore it? Hear him out?

The busy days spent in the café helped to take Tori's mind off her increasingly confusing love life. Izzy had called this morning to let her know that she was home-checking Simone and Tom, the couple who had offered to adopt Valentine, next week and, if all went well, they'd be able to take Valentine back to Brighton soon after. Izzy was thrilled and was already talking about which cat at the shelter might be able to take Valentine's spot at the café. Tori knew she was going to miss him, but she was happy he'd found his forever home. She hoped Tom and Simone knew how lucky they were.

Of all the customers that had passed through the café's doors during opening week, there was one in particular who had caught Tori's attention. She'd been in every morning at the same time, sitting at the same table by the window. She always ordered a pot of tea and a fruit scone: jam, no butter.

She was always immaculately dressed and sat quietly looking out of the window with Mr Wiggles curled up on her lap. Tori had discovered that her name was Cora, but beyond her name, Tori knew very little about her. Joyce hadn't seen Cora in the village before either. If she lived locally, wouldn't she have visited the café before now? Tori didn't want to pry, but she was intrigued.

'Morning, Cora,' said Tori, as she approached her table, order pad in hand.

'Good morning.'

'I see Mr Wiggles has found his usual spot,' she said, pointing at the cat, who was sleeping soundly in Cora's lap.

'Oh, yes. I think we're friends now. I'll have—'

'Your usual? A pot of tea, a fruit scone, jam, no butter?'

Cora nodded.

'Coming right up.' Tori walked through to the kitchen. 'A pot of tea—'

'I'm one step ahead of you, love,' said Joyce, nodding towards the tray she'd started preparing. 'I saw Cora come in.'

'She's a creature of habit, isn't she?'

'I could set my watch by her.'

'And Mr Wiggles seems to love her ... Hey, I wonder if she'd think about adopting him?'

'Maybe, but don't go forcing the idea on her.'

'But she might not realize the cats are adoptable? I could just mention it, in passing.'

'You've got about as much subtlety as a sledgehammer!'

'Hey, I can be tactful!'

'Hmm . . . best get that pot of tea over before it goes cold.'

Tori picked up the tea tray and walked back to Cora's table.

'Here we are – one tea, one scone, jam, no butter.'

'Thank you,' Cora replied.

'You know,' said Tori, tucking her order pad back into her apron pocket, 'all of the cats here are available to adopt. We're working with New Beginnings rescue—'

'Adopt a cat?' said Cora, stiffening slightly while holding her teacup in mid-air. 'I don't think so.' She nudged Mr Wiggles off her lap.

'They make great companions, if you're on your own, I mean . . .' Tori added quickly.

'And what would you know about it?'

'About what?'

'Living on your own.'

'Oh, well, I don't really . . .' Tori trailed off.

'Well then, I suggest you stick to serving tea instead of offering unwanted advice.' Cora turned her head away to look out of the window towards the village green.

'Oh God, sorry. I didn't mean to . . .' Tori stuttered, a wave of nausea washing over her. Cora was right – who was she to be offering anyone advice? She walked back to the kitchen, banging through the doors as she went.

'Careful!' said Joyce, looking up at Tori, concern flashing across her face. 'Hey, what's wrong, love? It's not Violet Davenport again, is it?' she asked, throwing down her tea towel and making towards the door. 'Maggie said she was in the shop again yesterday telling anyone who'd listen what a terrible idea the cat café is.'

'No, nothing like that, Mum. But why didn't you tell me about Violet?'

'Oh, I didn't want to worry you, I suppose.'

'Well, it's not Violet. I just overstepped the mark with Cora, I think,' she said sheepishly.

'You weren't pestering her about adopting a cat, were you?'

Tori screwed up her face. 'Well . . .'

'Tori! What did I tell you? She comes in here for a cup of tea and a bit of quiet. Not to have you poking into her business—'

'I know, I know, I'm sorry,' replied Tori, looking down at her trainers. 'But you have to admit, it *is* odd, isn't it? No one has seen her in the village before and now she's a regular here. I mean, it does make you wonder, doesn't it?'

'The sooner you learn to keep your nose out of other people's business the better, young lady.'

'I did try and apologize, but she wasn't interested.'

'Well, try again,' said Joyce, popping some bacon under the grill.

Tori walked back through the kitchen doors, only to find Cora's table empty, her scone untouched. Tori felt guilty about what had happened.

'Are you after the lady who was sitting there?' asked Claire, who was looking her usual glamorous self, her hair just as perfect as you'd expect, drinking a skinny latte and scrolling through her phone.

Tori nodded. 'Has she gone?'

'Afraid so. Just upped and left as soon as you'd finished talking.' Tori's face fell. 'What's wrong? She didn't leave without paying, did she?' asked Claire.

'Oh no, nothing like that,' replied Tori, twisting the tea towel she was holding. 'I just wanted to talk to her about something.'

'I'm in a bit of a hurry myself as well actually, do you mind if I get the bill?'

'Sure,' replied Tori. 'I hope that was okay,' she continued, pointing towards the latte on the table in front of Claire, which was barely touched.

'Perfect, thanks. I've just remembered I've got somewhere I need to be.'

'I can put it in a takeaway cup if you'd like?' said Tori, placing the bill on the table.

'Oh, I don't want you to go to any trouble, just leave it,' said Claire, pulling a five-pound note out of her blazer pocket and throwing it down.

'Honestly, it's no—'

'Just leave it, would you?' Claire snapped. 'Like I said, I've got somewhere I need to be.' She pulled a large pink holdall out from under the table and put the strap over her shoulder.

What was going on today? Tori had offended two people in less than ten minutes already. At this rate, she'd have no customers left by the end of the week. Just then, the bell to the café chimed to signal the arrival of a new customer, and Tori looked up to see Leo and Lara in the foyer, stepping aside to let Claire out. Lara was waving at her excitedly and Leo grinned as he ran a hand through his hair in a vain attempt to try to tame it.

'Well, this is a lovely surprise,' said Tori, as she greeted them. 'I wasn't expecting to see you two today.'

'Tori!' exclaimed Lara, wrapping her arms around Tori's waist and hugging her.

'We've not booked,' said Leo. 'We're hoping you can squeeze us in for an early lunch?'

'There's always a table available for my favourite customer,' said Tori, tussling Lara's hair.

'I didn't know I was your favourite customer,' said Leo with a conspiratorial wink.

'No, Uncle Leo! She's talking about *me*!' said Lara indignantly.

'You mean, *you're* her favourite customer?' said Leo, pointing at Lara with mock offence.

'Obviously!' replied Lara, rolling her eyes. 'I am, aren't I, Tori?'

'Oh yes, of course,' replied Tori, giggling, 'my absolute favourite. Now, let's get you sat down, shall we?' Tori led the way through the café, grabbing a couple of menus from behind the counter en route to the table that Cora had left empty. 'Let me get these out of your way,' she said hurriedly, reaching for the untouched scone and half-full teacup. 'You're not at school today then?' she asked Lara.

'Teacher training day,' replied Leo.

'Mum's at work,' said Lara cheerfully.

'So, Uncle Leo's stepped in,' Leo explained as Tori passed him a menu.

'Ah, that means Rose will still be at work then,' said Tori.

'Who's Rose?' asked Lara.

'You know, Rose,' said Leo, 'she's your teacher.'

'What?' replied Lara, open-mouthed. 'You mean Miss Hargreaves is called *Rose*?'

'Yes, didn't you know that?' said Leo, looking confused.

'I can't wait to tell everyone in class,' said Lara, clapping her hands together delightedly. 'We've been trying to guess her name for ages.'

'Uh-oh,' whispered Tori, 'I'm guessing it's not common knowledge among her pupils then. I'll be for it when Rose finds out.'

'Remind me never to tell you my secrets . . .' said Leo.

'Leo's secrets . . . Now that *is* a topic I'd like to find out more about,' said Tori, laughing. 'Now, what can I get you, Lara?'

'Hot chocolate with cream and marshmallows, please,' said Lara, closing her menu.

'Good choice. You can never go wrong ordering cream and marshmallows, Lara,' said Tori, casting a smile in her direction.

'And are you planning to order any food, Lara, or is it just cream and marshmallows today?' said Leo, raising an eyebrow.

'And a tuna panini, please,' replied Lara, giggling.

'Green tea for me and a ham sandwich,' said Leo, passing

his menu back across to Tori. Their hands touched for the briefest of moments and she felt a flash of electricity jolt through her. Leo's piercing blue eyes locked onto her and her insides turned to jelly. What was it about this man that the briefest of touches had such a dramatic effect on her?

By the time Tori returned to their table with drinks, Lara was playing a game of chase with Norris and Angel and a long piece of pink ribbon.

'Hey, Tori?' asked Lara, as she skipped around the café trailing the length of ribbon behind her. 'Where's Daisy?'

'Daisy? Oh, she's around here somewhere,' said Tori distractedly as she passed Leo his tea and he touched her arm discreetly.

'She's not,' replied Lara. 'I've looked everywhere.'

'She's probably just sleeping in one of the hidey-holes. Don't worry, I'll find her.'

Tori looked everywhere, but there was no sign of Daisy.

'See, I told you she's not here,' said Lara, who was now sporting a foamy milk moustache.

'She must be,' replied Tori, although she could feel a rising sense of panic. 'There's no way she could have got out, she must be here somewhere.' Tori made her way back through to the kitchen, her pace quickening. Perhaps Daisy had followed her through when she'd had the door open? 'Mum, is Daisy in here with you?'

'Daisy, no, why would she be?' said Joyce, shaking her head. 'She's not allowed in here anyway.'

'She's not in the café, she must have got through to the kitchen somehow.'

'I've not seen her, but let's double-check.' Joyce and Tori moved around the kitchen, looking under the worktops and opening cupboard doors to make sure Daisy hadn't snuck into somewhere she wasn't supposed to be.

'She's not here,' said Tori, her heart sinking. 'She can't have escaped can she, Mum?' The thought made Tori's heart race. The safety of the cats had been her top priority when they'd been redesigning the layout. She was sure the café was escape-proof.

'She'll just be hiding somewhere, don't worry. Let's have another look,' said Joyce, leading the way out of the kitchen.

'Excuse me, everyone,' said Tori, loud enough to get the attention of the customers. 'I'm sorry to interrupt your lunch but one of our cats is playing hide-and-seek with us. Would you mind having a look under your tables to see if she's there? Her name's Daisy and she's a tortoiseshell.'

Everyone began rising from their seats and peering underneath chairs and tables in search of Daisy. Leo was quick to spring to Tori's side, while Lara checked all of Daisy's favourite hidey-holes.

'She's got to be here somewhere,' said Leo, taking Tori's arm. 'This place is escape-proof; there's no way she's got through two sets of closed doors to make it out to the street. It's not possible.'

Tori hoped he was right. She looked around the room again, scanning every inch of the café for a sign of Daisy.

Running back to the counter, she grabbed a packet of treats from under the till.

'I'm so sorry, I just need to call her.' A hush fell over the café as Tori shook the treat packet frantically and called Daisy's name. Valentine, Mr Wiggles, Angel and Norris all rushed towards her, meowing in the hope of scoring a snack. All the cats were accounted for, all *except* Daisy. She couldn't explain how it had happened, but Tori now felt certain that, wherever Daisy was, she wasn't in the café.

Chapter 28

Most of the customers had returned to their seats and Tori could hear a few of the unfamiliar faces among them muttering in hushed tones: *a cat's escaped apparently . . . one of the cats is missing . . .*

Tori's head was spinning, and she could feel the room closing in around her . . . then Leo's arm was around her waist, steadying her.

'Don't panic, she can't have gone far,' said Leo, giving her a reassuring smile.

'He's right, love. She might be somewhere in here and we just can't see her. I'll keep looking,' said Joyce, giving Tori's hand a squeeze.

'Me too,' chorused Lara, 'cats are good at hiding. Domino got stuck under the dishwasher the other day and we didn't find him for ages.'

'Oh, bless you, Lara,' said Tori, forcing a smile. She took a deep breath and calmed herself. 'You're right, she must be around here somewhere,' she said, turning to Leo and automatically grabbing his hand.

'Why don't you and I head out to the green and see if she's made it out of the building? Lara and Joyce, can you keep looking inside in case she's hidden away somewhere we haven't looked yet?' said Leo.

'But what about this lot?' said Joyce, gesturing to the customers. 'Shouldn't we carry on serving?'

'Let's find Daisy first, then we'll worry about the customers,' said Tori decisively.

Tori and Leo made towards the lobby. As they approached, the door was flung open to reveal Claire, clearly out of breath, holding Daisy in her arms.

'Have you lost someone?' asked Claire.

'Daisy!' cried Tori, taking the little tortoiseshell from Claire and nuzzling her face in the cat's soft fur. 'Where did you find her?'

'I spotted her on the green when I was heading back to the salon. I thought she looked like one of yours and you were probably going frantic—'

'Oh, thank you!' said Tori, hugging Claire with her free arm. 'I was really starting to panic! I just don't understand how she could have got out; I mean she'd have to get through two sets of doors to make it out the front, it just doesn't make sense—'

'Oh, you know cats,' replied Claire, waving a hand. 'Ingenious little creatures, aren't they? Anyway, she's back safe and sound now, that's what matters.'

'You're right. I'd like to know how she managed it, though – I don't want it to happen again,' said Tori.

'Why don't we get Daisy settled inside and let Claire get on her way?' suggested Leo.

'Sorry, Claire, I know you said you were heading back to the salon, or I'd offer you lunch to say thank you. Why don't you stay next time, when you're not so busy?' said Tori.

'Did I? Oh, I've got plenty of time . . .'

'Perfect! Well, lunch is on me then, it's the least I can do. Why don't you join Leo and Lara? I'm just getting something for them too.'

'I'm sure Claire would rather—'

'I'd *love* to join you,' said Claire, interrupting Leo and slipping her arm through his. Tori noticed he looked decidedly uncomfortable all of a sudden.

'Well, that's decided then. Come and sit down and I'll get Daisy settled in,' said Tori, opening the internal door leading into the café.

As they walked back into the room, there were calls of 'Where did you find her?' from the regulars. Claire looked unsettled by all the attention and tried to brush it off by simply replying 'On the green.' Lara was eager to hear all about Daisy's rescue and the pair of them seemed to hit it off instantly. Tori couldn't say the same about Leo. As she watched from behind the coffee machine, she noticed Claire had inched her chair closer to his and was tossing her hair around flirtatiously. Leo looked unusually subdued and tight-lipped around her, which was weird given how friendly he usually seemed to be . . .

'Penny for them?' asked Joyce, returning to the counter and making Tori jump.

'You nearly gave me a heart attack!'

'You were miles away. Something on your mind?'

'No, not really,' said Tori, not quite meeting her mum's eye.

'Hmm, I'll wager it's something to do with a certain young man.' She nodded in Leo's direction. 'He seems like one of the good ones, you know.'

'You said that about Ryan and look where that got me.'

Joyce took a step back, visibly shaken by Tori's words. 'Oh, I'm sorry, Mum,' said Tori, her shoulders slumping. 'It's just been a stressful day already and I'm just a bit confused right now, to be honest.'

'Oh, love, come here,' said Joyce, wrapping an arm around her. 'No one's saying you need to go rushing into anything. But Leo's a good lad, that's all. You just need to see how he is with that niece of his to know that.'

'I know,' said Tori, nodding. 'We're just going to take things slow, see what happens. What harm can a date do?'

'Slow and steady often wins the race, love. I'm glad you're not writing him off because you're still hurting about Ryan.'

Tori wondered if her mum's advice might be different if she knew that Ryan had been in contact. She was right about Leo though. He was one of the good ones. Every moment she spent with him made that even clearer to her. She didn't want to let her experience with Ryan cloud her judgement, but she knew there was still something inside her that was warning her, holding her back. She was looking forward to having dinner with him on Thursday; perhaps spending some more time together on their own would help her to decide how she really felt about him ...

When Tori woke the following morning and switched on her phone, it pinged immediately with a message. She smiled when she saw it was from Rose. *Morning, hun I heard about what happened with Daisy yesterday, are you okay? I don't want to freak you out, but have you checked your Google reviews this morning?* She opened up the browser and typed *Cosy Cat Café* into the search bar, clicking on the reviews tab and saw that her average rating had dropped from 4.9 stars yesterday to 2.1. Rubbing her eyes, she looked at the screen again. 2.1? That couldn't be right. She scanned the most recent comments, which had been posted last night. *1.0 Terrible service, dreadful food and one of the cats even escaped during our visit! 1.2 What a joke this place is! Staff were distracted, too busy searching for a lost cat! 1.5 Dreadful place. Not hygienic having cats where food is served! Steer clear!*

She threw her phone down on to the bed and sank back into her pillow. That was it – the Cosy Cat was doomed. Doomed before it had even really got started. Surely no one was going to go out of their way to visit after reading those reviews? They made the place sound awful. Bad food ... unhygienic ... distracted staff ... and worst of all, they

implied she wasn't even able to keep the cats safe. *Oh God!*
She exhaled deeply and rubbed her temples. How could she
come back from this? She reached for her phone and called
Rose, who answered on the first ring.

'You've read them then?' Rose asked gently.

'Yep.' Tori let out a long, deep breath. 'I don't even know
what to say. They're awful, Rose, awful. They're right about
Daisy escaping, of course, but everything else is just, well,
it's just . . .'

'Lies!'

'Exactly! You don't think our food is bad, do you?'

'Not at all, it's bloomin' delicious.'

'Well, clearly some people do.'

'Not *some* people. *One* person.'

'What do you mean, *one* person? There's more than one
bad review.'

'Jake and I have got a theory . . .'

'Go on . . .'

'There's seven bad reviews and they were all left last
night, right?'

'Yep, looks like it.'

'Right, well, how likely do you think it is that seven
different customers yesterday went home and left a one-
star review?'

Tori paused while she considered the likelihood of that
happening. 'Erm, not very.'

'Exactly! And that's why Jake and I think all the reviews
were written by the same person.'

'But they're all under different names.'

'That doesn't mean anything, though, does it? I mean, anyone can open a fake email account and leave multiple reviews under made-up names. It would be easy enough. Plus, the way the reviews are worded, if you ask me, the same person wrote them all.'

'But who would do that? It's so mean.'

'Can't you think of anyone, Tori? No one that's been against the refurbishment from the start? Even used the word unhygienic when she was bad-mouthing the Cosy Cat at the meeting in the village hall?'

'You don't mean—'

'I do!'

'Violet?'

'Violet Davenport!' said Rose, with a touch of triumph in her voice.

'Seriously? You think she'd go that far?' asked Tori, squeezing her eyes shut.

'Why not? She's been against the cats from the start; there's no way she wants it to be a success. My guess is, she heard about what happened yesterday with Daisy and decided to use it to her advantage.'

'That bloody woman! I've absolutely had it with her!'

'You can't let her get away with it.'

'Oh, don't worry, I won't! I'm heading straight over there to have it out with her. Who does she think she is?'

'She thinks she runs the village. She could do with some-one standing up to her for once.'

'Thanks, Rose,' said Tori, her voice softening.

'For what?'

'For figuring it out. I don't think I'd have worked it out on my own.'

'You would have, and I spoke to your mum earlier – she agrees with me.'

'You did?'

'I had to talk to someone – you were still asleep.'

'I'll go and talk to her.'

'Try not to worry – it'll all sort itself out.'

'I hope so.'

'I *know* so.'

Tori pulled on her dressing gown, swept her hair up into a ponytail and rushed down the stairs, to find Joyce sat at the kitchen table, reading the newspaper, with a mug of coffee waiting for her.

'I know, I know,' said Joyce, holding up a hand to stop Tori before she could utter a word. 'I've spoken to Rose. Sit down and drink your coffee before you go flying off the handle, would you?'

Tori pulled out a chair opposite Joyce and plonked herself down. Taking a long, warming sip, she could feel the effects of the caffeine hitting the spot.

'What do you think, Mum? Could Violet be behind those reviews?'

'I have to admit, it does seem like a bit too much of a coincidence to me that all the bad reviews appeared in one evening. But do me a favour, love, don't go round there shouting the odds before you've got all the facts. We can't know for certain that it's her.'

'Who else in the village has got it in for me, though? It's got to be Violet,' said Tori, smoothing the tablecloth with her hand.

'Let's open up next door and you can have a think about what to do. Can you get the reviews taken down?' asked Joyce, getting up to refill her mug.

'I'm not sure – I'll look into it. I just hope it doesn't put people off, particularly if they're not from around here and wouldn't know the reviews are fake.'

'Let's not start worrying about things that haven't happened. We've got a café to run and cats to look after, in case you'd forgotten.'

'I'll get dressed and head next door. See you over there?' said Tori, standing up and making for the door.

'Right you are, love. But don't go stressing over this; Violet's not worth wasting your energy on.'

Tori nodded and muttered to herself. 'I wish it was that easy, Mum, I really do.'

By the time Joyce arrived at the café, Tori had fed the cats and was just about to start setting out the cakes in the glass display cabinet on the counter. Mr Wiggles had seemed more subdued than usual, but he'd eaten his breakfast and Tori decided to keep a watchful eye on him.

'Here, let me do that, love,' said Joyce, taking the tray from her. 'If you can pop the flowers on the table, we're almost ready to open.'

'No problem.' As Tori filled the final vase, she noticed Mr Wiggles walking oddly, staggering from side to side. 'Mum, there's something wrong with him,' cried Tori, rushing towards the cat, who had collapsed onto his side, panting heavily and looking dazed and confused. 'What's wrong, boy?' she said, dropping to her knees.

'Has he had a seizure maybe?' said Joyce, rushing to her side.

'I'll take him straight to Grace. Can you stay with him, Mum, while I grab his basket?' Tori sprinted to the supply cupboard at the back of the café and reached for the first cat basket she could find. By the time she'd returned to Mr Wiggles' side, the cat's breathing was starting to ease. 'How's he doing?'

'His breathing's a bit better but he's not right. He looks like he doesn't know where he is.'

'Come on, little man, let's get you to Grace,' Tori whispered as she scooped the large, black cat into her arms and placed him carefully into the wicker basket. He didn't even struggle as Tori lifted him inside, which worried her more than if he'd tried to take a chunk out of her.

As she dashed across the green to Brook House, she kept imagining the worst-case scenario. She knew Mr Wiggles was getting on a bit and had a thyroid problem, just like her mum, so what if there was nothing Grace could do? What if she was too late?

'Help!' Tori said breathlessly as she burst through the surgery doors. 'It's Mr Wiggles, I think he's had a seizure . . .'

'What happened?' said Tara, as she got up from behind her desk.

'Can I help?' asked a young woman dressed in scrubs that Tori didn't recognize, who had appeared through the double doors behind reception. 'I'm Kelly, the practice nurse.'

Tori explained what she'd seen: the staggering, the disorientation, the way Mr Wiggles didn't seem in control of his own limbs.

'That's really helpful, Tori, thanks. Grace is with another patient at the moment; let me just see if I can interrupt her. Pass him across to me,' said Kelly, her arms outstretched, as she disappeared through the set of doors to Grace's surgery.

Tori sat down silently on one of the plastic waiting-room chairs and tried to stay calm. What if something was seriously wrong with Mr Wiggles? Izzy had trusted her to look after him. She'd let her down ... she'd let everyone down. She kept going back to the evening her mum had collapsed at home ... what if ... *what if?* Her breathing was becoming more erratic now, her heart felt as though it was going to explode – if anything happened to Joyce ... She clutched the empty cat basket, she couldn't breathe ... she was having a heart attack—

'Tori? Are you okay?' Tori looked up to see Tara watching her, her face etched with concern. 'Tori, I think you might be having a panic attack. Here, take my arm, let's get you through to the staffroom ...'

'Now, just breathe into this for me,' said Tara, handing

Tori a brown paper bag. 'Long, deep breaths ... like this,' she said, taking a long, slow, deep breath in herself to demonstrate. Tori followed suit and began breathing into the bag slowly, taking steadying breaths. 'That's it,' said Tara encouragingly. 'How are you feeling? Better?' Tori nodded and slowly removed the paper bag from her mouth.

'I think so ... I'm so sorry, I don't know what happened.'

'Don't worry, you've had a stressful start to the morning, Mr Wiggles giving you a scare like that. Let me grab you a cuppa with lots of sugar.'

'Do you really think that was a panic attack? Nothing like that's ever happened to me before. I thought I was having a heart attack ...'

'That's exactly how it can feel; they're pretty scary if you don't know what's happening. Here, drink this,' she said, passing Tori a mug, 'it'll help.'

'Wow! How many sugars are in this?' Tori said, wincing.

'It'll do you good. Drink up! You know, I'm loving what you've done with the Cosy Cat, by the way. Those new kiwi and mango smoothies are delicious.'

'Thank you, that's good to know.'

'I love that you've kept all the old favourites, though – I do love Joyce's cream teas, you can't beat them. It still feels like the same old Cosy Cup.'

'Mum's cream teas are the best,' said Tori with a smile.

'In the whole of Sussex! Right, I'll go and see what's happening with Mr Wiggles.' Just as Tara turned to leave, Grace entered the room.

Julie Haworth

'Tori, there you are. Everything okay?' Grace asked. 'You look pale.'

'I'm fine now, I just had a bit of a panic attack. Tara's been looking after me. I feel fine now, honestly,' she replied, taking another mouthful of tea.

'Are you sure? I can always give Dr Marshall a call?' said Grace, taking a seat next to her.

'No need, honestly, I'm fine,' Tori reassured her, 'but what about Mr Wiggles? How's he doing?'

'Right, well, from the symptoms you described, it could be a few things. It could be as simple as a touch of dehydration right through to something a bit more serious.'

'Oh God, that sounds bad . . .'

'Well, let's not panic just yet. I'd like to keep him in this afternoon to run a few basic blood tests, if that's okay? He does seem a little dehydrated and, like I said, it could be that simple. Kelly's with him and getting him hooked up to a drip, but right now he seems fine, like nothing ever happened.'

'Okay, well, please do whatever you need to to get to the bottom of it, Grace. I don't care how much it costs.'

'I'll give you a call once we've got the blood work back as that will give us a clearer picture of what's going on. There's no point speculating until we've got all the facts. I'll fill Izzy in for you too.'

'I can't tell you how much it means that you were able to see him so quickly, I know how busy you are. It's just such a relief to know he's in good hands.'

'Ah, don't mention it, it's all part of the service.'

'Shall I head back to the café and wait for your call?'

'Please. I know it's easier said than done, but try not to worry. You making yourself ill too isn't going to be any use to Mr Wiggles, you know.'

'I'll try,' said Tori as she got up to leave. 'I'll keep everything crossed for some good news later and thanks again for all your help.'

The bad Google reviews certainly didn't appear to have affected business that morning. If anything, they seemed even busier than normal. All the regulars were in, as well as some new faces Tori didn't recognize. Perhaps the social media posts were starting to have an impact? Tori began to think that maybe it wasn't worth confronting Violet Davenport after all. The door to the café chimed and Tori looked up to see Cora waiting in the lobby. She picked up her order pad and hurried over to greet her.

'Cora! How lovely to see you! I wanted to apologize for—'

'Apologize? If anyone needs to say sorry, it's me,' said Cora as she followed Tori to her usual table and sat down.

'You? But I—'

'You were trying to be kind, Tori, and I jumped down your throat,' said Cora, hanging her head.

'I just thought that—'

'I know what you thought. You're right, I do love the cats and you thought adopting one of them might be a bit of company for me?' Tori nodded. 'Listen, if you've got time, can you get me my usual and perhaps today you could make it tea for two? If you can join me, that is?'

'I'd love to. Just give me a minute and I'll be right back,' said Tori as she hurried through to the kitchen to get Cora's order ready. She thought she'd mortally offended her yesterday and now the mysterious stranger who had shied away from revealing anything about herself was offering to have tea with her.

'How's Mr Wiggles?' Joyce asked, as Tori walked into the kitchen.

'Grace is running some tests; we should know something soon. She's said not to worry.'

'That's easier said than done.'

'I know,' said Tori, nodding. 'Let's try and keep busy, though.'

'Is that Cora?' asked Joyce, glancing up to the window in the connecting door. 'She's right on time as usual, I've got her order ready.'

'Thanks, Mum – could you throw an extra teabag in the pot? She's asked me to join her!'

'Really? Well, wonders never cease,' said Joyce, as she lifted the lid of the teapot and threw in another bag. 'There you go, love.' Tori smiled and placed a second cup and saucer on the tray before heading back to Cora's table.

'Thank you for joining me, dear. I really do owe you an apology after the way I spoke to you yesterday—'

'Oh no, it's fine. I was the one who—'

'I'd like to explain,' said Cora, holding up a hand to silence her. Tori nodded and drank her tea. 'Let me start at the beginning.' Cora took a deep breath, as if to steady herself. 'I only arrived in Blossom Heath recently; I've moved into Lavender Cottage, it's on the outskirts of the village. Do you know it?' Tori nodded. The cottage was in the row next to Jasmine Cottage and had been a holiday let for years; she wasn't sure she ever remembered it having a permanent resident. 'I wanted somewhere quiet, you see, after Dennis . . .' Her voice trailed off and Tori could see Cora's eyes misting with tears.

'Dennis?' she whispered.

'My husband of forty-five years. I lost him last year . . . cancer, you see.'

'Oh, Cora, I'm so sorry, I didn't know.'

'How could you? I've barely left the cottage since I arrived. Dennis and I bought the place years ago as an investment. We've been letting it out to tourists, but we planned to retire here ourselves.'

'I see,' said Tori solemnly.

'I've been keeping myself to myself since I moved in. It didn't seem right somehow, settling in without Dennis. But when this place reopened, I found I just couldn't stay away.'

'You wanted to see the cats?'

Cora nodded.

'Dennis and I had a little Ragdoll called Dolly; she was always more Dennis's cat than mine, though. The pair of them doted on each other. Wherever Dennis was, you'd find Dolly. She passed away a few weeks after I lost Dennis, kidney failure.' Cora pulled a tissue out of her leather hand-bag and wiped her eyes.

'Oh, I'm so sorry. I don't know what to say,' said Tori, reaching across the table and placing a hand over Cora's.

'The place doesn't seem right without her, but when you suggested adopting another cat, I just, I'm not—'

'Ready?' Tori asked gently.

'Exactly. I've had so much loss in my life recently, the thought of falling for another cat, who might not be around for long either ... it would just be too much.' Cora sat up straight and adjusted the collar of her blouse.

'I can understand that. I'm sorry I put pressure on you yesterday; if I'd known I never would have suggested it,' said Tori, swallowing hard. She just hoped Cora didn't ask her where Mr Wiggles was today; she couldn't bear the thought of having to break the news that he was unwell too.

'Like I said, you couldn't have known.'

'Well, you'll always find a warm welcome from the cats here, whenever you want to spend time with them.'

'Thank you,' said Cora, her smile lighting up her face. 'I have to ask you, dear, who is that ginger cat I see through the window some mornings?' she asked, pointing towards Ernie. 'He likes to make an appearance, now and again. Is he one of yours?'

'Ah, that's Ernie,' said Tori. 'He's my cat, he lives at home with us, but he likes to check in on us at the café.'

'Well, he's a beautiful boy, you're very lucky.'

'Thank you – I really am.'

'I must say, sitting here for an hour or so every day with a cat on my lap, watching the world go by, has helped me so much.'

'I'm glad,' smiled Tori. 'You know, there's much more to living here than just the café, though.' She hesitated slightly before continuing. 'Stop me if I'm pushing again, but I'm sure there are plenty of people in Blossom Heath who would love to get to know you . . .' Tori's voice trailed off as Cora held up a hand.

'I think just sitting with the cats is all I'm ready for now.'

'Fair enough, but if you change your mind, let me know. I'm sure the local WI would be thrilled to have you.'

'Well, if their cake-making skills are anything like your mum's, I'll have to give them a try. Oh, and Tori?'

'Yes?'

'Don't listen to a word of those Google reviews – they're absolute nonsense if you ask me.'

'You've seen them?' said Tori, her jaw clenching.

'I overheard someone in Harrison's talking about them, but like I said, absolute nonsense. Oh, and can you put my change straight in the collection tin.'

'Thanks Cora, I know the cat rescue centre will really appreciate that.'

Absolute nonsense. Cora's words rang in Tori's ears for the rest of the day. The fact that Cora had chosen to share her story with Tori had meant a lot to her. She'd been through so much in such a short space of time and Tori was glad that

287

spending time at the café was helping to restore her spirits. Wasn't that what the Cosy Cat was partly about? Trying to lift people's spirits and put a smile on their faces? She checked her phone and saw a message from Kate. *Don't worry about those silly reviews, you're doing a brilliant job and anyone with an ounce of sense knows it! x.* Tori smiled; she was grateful to have friends that she could count on when the chips were down. Although she still hadn't heard anything from Leo – perhaps he was still at work?

After the lunchtime rush had passed, an anxious Tori realized there'd been no news from Grace about Mr Wiggles, so it was with a shaky hand that she dialled the surgery's number.

'Hi, Tara. It's Tori. I just wanted to check in to see if there was any update on Mr Wiggles?'

'Grace is with a client right now, but I don't think we've had his blood results back yet. Hang on, let me double-check … Nope, nothing yet but he's awake and alert and he's had some food.'

'That sounds positive.'

'As soon as the bloods come back, I'll ask Grace to give you a call.'

'Thanks, Tara, I really appreciate that. Sorry to chase you, but you know what it's like when you're waiting for your phone to ring.'

'Oh, absolutely. Don't worry about it.'

'Thanks again and thank you for looking after me this morning,' said Tori, ending the call.

As she flipped the café's sign to 'Closed' later that evening, Tori decided that she had a stop to make before she could go home. Violet Davenport's house.

Chapter 29

As Tori walked towards the bottle-green door of Violet's tiny, thatched cottage, her stomach felt as though it was being squeezed in a vice. Was she doing the right thing? She didn't have any evidence that Violet was the one behind the Google reviews, but that was certainly what Rose and Jake thought. And her mum. It seemed unlikely they'd all got it wrong. Sometimes you just had to go with your gut. She took a deep breath and tapped the brass door knocker hard. She heard footsteps shuffling towards the door before it creaked open slowly.

'Yes,' said Violet sharply, when she spotted Tori on her doorstep.

'Mrs Davenport,' said Tori, drawing herself up to her full height and throwing her shoulders back. 'As I'm sure you're aware, someone has left some rather unflattering reviews for the café on Google . . .'

'I don't know what you're talking about, but I'm sure they're perfectly justified, if the way I was treated on my last visit is anything to go by,' replied Violet, folding her arms across her chest.

'It seems likely that these reviews were left by just *one* person, someone who has a grievance against the café perhaps; someone who didn't want us to open in the first place ...' Tori nodded curtly and stood waiting for a response.

'I hope you're not implying that *I'm* the one responsible?' asked Violet, her face reddening.

'That's exactly what I'm implying,' replied Tori, doing her best to keep her voice calm and steady.

'Well, I've never ... never been so ... *insulted*. How dare you come to my door throwing around unfounded accusations, Tori Baxter! Who do you think you are?'

'I just want you to think about all the trouble you're causing, Violet. We're trying to make the café a successful business and I don't want to see that ruined by some stupid vendetta you seem to have against it.'

'I can assure you that *if* I had a vendetta against your ridiculous business, you'd be the first to know about it. I wouldn't go skulking around leaving anonymous reviews. I'd proudly put my name to them.' Violet's face looked almost purple now. The last thing Tori wanted was for her to burst a blood vessel and keel over on the doorstep.

'You can deny it all you like, Violet; I just wanted to let you know that this stops right now. The cat café is very much here to stay, so you may as well get used to it.' With those words, Tori turned abruptly and strode off down the lane, leaving Violet Davenport very much lost for words.

*

'I can't believe you had it out with her,' said Rose as she let Tori into Jasmine Cottage. Tori wanted to calm down before heading home. She didn't want her mum to know she'd ignored her advice and confronted Violet on her own doorstep.

'Neither can I,' said Tori, slumping down on the sofa as Rose returned from the kitchen with a pot of tea.

'Don't get me wrong, I'm glad you did, it's just so out of character.'

'Let's just say the *new* me stands up for herself a little bit more than the old me used to,' said Tori, tucking her legs underneath her.

'Good. I'm glad. For what it's worth, I've always believed in you,' said Rose, seriously.

'Ah, but you're my best friend – that's your job,' said Tori, as Rose poured her some tea.

'You've had an epic showdown so I've added extra sugar,' said Rose, passing her the mug.

'That's the second cuppa I've had today overloaded with sugar, I'll be bouncing off the walls soon,' said Tori, taking a large swig. 'Mmm, I needed that.'

'Me too; running around after a class of eight-year-olds usually has me ready to collapse in a heap by six o'clock.'

'Honestly, I don't know how you do it.'

'Oh, I love it really. It's just been a long week. What are you up to tonight? Fancy the pub with me and Grace?'

'I'm waiting on a call from Grace actually – Mr Wiggles is with her. He had a funny turn today, so she's running tests,' Tori explained.

'Oh no! I hope it's nothing serious. When will you know?'

'I'll give her another call before I leave here,' said Tori, checking her phone again.

'Listen, if you're not up for the pub tonight, I totally get it.'

'I can't, I've got plans tonight . . .' Tori looked away, unable to meet Rose's eye.

'Who with?' asked Rose.

'Erm . . .' Tori pulled at a loose thread on her sleeve.

'With Leo?'

'Erm . . .' Tori hesitated.

'It *is* with Leo, isn't it? I can tell by your face!'

'Okay, it *is* with Leo,' replied Tori.

'I knew it!' yelped Rose gleefully.

'Oh, stop! You're as bad as Mum. She did a terrible job of hiding her excitement when I told her this morning.'

'I thought something's been going on between the pair of you for the last couple of weeks . . .'

'It's nothing really. I mean, we've only kissed once—'

'What? You've kissed? How did I not know this?' asked Rose, leaping up off the sofa. 'This is *huge*!'

'But you just said you knew there was something going on!'

'Oh, I was bluffing,' said Rose, tutting. 'I can't believe you've actually kissed! I totally called it,' she squealed.

'Alright it's just a kiss, that's all. We've not even been on a proper date yet.'

'But tonight's an official date?' asked Rose.

'Yeah, I guess so,' said Tori.

'You could sound a bit more excited about it, you know,' Rose said reproachfully.

'Oh, I am, or at least I think I am,' said Tori, 'but all this stuff with Violet has got me kinda preoccupied and I'm so worried about Mr Wiggles.' Tori glanced at her phone again.

'Where's he taking you then?'

'Who?'

'Leo, of course!'

'That new fish place in Rye, oh, what's it called ...'

'The Purple Prawn?'

'Yep, that's the one,' said Tori, nodding.

'Fancy! It's supposed to be lovely – gorgeous food and very romantic,' said Rose, raising her eyebrows suggestively.

'Oi! Stop!' said Tori, making a face.

'Oh, I'm pleased for you, you deserve a good night out with someone who gets your pulse racing.'

'Hmm, well, don't get too excited yet, let's see how things go, shall we?'

'It's going to be great, I can feel it in my bones, and my instincts on these things are never wrong.'

'There's always a first time,' muttered Tori under her breath. 'Listen, Rose, there's something I've not told you – I've had a message from Ryan.'

'What?' said Rose, sitting bolt upright. 'When? What did he say?'

'He commented on one of my Instagram posts and DM'd

me.' She fished her phone out of her bag and pulled up the message. 'It just says *I miss you*.'

'Well, of course he does; he was a bloody idiot to let you go in the first place. Have you replied?'

'No, I don't even know what I'd say.'

'How do you feel about things? Now you've heard from him, I mean.'

'Even more confused. I was just starting to get excited about seeing Leo and then Ryan decides to slide into my DMs.'

'Well, forget about him – for tonight at least. Go out and have a great time with Leo and see where your head's at afterwards. You don't have to reply to Ryan – it's your call, Tori.'

'Thanks. I think not replying is the best decision I can make right now. I'm just going to put Ryan and his stupid message out of my head,' she said determinedly. 'Do you think I should ring Grace again? It's been over an hour since I spoke to Tara.'

As if on cue, Tori's phone started ringing and she could see from the caller ID that it was Grace. She flashed the screen at Rose, who mouthed 'Spooky!'

'Grace! Any news? Is he okay, he's not—'

'Don't panic, it's good news – his bloods have come back normal, so I think dehydration might well be the cause of his episode.'

'Everything's normal, you're sure?' Tori felt her shoulders relax.

'For a cat of his age, he's actually in good shape.'

'But dehydration, that still sounds bad.'

'Cats can be reluctant drinkers, even when fresh water is on offer. If they're eating a diet of mainly dry food, they can get dehydrated quickly. It doesn't take much.'

'And that could really have caused what happened today?'

'Definitely. I can't completely rule out anything else, but if there is something neurological going on, he'll likely have another episode and if that happens, I'll refer him on to a specialist.'

'So, just wait and see and hope it's a one-off?'

'Exactly. I'm going to send you a couple of links to drinking fountains for cats; some cats prefer to drink from flowing water, which might encourage him to drink more frequently.'

'Ernie has one of those at home – he loves it! I don't know why I didn't think to get one for the café. Thanks, Grace, honestly, I can't tell you what a relief it is to know there's nothing seriously wrong.'

'You can come and pick him up whenever you're ready – he's itching to go home,' Grace laughed.

'Aw, bless him. I can't wait to see him. I'll be straight over to collect him and pay the bill. Thanks again for today,' said Tori, ending the call.

'Well?' said Rose, leaning in towards her.

'It's good news. All his bloods are normal. Grace thinks it could just be dehydration, so I'll order some water fountains so he drinks more.'

'That sounds promising, though, right? Something easily fixed?'

Tori nodded. 'Let's hope so,' she said, crossing her fingers.

'Do you mind if I get going? I want to go and pick him up. By the sound of it, he's itching to come home.'

'No, of course not, I'd be the same if it was Scout. And good luck for your date; I want to hear all the juicy details.'

'Okay,' said Tori, embracing Rose tightly. 'Thanks for today, talking's helped. I'm lucky to have you.'

'Likewise.'

When Tori arrived back home with Mr Wiggles, Joyce was waiting to greet them. Tori had called ahead to let her mum know that he'd had the all-clear from Grace, but Joyce had insisted on staying on at the café after closing to welcome Mr Wiggles home.

'Oh, there he is,' said Joyce, pressing her hand against the metal grille at the front of the carrier to give Mr Wiggles a scratch.

'He's loving that, I can hear him purring already,' laughed Tori.

'Thank God it was nothing serious. We'll just have to cross everything that we don't have a repeat performance.'

'I don't know why I didn't think to get water fountains for here, especially given how much Ernie loves his. I'm going to order a couple tonight and hopefully he'll be tempted to drink more,' said Tori, opening the basket to release Mr Wiggles. Angel trotted over and he rubbed his head against hers, purring loudly.

'Aw, how lovely. She's certainly pleased to see him,' said Joyce, smiling.

'She's not the only one; I couldn't wait to get him back home either.'

'Oh, I'm so attached to all of them now; I think I'm going to find it harder and harder each time one of them is adopted.'

'I know what you mean, but we're just a stepping stone for them on the way to their new lives, aren't we?'

'That's a great way of looking at it, love. A stepping stone,' Joyce repeated.

'And Izzy will always have new cats for us to take that need a helping hand too.'

'True. But I still think I'll shed a tear when Mr Wiggles leaves for his forever home.'

'Me too; he's made quite the impression already.'

'Oh, what are we like, love? said Joyce, pulling a tissue out of her sleeve and blowing her nose hard. 'Now don't you have a date that you need to be getting ready for?'

Tori had spent over an hour getting ready for her date with Leo. Finding the right outfit had been far more difficult than she'd imagined. She wanted to look her best but nothing she'd pulled out of the wardrobe so far felt quite right. Why hadn't she bought something new? She cursed under her breath. She had planned to wear her favourite blue and white dress but was horrified to find she couldn't zip it up. All those cakes at the café must be catching up with her. There was a tap on her bedroom door.

'How's it going, love?' asked Joyce.

'Don't ask,' Tori huffed. 'I was going to wear that blue and white dress, but it won't even do up!'

'Well, you can't do anything about that now. Let's find you something that will blow Leo's socks off.'

'Unless he goes for girls in jeans and old T-shirts, I'm going to be out of luck,' replied Tori, shrugging.

'Have you looked in that wardrobe in the spare room? I'm sure there's some of your old dresses hanging up.'

'I don't think so, Mum. I binned a ton of stuff before I went travelling.'

'Ah, you *thought* you binned a load of stuff, but I kept a few bits that I thought you might want to wear again . . .'

'*Really?* Oh, Mum, thank you!' cried Tori, leaping up from the bed and kissing her mother on the cheek. 'Come on, let's take a look.' Tori headed to the spare room, flung open the wardrobe doors and began looking through the clothes that were hanging on the rail. 'No, no, *God no,*' she said, making a face. 'I'm not sure there's anything here . . .'

'Keep looking, there must be something.'

'Hang on, what's this? Oh yeah,' she said, shooting Joyce a smile. 'I remember this dress!' Tori pulled a short black chiffon dress out of the wardrobe that was covered in tiny white flowers. 'I used to love this one.'

'I remember. Why do you think I took it out of the rubbish pile?'

'Mum, you're a lifesaver,' said Tori, turning to give her mum another kiss on the cheek. 'Let's hope it fits,' she continued, racing back to her bedroom and closing the door.

'Well? How does it look?' Joyce called through the door after a few minutes had passed.

'Ta-dah!' said Tori, as the bedroom door opened.

'Oh, Tori, you look beautiful.'

'You don't think it's too tight? It *is* pretty snug.'

'Not at all, it looks lovely.'

'Looks like we have a winner then,' said Tori, breathing a sigh of relief.

'It'll go well with those black sandals you've got.'

'Oh, they'll be perfect, yes,' said Tori, rummaging under her bed to fish the shoes out. She slipped them on and applied a fresh coat of mascara to finish her make-up off. She looked at herself in the mirror and took a deep breath. There was a knock at the front door. 'He's here!' Tori grabbed her clutch bag and stuffed her phone inside.

'Well, you best be off. Remember, Leo's a lovely boy, there's no need for you to be nervous.'

'Thanks, Mum.' Tori ran down the stairs as quickly as her heels would allow and opened the front door. As soon as she saw Leo, she felt her heart race. He was wearing a crisp, pale blue shirt, which matched his eyes perfectly, a pair of tan chinos and he smelt of fruity, citrus tones. He took a step backwards when he saw her.

'Wow, Tori, you look amazing.' He smoothed down his hair and straightened his collar. Was it possible he was feeling nervous too?

'Thanks,' she said. 'You don't scrub up so badly either, you know.'

He laughed, the lines around his eyes creasing.

'Ready?'

'Ready!' she said, grabbing her keys from the hall table. This was it. Her first date since she'd split with Ryan and she couldn't think of anyone she'd rather be on it with. She was really doing it and it felt great.

When they got out of the taxi in Rye, Leo automatically reached for her hand and slipped it into his.

'I'm still in shock, you know,' he said, turning to face her.

'About what?'

'That you finally agreed to go on a date with me. You were pretty elusive for a while there, you know,' he chuckled.

'Yeah, well, I . . .' she said, looking down at her feet.

'Hey, I didn't mean that in a bad way,' he said quickly, placing a hand gently under her chin and lifting her head.

'No, I know. Well, we're here now,' she said, stepping towards him, 'and just in case you're in any doubt about how I feel . . .' She placed her arms around his neck and kissed him. It was everything she had hoped it would be, she could feel Leo's body pressed up against hers and all she wanted was to stay in this moment, right here, right now, for as long as she could. When they finally broke apart, she was breathless.

'That was unexpected,' said Leo, pushing her hair off her face.

'I don't know what came over me,' she muttered.

'Well, whatever it was, I'm glad,' he said, leaning forward to kiss her again. 'Are you sure we have to go to dinner? We could just go back to mine . . .'

'Hey!' She tapped him playfully on the arm with her clutch bag. 'Let's have dinner first, see where the evening takes us.'

'Shall we go and find this restaurant then?' he said, taking her by the hand.

'Let's, I'm starving,' she agreed.

The waiter seated them at a window table in the Purple Prawn, and Tori's eyes widened as she scanned the room and took in her surroundings. The walls were painted in various shades of lilac, cream and purple and adorned with brass sea creatures. Across the whole of the back wall, the words *Go Wild Under the Sea* were stencilled in huge white letters. The tables were set with tiny purple lanterns and napkins with lobsters printed on them in gold leaf.

'Wow! This place is amazing,' she said as the waiter handed them menus.

'It's got really good reviews; I've been wanting to try it for ages. It's pretty ... quirky,' Leo said, looking around the room.

'I love how they've done it out; it's got such a great vibe.'

'I'm glad you like it,' said Leo, reaching across the table for her hand.

'I do. Thanks for organizing tonight.'

'Seafood's always a winner in my book. You can't live by the coast and not love it, right?'

'Absolutely. Let's get a look at this menu and see what sounds good.'

After devouring starters of king prawns and crab and a

main course of lobster and scallops, Tori felt as though she couldn't eat another thing. The food was as amazing as Leo promised it would be.

'I can't believe I've eaten so much! I won't fit in the cab on the way home at this rate,' she said, clutching her stomach.

'Hardly! You look stunning,' said Leo, giving her a look that made her insides soar.

'You don't look so bad yourself.'

'I'll take that,' said Leo, squeezing her hand. 'How are things going with the barn dance, by the way? I keep meaning to ask. I know I've not been much help; work has been keeping me pretty busy recently.'

'Oh, don't worry. The planning is coming along nicely; Mum's been a great help and Rose and Grace are pitching in too. It's all under control.'

'Good to know,' said Leo. 'Let me know if there's anything I can do.'

'I will. I'm guessing you know Rye well if this is where you're based for work?'

'Pretty well, although I don't get as much time to explore as I'd like while I'm working.'

'Too many cats-in-tree emergencies to deal with?' she said playfully, taking another glug of her wine.

'Rye has more emergencies to deal with than you might think for such a small town . . .'

'Like?'

'Well, road traffic accidents for starters; we get called out to some pretty nasty ones with all the narrow country lanes around here. The locals drive too fast, and the tourists don't know the roads which means . . .'

'Oh God, Leo, sorry, I didn't think. That must be awful. I honestly can't imagine dealing with something like that. I'd go to pieces.'

'It's what we're trained for, I guess, but it can be a lot to deal with sometimes. Certain incidents can just . . . well, they leave a mark.' She noticed the muscles around his jaw line tighten and she reached across the table and took his hand.

'It's amazing work you do, though, helping so many people.'

'We try to,' he nodded, his lips tightening. 'Listen, do you mind if we change the subject? I'd rather forget about work for tonight.'

'Oh, sorry, yes of course,' she said quickly. I didn't mean to—'

'Don't be sorry,' he said. 'I like that you want to know more about what I do, but let's focus on us, shall we?'

'Well, I'd say tonight's gone well, wouldn't you?' she asked, her voice cracking a little. 'Good wine, good food . . . excellent company.'

'I always knew it would, if I could get you to agree to come on a date with me,' he laughed, his eyes shining brightly in the candlelight from the lantern.

'What can I say? You wore me down!' she laughed.

'Hey!' Leo replied, pulling a face.

'I'm sorry, I'm sorry,' she said, leaning forwards and pecking him on the cheek.

'Can I be totally honest with you?' he said, looking serious.

Tori nodded. 'I don't want to play games, so I want to put all my cards on the table.' He took a deep breath. 'I really like you and I think we've got a shot at having something great together. I've not got the best dating history, but I've never felt like this before.'

Tori paused, unsure how to respond. She wasn't expecting such a declaration from Leo; it flummoxed her a bit.

'I, I . . .'

'Look, I know you've just come out of a relationship, and I don't want to put any pressure on you, but I wanted to let you know how I'm feeling. If you want to give this a go, I'm all in. I don't want you to have any doubt about where my heart is . . .'

'I appreciate the honesty,' she said, tilting her head to one side. 'I think we've got great chemistry. I just don't want to rush things, that's all. I've only been home a few weeks and, I guess, I'm still figuring things out. So much has happened since I've been back. How about we start by having a second date and seeing where things go?'

'I can live with that,' he said, smiling. 'If *you* plan it, that is. Although I'm not sure you'll be able to top this place,' he said, holding up his hands.

'Ooh, is that a challenge?' He nodded at her. 'Now I really will have to get my thinking cap on.'

As they walked back to the taxi rank hand in hand, Tori felt truly content. Leo's cards on the table speech had gone a long way to quashing any doubts she had about getting involved again so soon after Ryan. Not many men were brave enough to say what they were really feeling. It was refreshing. It was surprising. It was *hot*. She stopped, pulling Leo towards her, and kissing him hard. The temptation to go back to his place tonight was overwhelming and the touch of his lips against hers was electric.

'See, I told you we had great chemistry,' she said breathlessly. He ran his index finger down the side of her neck and her whole body shivered.

'I agree,' he said huskily. 'I'm so glad you came back to Blossom Heath, Tori.'

'Me too. Shall we go and find this cab then?' she laughed.

Tori and Leo spent the taxi ride home hand in hand. As they pulled up outside Leo's front door, they found they didn't want to let go, much to the annoyance of the driver, who tutted noisily and turned up the radio.

'Sorry,' said Leo sheepishly, 'I can't resist one more kiss.'

'Me neither,' Tori giggled.

'I won't invite you in, not because I don't want to,' he added quickly, 'but because, well, you know . . .'

'Thanks, I appreciate that. I'll call you tomorrow?'

'Only if I don't call you first,' he said, as he hopped out of the cab. Tori watched him walk up the path and let out a long, deep sigh of contentment. She felt happy, properly happy, which had seemed like a complete impossibility only a few weeks ago.

'Where to next, love?' the cab driver asked.

'Oh, sorry. The Cosy Cat Café, please.'

'Right you are.'

The short ride back to the café was over in minutes and, as she picked up her bag and exited the car, Tori thought she could see a figure in the doorway.

'Hello?' she asked, squinting in an attempt to see more clearly. 'Is there someone there?' The figure stepped out of the shadows towards her.

'Tori, hi. It's me, Ryan.'

Chapter 30

Ryan? *What?* But it couldn't be, surely? Tori took a step backwards, shaking her head. She felt winded, as though she'd been punched in the stomach.

'Ryan? What the . . .' She took another step backwards as he moved towards her and stumbled, losing her footing. Ryan grabbed her arm to steady her.

'Yes, Tori, it's me,' he said, his teeth flashing in the light from the café, a stark contrast to his tanned skin.

'But why are you here?' she asked, snatching her arm out of his grasp.

'I know,' he shrugged, 'it's crazy, isn't it?'

'But I don't understand why you're here?'

'I've missed you, Tori. These last couple of months without you have been hell. I've realized I made a terrible mistake—'

'No!' she shouted. 'You don't get to just turn up here in the middle of the night and say you've missed me. Things are over between us; you made that pretty clear when you dumped me five thousand miles from home!' Her eyes flashed with rage.

'I was an idiot, Tori, I didn't know what I was doing. Things were getting so serious between us, I just got scared. I knew marriage and kids was the next step and I just ... panicked.'

'So what's changed?'

'I still love you, Tori. Isn't that all that matters?'

She stared at him, unable to articulate a response. Her brain was whirring, trying to process his words. Less than five minutes ago, she'd been kissing Leo. And now?

'Why don't we go inside, I'll explain.'

'No way,' she said, pushing him away.

'Don't be silly, Tori. It's nearly eleven o'clock, I've been on a flight for hours, where am I supposed to go? My bags are—'

'Not my problem,' she said, folding her arms.

'Come on, Tori, you can't just leave me out on the street all night!'

'The Apple Tree's still open. If you hurry, you'll make it before closing, they'll have rooms for the night.'

'Whatever you want. I know it's a shock, me turning up like this, but when you didn't reply to messages, I just knew I had to—'

'Goodnight,' she said, opening the front door and slamming it behind her. Whatever else he had to say, she didn't want to hear it. The nerve of him, showing up on her doorstep like that, after everything that had happened. 'Arrrgggggh!' she yelled.

'Tori, is that you?' said Joyce, from the top of the stairs. 'What on earth's going on?'

'Oh, Mum, I'm sorry, I didn't mean to wake you,' cried Tori, running up the stairs.

'What's wrong? What's happened? Is it Leo?'

'No, the date was great. But when I got home . . . you won't believe who . . .' Anger was coursing through her, she couldn't find the right words.

Joyce pulled her into a gentle hug. 'Take some long, deep breaths . . .' Joyce breathed deeply and Tori followed suit. 'That's it, love . . . in . . . and out.' Tori's breathing began to regulate. 'Let's go and put the kettle on and you can tell me everything.'

With a cup of soothing chamomile tea inside her, Tori was feeling calm enough to tell her about Ryan's arrival back in Blossom Heath.

'I thought I heard the doorbell go earlier, but I was upstairs. It must have been Ryan. It's a lot to get your head around, that's for sure,' said Joyce, opening a packet of chocolate digestives. 'How do you feel about seeing him?'

'I honestly don't know. Six weeks ago, if you'd told me Ryan would be flying halfway around the world to tell me he still loved me, I'd have been overjoyed. But now?' She shrugged and rested her head on a hand. 'The nerve of him . . . just as I'm starting to move on.'

'I know,' said Joyce. 'He's certainly picked his moment. You don't have to make any decisions about what you want to do now though, do you? The two of you were together a long time, and he owes you an explanation, but he's got no right to put any pressure on you.'

'I genuinely don't know how I feel.'

'I think anyone would be confused – it's only natural, love,' said Joyce, getting up to answer the landline phone, which was ringing. 'Who the hell is that at this time of night?'

Tori could hear muffled voices coming from the other room. *No, I know, she's already seen him . . . yes . . . thanks for letting us know.*

'Who was that?' asked Tori, blowing her nose, as Joyce sat back down, digging into the biscuits.

'Oh, just Beth. Ryan's turned up looking for a room for the night and she wanted to make sure you knew he was back. Didn't want you to have any nasty surprises in the morning. She said she had half a mind to send him packing after the way he treated you, though.'

Tori forced a weak smile. 'I wish she had,' she said.

'Oh, and she's got a ton of fallen apples for us; I can finally get batch baking those apple pies this weekend.'

'That's kind of her.'

'Now, why don't we head to bed. We're going to have a busy day tomorrow.'

Tori grabbed the packet of biscuits and shoved them in her pocket. Somehow, she didn't think she'd be getting much sleep at all tonight.

As Leo kicked off his shoes and slumped down on the sofa, beer in hand, he couldn't stop thinking about how great Tori was. What a first date! He'd been on his fair share of dates, but he'd never felt as nervous as he had tonight. There was something about being with Tori that made him feel as though anything was possible. He really admired the way she'd picked herself up since being back home, she had something special about her – passion, drive . . . *a spark*.

He picked up his phone – was it too soon to message her? *Probably*, he thought, shaking his head. He scrolled through his Instagram, and a new notification popped up. *The Cosy Cat Café has added to their story*. He smiled and clicked through to a selfie of Tori with Angel; the caption read: *Don't forget all the cats at the café are adoptable*. He loved Tori's passion for the café, the way her face lit up whenever she talked about it made her enthusiasm infectious. All he wanted was to be near her; she was gorgeous, obviously, but the way he felt about her ran much deeper than purely physical attraction. There was a connection, something he'd not experienced before, with anyone, *ever*. He could talk to her, really talk to her. He found himself starting to open up in a way he'd never felt comfortable doing before. It didn't feel scary with Tori, though, and he found she was a great listener too. He knew he needed to tread carefully and take things slow; the last thing he wanted to do was to scare her off or come on too strong. But he was glad that he'd laid his cards on the table and told her how he felt. He wasn't going to rush things and, as he switched off his phone and headed up the stairs to bed, he knew in his heart that Tori was the woman he was ready to start building a future with.

*

By the time Tori arrived at work the next morning, news of Ryan's return to Blossom Heath had already spread around the village like wildfire and it wasn't long before the man himself showed his face at the café door. As Tori let him in, a hush descended across the room.

'Not here,' Tori hissed. 'I've got work to do – I can't talk now.'

'When then? You've got to give me a chance to explain—'

'How dare you! I don't have to give you a chance at all!'

'Sorry, Tori. Of course you don't,' he said, dropping his head. 'I was hoping that you might though . . .'

'Fine, I'll come to the pub tonight – we can talk there.'

'You won't regret it, Tori,' he said, his face brightening.

'I'll meet you at the pub at seven.'

'I'll be waiting. I don't suppose I could grab a coffee to go while I'm here, could I? The stuff they serve at the Apple Tree tastes like charcoal,' he said, screwing up his face.

'Fine,' she replied, grabbing the pot of filter coffee. 'That'll be £2.85,' she said, holding out the card machine.

'I'll have a G and T waiting for you,' Ryan said. Tori felt her insides knot into a tight ball. Why was he acting as if nothing had changed? 'This place looks amazing, by the way; you've done a great job. I'm proud of you,' he said, flashing her a smile as he left.

Had she done the right thing, agreeing to meet Ryan tonight? She had waited long enough to hear an explanation. She'd spent weeks wondering why he'd broken up with her so abruptly and maybe tonight she'd finally get the closure she needed to move on once and for all. Wasn't that what she had felt desperate for these last few weeks anyway? After all, what had she got to lose?

When the lunchtime rush was over and Tori was able to leave Joyce on her own, Tori pulled up on the driveway of Three Acres Farm to meet Jake's friend, Nathan.

'Hi, you must be Tori! I'm Nathan, pleased to meet you. Welcome to Three Acres!' said a tall, muscular man, wearing shorts and wellies, shaking her hand vigorously. She wasn't sure what she'd expected him to look like, but it certainly wasn't the handsome, twenty-something powerhouse in front of her.

'Lovely to meet you, and thanks so much for finding time for this. Jake said you were the man to speak to about cheese, as we're hoping to stock local suppliers in our café, the Cosy Cat? You might have heard of us?' Tori said, returning his smile.

'No problem at all, and yes, I've heard all about your café and your smoothies. I'm hoping to pop down myself one of these days to try out your avocado on sourdough, actually. I've got a great selection of our bestsellers for you to try, all set up in the barn.'

'Oh, wow! This place is amazing,' said Tori, following him.

'It's only recently we've been able to scale up our operation here. We were making everything in our kitchen for the first couple of years, but now the business is growing we've been able to take the leap and invest in all this,' he said, gesturing to the processing tanks and packaging machines.

'What kind of cheeses do you make?'

'We've got quite a big selection for a small farm; all the milk comes from the farm, we've got sheep, cows and goats, and every step in the process happens right here.'

'That's so impressive.'

'I've set up our most popular choices for you to taste and I've included some of our regional ones, like the Blossom Heath Blue and the Sussex Smoked,' said Nathan, pointing towards the biggest mound of cheese Tori had ever seen.

'Ooh, can I try this first?' said Tori, picking up a cocktail stick loaded with Blossom Heath Blue and popping it in her mouth. 'Oh wow, that's gorgeous,' she said, closing her eyes. 'It's so creamy. I love it! Definitely one for the café!'

'Excellent. Let me get you a bottle of water and feel free to just work your way through the tasting board.'

Tori spent a heavenly half hour sampling all the cheeses and chatting to Nathan. He'd lived on the farm all his life and had started making cheese when his father needed help diversifying the business. He'd been the driving force behind the cheese production, and it had been such a success, he was hoping to open a shop on site to sell direct to the public. Tori loved the flavours, the sustainable farming ethos and the great wholesale prices, so she decided to place a regular order for six cheeses to be delivered to the Cosy Cat weekly.

'These are going to be so delicious in our Blossom Heath Ploughman's. Do you have any leaflets at all? I'd happily put some in the café if you like and I can certainly tell people about the shop when it opens. I'm so glad Jake put us in touch,' said Tori.

'That would be great. Actually, Rose is up here later this week on a school trip with her class. I'm going to show them how to make our ricotta.'

'Oh, that sounds like fun, and I bet their parents will want to try your Blue as well.'

'That's the plan,' laughed Nathan. 'I'll see you Monday with your first delivery.'

Tori was glad the café was a bit quieter than usual for a Friday afternoon when she finally got back from the farm, full to the brim with cheese, and she was able to spend some time playing with the cats and thinking about what she wanted to say to Ryan that evening. Norris sensed that she was out of sorts and spent most of the afternoon following her around as she wiped down tables, reorganized the cutlery drawer and put fresh flowers on all the tables in readiness for the weekend rush.

'Honestly, Norris, I can't get rid of you this afternoon, can I?' she said, scooping him into her arms and, as she settled down in one of the chairs by the window, she saw Rose approaching the café and got up to let her in.

'Tori! I've just heard. How are you?' she said, hugging her friend close.

'Oh, you know, how are you supposed to be when your ex flies halfway across the world to win you back on the same night you've snogged the face off the local firefighter?' she laughed bitterly.

'Seriously?'

'Afraid so.'

'On the plus side, it sounds like the date with Leo went well? Do you want to talk about it?'

'Which part?'

'Any of it? None of it? Or we could just bitch about Violet if that will cheer you up?' Rose laughed.

'Grab a seat and I'll get us some coffee,' said Tori.

'Ooh, I don't suppose you've got cake?'

'Always,' said Tori, returning with a tray of coffees and lemon drizzle cake. 'Here we go. Help yourself. So, I'm guessing everyone knows Ryan's back then?'

'Pretty much. I just saw Kate; Maggie told her. You know what this place is like.'

'Nothing stays private for longer than twenty-four hours!'

'Exactly. Before I forget, Kate wanted to come and see you too, but she had to take Lily swimming. She said to call if you need her, though.'

'Sorry, I was going to message you both when I got home tonight to fill you in.'

'So, what did he have to say for himself?' asked Rose, stirring sugar into her coffee.

'Ryan?' Rose nodded. 'Not much so far. To be fair, I haven't given him much of a chance to.'

'I don't blame you.'

'But I've agreed to meet him at the pub tonight, hear him out.'

'Do you *want* to?' Rose asked, her eyes narrowed. 'Hear him out?'

317

'I honestly don't know. All he said last night was that he misses me and regrets ending things.'

'And how do you feel about that?'

'Stunned? Angry?' Tori shrugged. 'Maybe a little bit of me is glad; I'm honestly not sure.'

'And where does this leave things with Leo? How did the date go?'

Tori smiled at the mention of Leo's name. 'It was everything you'd hope for in a first date. Romantic, exciting, passionate . . .' Tori felt her insides fizz at the memory of the kiss they'd shared after dinner.

'You kissed?'

'Uh-huh.' Tori nodded.

'And how was it?'

'Let's just say it was a good kiss.'

'And was it only a kiss?' Rose asked, taking a huge bite of cake.

'Yep,' said Tori. 'Don't get me wrong,' she added quickly. 'It's not that I wasn't tempted; I just don't want to rush into anything yet.'

'Given that Ryan was waiting for you when you got home, that's probably a good thing.'

'You're not wrong,' said Tori, sighing. 'Can you imagine how much worse things would have been this morning?'

'Well, if it's any help at all, I'm Team Leo. Ryan had his chance, and he blew it. *Big time*. Hear him out if you want to, but don't let him suck you in with excuses.'

'But what if he's genuinely sorry? If he just panicked at the thought of settling down?'

'Then he should have spoken to you about it, worked things through. Not dump you without explanation, leaving you stranded.'

'We had a life together, though, Rose. I can't just switch off my feelings – it isn't that simple. If he is ready to settle down, maybe we could make it work?'

'I can't tell you what to do, Tori – it's got to be your decision. But if I was in your shoes, I'd be very wary. He's already let you down once.'

'I know, I get it. I know you're only looking out for me. You're right – it has to be my decision and I just know I won't be able to move on, not properly, unless I hear him out.'

'Fair enough. What are you going to do about Leo, though? You can't leave him hanging.'

'I know. I said I'd call him today. Do you think he's already heard that Ryan's back?' Tori asked, her gaze turning to her phone.

'Maybe, but you should call him anyway, in case he hasn't. Why don't I leave you to it?'

'God knows what I'm going to say,' Tori said, gripping the edge of her chair.

'Just be honest with him. You didn't know Ryan was going to turn up, so Leo can't hold it against you. Just tell him what you told me. Explain that you need some time.'

'I hope you're right. Thanks Rose, I'd best call him now,' agreed Tori.

'What time are you meeting Ryan?'

'Seven.'

'Okay, well, let me know how it goes. Whatever you decide to do, I'll be here for you.'

'What would I do without you?' said Tori, her eyes filling with tears.

'Oh, come here,' said Rose, hugging her friend. 'I know you'd do the same for me.'

'Somehow, I don't think you're going to end up in this state. You and Jake are meant to be, I reckon.'

'I hope so,' said Rose, 'I really do.'

When Rose left, Tori flipped the closed sign over the back of the café door, pulled up a seat and scrolled through her contacts to find Leo's number. Her finger hovered over it, her nerves building as she jabbed a finger on the call button. She took a deep breath as she waited for him to answer.

'Hello?' said Leo, his voice sounding groggy and hoarse.

'It's me, Tori. Are you okay? You sound . . .'

'Oh, I've just woken up, that's all,' he replied, yawning.

'Oh, okay.' Tori's hands trembled. Maybe Leo hadn't heard about Ryan's arrival from the Blossom Heath rumour mill yet.

'I'm on nights tonight – I'm getting some kip in before I start.'

'Oh God, I'm so sorry I woke you up,' she said quickly.

'I can't think of anyone else I'd rather have wake me up.' Tori heard the smile in Leo's voice.

'Listen, I know I said I'd call today anyway but . . . well, something happened last night after the cab dropped me off and I'm not really sure how to ... explain.'

'What happened? Are you okay?' he asked hurriedly. She could hear the tone change in his voice.

'I'm fine, it's just that ... I ... well ...'

'Tori,' said Leo, gently. 'Whatever it is, you know you can tell me, don't you? Whatever it is, it's okay.' She crossed her fingers and hoped that was true.

'Okay, well, when I got home last night Ryan, my ex, was here. He's back from Thailand and I think, well, he says, I mean, he wants us to ...'

'Get back together?'

'I think so, yes.' There was silence at the end of the line.

'Oh, I see,' said Leo, after a moment.

'And I'm not saying I want to get back with him. It was just, well, it was a bit of a shock, him just turning up like that and I'm feeling a bit confused. I know things between me and you are, well ... it's early days, and I'm just not sure that, I mean I'm not sure if ...' She was rambling now; she could feel it. Words were tumbling out of her mouth, and she was desperately trying to fill the awkward, painful silence with something, anything, that would go some way towards explaining what was going on in her head.

'How did you feel about seeing him?' Leo asked bluntly.

'I really don't know. I'm meeting him tonight for a drink.'

'You're *meeting* him?'

'Tonight, yes. I wanted to let you know, I want to be straight with you, Leo. I don't know what any of this means but I don't want to keep anything from you.' A painful silence hung in the air. Tori was desperate to fill it, but she didn't know what else she could say. After what felt like an eternity, Leo finally spoke.

'Listen, Tori. You don't owe me anything. Whatever's happening between us is pretty new, right? You've got history with Ryan and if you think he's what you want, I'm not going to get in the way.'

'Oh, okay . . .' She felt stung by his words.

'I appreciate you being honest with me – it took guts to tell it to me straight. Listen, I've got to get ready for work, so I guess I'll see you around.'

Before she had the chance to reply, Leo had rung off. His words echoed in her head. *I guess I'll see you around.* She sat there for a moment, staring at her phone. What had she expected him to say? Did she think he'd race over to the café and beg her not to meet Ryan? To tell her that he couldn't live without her? That she should forget Ryan and choose him? She shook her head. No, that would be ridiculous. Surely she should be pleased that Leo had reacted to her news so graciously? He'd been decent about the whole thing and let her off the hook without so much as a cross word. That was a good thing, right? Why, then, did she feel so utterly miserable? She knew one thing for certain, deep down in the pit of her stomach: she wanted Leo to put up some kind of fight for her, and the fact that he hadn't spoke volumes. Perhaps the decision she had to make about Ryan had suddenly got a whole lot easier . . .

*

Ryan, back? Now that was a curveball Leo hadn't been expecting. He put his phone down and sat up in bed. Talk about bad timing. After such a great date, to wake up today and find that everything had changed overnight, was ... well, it was a shock. A huge one. Leo pulled on a T-shirt and shorts and padded down the stairs to find Tinkerbell licking her paws, waiting for him in the kitchen. 'Oh, Tinks, what am I going to do?' he said, scooping the cat up into his arms. 'I finally find the perfect woman and her ex turns up the next day.' Tinkerbell purred in response. 'Look at me,' he said, putting her down on the floor and reaching for the kibble jar, 'I'm asking a cat for relationship advice.' Had he been naïve to tell Tori how he felt about her? It wasn't like him; he wasn't usually the one doing the chasing. If anything, he was normally the one making the excuses so he could get back to being free and single. Perhaps it was all for the best. If Tori was considering reconciling with her ex, he didn't want to be her back-up plan. He'd make things simple for her and take himself out of the picture.

Tori arrived at the Apple Tree at exactly seven o'clock, and nerves were bubbling up inside her. She spotted Ryan instantly, sitting in one of the corner booths. He was wearing dark blue jeans and a grey shirt, which showed off his glowing tan and drew Tori's eyes to his glossy dark hair and brooding eyes. God, he looked good. Really good. She pulled up a chair and Ryan leaned across the table to kiss her on the cheek, casting a glance around the room nervously. Ryan cleared his throat.

'Thanks for agreeing to see me – I promise you won't regret it. I got you a drink in,' he said, nodding towards the G and T on the table.

'Thanks.' She placed her handbag on the floor, folding her arms in front of her. 'So, where do you want to start?'

'By saying I'm sorry,' replied Ryan, tapping his leg against the table. 'I know sorry doesn't cover it, but I screwed up, Tori.'

'That's an understatement,' said Tori, through gritted teeth.

'I know it is.' Ryan hung his head. 'It doesn't come close. We'd had such a great time travelling, the thought of it coming to an end, of us coming back home and buying a place together, marriage and babies, well, I'm ashamed to say, I panicked. It felt like everything was happening too quickly – I didn't feel ready.' Regret was etched on his face.

Tori breathed deeply, trying to compose herself. 'So why didn't you say that to me? Why just dump me and leave me to come home by myself?'

Ryan shrugged. 'Because I'm an idiot? Because I didn't know how lucky I was to have you? I took what we had for granted, Tori, I know I didn't appreciate you,' he continued, wringing his hands.

'Do you understand what it's been like for me, Ryan? Coming back here, trying to figure out what I'd done wrong, why you'd ended things? Having to tell everyone that we were over but not knowing why? I didn't have any answers ... it was eating me up inside.'

'If it makes you feel any better, I've been miserable without you, Tori.' Ryan looked so sincere, and she felt a pang of sympathy for him.

'It makes me feel a *little* better,' she replied, her voice softening. She swirled the ice in her G and T, deep in thought. 'I don't understand what's changed, though. If you weren't up for buying a house together, for marriage and kids, then what's different now?'

'I've realized that I can't be without you, Tori. And if that means I need to go all in, that's what I'm prepared to do. Whatever it takes,' he said, taking a long, deep breath.

Tori studied his face; he looked in pain.

'But it's not what you want, though, is it? You'd only be going through the motions to keep me happy?'

'Whatever it takes, I'm willing to do.' He reached across the table for her hand. 'What do you say?'

'Honestly?' She shrugged, taking a deep, steadying breath. 'I appreciate the explanation, but I think it might be too late. You hurt me, Ryan ... I'm not sure sorry is enough, and I want to be with someone who truly wants the same future as I do,' she said, pushing the remainder of her drink aside and making to leave.

'Before you go,' Ryan said hurriedly, 'I know it's going to take time to rebuild your trust. I'm not going anywhere though, Tori, I'm not giving up – I'm here and I want to be with you, isn't that what's important?'

'I need some space, Ryan. I need time to think.'

'Understood.' He nodded. 'Well, you know where I am if you want to talk,' he said, gesturing to the bar.

'Aren't you going back to London to see your family?'

Ryan shook his head.

'Not this time. I'm staying right here. I'm hoping I'm still welcome at the café for a cuppa?'

'It's a free country,' said Tori, shrugging.

'Like I said, I'm not giving up,' Ryan repeated.

As Tori got up to leave, a few of the locals threw her furtive glances as she made towards the door.

'Tori, can I have a quick word?' asked Pete, the pub's landlord.

'Yeah, sure.'

'Listen, you know we've got Ryan staying but I don't want you to think Beth and I have taken his side. If I had my way, I would have sent him packing after the way he treated you,' said Pete, casting a furious look in Ryan's direction. 'But apparently that's not good business sense, according to Beth.'

'And Beth's right,' said Tori, placing a hand on his arm. 'Don't get yourself in trouble on my account.'

'If you don't want him here, Tori, just say the word and I'll kick him out, to hell with what Beth says,' he said, his fists clenched at his sides.

'No, it's fine, Pete, really it is. If Ryan wants to hang around, that's up to him – I don't have a problem with it.'

'Right you are, but if that changes, if he puts a foot wrong . . .'

'You'll be the first to know. And I'll happily watch you throw him out. Deal?'

'Deal,' said Pete, nodding. 'I still don't like him, though,

Tori. You can do so much better for yourself than someone who treats you like that.'

'Thanks, Pete.'

'You know Beth and I will always support you.'

'I know,' she said, leaning in to give the pub landlord a kiss on the cheek.

'We're all set to run the bar at the barn dance too. Beth's organized some extra staff for the night, so we can head up to the farm and take care of everything on site ourselves.'

'Thanks, Pete, you're a star.'

'Now before you go, Beth's got some apples for you,' he said, ducking behind the bar and returning with two full carrier bags.

'Thanks for these – Mum's pies will go down a storm in the café. I'll drop a couple back at the pub for you and Beth.'

'I'll look forward to it. It's hard to beat a proper home-made pie, particularly when it's packed full of good old Sussex apples.'

Chapter 31

Tori woke later than usual the following morning, having stayed up late into the night going over the events of the evening, first with Joyce and then with Rose, until she was too exhausted to think. She'd fallen into bed as though she hadn't slept in years, and if it hadn't been for Joyce banging on her bedroom door that the cats needed feeding, who knows what time she'd have woken up. She checked her phone ... nothing from Leo. There was a message from Claire though. *Just heard about Ryan turning up, what a grand gesture! He must be serious about wanting you back, maybe you should hear him out? Claire xx* Tori tossed her phone aside, she didn't want to think about Ryan right now, she'd reply to Claire later.

Pulling on a pair of jeans and a faded band T-shirt, Tori ran down to the kitchen, shoving an apple from the fruit bowl into her mouth.

'Slow down. You'll give yourself indigestion,' Joyce warned.

'I need to get to the café. It's Valentine's adoption day and I'm meeting Izzy before we open.'

'Oh yes, I'd forgotten. Our first official adoption, how exciting!' said Joyce, her face lighting up. 'You go, love.'

'See you,' said Tori.

When Tori arrived next door, Izzy was waiting outside.

'I'm so sorry,' Tori apologized, 'have you been here long?'

'Nah, I literally just got here, there's plenty of time to finish off your breakfast,' she laughed, pointing at the half-eaten apple in Tori's hand.

'God, you must think I'm so disorganized. It's not usually like this first thing, I promise.'

'Don't worry about it, you should see me at the centre, we're rushed off our feet most of the time. Anyway, how's Daisy? No more disappearing acts?'

'Ah, you heard about that. I wasn't trying to hide it from you, Izzy, life just got so busy, and—'

'Tori, it's fine,' said Izzy, resting a hand on her shoulder. 'These things happen – we have near misses up at the centre. Working with animals is always going to be a tricky business.'

'Thanks, I am sorry I didn't mention it, though. I should have. Right, let's get inside and you can say hello to the gang,' said Tori, beaming as she turned the key, ushering Izzy inside the foyer and closing the door behind her.

'I keep meaning to try and pay you a visit, but things are crazy busy up at the centre. The calls never seem to stop,' Izzy explained, a shadow passing across her face.

'Adoptions?'

'I wish,' said Izzy, shaking her head. 'No, it's mainly calls asking us to take animals in. We're completely full, but I can't bear to turn any of them away, especially if they're hurt or abandoned.'

'Oh God, Izzy, I had no idea things were so difficult,' said Tori.

'Oh, it's always bad this time of year. It's kitten season for starters so that means we're taking in way more expectant mums than we usually would. It makes it tougher for the older cats to find homes too, as they're competing with the cute, fluffy babies.'

'Can I help?'

'Tori, you already have. You've got five cats in the café – that's freed up five spots at the rescue so we can take new ones in.'

'Well, Valentine's leaving us today, aren't you, little man?' said Tori, scooping the small grey cat up in her arms. 'So that means we've got a space here. Can we take another?'

'You know, that's what I was going to ask. If you're sure that is?'

'Absolutely! Everything is going well, I think. The cats are getting along, they're happy and love meeting the customers, though we've had a few teething troubles,' she said, her mind turning to Daisy's disappearance and Mr Wiggles' vet visit, 'but nothing I can't handle.'

'I was hoping that's what you'd say,' said Izzy, visibly relaxing. 'I've got the perfect candidate in mind too. Pablo. He's a little black cat and he's been with us for ages. I've no idea why – he's affectionate, confident, gets along well with everyone, no medical problems either.'

'I'll never understand why people overlook the black cats,' said Tori, setting Valentine, who was getting squirmy in her arms, back on the floor.

'They just aren't as popular unfortunately.'

'Well, we'll happily take him and I'm sure he'll fit right in with this lot,' she said.

'Perfect, I'll bring him over tomorrow if that works?'

'I can't wait to meet him!'

'He's a sweetheart, you'll love him. How're things going with the barn dance? Anything I can do?'

'I'd say you've got enough on your plate right now. Everything's coming together nicely: Jake's friend is sorting the music, Jean and the WI ladies are on the case with the food and we've got an army of people signed up to help us set up on the night.'

'That's brilliant! Sounds like you've got everything in hand.'

'I think so. People have been really supportive; I'm hoping it'll raise a good amount for the rescue.'

'Fingers crossed,' said Izzy. 'We could certainly do with it right now. How's Mr Wiggles doing, though? Any more incidents?'

'Did Grace explain what happened?' Izzy nodded. 'Well, I think she was right, it was down to dehydration. He definitely prefers drinking from the fountain, so hopefully that's problem solved.'

'Excellent. Grace is usually spot on, to be fair.'

'She's great, isn't she?' Tori agreed, reaching for her phone which had buzzed with a message. It was another one from Claire. *Just heard you went on a date with Leo. I thought I'd warned you about him? I'd steer well clear, he's not a good guy.*

'Everything okay?' Izzy asked, reading the expression on Tori's face.

'Oh, it's nothing,' said Tori, placing her phone face down on the table with a shrug. She couldn't understand why Claire was so interested in her love life. Didn't she have better things to worry about?

Tori and Izzy spent the next half hour, before the café opened, going through the adoption paperwork for Valentine. The cats made a beeline for Izzy, which she put down to having a pocketful of cat treats.

At ten o'clock on the dot, Simone and Tom arrived, Simone clutching a pink and grey cat carrier.

'Hello, you two,' said Tori, opening the door to let them in.

'Sorry if we're a bit early, we're too excited!' said Simone, smiling.

'I know, me too!' replied Tori. 'You're our first official adoption and we're so pleased Valentine has found such a wonderful home.'

'Lovely to see you again,' said Izzy, shaking first Tom's, then Simone's, hand.

'I've saved a table for you. Would you like a drink while we go through the paperwork?' asked Tori.

'Two chai lattes, thanks,' said Tom.

'Can I have an almond croissant too?' asked Simone. 'Oh,

and some of those homemade cat treats? We can take a couple of bags home for Valentine.'

'Of course. Grab a seat and I'll be back in a jiffy,' said Tori. By the time she had returned with their order, Valentine was already curled up in Simone's lap. 'Looks like someone's found his happy place.'

'I hope so,' said Simone. 'Thanks so much for letting us adopt him.'

'Oh, it's not me you need to thank, it's Izzy,' she said, nodding in her friend's direction.

'But if it wasn't for the café, you'd probably never have met Valentine,' said Izzy.

'What you're both doing is fantastic,' Tom said gratefully.

'Thanks, I appreciate that.' Tori felt a lump forming in her throat. If it wasn't for the Cosy Cat, would Valentine still be waiting to find his forever home? The partnership between the café and New Beginnings had meant that Izzy had been able to offer a rescue space to more cats in need, including Pablo. What would have happened to them otherwise? She felt proud she was doing something helpful, useful, and realized she hadn't felt that sensation in a while.

Tori and Izzy chatted happily to Simone and Tom while the café was quiet, and Tori loved hearing about everything the couple had set up at home for Valentine. Simone was eager to show her pictures of Valentine's new bed, which was baby blue and covered in tiny navy pawprints, as well as all the toys and treats they had for their new family member.

'I think that's everything,' Tori said, as Tom and Simone finished signing the paperwork. 'Valentine is officially yours! Congratulations! Shall we get him loaded up and ready for his trip home?'

'Are you okay to put him in the carrier for us?' asked Simone. 'He knows you best so it might be a bit less scary for him?'

'Of course. Let's give it a go.' Tori took the carrier from Tom and scooped Valentine up from Simone's lap, where he had been purring contentedly, and held him close to her. 'Now you be good, little man. We're going to miss you around here, you know.' She kissed him on top of the head and, before he had the chance to realize what was happening, popped him headfirst into the carrier and shut the door behind him. 'There you are. He's good to go.'

'We'll take the best care of him, Tori,' said Tom.

'We really will,' agreed Simone. 'Thanks again for all your help. We'll let you know how he settles in.'

'Do! I'd love to see some pictures once he's made himself at home,' said Izzy.

'Before you go, do you mind if I grab a picture of you all for our socials?' said Tori.

'Of course,' said Tom, putting his arm around Simone and holding Valentine's carrier up for the camera.

'Perfect, thanks. Have a safe trip home.' Tori and Izzy waved at the window as they watched the couple drive away. It was a bittersweet feeling. Tori was pleased that Valentine was ready to start his new life, but she also knew she was going to miss him like crazy. She knew she'd feel the same way when the rest of the cats went off to their forever homes too, but reminded herself that she'd always have Ernie at home to love and treasure. He was going nowhere. Opening Instagram, she posted the picture of Valentine with the caption, *Happy Caturday! We're pleased to share our first ever adoption! Congratulations Tom, Simone and Valentine! #caturday #adoptdontshop #todayisagoodday*

The rest of the day passed in an endless flurry of coffees and cream teas. Saturday was always one of the busiest days at the Cosy Cat and there wasn't a table free for longer than two minutes all afternoon. Joyce's Sussex apple pie with whipped cream was proving popular and Tori remembered to stash a couple under the counter for Pete and Beth before they sold out. At four thirty, just as she was starting to think about giving the cats their early evening treats, Tori looked up and was surprised to see two men in uniform standing in front of her.

'I'm so sorry, we're fully booked this afternoon, but if you'd like a takeaway—'

'We're not here for coffee, I'm afraid, Miss. Are you the owner?' the taller of the two men asked, pulling an ID card out of his pocket.

'Erm, yes, well, along with my mum.'

'We're East Sussex Council's Animal Welfare – I'm Adam and this is my colleague, John. We've received some complaints over the conditions your cats are being kept in.

Today is a preliminary visit so we can assess the situation and remove any animals that may be suffering.'

'Suffering?' whispered Tori, her mouth dry, 'but they aren't suffering at all. We work in partnership with a rescue centre and our local vet has been helping us too. I don't understand who's said that . . .'

'The names of all complainants are entirely confidential,' John, who had a neatly manicured brown moustache quivering above his top lip, replied curtly.

'Don't worry,' said Joyce, who had appeared at Tori's side, 'we've got nothing to hide, have we? I'm sure once the inspectors have looked around, they'll see that.'

'The welfare of the cats has been Tori's number one priority since opening,' said Jean Hargreaves, as she rose from her seat using her walking stick for support. 'Do you imagine that any of us would come to a café where we thought animals were suffering, young man?' There were murmurs of agreement throughout the Cosy Cat, and the inspectors took a step backwards as Jean approached them. Tori was full of admiration for Jean's gravitas and hoped to have some of her bravery when she was in her eighties.

'I think you've been given some wrong information,' said Maggie, who had been having tea with Jean.

'If you find any cats are suffering, I'll eat my hat,' agreed Cora, pointing to Mr Wiggles who was in his usual place, curled up happily in her lap.

'We're regular visitors, and we've never seen any of the cats suffering,' piped up a man who Tori recognized but couldn't quite place. 'We live up on Meadowgate Mead and we're here every weekend, our kids love it.'

'Thanks . . .'

'Fred,' said the man, nodding at Tori.

'Nice to meet you, Fred,' said Tori, smiling, 'and thank you.'

'Did you know all the cats here are from New Beginnings? Izzy Sullivan approved the café before it opened and is fully supportive of the business,' said Jean.

'I didn't, no,' Adam said thoughtfully. 'Izzy certainly knows her stuff.' He turned towards Tori again, his tone softening. 'I hope you understand that we have to investigate any complaints that we receive, however false they might turn out to be.'

'If we can take a look around and see the cats, that's all we'll need to do today,' John added. 'We have to take all allegations of mistreatment seriously.'

Tori nodded as Grace burst through the door, rushing to the counter.

'What can I do to help?' she said, clearly out of breath.

'Grace? But how did you know?' asked Tori.

'I sent her a text message,' said Jean in a booming voice. 'I thought she should be here in case these two clowns got out of hand.' Both officers bristled at Jean's description.

'There's no need for that – we're just doing our job,' Adam replied.

'I'm Grace Ashworth, local vet. I've been helping to advise Tori ever since she set up the café, so I'm sure you'll find everything's in order. I can certainly answer any questions you might have if that helps?'

'That's much appreciated, Miss Ashworth. How about you accompany us on our inspection?' John replied, looking pointedly towards Jean.

'That sounds great,' said Grace. 'Shall we let Tori lead the way?'

As Tori and Grace took the inspectors around the café, Joyce, Jean, Maggie and Cora were watching eagle-eyed, muttering conspiratorially from a table in the corner. Tori explained the set-up and how the cats were fed and cared for. Grace pointed out all the features included in the design and layout of the space to ensure the cats had suitable enrichment and outlets to display their natural behaviours. Finally, Tori pulled out their vaccination records, which also contained microchip details and showed that their flea and worming treatments were up to date. Tori and Grace looked at each other anxiously, while the inspectors wrote furiously in their notebooks.

'Well, it seems as though we've had a wasted trip,' Adam said with a smile. 'From what we've seen here today, the cats seem to be well nourished and cared for, the environment is suitable for their needs, and we don't have any cause for concern as to their welfare.' Tori felt her shoulders relax; the knot that had formed in her stomach over the past thirty minutes started to untangle.

'Thank you,' she said, beaming.

'Like I said, we're just doing our jobs,' replied John.

'See? Told you you'd been sent on a wild goose chase,' Jean called across from her table, Joyce casting her a pointed look.

'I'm sorry for the disruption – we'll take up no more of your time,' said Adam.

'I totally understand, officer,' said Tori. 'Can I interest you in a coffee before you leave?'

'Thanks, we're parched,' said Adam, pulling out his wallet.

'And you're sure there's nothing you can tell us about who complained?' Grace asked, her eyebrows raised pointedly.

'I'm afraid not, no,' said John.

'It just doesn't seem right, though, does it? For someone to make up lies about us and waste your time like this?' said Tori.

'It happens sometimes, I'm afraid,' said Adam.

'Look, I'm just glad you're happy with what you saw today, that's the main thing,' said Tori.

'I think we can all guess who made the complaint,' said Jean, with a huff.

'It doesn't take a genius to work it out. I've heard all about Violet,' added Cora, peering over the top of her spectacles.

'Yes, it has to be Violet Davenport,' agreed Maggie. She watched the faces of the two officers closely for any sign of recognition at hearing Violet's name.

'Like I said—' said John.

'Honestly, don't worry about it,' said Tori, shrugging.

'I'd best be getting back to the surgery,' said Grace. 'Can I grab a soy latte before I go?'

'Of course, and thanks for coming over to help – I really appreciate it,' said Tori, 'and this one's on the house.'

'And we should be getting off too, thanks,' said Adam, as Tori passed him a takeaway cup. 'Sorry for any inconvenience today's visit may have caused,' he continued.

Tori let the officers out and returned to the counter.

'Well, I wasn't expecting that today,' said Joyce, exhaling deeply. 'Do you really think Violet's behind it?'

'I'd bet my pension on it,' said Jean. 'Once Violet takes against you, you'd better watch out.'

'But seriously, I don't understand why she's got it in for me? What have I ever done to her?' Tori felt a wave of despondency wash over her. She'd put her heart and soul into the Cosy Cat, done everything she possibly could to make the business a success, but for some reason, Violet was against her, wanting them to fail. Her recent showdown on Violet's doorstep wasn't likely to have improved the situation either.

'Oh Tori, don't worry about Violet. We all love coming here, you've done a great job, the cats are happy, and you should be so proud of yourself. Ignore her, she's not worth it,' said Cora, putting an arm around her.

'Thanks Cora, that's really kind of you,' said Tori.

'I couldn't agree more,' said Jean, nodding approvingly at Cora. 'I don't think we've been introduced – I'm Jean, Jean Hargreaves.'

'Cora Tomlinson,' Cora replied. 'I've not been in the village long, but I can already see you've got some wonderful friends here, Tori.'

'Cora's right,' agreed Maggie. 'And this place is a credit to you and you're doing your mum proud.'

'Thanks, Mags,' Tori sniffed.

'Listen, love, you've had a rough couple of days. Why don't you get on home and I'll close up here,' said Joyce.

'But Mum . . .'

'No arguments,' said Jean. 'If your mum needs any help, we can all pitch in, can't we girls?' Cora and Maggie nodded in agreement.

'That's settled then, love, off you go,' said Joyce.

Knowing better than to try to argue with Jean once she'd made up her mind about something, Tori grabbed her bag and a slab of bread pudding to go. As she headed towards the door, she could hear Jean asking Cora to join her and Maggie, and suggesting that she go along to the next WI meeting. Tori smiled to herself. She had been touched at how quickly Jean and Cora had leapt to her defence today. Grace had dropped everything to support her. Clearly someone wasn't a fan of what she was doing with the café, but with friends like Grace, Rose, Maggie, Cora and Jean in her corner, did it really matter?

Chapter 32

'I still don't know how you managed to talk me into this,' muttered Tori, as Rose greeted her at Blossom Heath Primary School on Monday afternoon. Tori had Angel and Daisy with her, and she could hear both cats meowing indignantly, clearly unhappy at being away from the comfort of the café.

'Thank you *so* much for doing this – you're a star.' Rose reached out a hand to take one of the carriers from Tori, who was struggling to get through the double doors.

'You might change your tune if these two cause havoc,' Tori laughed, as Mrs Connolly appeared from behind her office door to welcome them.

'Ah, Tori, we're so pleased you could join us today. I can't tell you how much the children in Butterfly Class are looking forward to meeting the cats.' Bertie, Mrs Connolly's elderly chocolate Labrador, made a surprisingly speedy rush towards them but Mrs Connolly managed to stop him in his tracks. 'No you don't, Bertie my boy,' she said, reaching down to grab his brown leather collar. 'Those cats have got enough to contend with today – they won't welcome your unwanted attention. Honestly, every time I think Bertie's ready to retire from school life, he proves me wrong by charging about the place like a puppy!'

'He certainly looks full of beans today,' agreed Rose.

'Thanks for arranging this, Mrs Connolly. The cats are definitely going to be the main attraction; I'm not sure how interested the kids will be in hearing what I've got to say, to be honest . . .' said Tori.

'Not at all, they're desperate to hear about what the cats do at night when the café's closed, and the secret ingredients in your famous hot chocolate. And I have to say, I'm really interested as well. When Rose told me about the changes you'd made to your mum's tearoom, I was really impressed. The young people we teach here need to know that there are opportunities for them in Blossom Heath; that they don't have to leave the village to make something of themselves. Tell me, how did you come up with the idea of having cats there in the first place? It's so unique.'

'They're really common in Asia; I went to loads of them while I was travelling and when Mum suggested turning the Cosy Cup into the Cosy Cat, I just knew it would work,' Tori explained.

'Isn't that marvellous?' said Mrs Connolly appreciatively. 'I've certainly enjoyed my visits. I can't have a cat as Bertie would eat it alive, so it's been lovely to spend time with yours. We're lucky to have such an enterprising young woman in to talk to the children, don't you agree, Rose?'

'Oh absolutely,' said Rose, nodding her head vigorously.

'Actually, while I'm here, Mrs Connolly, I was wondering if I could run something past you?' Tori said.

'Of course,' replied Mrs Connolly.

'Well, a few of us have been trying to think of ways to raise funds for New Beginnings, and we've got a barn dance planned up at Harper Farm in a few weeks' time,' continued Tori.

'I've already got it in my diary,' said Mrs Connolly, nodding.

'And I was thinking, how would you feel about supporting a "Sponsor a Cat initiative", here at the school? I haven't worked out all the details, but I was thinking that for something like a twenty-pound donation, you'd get two access all areas visits a year to the shelter and a card for fifty per cent off hot chocolate at the café. I've spoken to Izzy and we both thought the school would be the perfect place to launch it.'

'That sounds wonderful. I'll need to know all the details, of course – email them over once you and Izzy have worked everything out. The pair of you could come to assembly one morning to explain it to the children and if you want to put a letter together, we can send it home to explain the scheme to parents. How does that sound?'

'That sounds brilliant, thank you, Mrs Connolly. I'll get in touch as soon as we've worked out all the logistics,' said Tori.

'If all goes well, perhaps we can arrange an outing to the café for those children who have sponsored a cat, so they can see the work you're doing to help rehome the cats from the rescue centre,' said Mrs Connolly.

'Oh, we could definitely do that, and perhaps the children could help with grooming and feeding the cats we've got as well, with their parents' permission, of course. I'd have to check with Izzy, though, and make sure we've got all the right insurance cover in place,' replied Tori.

'That sounds great. There'll be a risk assessment to do, of course, but Rose can help with that. Now, if you'll excuse me, I've got a mountain of paperwork to get through this afternoon; William Braithwaite has been up to his tricks again and I can't tell you the amount of extra work that young man causes me.'

'Oh no, what's he done now?' asked Rose with a sigh.

'Forged his mum's signature to try and get out of PE – again. Honestly, that boy is going to drive me into early retirement,' said Mrs Connolly, as she closed her office door.

'You can't blame him,' whispered Tori, waiting to make sure she was out of Mrs Connolly's earshot. 'I used to do everything I could to get out of PE too.'

'I certainly admire his ingenuity,' laughed Rose. 'Right, let's go to my classroom and we can set everything up before the lunchtime bell goes. I love your sponsor a cat idea, by the way – you can sign me up for sure.'

'Thanks, Rose, I can always count on you.'

Tori and Rose had fifteen minutes to get set up in the class-room before the children arrived. Tori had brought over a mesh fabric puppy pen for Daisy and Angel to get comfort-able in, while she set up some cupcakes for the children to enjoy after her talk. The thought of trying to hold the attention of a class of eight-year-olds terrified her and she figured if she had treats, she'd hopefully win them over.

'I wasn't expecting these,' said Rose, picking up a cupcake and licking off the yellow frosting.

'Hey, they're for the kids,' said Tori, tapping her hand away.

'Well, there have to be some perks to my job,' Rose laughed, taking a bite.

'Hmm,' said Tori, her eyes narrowing. 'I know you've got a few pupils with nut allergies, so they're all nut-free, and Mum baked a few that are gluten-free as well – they've got the blue icing, in case you've got any coeliacs.'

'Ah, excellent. Yep, Hayden has a nut allergy, we had a really close call with him last year, I had to use an EpiPen – it was all pretty terrifying to be honest,' said Rose, a shadow crossing her face. 'Anyway, what's the plan?'

'Well, I thought I would start by telling the kids about the café and how we took inspiration from my travels, then I'll talk about the work Izzy does at the rescue and how it all fits together, then maybe get the cats out, let the children pet them and answer any questions they've got?'

'And the cupcakes? When are you dishing them out?'

'At the end? My plan was to get the kids hyped up on sugar just before I leave and let you deal with the consequences.'

Rose groaned. 'Cheers for that,' she sighed.

'Well, I wanted to give the kids a true café experience and I can't really do that without cake.'

'Fair enough.' Rose nodded. 'Any possibility this is

payback for me roping you into doing this in the first place?'

'I guess we'll never know,' Tori laughed.

'Oh, I meant to tell you,' said Rose, suddenly changing the subject. 'I went to see Claire for a haircut on Saturday, she gave me a right grilling about you and Leo.'

'Did she?' asked Tori, arching an eyebrow.

'She really did. She heard you'd been on a date and wanted to know if you were still seeing him now Ryan's back.'

'What did you tell her?' asked Tori, taken aback.

'Nothing really, I kinda changed the subject. I didn't think you knew each other that well.'

'We don't. We went out for lunch a few weeks ago but I wouldn't say we were close. She's been a bit frosty with me the last couple of times I've seen her.'

'Weird that she's asking then,' said Rose, shrugging.

'It is a bit. Hey, it looks like we've got company,' she said, nodding towards the door, through which a stream of children was being led into the classroom by a lunchtime assistant in a fluorescent tabard.

Rose immediately snapped into teacher mode. 'Good afternoon, Butterfly Class, come straight in and sit down on the carpet for me ... quickly Billy, Mason, Tiffany.'

Tori smiled at the wide-eyed children as they murmured to each other at the sight of a visitor in their classroom.

'Tori!' shouted Lara from across the room, 'what are you doing here?'

'Just sit down quietly, please, Lara, and I'll explain everything in a moment,' said Rose.

'What's in there?' said a boy with the remains of his lunch smeared around his cheeks, pointing towards the pet pen.

'I said sit down quietly, Billy,' said Rose.

'Wow, Miss, there's cats in there,' squealed a girl wearing red patent shoes and, as if on cue, Daisy let out a little meow.

'There *are* cats in there, aren't there, Miss? I heard them,' a girl with her hair in pigtails said excitedly.

'I said, sit down, Poppy,' Rose repeated.

'Where? Let me see?' A cacophony of voices echoed around the room.

'Butterfly Class, if you don't all sit down this instant, none of you will be meeting the cats.'

A hush descended and Tori was impressed at how quickly Rose was able to bring the excited group under control. She made a note never to mess with Rose when she was in teacher mode.

'Thank you. Now everyone is listening,' said Rose slowly, staring pointedly at Billy and Poppy, 'we've got a very special guest joining us this afternoon. This is Tori and she runs the Cosy Cat Café—'

'Oh, I've been there!'

'Billy, we do not shout out in class, do we?' said Rose.

'Sorry, Miss,' said Billy, looking crestfallen.

'I'm sure many of you have visited with your mums and dads, but who can tell me what's special about it? What makes it different to other cafés you might have been to?' Rose asked.

A sea of hands shot into the air. Rose scanned the room. 'Tiffany?'

'It's got cats in it, Miss.'

'That's right, Tiffany. The Cosy Cat isn't a regular café, it's a cat café. And Tori, who runs the business with her mum, Joyce, has been kind enough to come and join us today to tell us more about the café and let us meet some of the cats that live there. Isn't that exciting?'

Thirty little heads nodded enthusiastically. Tori noticed lots of the children whispering to each other and smiling and she could feel her nerves ease a little.

'So, let me hand you over to Tori and she can tell you all about life at the café,' Rose continued, giving Tori a small nod of encouragement.

Tori took a deep breath, stood up and smiled warmly at the children sat in front of her.

'Hello, Butterfly Class, it's lovely to see you all today. Rose, oh, I mean Miss Hargreaves ...' The children burst into hysterical laughter. Tori cringed, she was only one sentence in and already she'd put her foot in it.

'Alright, alright,' said Rose, trying to calm the children's laughter as Tori attempted to compose herself, 'my name's not that funny.'

When the kids had finally stopped giggling, Tori went on to explain about the idea for the partnership between the Cosy Cat and New Beginnings – to help find homes for cats in need. The children listened patiently until Daisy and Angel started to meow more loudly, and Tori could sense they were becoming fidgety.

'How about we get Daisy out now? Remember, we need

349

to be very calm and quiet around her, as we don't want to frighten her, okay?' said Tori.

'Yes, Miss,' said Billy, 'we'll be really quiet, honest.'

'Thanks, Billy. How about you come up here first and help me with Daisy? You can show everyone how it's done,' said Tori.

Billy stood up, puffed his chest out with pride and made his way over to sit on the floor next to Tori. Tori unzipped the top of the pen, reached in and scooped Daisy up. A chorus of 'Awwww' rippled through the classroom.

'Daisy, I'd like you to meet the children of Butterfly Class.' Tori tickled Daisy under the chin and the cat instantly began to purr. 'Now, Billy, I'm going to pop her on your lap, so can you keep very calm and still so she can get used to you a little bit first?' Tori placed Daisy gently on Billy's lap and the little cat instantly nuzzled into his arm for a cuddle. 'I think she likes you, Billy,' said Tori, smiling.

'I can hear her purring,' whispered Tiffany.

'That means she's feeling happy,' said Tori, and Billy beamed at her. 'How about if we split the class into two, Miss Hargreaves? I'll stay with Daisy, and perhaps you can get Angel out, please?'

'What a good idea,' said Rose, reaching down to take Angel out of the pen. 'This half of the class, you're with me,' she said, waving an arm. 'Everyone else stay with Tori.'

Tori enjoyed introducing the children to Daisy and answering all their questions.

'Miss?' asked one of the boys just as Tori was getting ready to put Daisy back in the carrier.

'Oh, you can call me Tori as I'm not a teacher,' Tori laughed.

'Tori?' asked the boy. 'Do you think I could take Daisy home? We were going to get a kitten from the pet shop in Hastings, but I'd rather get a rescue and I really like Daisy . . .'

'That's so sweet, but you can't just take her home with you now, I'm afraid,' said Tori, smiling broadly. 'What's your name?'

'Mason Jenkins,' replied the boy.

'Well, Mason, why don't you and your mum come and visit the café and we can talk about how you can go about adopting Daisy? What do you think?'

'Yes, please. I'll ask Mum tonight,' said Mason, nodding his head, before going to join his friends at the back of the class.

'Right, it's time to say goodbye to Tori and the cats, I'm afraid,' said Rose, putting Angel back into her carrier. 'But we're very lucky as Joyce has kindly baked some cupcakes for us all,' she said.

'Cakes!' the children chorused.

'Just one each,' said Rose, 'and don't worry, Hayden, they're all nut-free so you're fine to have one.'

'Thank you, Miss!' a cute little boy, who Tori assumed must be Hayden, called.

'Well, I think that was brilliant, Tori, thanks so much for coming, the kids had a great time,' said Rose.

'It definitely went better than I was expecting; I don't know why I got myself in such a tizzy about it,' said Tori.

'Well, you didn't show it, you did great. What was Mason talking to you about, by the way?'

'Oh, he's hoping his mum might let him adopt Daisy. They were going to buy a kitten from that big pet shop in Hastings, but he'd like to get a rescue, so I've told him to come to the café for a chat.'

'Wow! I love that. How great would it be if Daisy finds a home because of today?'

'It'd be fantastic. Let's wait and see, though – his mum might say no.'

'Mason's a sensible lad; I don't think he'd have asked unless his mum had said he could get a cat, to be honest. I'll keep my fingers crossed for Daisy.'

'Me too.'

As Tori walked along the corridor from Rose's classroom, she felt proud of what she'd achieved today, and she felt more determined than ever to make the Cosy Cat a success. And if Daisy had found a home because she'd visited the school, well, that really would be the icing on the cupcake.

Chapter 33

Feeling buoyed by the excitement of her visit to the school, Tori spent some time updating the social media accounts and replying to comments on her posts. Despite being a relative Instagram newbie, she had got the hang of it pretty quickly, with a little help from Jess, and she was amazed at how fast the Cosy Cat's account was racking up followers.

'You okay, love?' asked Joyce, as she came out of the kitchen. 'You look deep in thought.'

'Sorry, Mum, I'm just looking at our Instagram,' said Tori, showing her mum her phone. 'We've got nearly three thousand followers already and I've only had the account open a few weeks.'

'Is that good?'

'Well, yeah, I think so – all the comments are really positive. People seem to love the work we're doing with the rescue, lots of people saying they're going to check out their local adoption centres too, and look, there's even a comment from Millie Martin, and she's followed us too!'

'Ah, you should be so proud of yourself, love,' said Joyce, taking a closer look at Tori's phone. 'Who's Millie Martin when she's at home?'

'She's an influencer, Mum. She was on a reality dating show last summer, and she's all over Instagram. Look at what she's written. *Wow! Love the work you're doing to support pet adoption. I'll have to pop by when I'm next in Sussex.* Do you think she would, though?'

'I don't see why not.'

'But she's proper Insta famous, Mum. Would she really come *here*?'

'Why not ask her?'

'Ask her?'

'Why not?'

'She's probably really busy … she wouldn't come to Blossom Heath … would she?' Tori picked at her cuticles. Could she really just send Millie Martin a message inviting her to the Cosy Cat? Surely she'd never get a reply. But what harm was there in asking? Tori took a deep breath and typed out a message. *Thanks so much, Millie. The cats would love to meet you xx* She hit send and shook out her hands.

'Got to be worth a try, love,' said Joyce encouragingly. 'Oh, I nearly forgot. Jess dropped off the jute bags, mugs and keyrings you asked her to order,' she continued, pulling a box out from behind the counter.

'Wow, these look amazing,' said Tori. 'I hope they sell okay.'

'I'll price them up now and put them on display on those

hooks the carpenter put up. I think they'll look great there, right next to the till. Everything's really coming together, isn't it?'

'What about Ryan?' said Tori, slumping down on to the counter. 'I've got no idea what I'm going to do about him. I haven't heard from him since we met at the pub last Friday.'

'Well, I can't tell you what to do, but you've got good instincts, so listen to them – you'll make the decision that's right for you.'

'But what if I get it wrong? What if Ryan lets me down again?'

'Well, he might,' said Joyce, taking Tori's hand. 'But all you can do is follow your heart. Things don't always work out the way we'd like them to, but none of us have a crystal ball, love.'

'I don't doubt his feelings; what worries me is that he's only saying he's ready to settle down because he knows that's what I want. I need to be with someone who wants the same things as me, who wants to build a future together and I'm not sure he does,' Tori said, mustering a weak smile.

'Oh love, I know it's a difficult decision but it's one only you can make.'

'I know, I just hope I get it right.'

'Why don't we get off home? I'm nearly done in the kitchen, so you just need to tidy up out here. The yoga club had me rushed off my feet while you were at the school; I still don't think I've got the hang of those smoothies, to be honest,' said Joyce with a sigh. 'They're so popular, though; the new additions to the menu are going down a storm and the regulars love that we've kept all the old favourites.

'Thanks, Mum.'

'How about we treat ourselves to fish and chips for tea?'

'That sounds lovely,' said Tori.

As Tori stood to flip the door sign to 'Closed', she spotted a familiar face running towards the café.

'Mason!' she said, pulling the door open.

'Hi, Tori. This is my mum,' replied Mason.

'Sorry, are you closing up?' asked Mason's mum, out of breath from jogging to keep up with her son. 'I told Mason we'd come first thing in the morning, but he was desperate for us to try and catch you tonight.'

'Ah, no worries. We don't close for another twenty minutes or so, so come in. What do you say to hot chocolate, Mason? If that's okay with Mum, of course,' Tori added quickly.

'That would be lovely, thank you. I'm Hayley, by the way.'

'Lovely to meet you,' replied Tori. 'Grab a table any-where – I'll bring your drinks over.'

'Thanks. We wondered about Daisy. Mason told me you'd visited the school and said we might be able to adopt her?'

'Yes, that's right. We look after some of the rescue centre's cats that are looking to find their forever homes,' said Tori.

'Daisy!' cried Mason, as soon as he spotted the little tor-toiseshell cat, who was stretched out in a basket next to Pablo, who Izzy had brought over that morning, and was already settling in beautifully.

'Why don't you grab some toys from the basket over there, Mason, and you two can play, while I chat to your mum.' Mason nodded enthusiastically, grabbing a fishing rod toy from the toybox.

'It's so lovely to see him with a smile on his face,' said Hayley as Tori returned to the table with a tray of hot chocolates. 'We lost Mason's dad last year and it's been a tough time for him.'

'Oh, I'm so sorry to hear that. How awful for you both.'

'Thanks,' said Hayley, taking a swig of her drink. 'It's taken Mason a while, but I think he's doing much better now. He had some issues settling at school last year, but Miss Hargreaves has been great.'

'Oh, Rose is just brilliant, isn't she?'

'You're friends?'

'Yes, since we were kids. Rose is a brilliant teacher.'

'She's been fantastic. Mason's making friends and he's really enjoying being at school; I don't think we could imagine living anywhere else now. That's one of the reasons I've been thinking of getting him a cat. He absolutely loves them,' she said, nodding towards Mason, who was laughing while throwing a catnip mouse for Daisy and Pablo, 'and I think he could do with a little buddy at home.'

'I think that sounds like a great idea,' agreed Tori. 'I've got my own cat too, Ernie, and we've got such a special bond. He sleeps on my bed and always listens without judgement when I've got a problem – I adore him. I was lost without him when I was away travelling. I'm sure Mason will have a similar bond with Daisy.'

'Aw, that's exactly what I'm hoping for. I was going to get him a kitten from the pet shop in Hastings, but after your visit to the school, Mason has fallen completely in love with Daisy.'

'Well, it looks like the feeling's mutual,' said Tori, casting a smile in Mason and Daisy's direction. 'There's some paperwork to fill in from the rescue centre, which I can get Izzy from New Beginnings to email to you, then she does a home visit and once you're approved, we can book in a time for you to come and take Daisy home.'

'Well, we've got a lovely garden and I only work part-time, so I'm hoping the home check will be okay. Thanks, Tori, I don't know why I didn't think of adopting before, I just assumed rescues wouldn't rehome to families with younger children.'

'Izzy looks at each adoption on a case-by-case basis, so there are no hard and fixed rules; it's so important to find good homes for abandoned and unwanted cats.'

'Absolutely,' agreed Hayley. 'Here's my email address and we'll get out of your hair so you can close up.'

'Great, thanks, I'll forward it on to Izzy and she'll be in touch soon, I'm sure.'

'Oh, before we go, could I grab a ticket for the barn dance up at the farm? I saw a poster saying you were selling them here?'

'That's right.'

'A few of the mums from school are planning on going, we thought we'd make a night of it. Get glammed up and escape the kids for a few hours.'

'Oh, that's a nice idea, it would be great to see you there. I'll get the ticket book.'

As Hayley and Mason said their hopefully temporary goodbyes to Daisy, Tori fired off a text to Izzy. *Looks like we've found a potential home for Daisy.* Within seconds Tori's phone buzzed with a reply. *You absolute superstar xx* Tori bent down and gave Daisy a tickle under the chin. 'Did you hear that, little madam? It looks like you might be leaving us soon as well.'

The queue at the fish and chip van was particularly long and Tori was aware of her stomach growling loudly as she waited in line to place her order. Pulling her phone from her bag, she spotted an unread message from Ryan. *Can we meet tomorrow?* Before she had a chance to think about replying, she heard a familiar voice behind her.

'Tori, hi,' said Leo, and she felt flooded with warmth at the sight of him – his smile, his kind eyes and adorably messy hair . . .

'Oh, hi,' she replied in a squeaky, unfamiliar voice. This was the first time she'd seen Leo since their date last week and her mind drifted back to the parting kiss they'd shared . . .

'Looks like we both had the same idea then?'

'Sorry?'

'Fish and chip supper?' he said, nodding towards the van.

'Oh, yeah, right.'

'So . . . how are you?' he asked gently, shifting his feet and not quite meeting her eye.

'Oh, erm, good, I guess,' she shrugged. *God this was awkward.* 'You?'

'Yeah, fine, you?' he replied, taking a deep breath.

'We already did me . . .' Tori smiled, desperately hoping to break the tension. 'Oh, I saw Lara at school today, by the way,' she said, eager to fill the silence.

'Did you?'

'Yeah, I was doing a talk about the café and took Daisy and Angel with me – the kids loved them,' she said, smiling.

'I'm sure they were a big hit,' he said, still not quite meeting her eye.

'Actually, Daisy might have found a forever home with one of the boys in Lara's class – his mum's just been in.'

'Oh, that's great news,' he said, pushing up his sleeves. 'I'm really pleased for you; it's brilliant that the adoption side of the café is taking off.'

'Thanks, Leo.'

'Next!' cried a voice from the serving hatch of the van. 'What'll it be?'

'Two large cod and chips, please,' said Tori.

'Is that everything?' the woman asked.

'Yes, thanks.' Tori pulled her purse out of her bag to pay and then stood awkwardly waiting for her order.

'Next!' the woman cried, and Leo stepped forward.

'Bye then,' said Tori, waving weakly at him, as the server passed across her order.

'Tori, listen, I—'

'Next?' the woman repeated with increasing volume.

'That's you, I think,' said Tori.

'Oh, yeah … Well, it was good to see you, Tori. Look after yourself,' Leo said, turning back towards the fish and chip van as Tori walked away.

Why? Why hadn't he said something to her just now? thought Leo as he walked home, a warm bundle of fish and chips stashed safely under his arm. The prospect of his fish and chip supper suddenly seemed a whole lot less appealing. That had been the perfect opportunity for him to find out what was going on with Ryan. He tried to put Tori out of his mind, but he couldn't, and he realized he didn't want to. He wanted to build a future with her; he wasn't interested in dating anyone else. As he walked home past the Apple Tree in the warmth of the evening sun, he found himself wishing he was there with Tori, enjoying a drink together and talking about their future. Since Tori broke the news of Ryan's return, she was all he'd been able to think about – at work, at home, day and night, she was constantly in his thoughts. Could he really just walk away and let Ryan pick up where he'd left off? Shouldn't he put up a fight?

He knew his reaction to Ryan's return had sounded too flippant; he'd acted as though it was no big deal, and he could hear the hurt in her voice when he'd said that he'd see her around. He thought it would be easier for Tori that way, to let her think he wasn't bothered, but, as it turned out, he couldn't have been more wrong. He felt an overwhelming urge to throw his fish and chips in the bin, run straight to her house, bang on the door, and remind her how great they were together, that what they'd both felt on that first date shouldn't be discarded so easily. Leo shook his head. No, he'd only make a fool of himself. If Tori thought her future was with Ryan, he shouldn't get in the way of that, but if she didn't, she needed to figure that out for herself. Leo could only hope that their date had meant as much to her as it had to him.

As he walked slowly up the road towards home, he saw Tinkerbell waiting to greet him at the end of the cul-de-sac. She ran towards him meowing as he approached. 'Hey there, girl,' he said, scooping her up with his free hand. She sniffed at the fish and chip wrapper with interest. 'Fancy joining me for some cod and chips?'

Tori ate her supper in silence in front of the TV that evening. She couldn't finish her cod; she'd lost her appetite. She pushed her plate to one side, deciding to save the fish as a treat for Ernie when he next appeared through the cat flap. She couldn't stop thinking about seeing Leo at the fish and chip van. Even just a few moments with him were enough to stir up her feelings again and she couldn't deny the way she felt about him. It was more than just a physical attraction, it was something real, and she felt as though he was someone she could trust, someone she could build a future with. But did he feel the same? He'd been so laid-back when she told him about Ryan's return, he didn't seem to even care. What was it he'd said? *I'm not going to get in the way.* But there was something tonight, something in the way he'd looked at her . . . Should she go and see him? Tell him how she felt? Should she make the first move, even if she risked being rejected? She felt a wave of nausea wash over her at the thought. Her phone buzzed with another message from Ryan. *Tori, can we meet tomorrow? I've got something I need to tell you xx* She typed out a reply. *Meet me at the café at closing time.*

The following evening, Ryan arrived at the Cosy Cat just as Tori was closing up. He was dressed smartly in black jeans and a grey, collared T-shirt and he was carrying a bouquet of pink roses.

'Hi,' he said nervously as she opened the door to let him in. 'I got you these, I know they're your favourite.'

'Thanks, you shouldn't have.'

'Ah, there you are, Ryan. Tori mentioned you were picking her up,' said Joyce, keeping her tone neutral.

'Great to see you, Joyce,' said Ryan, giving her a kiss on the cheek. Tori noticed her mum stiffen slightly.

'Let me take those,' said Joyce, reaching out a hand. 'I'll put them in some water,' she said, disappearing through to the kitchen.

'So, what's the plan then? If we're going to talk, I'd rather go somewhere else,' said Tori.

'I thought we could take a drive out to Hastings, go for a walk along the front? Get dinner somewhere?'

'Dinner? I'm not really dressed for anything fancy,' said Tori, looking down at the pale pink T-shirt dress she was wearing.

'You look perfect to me,' he said, flashing her a smile. 'God, sorry, did that sound super-cheesy?'

'Just a bit, yeah,' she said stiffly.

'Well, I never was much of a smooth-talker,' he replied, looking away.

'Right, well, if we're going to Hastings we may as well hit the road,' she said, grabbing her handbag and denim jacket from the hook behind the door.

The short drive to Hastings passed in awkward silence. Ryan tried to make small talk, but to Tori it just felt odd and uncomfortable. When Ryan finally found a parking space along the seafront, Tori couldn't wait to get out of the car.

'Let's have a walk along the front, shall we? And then maybe find somewhere to eat? I thought we could go to that pizza place you used to like ...' said Ryan.

'Let's just see how things go, shall we?'

'Oh, of course, yeah ... sorry.'

They walked for a few minutes before Ryan turned to her and said, 'Tori, this is crazy – we're acting like strangers.

Let's sit down and talk properly,' he said, taking her hand and guiding her towards the nearest bench.

'I'm listening,' she said, pulling her denim jacket around her; it was chillier than she'd expected for July, and the sea breeze was cutting right through her.

'It's like I said the other night – I know I screwed up in Thailand. I want you back, Tori. I want us to try again and if all that other stuff is important to you, we can do it, all of it.'

'What other stuff?'

'You know, marriage, kids, houses. It's all in the plan *eventually*,' he said, placing great emphasis on the word, 'but we're only young, it's not like there's any rush, there's no deadline.'

'But that other stuff is important to me, Ryan. I need to know that we want the same things.'

'And we do. Like I said, I'll do whatever it takes – I want you to be happy,' he said, taking her hand.

'And you're ready for that? Buying a house together? Getting married?'

'Whatever it takes, I just want you back in my life,' he said, placing a hand on her knee.

'Really?' Tori said, feeling her resolve weaken as he pulled her in closer to him.

'I've always loved our adventures together, the travelling, the exploring, the places we've been … all of it. I can't imagine doing those things with anyone else. I want my next adventure to be with you, Tori, only you. I promise. I *love* you,' whispered Ryan, leaning towards her and bringing his lips closer, kissing her softly and she felt his arms tighten around her waist. The kiss was warm, familiar and comforting. When they finally broke apart, Ryan gently stroked her face, murmuring in her ear, 'Does this mean I'm forgiven?'

Tori stared at him, her heart pounding. 'Let's take it one day at a time, shall we?'

'I can live with that,' said Ryan, tucking her hair behind her ear.

Chapter 34

Tori barely slept again that night, replaying the conversation with Ryan over and over in her head. He was finally offering her everything she wanted. A life together, marriage, maybe even kids one day too? And yet she had a nagging little voice in her brain telling her something wasn't right. If they'd had this conversation before she'd left Thailand, she'd have been overjoyed. So why didn't she feel like that now? What had changed? Were her feelings different? The way Ryan had talked about their future together had bothered her too. Was he just trying to placate her to win her back? Sure, he said he wanted to marry her one day, but did he really mean it? Their kiss had felt off too. It wasn't that it was a bad kiss – the chemistry between her and Ryan had always been there, she'd felt it yesterday, but something was missing. It just wasn't as passionate as the kiss she'd shared with Leo. That had been electric; fireworks, earth-shattering, mind-blowing. Tori buried her head in the pillow. *Pull yourself together.* You've not told Ryan you're getting back together. You're taking each day as it comes, that's all.

Tori's phone buzzed. She made a grab for it, feeling a wave of disappointment wash over her when she realized the message was from Ryan, not Leo. After their encounter yesterday, she'd hoped he might get in touch. Her finger hovered over Ryan's words. *It was like old times again last night, miss you already xx* She stared at the screen for a while, unsure of how to reply. Deciding that avoidance was probably the best strategy, she opened Instagram and saw she had a new message. *Hi Tori, I'm filming in Brighton today and I'd love to pop by and see you. Would that be cool? Millie x* A message from Millie Martin? *The* Millie Martin? Tori rubbed her eyes. *Millie Martin in Blossom Heath?* How exciting! She let out an involuntary whoop, threw the duvet back with a start and raced down the stairs.

'Mum! You're not going to believe this,' Tori cried as she burst into the kitchen.

'Blimey, Tori, you nearly scared me half to death! What's happened?' said Joyce, her tea slopping over the sides of her mug.

'You're not going to believe it, but you know I sent that message to Millie Martin, the influencer?'

'I remember, yes,' said Joyce, nodding.

'Well, she's only gone and replied! She wants to come to the café today!' she explained, a little breathlessly.

'I told you it was worth a try.'

'I can't believe it. What shall I say to her?'

'You say yes, obviously,' Joyce laughed.

'Okay, hang on,' said Tori, typing out a reply. *We'd love*

to see you Millie, I'll keep a table reserved for you. 'There, done,' she said, exhaling. Before Tori could draw breath, her phone buzzed again, *Thanks hun xx* And just like that, the Cosy Cat had its first celebrity customer . . . and she was on her way!

After the initial burst of adrenalin had passed, Tori and Joyce spent the morning preparing for Millie's arrival. Joyce pulled out all the stops in the kitchen and Tori cleaned every inch of the café until she could see her reflection in the table-tops. She'd put a reserved sign on her favourite table in the window, and she'd fired off messages to Rose, Kate, Grace, Izzy, Harriet and Melissa to let them know about Millie's planned visit, so they could pop in and meet her themselves. Tori had thought about sending Leo a message to tell him too, but something had stopped her, and she'd deleted the draft without sending it.

Once the lunchtime rush was over, Tori's excitement began to turn to anxiety. She looked up at the clock for what seemed to the hundredth time: 2.20pm. The café usually closed at four and there was still no sign of Millie. What if she didn't show? Tori took a deep breath and tried to quash the nerves that were building inside her. Millie said she'd be here, hadn't she? Tori had no reason to doubt her, but as the minutes ticked by to 3.20pm, Tori let out a defeated sigh. Still no sign of Millie.

'I forgot to tell you, love,' said Joyce, trying to distract her. 'I bumped into Claire earlier, she wanted to know if you're planning on giving Ryan another chance?'

'Really? She was asking Rose whether I was still dating Leo. Since when is she so interested in my love life?' said Tori, bristling.

'I was inclined to tell her to mind her business, but I think she's only concerned for you. Beth said she's seen her chatting to Ryan in the pub a few times, perhaps she thinks she can plead his case?'

'It's going to take more than a word from Claire to help make things clearer,' said Tori, looking at the clock again.

'Oh, love, don't worry, there's still time for Millie to get here – we don't close for another forty minutes,' said Joyce, with an encouraging smile.

'I knew I shouldn't have gotten so excited,' Tori sighed, as the café door opened with a bang.

'Has she been? Am I too late? I practically chased the kids out of school,' said a sweating Rose, leaning on the door to catch her breath.

'Nah, not yet. I don't think she's coming,' replied Tori with a shake of the head.

'There's still time,' said Rose, nodding at the clock on the wall.

'You sound just like Mum,' said Tori with a half-smile.

'Well, great minds and all that, eh Joyce,' said Rose with a wink.

'Exactly, Rose, dear,' Joyce agreed.

'How about you and I have a catch-up coffee before Millie arrives?' said Rose.

'But what if she doesn't—'

'Hey, she's coming, okay?' said Rose, hugging Tori firmly.

'You don't know th—' said Tori.

'Actually, I do,' Rose said with a grin. 'Look …' She nodded towards the window. Spinning round, Tori stared wide-eyed, as Millie, who was easily six foot plus and dressed in a show-stopping pair of bright green high heels and a leopard print catsuit, headed straight for the café, accompanied by a group of what Tori assumed must be her staff. Tori ran her fingers through her hair, took a deep breath and rushed to open the door.

'No, I said 9am is too early, Dimitri,' Millie barked. 'Tell them it's midday at the earliest or I'm cancelling the whole thing.' A slender man, dressed all in black, nodded compliantly. 'Oh, and Flavia, ring ahead to La Maison de Blanc, will you, and let them know I'll be there for seven.'

'Sure, Millie,' answered a petit assistant who was busy tapping away on her phone.

'Millie?' Tori said, her voice cracking a little. 'Hi, I'm Tori, welcome to the Cosy Cat Café, I'm so glad you made it. Let me show you to your table.'

'Ah, Tori, thanks for having us – I love your Insta grid! Can I meet the cats?' Millie asked.

'Of course!' replied Tori, before turning to mouth the words 'Ring Grace and Izzy' at Rose.

'Is it okay if my staff set up somewhere? You have Wi-Fi, right?'

'Absolutely, feel free to set up anywhere you like, guys,' said Tori. 'The Wi-Fi password is on the menus.'

'Thanks,' said Dimitri, as Millie's team began plugging all sorts of tech into the sockets.

'And who's this little darling?' asked Millie, bending down and scooping Daisy up in her arms. 'Isn't she just adorable?'

'This is Daisy,' said Tori. 'She's actually just found a forever home, so she should be going to her new family in the next few days.'

'How wonderful,' said Millie, beaming, 'what a lucky girl.'

'We've got four other cats with us at the moment, who are available to adopt. Angel, Norris, Pablo and Mr Wiggles,' Tori explained.

'And they're all from New Beginnings?' asked Millie.

'That's right.'

'I can't tell you how much I love this place, Tori. My own cats are rescues – I've got a Bengal and a Burmese, Primrose and Saffy. I couldn't be without them, you know. When all this,' she said, waving an arm in the direction of her entourage, 'gets too much, I know I can always go home to them. They don't judge me. They don't care who I'm dating or what the press are saying about me, they just love me ... well, for me, I guess.' Tori noticed Millie's voice crack a little and couldn't help herself, reaching out to give Millie's arm a squeeze.

'Oh, sorry,' said Tori, 'I didn't mean to—'

'Don't be silly,' said Millie, putting Daisy gently back on the ground. 'You get it, don't you? I can see that you do.' Tori nodded and Millie leant forward and gave her a quick hug.

'Wow,' mouthed Rose, from the other side of the café, as she gave Tori an enthusiastic thumbs-up.

'I'm guessing that you've got your own cat at home too?' asked Millie.

'That's right, Ernie, he's a rescue too,' said Tori, pulling out her phone to show Millie a photograph of Ernie curled up on the sofa.

'Oh, he's stunning,' cooed Millie. 'A Maine Coon?'

'That's right,' nodded Tori.

'Just gorgeous. Oh. My. God! Are those anpans?' said Millie, peering at the display of cakes on the counter.

'They are indeed. I baked them myself. I'm Tori's mum, and you must be Millie? Welcome to the Cosy Cat Café!' said Joyce, emerging from the kitchen with flour in her hair and her apron askew.

'Well, hello, Tori's Mum, thank you! You know, I haven't seen them since I was last in Japan. I was addicted when I was in Tokyo,' said Millie.

'I'll get you some,' said Joyce, picking up the serving tongs.

'Oh, I really shouldn't . . . the calories,' said Millie, screwing up her face. 'Oh, what the hell. Go on then, I'll take two. It's not every day you get to indulge, is it? You know what, I don't think I've ever seen them in the UK, not even in London.'

'I've recently returned from travelling around Asia,' said Tori, 'so when we reopened Mum's tearoom, we thought we'd add some of the tastes and flavours from the places I'd visited to the new menu. It's where cat cafés originated too, so it feels appropriate to incorporate them and give our customers a more authentic experience without having to travel.'

373

'Wow! These are delicious,' said Millie, closing her eyes as she savoured the sweet taste. 'Now, Tori, anything I can do to get these beautiful babies adopted? You name it.'

'We could take some photos of you with them?'

'Sure,' Millie laughed, pulling out her phone. 'Hang on, let me grab one of these cute bags too – we should get your logo in the shot,' she continued, typing away furiously. 'There, you look gorgeous,' she said, showing Tori her Instagram post, the caption read: *Hanging out @TheCosyCatCafe in Sussex with some super cute cats who are looking for their furever homes #adoptdontshop #rescuedismyfavouritebreed*. 'But what I meant was, how can I help support the rescue centre?' Tori spotted Izzy rushing across the village green and smiled.

'Ah, here comes Izzy, she's the person to talk to about that,' said Tori, as a very out of breath and red-faced Izzy came bursting through the door.

The rest of Millie's visit passed by in a flurry of activity; she was keen to chat to both Izzy and Grace about the work at New Beginnings and the challenges it faced. Tori and Joyce kept the best of the new menu coming, with the local cheeses in the Blossom Heath Ploughman's going down particularly well. Millie posted a picture of the Blossom Heath Blue on her grid, tagging Nathan's farm in, which had already raked up over one hundred likes. Tori was amazed at how much her team managed to eat, while Rose was kept busy snapping photos for them all to share across their channels.

'There's no time like the present – let's go,' said Millie, standing up and grabbing her handbag.

'What? Right now?' said Izzy, looking genuinely surprised.

'Definitely, if that's okay with you? Who knows when I'll be back in the area again,' said Millie.

'Tori, Millie's going to come up to the rescue ... now.'

'Oh, that's a great idea,' said Tori excitedly. 'It'll give you a real insight into what we're both trying to achieve here.'

'And just how fit to bursting the centre is,' said Grace. 'Anything you can do to raise funds and awareness would be brilliant – thanks, Millie.'

'Well, if I can help at all, I'm happy to,' said Millie, flashing her perfect smile. 'And who knows, I might even find a kitty to add to my feline clan.'

'Are you thinking of adopting again?' asked Izzy.

'If I can find the right match for my two babies, then yes, absolutely. I don't think they'd tolerate an adult cat, but maybe a kitten ...' Millie explained.

'Oh, we've got loads of kittens right now and I've got just the one in mind ...'

'You're in good hands with Izzy,' said Grace.

'Well, then, let's go,' Millie laughed. 'Tori, can I get a few bags of those dog treats you've got by the till? Are they homemade? My friend's Cavapoo will go mad for them.'

'They are, and a percentage of the profits goes back to the rescue centre too,' said Tori.

'They do? In that case I'll take every bag you've got,' said Millie, beaming. 'Dimitri, settle up our bill, will you? And this is for the donation tin,' said Millie, pulling a thick wedge of fifty-pound notes out of her purse and pushing them into the jar on the counter.

'Wow, Millie, that's so generous of you,' said Izzy, tearing up a little. 'This will make a huge difference.'

'Don't mention it,' said Millie, smiling, as she swept out of the café, her team trailing behind her.

Before Tori fell asleep that evening, she scrolled through Instagram one last time. She couldn't believe how generous Millie had been, not just adding multiple photos of Angel, Pablo, Norris and Mr Wiggles to her grid, but also sharing her favourite treats from the new menu. The Cosy Cat's account had seen a surge of new followers as a result and the daily allocation of pre-bookable tables was now full for the next four weeks. She'd even had an email from a reporter at the local paper who'd heard about Millie's visit and wanted to run a piece on the café. As thrilled as Tori was with the buzz around the café, she was even happier to see the stories and reels Millie had posted from New Beginnings, and Millie had adopted not one, but two, tabby kittens, the aptly named Dolce and Gabbana, who looked utterly adorable and very at home in Millie's arms. Izzy had been straight on the phone to Tori to thank her for getting Millie involved with the rescue and New Beginnings had already had a flurry of donations via PayPal. Izzy and Millie had got on so well, and spent so much time together, she'd even persuaded the social media star to become a patron of the rescue. Now if that wasn't a good result all round, Tori didn't know what was.

As Tori settled herself under the duvet, with Ernie resting at her feet, her phone buzzed. Tori's heart raced when she saw it was a new message from Leo. *Just heard about Millie Martin's visit! Great result for the café and the rescue. Proud of you Leo x* A smile spread across her face as she typed out a reply. *It wasn't just me, it was a team effort, but thank you xx* Leo responded quickly. *See you at the barn dance tomorrow evening. Maybe we can talk?* The dance. Amidst all the excitement of the day, Tori had completely forgotten about the fundraiser at Harper Farm. She blinked rapidly, thinking of how to reply. She deleted several messages before she finally hit send. *Sounds good. Looking forward to it. See you there xx* Tori stared at her phone for a while thinking about what she'd actually say to Leo tomorrow. She needed to get things clear in her mind first, but she still felt so confused. As she flicked off the bedside lamp and snuggled down under the duvet, she realized that she still hadn't replied to Ryan's message from earlier. She closed her eyes and decided that particular task could wait until the morning . . .

Chapter 35

Tori arrived at Harper Farm earlier than planned the next day. She was part of the team helping to set up the event, but she hoped to talk to Rose before any of the other volunteers arrived. She needed to work through her feelings about Ryan and Leo, and she knew talking to Rose would help. There were just some things that she couldn't discuss with her mum and her steamy feelings towards Leo definitely fell into that category.

'Tori!' Jake called from the yard as she pulled up at the farm. 'We weren't expecting you for a couple of hours yet,' he said looking at his watch.

'I know, but I wanted to try and catch up with Rose, so I thought I'd get here early,' replied Tori, as she climbed out of her car.

'She's just taken the dogs out for a walk, but she should be back any minute. Cuppa?'

'Please.'

'Come in, I'll stick the kettle on,' he said, gesturing

for Tori to follow him into the farmhouse. 'Milk, two sugars, right?'

'Yep, thanks, Jake.'

'So, how's things?' he asked. 'I heard about Millie Martin rocking up at the café. Impressive,' he said, raising an eyebrow. 'Nathan said she even gave his cheese a shout-out – he's had loads of online orders today.'

'That's great! I still can't believe she turned up. We're fully booked for the next few weeks now.'

'I'm not surprised – hasn't she got about two million followers?'

'Two point six million, to be exact.'

'Wowser,' said Jake, whistling.

'I know, crazy, isn't it?'

'Mental,' Jake agreed, 'and what about Ryan? I'd heard he was back. How are you doing with all that?'

'Not great,' she said, groaning. 'It's a bloody mess if I'm honest, Jake.'

'I'm guessing that's what you want to talk to Rose about?'

'Is it that obvious?'

'Well, it doesn't exactly take a genius to work it out.' Jake smiled. 'You know, I'm a pretty good listener, if you want to talk while you're waiting for Rose?'

Tori eyed him suspiciously. 'Hmm . . .'

'You don't look convinced . . . Just try me, okay? What harm can it do?'

'Okay, okay,' said Tori, exhaling, 'why not?' Jake passed

her a steaming mug of tea and pulled up a seat next to her. 'Well, I'm guessing Rose has told you what Ryan did just before I flew home.'

'She filled me in, yes,' he said, nodding.

'And things with Leo were going well, pretty well. And then up pops Ryan wanting us to get back together again and I'm just not sure if I can . . .'

'Trust him?'

Tori nodded and took a huge gulp of her tea. 'He let me down badly, Jake. I know he didn't cheat or anything like that, but he just dumped me without any explanation. I was left to come home alone from the other side of the world. I'm just not sure if his heart is really in building a future together or if he just wants me back cos he says he misses me.'

'And Leo? How do things stand there?'

'I don't know,' she said, shrugging. 'I thought things were going really well but when I told him Ryan was back, he acted as though he wasn't bothered at all. I guess we've only had one date, so he probably isn't—'

'He is.'

'Is what?'

'Bothered,' said Jake.

'How do you . . . Has he said something?' Tori asked quickly.

'Well, not directly, no. But I can tell something's up with him.'

'You can?'

'Oh yeah, definitely. He's not his usual . . . well, he's not

Leo. He's been really down and grouchy. It's not just me – all the lads at football have noticed something's up. He's grumpy at practice, not wanting to come to the pub. If I didn't know better, I'd say he was missing someone . . .'

'What? But that doesn't make any sense,' said Tori, shaking her head. 'He's not said anything to me, he's not shown any sign that he's not okay about Ryan.'

'Well, he wouldn't, would he?'

Tori threw him a confused look.

'Come on, Tori, he's a bloke. What do you expect him to do? Turn up at the café and tell you not to take Ryan back?'

'Well, if that's what he wants, then yes!'

'But he doesn't know that's what *you* want, does he? I'm guessing you haven't told him how you're feeling either, have you?'

'Not exactly, no,' she said, shifting in her seat awkwardly.

'There you are then,' said Jake, with an exasperated look on his face. 'You think Leo doesn't care, but I'm telling you he does. He thinks he's doing the honourable thing by letting you decide how you feel about Ryan without pressurizing you. He'll string me up if he knew I'd told you that, by the way, so don't tell him I told you, okay?'

'But I had no idea.'

'Why would you? And you haven't opened up to him either.'

'I guess not.' Tori shrugged.

'You're as bad as each other.'

'That doesn't make it any easier, though, does it? I'm still

381

confused. I'm scared of getting hurt again and I feel like I don't know who to trust.'

'Ah, well, that's love for you, I guess; none of us know if we'll get hurt. Sometimes you just have to go with your heart and work the rest out later.'

'And if you're not sure what's in your heart?'

'Well, how do you really feel about Ryan? Do you actually want to try again with him?'

'Argh, that's just it, I don't know. If he really does want marriage and kids, then maybe.'

'That's something I can't help you with, I'm afraid – you've got to make that decision on your own.'

'But what if I get it wrong? What if I make a mistake?'

Jake shook his head. 'You won't,' he said reassuringly. 'I know that you've got good instincts – you just need to start trusting yourself again.'

'When did you become so wise, Jake Harper?' said Tori, her voice catching a little.

'I always have been. You've just never needed my advice before.' He smiled.

'I'm so glad you and Rose found each other. I hope you know how lucky you are?'

'Oh, don't worry, I do,' said Jake, beaming. 'I make sure she knows it too.'

'I know what too?' said Rose, appearing in the doorway of the farmhouse with Scout, Finn and Tagg right behind her.

'How lucky I am to have found you, my love,' said Jake,

standing up from the table and wrapping his arms around her waist.

'I'm glad you realize,' said Rose, putting her arms around his neck and planting a kiss on his cheek. 'Is everything okay, Tori? I wasn't expecting you for another hour or so.'

'Oh, I just needed a bit of advice but, as it turns out, I think I'm sorted on that front now,' said Tori, nodding in Jake's direction.

'Jake gave you advice?' said Rose, her eyes widening. 'Seriously?'

'Hey, I'll have you know I'm a great agony uncle,' replied Jack, feigning offence.

'Actually, on this occasion, I think he was exactly the man I needed to speak to,' said Tori, nodding decisively.

'Seeing as my work here is done, I'll head up to the barn and start setting up for tonight,' said Jake, pulling on a base-ball cap and grabbing his sunglasses from the table.

'Thanks, Jake,' said Tori, 'I mean it – thanks for listening.'

'Anytime,' he replied, the three Border Collies following closely behind him.

Tori, Rose, Jake and the rest of the volunteers had trans-formed Harper Farm into a stunning party venue. The dance itself was taking place in the main barn, which Tori now barely recognized, such was the extent of its transformation. Jake had arranged hay bales, so that everyone had some-where to sit, the WI had decorated tables at the back of the barn, with wildflowers in tiny milk bottles and corn dollies dressed in mini farmer outfits, ready for food to be brought out on later. Joyce had been baking all morning at the café and Tori knew Jean's WI ladies were great cooks, so she couldn't wait to see what they were going to bring too. Jess was going to be selling the Cosy Cat's branded merchandise to help raise funds and the stall was stocked with mugs, bags and coasters, as well as batches of their homemade cat and dog treats, which had been packaged up in cute brown paper bags decorated with tiny pawprints. Jess had even drawn a series of limited-edition sketches of the cats to sell, calling them 'Paw-traits', much to everyone's amusement. Tori had already decided she would be buying Mr Wiggles' portrait to display in the café and had asked Jess to draw Ernie too. Grace and Rose had spent an age tying strings of fairy lights around the wooden beams and filling jam jars with tealights to use as makeshift lanterns. Now, with dusk beginning to fall, the band had arrived, and the space looked truly magical.

'Well done everyone!' cried Mrs Connolly, clapping her hands to attract everyone's attention. 'I'd say that's a wrap, wouldn't you, Jake?'

'Absolutely – thanks so much for all your help this afternoon. You've just got time to go home if you want to change before the party starts!' The volunteers gradually began to filter out of the barn and Tori saw that Claire was making a beeline for her.

'Tori, hi! Can I have a word?' Claire asked.

'Look, sorry I've not replied to your messages, life has been a little crazy recently.'

'I've got to know Ryan the past few days and I just don't understand what's wrong with you, Tori. Why won't you take him back? As far as I can see, he's bending over backwards trying to make things right with you.'

'What?' said Tori, shocked. 'I can't see what business it is of yours.'

'You should count yourself lucky he's trying to win you back, rather than throwing yourself at Leo. It's not a good look, Tori,' said Claire, staring daggers at her.

'Everything okay?' Rose interrupted.

'Yep,' Claire nodded, through a tight-lipped smile. 'I need to get going anyway.'

'What on earth was all that about?' Rose asked, watching Claire walk away.

'She was giving me a lecture over Ryan. I should be grateful he wants me back apparently.'

'Seriously?'

'Yep. I thought she'd understand why I'd be cautious about him but obviously not. Maybe I've got her all wrong.' Tori shrugged.

'How are you feeling about things?' Rose whispered. 'Any idea what you're going to do?'

'I'm going to play it by ear. I'm so nervous about seeing Leo but I've not told Ryan about tonight; he's bound to have seen the posters up in the pub, though, so I'm guessing he might turn up. The thought of seeing them both together feels pretty nerve-racking,' she said, clutching her stomach. 'I feel like I owe Ryan the chance to try and put things right.

Talking to Jake helped, though, and I know I just need to be honest with Ryan and with myself. I need to be sure about what it is I really want.'

'And you're not?'

'I don't think so, no,' Tori said, shaking her head.

'Maybe everything will feel a bit clearer if you do see Ryan tonight? Trust your instincts, Tori, they won't let you down,' said Rose with a nod.

'I really hope you're right, Rose ...'

And with that, Tori went home to change.

Chapter 36

When Tori arrived back at the barn an hour later, she spotted Ryan immediately. She had hoped when she saw him again that her gut instinct would help guide her, but she was still feeling as confused as ever.

'Wow, Tori, you look amazing,' he said, walking slowly towards her.

'Thanks,' said Tori, her legs feeling a little shaky. 'I couldn't decide whether to wear a Cosy Cat or New Beginnings T-shirt, so Jess had this one made with both logos. Isn't it great?'

'Yeah, it looks really cute on you,' said Ryan, smiling. 'Drink?'

'Yes, please.'

'I'll see what I can find.'

As Ryan disappeared off towards the bar, Tori scanned the room looking for Leo, when, out of nowhere, a small body engulfed her in a hug.

'Hi, Lara,' said Tori. 'How are Domino and Dexter?'

'Oh, they're great, they've grown so much already, they don't really seem like kittens anymore,' said Lara, her voice tinged with disappointment.

'I know what you mean. I've almost forgotten how tiny my Ernie was as a kitten. I'll have to show you a photo one day – he could fit in the palm of my hand when he was a baby,' said Tori.

'Lara, there you are!' said Leo, jogging over. 'I told you not to go running off.'

'Oh, she's fine,' said Tori, 'we were just catching up, weren't we?' Lara nodded enthusiastically.

'It's good to see you,' said Leo, flashing Tori a smile that made her legs turn to jelly. 'I've missed you,' he said, fixing his gaze upon her. 'I was hoping we could talk—'

'Cider okay?' asked Ryan, passing Tori a recyclable paper cup. 'There wasn't much choice, to be honest—'

'Oh, sorry. I didn't mean to interrupt,' said Leo awkwardly. 'Come on, Lara, let's go, Tori's busy.'

'Oh no, it's fine, you don't have to,' said Tori quickly, but Leo and Lara were already out of earshot.

'Who was that?' asked Ryan, taking a swig of his pint.

'Oh, that's Leo and Lara, Leo is—'

'Look, can we go somewhere a bit quieter?' said Ryan, shouting into Tori's ear. 'Now the band's started up, I can't hear myself think. I've got something important I want to ask you.'

'Yeah, okay,' said Tori, wondering what could be so

important so early on in the evening. He guided her through the crowds of people that were heading towards the dance floor.

'Ah, that's better,' he said, as they stepped into the cool night air, 'I couldn't hear myself think in there. God, barn dances are the worst, aren't they? Let's sit on that bench over there, shall we? Like I said, I wanted to talk to you about something.' He reached towards his inside pocket.

Oh God, he wasn't going to propose, was he? Tori knew she'd told Ryan getting married was important to her, but she didn't mean here ... now ... tonight. She wasn't even sure that she wanted to get back together with him, let alone marry him. She felt her jaw muscles tense, her heartbeat quicken and her breathing become more shallow. *God, was she going to have another panic attack?* Ryan pulled an envelope out of his pocket and passed it to her. An envelope? Okay, so it definitely wasn't a ring. She felt her shoulders relax a little and her breathing steadied.

'What's this?' she asked, her curiosity peaked.

'Well, now we're giving things another go—'

'Hang on, I've not said—'

'I wanted to show you how serious I am about our future, Tori. Open it ...'

Tori tentatively peeled the envelope open, to find two one-way plane tickets to Thailand and a leaflet for an outdoor activity centre inside. She looked at him, confused.

'I don't get it.' She shrugged.

'Isn't it obvious?' Ryan laughed. 'The tickets are for us – to go back to Thailand together. I've found this great adventure centre that has jobs for us both, maybe even management roles in the future. We can start again together there, Tori, maybe even stay long term. What do you say?'

'What are you talking about? Go back to Thailand? Why would I do that? I've got the café here.'

'Don't be silly, Tori, it's only a café,' he said, throwing his hands in the air. 'I'm talking about a *real* life together, an adventure, not some boring humdrum life.'

'But what I'm doing here isn't boring or humdrum, it *is* an adventure. It means something to me. It's important. Don't you get it?'

'Important? Seriously? A cat café in Blossom Heath?' he said, shaking his head. 'Do you really want to follow in your mum's footsteps and spend your entire life running a village café?'

'And what's wrong with following in my mum's footsteps?' Tori asked, her shoulders stiffening.

'Well, nothing I guess.' Ryan shrugged. 'It's just a bit pedestrian, isn't it? You'd be settling, Tori,' he said, reaching out for her hand. She jerked away from him.

'Settling? By staying here in Blossom Heath, you mean?'

'Exactly. I thought you were aiming for something better, Tori. I thought you were ambitious.'

'I think all the work I've put into the café is pretty ambitious,' she said, hurling the plane tickets back at him. 'And

I think what I've achieved since I've been home is pretty good, actually.'

'Calm down, will you. I'm not having a go; I'm just saying running a café isn't really—'

'I know exactly what you were trying to say, Ryan,' she said, the heat rising in her cheeks. 'Did you really think I would just abandon the café? The cats? The work I've been doing with the rescue centre? Just because you've got some half-arsed plan to go back to work in Thailand?'

'For God's sake, Tori, you're taking this the wrong way. I'm telling you that I love you, that I want to be with you. I've said I'll do marriage and kids if that's what you want, but we don't have to do all that right now. I thought you'd be up for something more fun before we think about settling down. I want you to come back to Thailand with me.'

'And if that's not what *I* want? If I want to stay right here, to make a go of things at the café? Build a life here?'

'Then I'd say you're missing out on the opportunity of a lifetime. Come on, Tori, just say yes. If you still want to do the whole marriage thing in a few years' time, we can talk about it then, re-evaluate.'

'*Re-evaluate?* What does that even mean?'

'It means, we're young. We should be travelling, having adventures, having fun. Not stuck in the middle of nowhere, running a café and tying ourselves down.'

'Tying ourselves down?' she repeated. 'Is that how you see our relationship? As a tie?'

'Of course not, you're twisting my words. Honestly, I thought you'd be happy about this; Claire said you'd jump at the chance—'

'Claire? What's she got to do with any of this?'

'Well, nothing really. We've just been chatting a bit since I've been staying at the pub and she said you'd love to—'

'Do you know what?' said Tori, feeling calmer than she had done since Ryan had arrived back. She had clarity. She knew exactly what she wanted to do. 'I don't want to come with you, Ryan. We're not right together. I thought I needed you to be happy, but I was wrong. You don't understand or care what's important to me and I can't be with someone who doesn't get me. Really get me . . .'

'Of course I do.'

'You really don't, Ryan, but that's okay because I think—'

'Help! Help!' Tori's head snapped round to see Maggie frantically waving her arms next to one of the outbuildings. 'Over here! Help!'

'What the—' said Tori, leaping up from the bench.

'Are those flames?' asked Ryan, pointing towards a fire that was licking up the walls towards the wooden roof at an alarming rate.

'Oh God, it's on fire,' Tori cried, running across the yard. 'Get help. Go! Quickly!' she barked at Ryan. 'Mags! Are you okay? Help's coming,' she coughed as smoke filled her lungs and the heat from the flames burned her cheeks.

'I'm fine!' cried Maggie, her face streaked with tears. 'I came out for some fresh air and spotted the flames.'

Tori could hear Jake and Leo's voices behind her, getting louder, and was grateful that Ryan had clearly raised the alarm.

'Tori? Are you hurt?' Jake called, sprinting towards her.

'No, I'm fine,' she stammered. 'Mags spotted the flames.'

'Is there anyone inside?' Leo asked, pulling off his jacket.

'I don't know, I don't think so,' said Maggie, tears streaming down her face.

'Any livestock in there?' Leo asked Jake.

'No, it's just the feed store.'

'I've called the fire brigade,' shouted Rose, clutching her phone. 'They're on their way.'

'Great,' replied Leo. 'Jake, have you got an outside water tap and hose? Let's try and get this thing under control if we can, shall we?'

'On it,' said Jake, running across the yard.

'I'll help,' said Maggie.

'There are buckets in the cow shed, we can fill them with water from the animal troughs,' yelled Rose. The music from the barn dance stopped as word of the fire spread, the yard was suddenly filled with people.

'Lara?' cried Nina. 'Has anyone seen Lara?' she screamed. 'Leo? Was she with you?'

'No!' Leo shouted and Tori could see the look of panic etched onto his face. 'Lara!' he yelled. 'Lara, where are you? You're not in trouble, we just need you to come out now, okay?'

'Lara? Lara?' an echo of voices called from around the yard

as more partygoers became aware of the emergency and left the dance to help. There was no response.

Rose, Jess, Pete and Beth began throwing buckets of water on the flames that were now threatening to engulf the whole building.

'We need more!' yelled Jess, running back to the troughs to refill the buckets.

'Lara's not in the farmhouse,' shouted Mrs Connolly from across the yard.

'She's definitely not still in the party,' said Cora, 'I've completely scoured the barn.'

'There's no sign of her in the lambing barn,' shouted Grace.

'I've checked the hayloft too, just in case she'd decided to climb the ladder,' said Izzy, jogging back to the yard to find a desperate Nina with tears running down her face. 'She's not there, Nina.'

'You don't think she could be . . .' said Nina, nodding towards the flames. 'Oh God, Leo,' she said, as the blood drained from her face.

'Lara!' Leo yelled again, ripping a sleeve from his shirt and tying it around his face.

'Leo? What are you doing?' yelled Tori. 'You're not going in there, are you? It's too dangerous—'

'This is what I do, Tori – it's what I'm trained for.'

'Leo, no! You need to wait for back-up. You don't have the right equipment.' Tori tried to pull him back.

'I have to,' he said. 'It's Lara.'

Tori nodded; she knew she couldn't stop him. If there was

any chance Lara was in that building filling with flames, then Tori knew he had to go. She held her breath as she saw him disappear into the smoke.

'Where's Leo?' said Jake, as he returned with a hose. Tori lifted her arm slowly and pointed towards the burning barn. 'What? He's gone in? Is he mad?'

'It's Lara,' Nina said weakly. 'She might be inside.'

'Jesus!' said Jake, grabbing Nina around the waist as her knees buckled. 'Let's give him a hand then, shall we?'

Tori took Nina's weight from Jake, and he aimed the hose at the fire raging in front of them. The stream of water seemed weak and ineffective against the wall of flames. Rose and her team of volunteers continued to hurl water from their buckets at the fire, but the flames just seemed to get fiercer, hotter and bigger.

Tears were streaming down Tori's smoke-streaked face now, and despite the heat from the fire, terror had frozen her insides. Why hadn't she tried harder to stop him? She should have forced him to stay, to wait for the fire service to arrive. *If he didn't . . . if he couldn't find Lara . . . if they didn't make it out . . .* She thought she might vomit. She was clutching her hands together so tightly that her fingers were numb. *Come on, Leo . . . where are you?* She stared at the entrance to the barn, looking for any sign of movement among the thick, black smoke. A flicker, a sign . . . *anything.* She stared hard, her eyes watering, burning as she gazed through the smoke. *Come on. Please.* She could hear voices around her, sirens in the distance, someone saying her name, but she couldn't look away. Suddenly men in uniform were all around her, trying to move her aside, barking orders at each other. She wouldn't, she couldn't, move.

And then, there he was. The sight she had been waiting to see for what felt like an eternity. A silhouette framed in the doorway, carrying a small, limp figure in his arms. It was Leo. Leo *and* Lara. Firefighters rushed forwards and took Lara from him, as Leo fell to his knees, coughing, gasping for air. He was barely recognizable beneath all the soot. A paramedic rushed to his side placing an oxygen mask over his face and patting him on the back. Lara was wrapped in a silver blanket, a tiny oxygen mask placed over her nose and mouth. Her eyes were open, and she was nodding. Nina was at her side, crying, hugging her daughter close to her. Tori couldn't wait any longer; she rushed towards Leo and threw her arms around him. He hugged her hard and wouldn't let go, and Tori knew it was now or never – she had to tell him how she felt. Leo pulled his oxygen mask away from his face.

'Sir, I really must insist you keep—' said a paramedic, trying to reattach the mask.

'I'm fine now, seriously,' Leo said, taking a deep breath and coughing violently.

'Leo,' cried Tori, 'I thought I'd lost you ... I don't know what I'd have done ... I haven't told you—'

'Ssssh,' he said, placing a finger to her lips. He pushed a strand of smoke-streaked hair behind her ear as she leant in towards him.

'What's happened to Lara?' Tori whispered.

'I need to make sure she's okay,' said Leo.

'Let's go find her,' said Tori, taking his hand.

Chapter 37

Lara was sitting upright in the back of an ambulance, Nina at her side, clutching her daughter's hand.

'How's she doing, Will?' Leo asked the paramedic.

'Her vitals look good, but we're going to head to A and E to get her checked out. She's had a lucky escape, mate,' replied Will, clapping Leo on the back.

'Leo, if it wasn't for you ...' Nina whispered.

'Don't even go there, Sis,' said Leo, his voice cracking. 'Do you know what happened, Lara?'

'It's all my fault, Uncle Leo, I took one of the magic jam jars into the barn to look for fairies ...'

'Magic jam jars?' asked Nina.

'I think she means the ones on the tables – Rose and I put tealights in them,' replied Tori.

'But it was dark, I dropped it and the straw caught on fire. I thought I'd be in trouble, so I hid ... and then, then ...' Lara sobbed.

'Hey, you're not in trouble,' Leo said soothingly, putting

his arm around Lara's tiny shoulders. 'We're just glad you're okay, that's all. That's the only thing that matters, right?'

'Okay,' sniffed Lara.

'Why don't you ride with us to the hospital?' said Will. 'You should get checked out too.'

'I'm fine,' said Leo, coughing again.

'I want you to, Uncle Leo,' said Lara.

'As long as there's still room for Mummy,' said Leo, looking at Will.

'Well, it's bending the rules a little but I'm sure we can take all three of you,' said Will, smiling at Lara. She beamed at him.

'I'll leave you to it,' said Tori, turning to go.

'Hang on,' said Leo, jumping out of the ambulance. 'Will, just give me a second, will you? Tori, wait . . .'

'Leo, I'm so sorry, this is all my fault,' said Tori, full of shame.

'Your fault? And how's that exactly?'

'It was my idea to put tealights in the jam jars. That's what caused the fire.'

'You didn't know what was going to happen, you couldn't have.'

'But even so . . .'

'Don't blame yourself, okay? I'm fine, Lara's fine, that's what matters,' he said, wiping away the tears that were now streaming down Tori's face.

'I know but—'

'Listen, before I get in that ambulance, I need to tell you

something.' Tori opened her mouth, but Leo put a finger to her lips. 'I wanted to say this the other night at the fish van, but I lost my nerve. I think we're great together, Tori. I think we could have a shot at a real future. I know this Ryan bloke is back on the scene, but he's got competition on his hands. I'm not giving up, Tori. If you pick Ryan, that's ... fine. But I can't let you choose him without telling you how I still feel about you.'

'There is no competition,' said Tori.

'What?'

'I mean,' she said, putting her finger to his lips, 'I mean, I choose you, Leo – *you're* the one I want to be with.'

'And you couldn't have told me that before I did that whole embarrassing speech thing?' he said, smiling broadly.

'Well, you were doing such a great job that I didn't want to interrupt you ...'

Leo pulled Tori towards him and kissed her, the whoops from the onlooking crowd eventually breaking them apart.

'About time!' shouted Mags.

'Finally!' said Rose.

'I knew it!' cried Grace.

'Come on, Romeo, time to go,' shouted Will from the back of the ambulance.

'Can I take it that means Ryan is out of the picture then?' Rose whispered in Tori's ear as the ambulance pulled away.

'You can,' said Tori, nodding. 'I guess I'd better go and find him – I'd just told him I didn't want to get back together when we spotted the flames.'

'Oh, he's literally just gone,' said Beth. 'Once he saw you and Leo kiss, he told me he was heading straight back to the pub to check out.'

'I think once he saw you two together, he realized it was game over,' added Jake.

'Jake, I'm so sorry, your beautiful barn,' said Tori, looking up at the remains of the building in front of her.

'Oh, don't worry, honestly. We've got insurance, no one's hurt, that's all I care about,' said Jake, putting an arm around Rose. 'In fact, you should all get off home. The fire crew can take it from here. You've done more than enough tonight.'

'Only if you're sure?' said Mrs Connolly.

'We're happy to stay and lend a hand,' said Grace.

'No, we can manage, honestly,' said Rose. 'You all go home and get some sleep.'

'I'll come back tomorrow with some of the lads from work and we'll help with the cleanup,' said Greg, who Tori noticed was holding her mum's hand.

'That would be much appreciated, Greg, thanks,' said Jake.

'Come on, love,' said Joyce, 'I think you've had enough excitement for one night. Let's try to get some rest and you can check on Leo tomorrow.' Tori nodded and followed her mum towards the car. 'I'll drive,' said Joyce, taking the keys from her daughter, 'I don't think your mind's going to be focused on the road.'

'You're one to talk,' laughed Tori, climbing into the passenger seat. 'What about you and Greg? He's pretty smitten if you ask me.'

'We're going on a date next Thursday actually,' said Joyce, struggling to contain the excitement in her voice. 'He finally worked up the courage to ask me.'

'Ah, that's brilliant, Mum. I'm so pleased for you.'

'Don't go getting too ahead of yourself, it's just a date, but it's a step in the right direction.'

'It certainly is,' agreed Tori.

'We're going to go to that new Italian place in Rye for dinner,' said Joyce, smiling and starting up the engine.

'I might have to pop in for a drink then, check how you're getting on.'

'Don't you dare, Tori Baxter!' laughed Joyce as she hit the accelerator and pulled away from Harper Farm.

When Tori and Joyce arrived back home, their usual parking space outside the café had been taken, so Joyce parked further up the street and, as they walked along in silence towards the house, Tori reflected on the events of the evening. Just as she pulled her phone out of her pocket to send Leo a message, she was startled by the sound of breaking glass.

'Mum, did you hear that?' she whispered, stopping sharply and grabbing Joyce's arm.

'Yes! You don't think someone's trying to break into the café, do you?' whispered Joyce.

'Wait here, I'll take a look.'

'Tori, no! It could be dangerous,' hissed Joyce, but it was too late, Tori was already jogging down the street towards the café.

'Hey! What's going on?' she shouted as she neared the café. 'I'm calling the police!' she yelled, phone in hand. As she got closer, she could see the front window of the café had been cracked rather than broken, so hopefully the cats were still safely inside, and there was someone peering in through the window.

'Tori!' squeaked a familiar high-pitched voice.

'What on earth . . .' Tori knew that voice, she was sure of it. She shook her head, willing herself to remember . . . 'Who's there?' The figure in front of her stood frozen to the spot. Tori strained her eyes in an attempt to see who it was. 'Oh my God, Claire is that you? Are you alright?' she asked, rushing forwards. 'You're not hurt are you?' Claire shook her head, but didn't utter a word. 'What happened? Has someone tried to break in? Did you see who it was?'

'I think so,' said Claire, her hands shaking, 'it was just kids . . . they went that way,' she stuttered, pointing towards the village green.

'I'm calling the police,' said Tori. 'Don't worry, you're okay, that's the main thing, any damage can be repaired—'

'Hello? Tori?' called Maggie, making towards her across the village green. 'Is something wrong? I heard shouting.'

'Tori! What's going on?' asked Joyce, suddenly appearing out of the darkness.

'Claire's just seen someone trying to break in. I'm calling the police,' Tori explained.

'Tori, wait!' said Claire, reaching out a hand to stop her. 'Don't call the police . . .'

'But why? Claire, I think you're in shock,' said Tori gently. 'Let me call for some help—'

'No, don't! What I said just now about some kids running away ... it wasn't true,' said Claire, hanging her head.

'Well, don't worry, it's dark, the police won't expect you to identify—'

'I didn't see anyone running away ... because it was me,' said Claire, taking a deep breath in. 'It was an accident, though, Tori. You have to believe me,' she added quickly. 'I didn't mean to do any damage ... I just swung my bag at the window and, well, you can see what happened,' she said, pointing at the glass.

'Claire!' said Maggie, looking shocked.

'But I ... I don't understand. Why would you do that?' Tori asked, looking down at Claire's designer bag, which was large enough to make a serious dent in pretty much anything.

'Oh God, Tori, I'm so sorry, I don't know what I was thinking,' said Claire, wringing her hands. 'I spotted you and Leo kissing and ... I just got so ... angry. One minute I was driving past the café and the next I was stood outside hurling my bag at the window. I'm so sorry, I shouldn't have acted like this over a man ... I'm not this person.'

'But Claire, why? I don't understand – what's Leo got to do with any of this? With you?' Tori asked, shaking her head.

'Well,' said Claire, looking up at Tori. 'We'd been on a couple of dates, and I was ready to take things further, to be a couple, but that wasn't what he wanted. Then you arrived back in the village ...'

'Oh, Claire,' said Joyce, 'this really isn't Blossom Heath behaviour.'

'At first, I thought if Tori took Ryan back, Leo and I might have a shot. When I realized that wasn't going to happen, I just saw red, I wanted Tori to ... the café to ...'

'Fail?' said Tori.

Claire nodded. 'But it didn't, not even after I got Violet involved. I thought she'd be able to stop the café before it even reopened. But when that didn't work, I took things further ... the reviews, the call to animal welfare ...'

'That was you? All of it?' said Maggie, frowning. Claire nodded.

'And Daisy?' Tori said slowly, trying to process this information, 'that day she went missing, don't tell me you—'

'I sneaked her out in my gym bag,' said Claire quietly. 'I hoped that if people thought you couldn't keep the cats safe, it might stop them coming ...'

'I thought we were friends, Claire,' said Tori. 'I confided in you; God, I even asked you for advice ...'

'I know, I know,' said Claire. 'When Ryan arrived in the village, I thought you guys would get back together. I got chatting to him in the pub one night and he was so keen on you going back to Thailand with him. I encouraged him, suggested he surprise you with the tickets—'

'You did what? Is that why you kept trying to push me and Ryan together? And kept asking if Leo and I were still dating?' asked Tori. Claire nodded. 'How dare you try and interfere like that!'

'I'm so sorry, Tori, I know I've behaved badly.'

'Behaved badly?' yelled Tori. 'Apart from anything else, this is criminal damage – I should call the police!'

'Please, Tori, can we sort this out between us? There's no need to call the police. I've been an idiot. I saw you and Leo kissing and I was hurt. I was driving past the café and I just ... Oh, I don't even know what I thought ... I was so upset,' Claire said miserably.

'What if you'd broken the window and the cats escaped? They could have been killed,' said Joyce.

'I know, I know. I wasn't thinking. I don't know what came over me ... I'll make sure I pay for the repairs, I'll have someone out first thing to fix it ... Please, can you forgive me?'

'That's asking a lot, Claire,' said Tori, folding her arms. 'What's changed? Is it just that you've been caught out?'

'No, absolutely not,' said Claire quickly. 'If that's all it was, I could have lied and blamed it on someone else. I can see Leo's crazy about you. I just need to accept he's not interested in me.'

'And can you?'

'Yes. I wanted ... I hoped me and Leo had something, but there was never anything on his part, not really. I'm sorry. You tried to be my friend and I ...' Claire trailed off unable to finish.

'I don't know, Claire,' said Tori slowly, still stunned by what she'd just learnt. 'This is a lot to take in. Look, it's been a rough night – I'm not going to call the police but I'm not sure we can move past this either.'

'Are you sure you don't want to get the police involved?' asked Maggie, looking Claire up and down. 'What she's done is pretty serious.'

'I know what it's like to be let down, Mags, it doesn't always leave you thinking straight. What you did wasn't right, though, Claire, you need to make amends,' said Tori.

'I know exactly how she can do it too,' said Joyce. 'Wasn't Izzy saying just the other day how short they are for volunteers up at the centre? If Claire is serious about wanting to put things right, she can go and see Izzy in the morning and sign up.'

'I absolutely will,' said Claire. 'A second chance is more than I deserve after everything I've put you through, Tori. And I promise, I really will have someone out first thing to sort that window.'

'You'd better,' said Tori.

'I think it's about time we all called it a night. There's been more than enough drama to deal with this evening. Thanks for your help, Mags. We'll see you tomorrow,' said Joyce, putting an arm around Tori and ushering her back towards the house.

As Tori tried to process the events of the evening and turned her key in the front door, she suddenly realized something . . . she owed Violet Davenport a very big apology.

Chapter 38

Tori was awoken the next morning by the sound of her phone buzzing. She grinned and threw back the duvet when she spotted a message from Leo. *Lara and I got the all clear from the doctors. When can I see you? Miss you already xx*

Tori hugged her knees close to her chest and smiled. She had a message from Rose too. *Can you meet me at Jasmine Cottage when you get this? Jake and I need your help with something xx* Intrigued, Tori typed out a reply. *Of course. Hope everything's okay? Can I bring Leo?* Tori pulled on her dressing gown as the reply from Rose came through: *Yes and yes.* She fired off a message to Leo: *How about now? Fancy meeting me at Jasmine Cottage?* Before she could put her phone down, Leo had replied. *On my way xx*

Tori ran down to the kitchen to find a note waiting for her on the table. *Morning, love. Cats have been fed, repairs have started on the window, there's nothing for you to do, just come and meet me at Jasmine Cottage.* What? Her mum was at Jasmine Cottage? What was going on? Her curiosity getting the better of her, Tori showered in record time, threw on a pair of jeans and a vest top and opened the front door to find Cora with her arm poised, ready to knock.

'Cora?' said Tori, as she pulled on her jacket.

'Tori, is everything okay with the café? I just spotted the window?'

'Oh, yes, just a bit of an accident but it's being fixed.'

'Well, as long as you're okay. I was going to pop in later to speak to you about something, but I may as well ask you now . . .' Cora took a deep breath. 'I was wondering if I could adopt Mr Wiggles?'

'Seriously?' said Tori, beaming. 'That's wonderful!'

'Really?' said Cora, her eyes brightening. 'I was afraid you might think . . . if Izzy might think . . . well, that I'm too old.'

'I'm fairly certain there isn't an upper age limit, but I can check and let you know first thing tomorrow if that's okay?'

'Oh, Tori, thank you,' said Cora, her eyes shining brightly. 'I can't tell you what that means to me.'

'Can I ask what made you change your mind? I know you said you weren't ready . . .'

'Jean. Well, Jean and the other ladies at the WI. They're a lovely bunch, Tori, I'm so glad you told me to go along and meet them. They've made me realize that, well, that I've still got a life to live, even without Dennis, and the sooner I start living it again, the better.'

'Oh, Cora. I'm so pleased. From all you've told me about Dennis, I'm sure he'd be pleased too.'

'He would,' agreed Cora, smiling. 'He'd have told me that

there's a cat without a home and a home without a cat and I've had the solution to that problem right under my nose.'

'He sounds like a very wise man.'

'He was,' said Cora, smiling fondly. 'I've got you and your café to thank. If I hadn't started coming in, I'd probably still be holed up inside the cottage feeling hopeless. You gave me a reason to get out again and I'm grateful to you for that.'

'Oh, Cora,' said Tori, swallowing hard. 'It's my absolute pleasure. I'm pleased I was able to help.'

'I can see you're going out, so I won't keep you.'

'I'll drop Izzy a message now and get the ball rolling, so you'd better start stocking up on cat food,' Tori laughed.

'My next stop is Harrison's,' said Cora. As Tori watched Cora walk across the green, she felt a surge of happiness for the bright future Cora and Mr Wiggles had to look forward to.

Before Tori set off to Jasmine Cottage, she knew she had a detour to make on the way. Violet Davenport's house. She couldn't believe how wrong she'd been about Violet; how could she even begin to apologize? She took a deep breath before tapping gently on the brass knocker.

'Violet, hi,' she said nervously as the front door swung open.

'You! If you're here to accuse me again . . .'

'No, Violet, I'm not,' said Tori sheepishly.

'No?'

'I'm here to apologize.'

'Go on . . .' said Violet, challenging her with a steely glare.

'Well, I know now I was wrong about you being the one causing trouble for us at the café, the bad reviews, the animal welfare complaint . . . all of it. I know it wasn't you, Violet and for what it's worth, I'm sorry. Really sorry. I shouldn't have accused you like that, not without any actual evidence, it was wrong of me. I know I don't deserve it, but I was hoping you could find it in your heart to forgive me and maybe we could make a fresh start?' said Tori. 'Hang on, who's that?' she asked, spotting a small black and white cat curled up on the hall chair.

'Maximus, my cat. I call him Max,' said Violet, her face softening.

'But . . . but . . . I thought you hated cats?'

'Why would you think that? I've never said that I hated cats, I simply said that—'

'But that's why you didn't want the cat café to go ahead because—'

'Oh, you've got it all wrong – it was never because of the cats, it was all about the parking.'

'It was?' said Tori, looking stunned. 'But why haven't you been in since we've reopened? Since the cats arrived? You used to be a regular.'

'I feel foolish,' said Violet, dropping her head.

'Foolish? I don't understand . . .'

'I'd made such a fuss about the parking and then when you came up with a solution so easily, I could see that . . . well . . . that I'd wasted everyone's time,' said Violet, not quite meeting her eye.

'Oh, Violet. Of course you didn't look foolish. You had a

valid concern and you raised it, that's all. If you'd just spoken to me, we could have straightened everything out.'

'Yes, well . . .'

'Actually, I could do with some help at the café now if you're free?'

'Help? From me?'

'Well, yes. There're some repairs going on and I'm worried the cats might get a bit spooked; Mum and I are both out, you see. I was wondering if you might be free to sit with them for a while, just for a bit of company?'

'Oh, the poor loves. If you think that would help?' said Violet, her eyes brightening.

'It really would. It would be a huge weight off my mind. And you can help yourself to cake too. If there's anything that takes your fancy, that is? I promise I haven't baked it.'

'That's something at least. Just let me grab my bag.'

As Tori walked back across the green with Violet at her side, she couldn't remember when she'd ever been happier than she was right at that very moment.

When Tori finally reached Jasmine Cottage, having settled Violet into the café and showed her how to work the coffee machine, she could see that Leo had already arrived. Scout, Tagg and Finn rushed out to greet her and she bent down to fuss them.

'Are you guys in on this plan too?' she whispered, before following the dogs inside. 'Mum? Rose? What's going on?' she called.

'Ah, you made it then?' said Leo, engulfing her in a hug.

'How are you feeling today?' she asked, resting her head on his shoulder. He slid his arm around her waist, kissing her on the cheek.

'I'm good. I'm more interested in why we're here,' he said.

'You mean you don't know either?' said Tori.

'No! You're the one who invited me, remember?' he laughed. 'Hey, Rose, where are you? What's with all the boxes?'

'Oh yeah,' said Tori, 'what's the deal, Rose?' And where is everyone?'

'We're here!' said Jake, descending the stairs balancing a huge box in his arms, with Rose, Joyce and Jean following behind him.

'Ah good, you've arrived!' cried Jean gleefully.

'Tori, hello, love,' said Joyce.

'Will one of you tell me what's going on?' said Tori, resting her hands on her hips.

'Ah, I guess I better explain,' said Rose. 'You've noticed all the boxes, yes?' She pointed towards piles of boxes in the hallway.

'They're hard to miss,' said Tori.

'Well, Jake and I have some news.' Rose took Jake's hand and looked up at him expectantly.

'Rose and I are moving in together!' said Jake.

'What? Seriously? Guys, that's amazing news!' squealed Tori.

'I know!' agreed Rose. 'It's not just me – Aunt Jean's coming too.'

'There's plenty of room in the farmhouse and neither of us like the idea of Jean being on her own anymore,' explained Jake.

'Now I'm going to have three collies to fuss over,' said Jean, bending down with the help of her walking stick to stroke Scout on her head.

'We'd planned to move in together in a few months, but after everything that happened last night, it made sense to bring it forward, we don't want to be apart anymore,' said Rose.

'But it does leave us with a bit of a quandary, Tori. What with me moving too, Jasmine Cottage will be sitting empty, and I don't want that. This place is too special for it to just languish, unloved,' said Jean.

'Why don't you rent it out?' Leo suggested.

'That's exactly what I was thinking, Leo,' Jean agreed.

'One of my football mates is a letting agent – I could get him to pop by if you like?' said Leo.

'Hang on a minute,' said Tori, her eyes shining with excitement. 'What about me? I could rent Jasmine Cottage!'

'You?' said Jean thoughtfully.

'Yes! The café's starting to turn a bit of profit, it would be a stretch, but I'm pretty sure I could pay you the going rate. The plan was always to buy somewhere but—'

'You could still do that, dear,' said Jean.

'Oh no, I wouldn't be able to pay rent *and* save for a deposit . . .'

'But you haven't even asked what the rent is yet,' continued Jean.

'Well, a two-bed cottage,' said Tori, mulling it over, 'that's got to be at least—'

'Four hundred a month?' said Jean.

'What? No, more like eight,' said Tori, shaking her head.

'Tori's right, Jean, a cottage like this would go for at least eight hundred,' agreed Leo.

'Unless I set a peppercorn rent, just to tide the tenant over until they're able to buy the place off me,' said Jean.

Was Tori imagining it or was there a twinkle in her eye? 'But I don't understand why you'd do that for someone, Jean?' said Tori, looking from Jean to her mum.

'Not just someone, Tori dear – you. I'm suggesting you move in here and pay me a peppercorn rent on the under-standing that you'll buy the place off me once you've saved up the deposit you need.'

'But, Jean, I couldn't possibly, that's too generous . . .'

'Well, I think it's a wonderful idea,' said Joyce, giving Jean a knowing glance.

'Wait! Did you have this already worked out?' asked Tori, realization dawning.

'You did, didn't you?' cried Rose, clapping her hands together. 'Oh, I love it!'

'Tori, my dear, I'd love you to be the tenant of Jasmine Cottage,' said Jean.

'I don't know what to say,' said Tori, her eyes wide with shock. 'This is overwhelming.'

'Just say yes, dear,' said Jean, smiling.

'Yes!' said Tori, and Rose whooped with delight, embracing her friend.

'You'll be needing these then,' said Rose, taking a set of keys from her pocket.

'I don't know what to say – this is beyond anything I could imagine,' said Tori.

'Seeing the look on your face is thanks enough, my dear,' said Jean. 'Now, Jake, Rose and I were about to take the jeep back up to the farm to unload some of these boxes, so we can drop Joyce home on the way. I think you need a bit of time to explore your new home. And Leo, why don't you stay and give Tori a hand?' said Jean, with a mischievous look.

'Oh, yes, definitely,' said Leo, flushing. 'Thanks, Jean.'

'I honestly can't thank you enough,' said Tori, gently hugging Jean.

'Oh, don't mention it, my dear. You've got the keys now and all the furniture is staying put, so you can move your things in whenever you're ready,' said Jean.

'How long have you known about this?' Tori whispered to her mum as she was leaving.

'A while,' said Joyce, smiling at her daughter. 'I'm just incredibly good at keeping secrets.'

'Clearly,' said Tori, raising her eyebrows.

As Jake and Rose carried the last few boxes out to the jeep, Leo closed the door behind them.

'Can you believe this?' asked Tori, looking around the room wide-eyed.

'Hey, don't look at me, I had no idea,' laughed Leo. 'It's pretty great, though, isn't it?'

'Great? It's amazing!' She took a step closer towards him. 'Although it's not even the best thing that's happened to me this week.'

'It isn't?' asked Leo.

'Nope, not even close,' she replied. She held out a hand and Leo took it, pulling her in closer to him.

'So, if moving in here isn't the best thing to happen to you this week, what is?' he asked, stroking her cheek with his fingertips.

'This is,' she said, leaning in for a kiss that was just as passionate as the very first one they had shared together all those weeks ago. When they finally parted, Tori looked around Jasmine Cottage and smiled. She knew her future here was going to be happy – very happy indeed.

Acknowledgements

So, here we are again. The second book in the Blossom Heath series is out in the world and I still can't quite believe it! I think I *might* be starting to accept that I'm now a published author (although even writing that sentence still makes me feel like this whole thing is happening to someone else!).

Thank you for reading *New Beginnings at the Cosy Cat Café*, I can't tell you how much I appreciate it. I hope you enjoyed your return trip to Blossom Heath just as much as I did. I've been blown away by the reaction to my debut novel, *Always by Your Side*, and saying a simple thank you doesn't seem even nearly enough to convey how much it means to me, but *thank you*!

There are so many people I'd like to thank for helping me in my writing journey, but I want to start with a huge shout-out to the wonderful Sara-Jade Virtue at Books and the City. Thank you for helping me to make my dream a reality and an even bigger thank you for everything you do for the romance genre. Us romance authors are incredibly lucky to have you as our champion! To Louise Davies, thank you for your expert eye and for helping me to make this novel the absolute best possible version of itself.

The Romantic Novelists' Association is an organization that has played a huge part in my author journey, and I'd like to say thank you to them for building such a supportive and encouraging community of writers. I genuinely don't think I'd be sat here writing this today if I hadn't joined the New Writers' Scheme back in January 2021. I'd also like to give a mention to the RNA's Essex Chapter, where I've met so many wonderful authors and made the best of friends. Romance authors really are the loveliest of people! A huge thanks goes out to Carrie Elks in particular for organizing our, now legendary, Thursday lunches and for always being such an inspiration.

To my wonderfully supportive family and friends, thank you once again for bearing with me as I remain buried deep in plot twists and manuscript edits. It may seem like I'm permanently writing away at my laptop and oblivious to the outside world, but your love and support means everything. I want to give a special mention to my incredible friend Joanne Barnetson – in what has been the toughest of years for you, you've remained my biggest supporter and I honestly can't thank you enough for that. I am one lucky human to count you as my friend.

I also want to thank the real-life Cosy Cat Café, in Herne Bay, Kent, for kindly allowing me to make use of their name in my novel (it really is the purrfect name for a cat café!). If you ever find yourself in Herne Bay, do pay the Cosy Cat a visit and treat yourself to a cup of something delicious and a slice (or two) of cake. Tori and Joyce would most definitely approve!

I'd like to give a final shout out to all the cat owners of the world. If you're lucky enough to share your life with a feline friend, I'm sure you can relate to some of Tori's trials and tribulations at the Cosy Cat! I've been fortunate enough to share my life with a number of rescue cats over the years and they've all left their very own unique pawprints on my heart. It's them I have to thank for being the inspiration behind the Cosy Cat, and I'm sure they'd all have made themselves right at home there.

Always By Your Side

'A warm, romantic story about community,
friendship and following your heart, *Always By
Your Side* is a feel-good delight, I adored it!'
HOLLY MARTIN

When school teacher Rose loses her dream job at a London
primary school, her self-confidence takes a knock. Worse still,
her stockbroker fiancé, Ollie, sees it as the perfect opportunity
for her to join his firm, which only adds to the feelings Rose
has that their relationship might be coming to an end.
An unexpected phone call, and an elderly aunt who's taken a
fall, means Rose must drop everything – including Ollie – and
return to Blossom Heath, the Sussex village she grew up in.

With no job to rush home to, Rose decides to stay in
Blossom Heath for the summer, trading London for the
idyllic countryside. Here, Rose finds herself reconnecting
to the village life of her childhood in more ways than one,
including falling head-over-heels for local farmer, Jake.
So when her London life comes calling, Rose is faced with
an impossible choice . . . to return to the high-pressure life of
her past, or embrace the joy of a new life in the country.

AVAILABLE IN PAPERBACK, EBOOK AND AUDIO

**SIMON &
SCHUSTER**

booksandthecity.co.uk
the home of female fiction